FEARED

This Large Print Book carries the
Seal of Approval of N.A.V.H.

A ROSATO & DINUNZIO NOVEL

FEARED

LISA SCOTTOLINE

WHEELER PUBLISHING
A part of Gale, a Cengage Company

Farmington Hills, Mich • San Francisco • New York • Waterville, Maine
Meriden, Conn • Mason, Ohio • Chicago

LIBRARY OF CONGRESS CIP DATA ON FILE.
CATALOGUING IN PUBLICATION FOR THIS BOOK
IS AVAILABLE FROM THE LIBRARY OF CONGRESS

ISBN-13: 978-1-4328-5596-3 (hardcover)

Published in 2018 by arrangement with Macmillan Publishing Group, LLC/St. Martin's Press

Printed in the United States of America
1 2 3 4 5 6 7 22 21 20 19 18

For Francesca, with love

It is better to be feared than loved,
if you cannot be both.

— Niccolò Machiavelli

CHAPTER ONE

"Surprise!" everyone shouted, as Mary Di-Nunzio opened the door to the conference room. The office was throwing her a baby shower, and she almost burst into tears of joy. Pregnancy had boosted her emotions past normal Italian-American levels, and for the past seven months, she'd been a walking bowl of estrogen.

"Aww, you guys!" Mary wiped her eyes while they all rushed over.

"Were you surprised?" Judy Carrier, her best friend, gave her a big hug.

"Or did you guess?" Anne Murphy, the firm's gorgeous fashionista, enveloped Mary in a perfumed cloud.

"DiNunzio, you couldn't have been surprised, could you?" called out Bennie Rosato, Mary's partner and former boss. Bennie stood at a distance because group hugs were against her religion, folding her arms in her characteristic khaki suit, unruly blonde topknot, and vaguely ironic smile. "Where did you think we all were?"

"I don't know!" Mary sniffled happily. "I figured I was the first one in this morning."

"You? Ha!" Lou Jacobs laughed, giving her a hug. Bald and nearing seventy years old, Lou was a former cop who worked as their investigator. He was trim, fit, and perennially tan from weekends fishing in Margate. His eyes were a flinty gray-blue, with a nose like the bill of a seagull.

"Congrats, Mary!" Marshall Trow, their receptionist, smiled from ear-to-ear.

"Congratulations, Mary!" John Foxman gave her a stiff hug, and Mary hugged him back warmly. She had thought he was too preppie when they first met, but he'd proved his mettle on one of her most important cases.

"You guys went to so much trouble!" Mary took in the scene. Pink and blue streamers hung from the ceiling, obscuring Bennie's beloved Eakins rowing prints and the view of the Philadelphia skyline. Stacks of trial exhibits had been pushed aside to make room for pink- and blue-frosted cupcakes, a pile of gaily wrapped gifts, and paper plates and cups.

"It was no trouble." Judy waved her off with a grin.

"We wanted to!" added Anne.

Bennie snorted. "DiNunzio, I agree with you, but they said we had to." She gestured Mary into a seat at the head of the table, usually hers. "Now sit down and have a cupcake, so we can get back to work."

"Got it." Mary waddled to the seat. "Sit down, everyone, please. I can't take the guilt if you're standing."

"Bennie, give us a toast." Judy sat down, reaching for a pink cupcake and taking a typically big bite.

"Okay." Bennie raised her I CAN SMELL FEAR mug. "Everybody, join me, get a drink."

Mary felt her eyes well up again. She loved them, and as thrilled as she was about the baby, she would miss them during her maternity leave. And seeing Bennie standing proudly, her mug raised, made Mary flash on the arc of their long relationship. Mary had joined the law firm as an insecure associate and had grown into a somewhat-less-insecure named partner, which was progress.

"To Mary DiNunzio." Bennie's expression softened. "I speak for everyone at Rosato & DiNunzio when I say that we wish you, Anthony, and your new baby all the happiness in the world — but we can't wait

11

until you come back to work."

"Hear, hear!" Lou called out, and everybody cheered, raising their cups. "To Mary!" "To the baby!" "To the new lawyer!"

"Thank you!" Mary smiled, taking a sip of seltzer, which would probably make her gassy. These days she could barely walk for having to hold her sphincter closed. At home, she let it rip, and her husband, Anthony, wasn't allowed to complain. Her breasts had grown to gargantuan proportions, and he had to take the bad with the good.

Suddenly there was a noise outside the conference room, and a man in a sportcoat arrived at the threshold. "Excuse me," he said, "there was nobody at the reception desk. I have hand-deliveries for Bennie Rosato, Mary DiNunzio, and Judy Carrier."

"That's me," Bennie said, rising and walking around the table.

"I'm Judy." Judy stood up and went over.

"I'm Mary, but hang on." Mary got up, slowly.

"Okay, here we go." The man handed Mary, Judy, and Bennie each a thick manila envelope. "I'm with AMG Process Servers. You've been served."

Bennie blinked. "You mean a client of ours has been served."

"No. *You've* been served. Bye." The man left, with a surprised Marshall escorting him out.

"What?" Mary asked, aghast. She'd never been sued in her life. She'd never even colored outside of the lines.

"Let me see." Bennie had torn open the envelope and was already reading the papers with a deepening frown. "It's a copy of a Complaint that was just filed with the Pennsylvania Human Relations Commission. We're being sued as a firm and individually, as partners."

"Who could be suing *you guys*?" Anne rose quickly, crossing to read the papers.

Lou snorted, getting up. "Who would be crazy enough?"

"And for what?" John asked, indignant, crossing the room to read over Bennie's shoulder.

Bennie read through the papers. "We're being sued for reverse sex discrimination."

Mary read over Bennie's shoulder, aghast. "The plaintiffs are three male lawyers who allege they applied for jobs and weren't hired because they're men."

"Are you *serious*?" Judy recoiled. "We're being sued?"

Lou asked, "What's the Pennsylvania Human Relations Commission?"

13

Bennie kept reading the Complaint. "It's an agency that enforces state law prohibiting discrimination on the basis of gender and for other reasons. The federal analogue is Title VII of the Civil Rights Act."

Judy looked over at Lou. "The Pennsylvania Human Relations Act covers smaller employers like us. This is the beginning of a lawsuit, because you have to file a complaint with the Commission before you can go to court."

"Here, I'll read the allegations." Bennie cleared her throat. "The law firm of Rosato & DiNunzio was unlawfully founded as a 'women-only' law firm. On many occasions, its principals Bennie Rosato, Mary DiNunzio, and Judy Carrier have even admitted as much, stating in interviews that their law firm is 'comprised of all women' and is 'all-female.' "

Mary felt a wave of nausea, only partly pregnancy-related. "We said that because reporters would ask us if we were all-female. That doesn't mean it's a *job requirement.*"

"Who *are* these plaintiffs?" Judy's fair skin flushed with emotion, turning almost as pink as her hair. "When did we fail to hire them? Besides, we're not an all-female law firm anymore. We have John now. Doesn't he count?"

"Yeah, right." Anne gestured to John. "You hired him yourself, right, Judy?"

"Yes, totally." Judy nodded, emphatic. "Bennie, that disproves their case right there, doesn't it?"

"No, it doesn't." Bennie looked over, frowning. "Point of law, the fact that a company hired a man doesn't prove that it didn't discriminate against another male plaintiff. Secondly, the fact that we don't interview more widely doesn't cut in our favor. Failing to interview widely tends to perpetuate discriminatory employment practices. In an all-male firm, it would perpetuate an old-boy network."

"Like an old-girl network?" Mary felt defensive. "Gimme a break. We don't discriminate against men. This suit doesn't have any merit. These guys have a lot of nerve."

"Because they're men," Judy shot back, but nobody laughed. "Okay, not allowed to joke around anymore. Bennie, who are the plaintiffs?"

"Their names are Michael Battle, Graham Madden, and Stephen McManus, corporate litigators. They allege they were 'more than qualified' to be associates. They applied and were rejected. It says we interviewed one, McManus." Bennie looked up, puzzled.

"Who interviewed McManus?"

"I did," John answered. "I thought we needed an associate to help on *London Technologies.* I asked Anne if I could hire somebody. Remember, Anne?"

"Yes." Anne nodded, frowning. "You were supposed to interview the candidates, make a recommendation to me, and I'd run it up to Bennie."

"Okay, so I put an ad online and in the *Intelligencer,* went through the resumes, and interviewed a bunch of candidates, including one of these three, the plaintiffs." John looked nonplussed, turning to Bennie. "I liked Steve McManus and recommended to Anne that we hire him. She said no and told me to go back to the drawing board. Instead I hired a contract lawyer because I didn't have time to start the whole process over again."

Bennie faced Anne. "Why didn't you want to hire McManus? Did you interview him?"

"No." Anne thought for a minute, a worried crease marking her perfect features. "I looked at the resume and didn't like it. He didn't seem to have any personality. I didn't think he would be a good fit."

Bennie arched an eyebrow. "What do you mean by 'good fit'?"

"He seemed really boring, like, too quiet.

None of us is, and that's why this is a fun place to work. He didn't strike me as the kind of person we need, completely regardless of his gender." Anne straightened. "I can totally defend my decision. Under the law, we can decide not to hire someone for any reason, or even no reason, as long as it's not discriminatory."

"Correct." Bennie returned her attention to the Complaint. "Foxman, you're mentioned here, too."

"I am?" John swallowed hard, and Mary noticed he suddenly seemed nervous, which was unusual because not much ruffled his patrician cool. He was good-looking, with intelligent blue eyes behind rimless glasses, a small nose, and precisely layered reddish hair. Tall and perennially well-dressed, he always looked to Mary as if he'd been born in a rep tie. But she could see his mouth go suddenly dry.

Bennie cleared her throat again. "Let me read aloud. 'Plaintiff Stephen McManus was interviewed by associate John Foxman in his office at Rosato & DiNunzio. During the interview, Foxman told Plaintiff McManus that he himself felt 'out of place at Rosato & DiNunzio because he was a male.' " Bennie looked up slowly, appalled. "Did you say that, Foxman?"

Mary sensed the answer. John tended to make his opinions known, and she remembered that on the last case they had worked together, he had spoken imprudently to the media. In other circumstances she would have termed it mansplaining, but not today.

"Whoa." Judy grimaced at John. "Did you really *say* that?"

"John, do you really *think* that?" Anne's lovely green eyes focused on him, awaiting his answer, as was Lou.

"Um." John swallowed visibly, his Adam's apple getting stuck on his cutaway collar. "I said that."

Mary moaned inwardly, and everyone fell silent. A pink streamer fluttered from the ceiling to the carpet.

"Foxman." Bennie controlled her tone. "You said that to an *interviewee*? Explain."

John went ashen-faced. "I'm the only male lawyer. If we're being honest, I do feel that way, sometimes."

"Like when?" Judy and Anne interrupted, in outraged unison.

John gestured vaguely at the streamers. "For starters, at a baby shower."

Judy threw up her hands. "John, *I* feel out of place at a baby shower."

"But I do feel out of place here, at times."

"John, really?" Judy blurted out. "You're

not out of place here. You're one of us, whether you're a man or woman. You know that."

"Bummer." Anne was shaking her head, her glossy red hair shining. "You never said anything like that to me."

Mary could see that John felt terrible, but now they were on the legal hook. Litigation was a nightmare, especially when you were on the receiving end, and it was the last thing she needed in a difficult pregnancy. She tried not to throw up.

Bennie raised a hand. "Foxman, I asked you to explain the circumstances in which you made this statement to an interviewee."

John stiffened. "Well, during the interview, I guess McManus and I got to talking. He was a nice guy. I felt we had a rapport. That's why I wanted to hire him. I might've admitted that I felt out of place here, sometimes. As a guy."

Bennie squared her shoulders. "Foxman, I'm disappointed. If you'd brought it to me, we could have addressed it. Instead you chose to make your views known to an outsider, who's using it against us in a base-less lawsuit."

John swallowed, mortified. "It was a mistake."

"No, it was treason."

John flinched. "Bennie, I'm sorry. Do you want me to resign? I don't want to, but I will if you want me to."

"And add fuel to the plaintiffs' fire? No." Bennie glared at him, creating the most awkward moment in legal history. "Where do you think those resumes would be? Or a copy of the ad that we ran? Do you have them?"

"Yes, somewhere."

"Find their resumes and any other communications you had with them — email, text, phone calls, whatever. Prepare a chronology so we understand exactly what happened. We have to know what they know." Bennie glanced at Anne. "Murphy, I'm tasking you with preventing this from happening again. We have to institute a formalized way of dealing with interviewees from now on. We can't do it by the seat of our pants anymore. Please coordinate with Marshall, set up a system, and let us know your recommendation. We need to implement it immediately."

"Will do," Anne said quickly.

Judy turned to Bennie. "Who represents the plaintiffs?"

"Hold on, let me see." Bennie flipped through the Complaint, then looked up. "Guess who, DiNunzio."

"Tell me." Mary hated guessing games from before she was on progesterone, which left her feeling dumber than usual.

"It's your mortal enemy."

"I don't have any enemies."

Judy smiled. "Truth. She's universally beloved."

Bennie met Mary's troubled gaze. "You beat him last time, and he's back with a vengeance. Nick Machiavelli."

"Oh no." Mary's heart sank. Unfortunately, her gorge rose. The real Niccolò Machiavelli had thought it was better to be feared than loved, and his alleged descendant, South Philly lawyer Nick Machiavelli, followed suit. He was feared, not loved, while Mary was loved, not feared. She knew Machiavelli would come back for an ultimate lawyer battle, like a fight between good and evil, with billable hours.

Bennie closed the Complaint. "Folks, the party's over. Sorry, Mary. Open your presents later. We have to talk about this lawsuit, and everybody has to clear the room except for the three partners."

"I need a wastebasket," Mary said, looking around.

CHAPTER TWO

Mary nibbled a cupcake, hoping it would calm her stomach, but it didn't work. That was the double-edged sword of pregnancy; if you didn't eat, you felt nauseated, but if you ate, you threw up. It didn't help that she was being sued, and by Machiavelli. Her thoughts churned while she watched Judy wolf down a cupcake and Bennie pace the conference room, in front of the skyline of Philadelphia, topped by Billy Penn on City Hall. From this angle, he famously looked like he had an erection, but Bennie didn't notice.

"I cannot believe this!" Bennie shouted, throwing up her hands. Mary and Judy exchanged glances as they sat at the table. They knew from experience that when she started pacing, it was best to stay out of her way, like the Acela racing up and down the Northeast Corridor. And not the quiet car.

"This is outrageous!" Bennie pivoted

when she reached the credenza, then paced in the other direction, waving the Complaint in the air. "A failure-to-hire case, brought by men, against us! Do you believe it? Do you even *believe it*?"

Mary gathered the question was rhetorical, and Judy reached for another cupcake, this time a blue-frosted instead of a pink, wondering if the choice was intentional or politically correct.

"I worked my whole life, my *whole entire life* to have my own law firm!" Bennie shook her head as she strode to the wall, then snap-turned around like an Olympic swimmer at the end of the pool. "I was on my own, and you guys both know it, then I met you two! I wasn't hiring only women! The gender didn't matter to me, at all! Remember when you started with me, as associates?"

"Totally," Mary answered, since Judy's mouth was full. Her worries were already turning to the potential costs of the lawsuit. The firm had an insurance carrier, but it wouldn't cover acts outside the scope of employment, which could arguably include intentional employment discrimination. The three of them could be on the hook for the damages, and her husband, Anthony, didn't have a job.

"You remember, you were big-firm refugees! I hired you both because you were the best! Because you're terrific! And we crushed it, the three of us, case after case. We made the firm a success, thriving through thick and thin! Remember when we almost went bankrupt?"

"Yes," Mary answered again. They had almost been evicted from their offices. The caseload had gone up and down, and so had their cash flow. Bennie had kept them all together, doing everything she could to make payroll and not fire anyone. Back then, Mary hadn't been sure she even wanted to be a lawyer, but then she'd found special-education law, which was her true niche. She did well *and* did good, for children.

"Now here we all are, over a decade later, and all of us partners, and *this* happens?" Bennie raised the Complaint like a flaming torch, but not like Lady Liberty, more like an angry mob. "You know whose fault this is? Mine, all mine. I've been too lax."

"No, you haven't," Mary said, meaning it. She was already thinking along different lines. "Bennie, with respect, you're on the wrong track."

"How?" Bennie whirled around. "Are you going to tell me this isn't a disaster?"

24

"No, it is. But I have some ideas about how it came about." Mary gestured to the chair catty-corner to hers, opposite Judy. "Please, sit down. I have a hunch."

Judy wiped crumbs off her chin. "Good, Mare. I like your hunches."

"Thanks." Mary rallied as Bennie stalked over, threw the Complaint onto the polished conference table, and sat down. "So Nick Machiavelli filed this suit against us. He threatened that someday he'd get a rematch, you remember."

"I remember." Bennie folded her arms.

Judy reached for the coffee carafe. "I hate that guy, I hate everything about him. He's a phony, a fraud. Can you imagine, trying to convince people that you're a direct descendant of the real Machiavelli?"

"It is his real last name, and I know his family from the neighborhood." Mary had gone to Goretti, a sister high school to Nick Machiavelli's school, Newman, and his pretensions were the least ridiculous thing about him. "The problem is, the man is an excellent lawyer, mainly because he's ruthless. Nothing stops him. The ends justify the means, so maybe it's in his DNA."

"He's not going to get away with this. He won't even know what hit him. I'm going to devote the full resources of this firm to this litigation. We're going to pulverize him." Bennie's blue eyes flashed, in battle mode, and Mary had never seen her like this. She knew that Bennie loved a good fight, but she didn't know that Bennie loved a good war.

"My point is, think about what's going on here. We know the shenanigans he pulled on that last case, right? He waged a proxy war. He sent lawyers to oppose me. So now we know how he works. He's indirect."

"Right," Bennie answered, nodding.

"And?" Judy shifted forward in the chair. "Where are you going with this? What's your hunch?"

"Think about this. Two of these plaintiffs are lawyers none of us met. We don't even know where their resumes are. We have to go hunt them up." Mary slid the Complaint over, checking the caption. "But the third, Stephen McManus, is the one from that interview with John —"

Bennie interrupted, "I *still* cannot believe Foxman said what he said. I don't want to fire him, I want to kill him. How imprudent can you possibly be? And —"

"Wait." Mary raised a hand, probably the only time she had ever silenced Bennie Rosato. "John told us that the interviewee was chatty. And somehow, the conversation must've come around to how it is to work with women. And that's when John throws in his two cents, that he feels out of place, which ends up in the Complaint. Now what does that tell you?"

"That John should be fired!"

"No, think about it." Mary got so excited she felt the baby kick, but this wasn't the time to say so. "We know Machiavelli has wanted a rematch. There hasn't been another case on which we're opposing counsel, so he *made* one. I bet that, one way or another, these plaintiffs were connected to Machiavelli before he became their lawyer."

Bennie blinked.

Judy's mouth dropped open.

"Right?" Mary felt the baby kick again. "John advertised for an associate, and I bet that Machiavelli saw the ad, sent McManus to us for a job interview, and coached him to get John talking about what it was like to work with us. And he had the others send in resumes, too. In other words, he *manufactured* the lawsuit against us."

Bennie's blue eyes rounded. "Yes, that's completely possible. They don't have much of a case without Foxman's statement. It's essentially an admission."

Judy gasped. "That must be what happened. John was set up. He was *entrapped.*"

Bennie looked over. "He still shouldn't have said it, Carrier."

"I know, and I feel terrible that he thinks that."

"I don't care what he thinks, I care what he says." Bennie snorted. "And it was wrong and disloyal for him to say such a thing to anybody outside of this firm, especially an interviewee. I would've fired him if I thought it wouldn't hurt our defense — or if he wouldn't file a retaliation claim against us."

Judy frowned. "He would never do that."

"Never say never," Bennie shot back, but Mary wanted to return to the subject. John was a great guy, and she knew he had a great heart, even serving as the devoted guardian of his brother, William, who had cerebral palsy. Something told Mary that John had been taken advantage of by Machiavelli, and all she had to do was convince Bennie.

"So Bennie, my point is that nothing we or John did really caused this lawsuit. It's not that we're too lax, and we certainly don't discriminate against men. We were set up, too —"

Bennie's smartphone started ringing, and she slid it out of her pocket, checked the screen, and pressed a button to decline the call. "That's a reporter I know from the

28

Inquirer. It must be about this case. The timing can't be coincidental."

"Agree." Judy's phone started ringing, faceup on the conference table. She glanced at the screen, declining the call. "And that's somebody from the *ABA Journal.*"

Mary's phone rang, too, but she let it go, assuming it was more of same. The baby kicked again, and she wondered if he or she would be a lawyer or a reporter one day. After he/she stopped causing so much gas.

Suddenly there was a knock on the door, which opened, and Marshall popped her head through. "Excuse me, but there's media calling for you about the lawsuit. Do you want to take these calls? What do we say?"

"No comment," Bennie, Mary, and Judy answered, in lawyerly unison.

"Got it, thanks." Marshall flashed a shaky smile before she closed the door.

Mary heaved a sigh. "Honestly, this is how Machiavelli operates. He'll try to ruin our reputation. His goal isn't just to win this lawsuit, it's to crush us."

Judy cringed. "You're exaggerating, right?"

"Not this time," Mary answered, without hesitation.

Bennie mulled it over. "DiNunzio, come on. The damages can't be that much."

"It's not the damages, it's what just happened. The press. He's trying to ruin our reputation as a firm. And it's so gossipy, they'll all run with the ball. How do you think potential clients will react? They'll stay away in droves."

Bennie bore down. "Then we lock and load. Machiavelli has been circling us for too long, and it's time that we finished him off, for good."

Judy nodded. "Agree. We can take him."

Mary forced a smile, but she knew Machiavelli better than they did, so she was less than optimistic. In fact, less-than-optimistic was her middle name.

Bennie checked her watch. "We need a lawyer, ASAP. We can't represent ourselves since we're going to be fact witnesses."

"Who would you hire, Bennie? Should we go big firm or little?" Mary shifted, trying to get comfortable, but there was a human being on her bladder. "Machiavelli runs his own shop. He's probably got twelve associates working for him. He's going to throw everything he has behind this case, too."

Judy sipped her coffee. "I say small firm. There are plenty of great boutique firms in the city. We want somebody who will dedicate themselves to us. Who identifies with us."

Mary didn't agree. "Hmm, I say big firm. We want a show of force. But do we hire a man or woman? I say a man, for obvious reasons."

"I say a woman, because we want to win." Judy smiled crookedly.

Bennie scoffed. "I'll be damned if I pick a lawyer by gender. I never have and I'm not about to start now."

"Then who?" Judy turned to Bennie, waiting for her answer, and Mary did the same. Even though they were both Bennie's partners, they used to be her associates and old habits die hard.

"We need to think strategically in our choice of counsel. It kills me that we can't represent ourselves, because we're the best."

"I second that emotion." Judy smiled.

Mary added, "And obviously, we need somebody who's brilliant, but who won't be intimidated by Machiavelli."

Bennie's eyes narrowed in thought. "Not just somebody who's not intimidated, but somebody who can deal with how manipulative Machiavelli is and the fact that he plays outside the rules. Machiavelli is intense, relentless, and unconventional, which can throw even the best of lawyers off their game. It's like guerilla warfare against conventional warfare."

"You're right," Mary said, changing her mind. "So that would leave out most big-firm lawyers because they tend to proceed in an orderly fashion."

Judy shifted forward. "And come to think of it, it would eliminate smaller firms, too. We need a shop with the horsepower to deal with the crapstorm that's coming, even the media."

"I got it!" Bennie snapped her fingers. "I know exactly who we need. Roger Vitez. He's the lawyer's lawyer."

"I've never heard of him." Judy frowned.

"Me neither," Mary said, worried. She wasn't sure she wanted to place her legal career in the hands of some unknown quantity.

"Because that's the way he likes it. He's a secret weapon." Bennie picked up her phone. "I hope I can reach him. He doesn't have a cell phone."

Mary didn't like the sound of that, either. "What kind of lawyer doesn't have a cell phone?"

"One who doesn't need the work," Judy interjected. "Bennie, does he specialize in employment discrimination?"

"No, legal malpractice. Lawyers hire Roger when their ass is in a sling." Bennie thumbed through her phone contacts. "He's a little odd, no suit-and-tie, no phone, no watch, but he never loses. He has a great reputation."

Judy caught Mary's eye. "Then how come I never heard of him?"

"Think about it." Bennie lifted an eyebrow. "Didn't you ever wonder why you never read about legal malpractice cases in the newspaper? Even in the legal journals? Because lawyers who get sued *don't* talk about it, the bar takes care of its own and newspapers take care of advertisers."

Judy frowned. "So legal malpractice is booming, which is good and bad news."

Mary remained worried. "But does he know employment law?"

Bennie put the phone to her ear. "I'm sure he knows enough, and he's the strategic choice for this case. The only question is, will he take us?"

Judy scoffed. "Who wouldn't? We're arguably the most high-profile firm in the city."

"Plus we're nice," Mary added.

"Speak for yourself," Bennie said, without a smile.

CHAPTER THREE

Vitez, LLC, was housed in a unique office building, a brownstone that had been stripped to its exposed brick walls, then glassed in and dramatically renovated as a glass box, with an atrium in the center that served as a waiting room, furnished with glass end tables and modern sectionals that matched a large square of sisal. Glass balconies ringed the atrium at the second and third floors, where the associates' offices were located, also with glass walls, through which they could be seen working. All Mary could think was how much Vitez spent on Windex.

Roger Vitez himself looked in his late forties, thanks to salt-and-pepper hair cut in careful layers and long sideburns that tapered to a matching beard, immaculately trimmed. He was tall, trim, and handsome, though his features were precise to the point of delicacy, with a long narrow face accentuated by a long thin nose, intelligent blue eyes bracketed by fine crow's-feet, and fine lips pursed as tightly as a coin slot turned on its side. He was dressed in a black turtleneck and light gray wool pants, more like an art director than a lawyer. He didn't have a wedding ring, which didn't surprise Mary, because he seemed like a super-picky kind of guy, which was her least favorite.

She and Judy remained quiet as Bennie pitched Roger their case, and Mary took in his office, which was equally unique. It was another large glass box, with a glass desk, glass table, and more glass walls. Transparent halogen pendants shone from black tracks that coordinated with the black frames of clerestory windows, and except for Vitez's laptop, there was no lawyer paraphernalia like legal pads, memos, red accordion files, family photos, framed diplomas, or Lucite awards. The bookshelves were also glass, and the books weren't the typical *Federal Rules of Civil Procedure* or *Purdon's Pennsylvania Statutes,* but *Lao-Tzu, The Way of Buddha,* and *The Tibetan Book of the Dead.*

"Well, Bennie," Roger said, after Bennie was finished. He tented his slim fingers and leaned back in his black mesh chair. "Thank you for coming over. I'm afraid I'll have to decline the representation. With gratitude, of course."

Mary and Judy exchanged looks, but didn't say anything, since Bennie wanted to do all the talking. This was a revolting development, as far as Mary was concerned. Bennie had spent the cab ride here raving about Vitez, that he'd graduated from Harvard Law, clerked for the Supremes, and was notoriously choosy about his caseload. Now that he didn't want them, Mary wanted him even more. She fell for the Supply-Limited sales pitch every time.

Bennie leaned forward. "Roger, you have to take this case."

"I'm very flattered, but I'm sure anybody in the Bar Association would jump at the chance to represent you. You know absolutely everyone. I suggest you give any one of them a call."

"But you are my first and only choice. I want you. We all do."

"We do," Mary said, but didn't say more.

"We really do," Judy chimed in.

"I wish I could, but I can't." Roger smiled, tenting his slim fingers, but Bennie was getting frustrated.

"Roger, why not?"

"For starters, I have a bad feeling about this lawsuit. I read the Complaint you emailed me and the Pennsylvania Human Relations Act. I sense that there's more here than meets the eye. You know in movies, when they say, 'this time it's personal'? I get the same sense about this lawsuit."

Bennie hesitated. "Okay, you're right, it's personal. The attorney on the other side is Nick Machiavelli, do you know him?"

"I've heard of him."

"He's an old nemesis of Mary's, and she beat him last case and he's coming back with a vengeance. We believe he put the plaintiffs up to this matter. He manufactured the case."

Roger blinked. "So my intuition was correct."

"Yes."

"Then I decline the representation."

"Roger, come on. You represent lawyers accused of legal malpractice. How much more personal can it get?"

"This. A personal vendetta."

Bennie blinked. "How did you even know that from the Complaint?"

"I asked myself why the plaintiffs are proceeding under the Pennsylvania Human Relations Act as opposed to Title VII."

"Our firm is too small to be covered by Title VII. We're only four employees and three partners."

Roger raised a hand. "That's not what's significant here. Although both the federal and state statutes outlaw discrimination on the basis of gender, the Pennsylvania Human Relations Act has sharper teeth. Most significantly, under the PHRA, a plaintiff can sue a defendant personally and individually. That's what they're doing in this case. You three were named as individual defendants. That's not possible under Title VII."

"Damn, I should have realized that." Bennie pursed her lips, frowning. Judy and Mary exchanged glances. They should have realized that, too, but they'd been too upset. The baby kicked hard, like a rebuke.

Roger frowned slightly. "This provision weaponizes the statute. You're personally liable for any damages. It also throws your liability coverage into question. If you're not covered by insurance, then each of you would have to pay damages personally."

"Understood." Bennie nodded, and Mary felt a wave of fear. She and Anthony didn't have the financial cushion to withstand a personal judgment. And she felt a wave of guilt, too, for getting him, Bennie, and Judy, into this mess. She was Machiavelli's real target, but they were caught in the crossfire.

Roger continued, "Secondly, under the PHRA, there's no cap on compensatory damages, as under Title VII. Under Title VII, damages against even a firm of fourteen employees are capped at $50,000. Punitive damages are available under Title VII, but not under the PHRA, but they're so rarely awarded that it doesn't make a difference for your purposes."

"So the exposure is broader."

"Correct." Roger untented his fingers. "You have thirty days to answer the Complaint. Though extensions are freely given, I would suggest you do not extend."

"I absolutely agree. That's how we litigate. Even as defendants, we're aggressive. We take the lead and never let go. In fact, we need to file an answer to this, right away."

"No, you don't."

Bennie frowned. "Why? Don't you want to take the initiative?"

"Yes, I do. That's why I would wait."

"How is waiting 'taking the initiative'?" Bennie asked, but Roger only smiled, somewhat condescendingly, to Mary's eye.

"I have the same question," Mary said, backing Bennie up.

"Then I'll explain," Roger answered calmly. "To answer quickly is to react to Machiavelli. When you react to Machiavelli, you give him the initiative by your actions. Under the rules, you have ample time to answer. You respond to the rules, not to Machiavelli. Do you see the difference?"

"Fine," Bennie answered.

"After the Complaint is answered, the Pennsylvania Human Relations Commission begins its investigation. As you may know, you'll be deposed and there will be additional discovery. The focus will be the decisions you made not to hire the plaintiffs, as well as anecdotal or statistical evidence of gender bias in favor of women at your firm."

"How long do you think that takes? Six months to a year?"

"Yes, and after a year, the plaintiffs can go to file suit in court. Before that, as you know, the Commission will pressure you to settle."

"We'll never settle." Bennie folded her arms, and Mary realized they hadn't even discussed the possibility of settlement. Still, she felt the same way and suspected that Judy did too.

Roger frowned slightly. "I would advise you to keep an open mind about settlement."

"No, absolutely not. It would be an admission. I know you're going to say it's not, but it is, in reality."

"Nevertheless. Settling this dispute without prolonged litigation benefits you and the firm." Roger blinked. "Time is also a factor. The fact that they have a year to investigate prolongs the damage to your reputation, given that they're off to a fast start. Reports of the allegations are already popping up online."

Bennie grimaced. "That's why I wanted to meet right away. I also think we should hold a press conference today at the firm. We need to take our case to the media, too. I texted our associate Anne Murphy to set it up for two o'clock this afternoon."

"Good, go ahead even though you're not represented yet. In fact, it plays better. Their complaint is colorable, given the admission by your associate John Foxman, and he is the only male lawyer employed by you."

"It's not intentional." Bennie flushed, defensive.

"I'm sure it isn't. But the optics are poor and the numbers cut against you. In addition, your firm had its genesis as an all-female law firm. You have made many comments to that effect. It's not an illogical conclusion to think that what you manifested, you intended. The plaintiffs' position has a commonsense appeal."

Judy cringed, and Mary was feeling more worried. They needed Roger to take their case, and fast.

Bennie pursed her lips. "Don't tell me you think they can win, Roger."

"On the contrary, I do."

"The hell they will. We'll fight them tooth and nail. Tooth and nail!"

Roger blinked. "I'm sure that whichever lawyer you go to will be thrilled with the representation. You know everyone and you'll have your pick."

"Roger, seriously?" Bennie raised her voice. "You can't be turning me away. We've known each other forever."

"That's why another lawyer will do better for you than I would."

"Why? This case could *not* be more important to me!"

"That's why." Roger leaned back in his chair, spreading his elegant hands in appeal. "You're facing an existential threat to your law firm. For you, it's your reason for being. Your baby, your way of life. Your emotions are at an all-time high."

"Of course they are! What else would you expect?"

"Nothing else." Roger turned to Judy and Mary. "I don't know either of you, but I'm sure as partners, you share her concerns, temperament, even energies. Yes?"

"Yes, we do," Judy answered, and Mary

let it go. She didn't know whose energies she shared. Lately she didn't have any energy.

"Thought so." Roger nodded. "I operate very differently from you three."

"Oh come on!" Bennie scoffed. "Don't be such a control freak! We're all litigators, for God's sake!"

"True, but we litigate in our own way." Roger paused. "Ours is a Darwinian profession. Litigators are strong. We self-select. Only the toughest survive, so there's lots of toughness. Talk of force. Force meeting force. Conflict. Clashes. Battle imagery. War. Fighting. Like this." Roger smacked his hands together, a harsh sound echoing in the still, quiet office. "In addition, our justice system is adversarial. There's two teams, two sides. They fight, and one wins."

"So?" Bennie shot back, and Judy looked over, surprised at the crankiness in her tone. Mary was getting cranky herself, since evidently, Roger spoke haiku.

"I'm strong, but there are different forms of strength. I don't fight. I don't use force. I assert my position but I remain flexible. My associates are strong, too. But we're strong in a different way. I'm not sure the Vitez firm and the Rosato firm are well-suited."

"Roger, we're not getting married! We're

43

not even merging!"

"And that's what I mean." Roger smiled slightly. "I don't see things the way you do. I don't see the labels and divisions. Relationships are relationships. To me, the relationship between client and attorney is no different from the relationship between lovers or corporate entities. It's about my relationship to myself, ultimately."

"Oh please." Bennie groaned, but Judy tilted her head, obviously intrigued. Mary tried not to throw up again, thinking of all the money that was about to go down the tubes because of Machiavelli.

Roger shifted forward. "Bennie, to achieve a successful result, we need to work together. I don't think we'll work together well."

"Of course we will!" Bennie threw up her hands. "We're a *dream client*!"

"Or a nightmare client."

"How dare you!" Bennie spat out, and even Mary was taken aback. Only Judy was still listening.

Roger put up a palm. "Bennie, don't mistake me. It's not personal. That's exactly my point. A personal lawsuit means drama. I call plaintiffs like this 'paintiffs' because that's what they want to inflict."

"That's cute, but all plaintiffs cause pain

and drama."

"Not like this. I abhor drama. It dissipates energy and squanders clarity."

"Why won't you take us, *really*?" Bennie bore down. "It's because you don't think I'll listen to you, is that it? You think we'll have a power struggle?"

"No. I don't seek your obedience, I seek your cooperation. Not everything is binary. Yet that's how you see the world. You will be unhappy with my representation. Inevitably. As I will be unhappy representing —"

"If I may, Roger?" Judy interrupted. "I understand what you're saying. I agree that we have a difference in our energies. I know that our philosophies aren't necessarily compatible."

"Oh?" Roger tilted his head, and for the first time, Mary thought his blue eyes showed signs of life.

"Yes, and it's demonstrated in this very meeting. Bennie wants to argue you into taking our case, but she can't."

"Exactly."

Bennie looked over with a frown, but Judy kept talking.

"I've done a fair amount of reading on Eastern philosophy, as you have. I own most of these books, too. I've studied them." Judy gestured at the shelves. "After college, I was even thinking about becoming a Buddhist nun."

"What?" Mary blurted out, incredulous. She thought she knew everything about Judy. She'd even seen her bra drawer, which was a mess. Meanwhile, Mary's sister was a nun, but a Catholic nun, like normal. Mary didn't even know that Buddhists had nuns.

Roger beamed at Judy. "So why didn't you pursue becoming a nun?"

"I felt I could do more good as a lawyer. I handle the *pro bono* work that Bennie brings into the firm. I think of that as my reason for being, not the firm, the service. I follow The Way."

"You do?" Bennie's eyebrows lifted.

"Which way?" Mary asked, bewildered.

"The Way of the Tao," Judy answered with an unusually placid expression.

Mary looked at Judy, nonplussed. She knew her best friend had pink hair and minored in woo-woo, but Judy had gotten even wackier since she'd bought a loom. Mary wasn't sure how these two things were related, but nobody needed to weave things you could buy woven.

Roger folded his slim fingers on the glass desk. "So then, Judy, you understand. Your firm's way of doing things, and the fact that this lawsuit is so personal, counsels against my involvement."

"Perhaps," Judy said, equally calmly. "I see your position."

Bennie's eyes flared in anger. "Carrier, whose side are you *on*?"

Mary was pretty sure that Bennie was proving Vitez's point. Meanwhile, she'd never heard Judy say *perhaps* before. Mary didn't know what was coming over her best friend and prayed it helped the cause. That is, she prayed to the real God, not whoever they were talking about.

Judy nodded. "I do understand, Roger. It's interesting, though, that one of my favorite lessons from Lao-Tzu is about the Sage and his philosophy of service."

"How so?" Roger asked pleasantly.

"Lao-Tzu teaches, 'the more the Sage helps others, the more he benefits himself. The more he gives to others, the more he gets himself.' That is The Way of the Sage."

Roger didn't speak for a moment, and Mary was totally confused, since she thought they were talking about the Way of the Tao, not the Way of the Sage, and in any event, she had been raised Catholic, which was My Way Or The Highway.

Judy paused. "So I hope you'll revisit your decision not to represent us. After all, in the words of Lao-Tzu, 'The flexible are preserved unbroken.' "

"Excuse me, ladies." Roger closed his eyes and sat perfectly still for a moment.

Judy said nothing.

Bennie said nothing.

Mary held her breath.

Roger opened his eyes. "I have reached a decision."

CHAPTER FOUR

"I'll take the case," Roger said, and just as Bennie, Mary, and Judy were getting ready to cheer, a black landline phone buzzed on his desk, and Roger raised an index finger, pressed the intercom button, and answered the phone. "Yes? . . . Will do . . . Thank you," he said, hanging up and returning his attention to them. "Ladies, Machiavelli is currently holding a press conference regarding the lawsuit. It's being streamed live."

"Damn it!" Bennie smacked the desk. "He beat us to the punch!"

"Oh no," Judy said, dismayed.

"Bear with me." Roger turned to his laptop, pressed a few buttons, and turned the laptop face out as a video began to play. Mary felt stricken, just seeing Machiavelli, his dark eyes flashing and his hair slicked back. He had on a tailored Zegna suit and he sat in the middle of an ornate conference table at his office. Next to him sat three young men in suits, and the room was filled with reporters.

Machiavelli was saying, "Thank you for coming, and I hope you have the copy of the Complaint we distributed. This is a very important event, not just an ordinary lawsuit. Before you begin, let me say first that it's undoubtedly true there is sexism in society and that women are discriminated against in many professions. I don't deny that, and neither should you. History proves that it's true, not only in employment. Recent social movements show that it's also true in general. It seems like every day there's another hashtag." The reporters chuckled, and Machiavelli continued. "But of late, it's also true that there is discrimination that isn't talked about as much — and that's reverse discrimination against men."

Roger watched the video, saying nothing.

Mary felt her blood boil. "Now he's going to make it sound noble, when really he's just trying to get me back."

Bennie growled. "I want to crush this kid."

Machiavelli continued, "Many women who have attained positions of influence in the profession use their empowerment as a sword, not a shield, and on occasion, they use it against men. Nowhere is this more true than the case that we filed today with

50

the Pennsylvania Human Relations Commission, on behalf of these three young lawyers."

Machiavelli gestured at the three men, and they smiled as he introduced each one, their appearance confirming to Mary that the lawsuit was manufactured, if not cast, like a movie. Nobody she went to law school with was as handsome as any of these plaintiffs, who looked like three male models in a racially balanced ad campaign. They were all about the same height, which was tall, and the same weight, which was superhunky. Michael Battle, who was Asian, had a dazzling smile and a spray of glossy bangs. Graham Madden was African-American, and he wore glasses but didn't look as if he needed them. And the whitest of white guys, with blond hair and blue eyes, was Stephen McManus, who sat next to Machiavelli.

"These three men are brilliant young graduates of top local law schools, but they were not hired by Rosato & DiNunzio simply because they are male." There was murmuring among reporters, and Machiavelli continued, "Rosato & DiNunzio was founded by Bennie Rosato, a proponent of women's rights, and she intended her firm to be an all-woman's law firm. She bragged about it whenever she could, in public. For over a decade, Bennie Rosato hired, cultivated, and promoted only female lawyers, specifically, now-partners Mary Di-Nunzio and Judy Carrier, and associate Anne Murphy. All these women have, at one time or another, described the firm as 'all-female.' Imagine what outcry there would be — justifiably so — if any of the defendants had described their law firm as all-white, all-black, or all-Asian. I submit to you that, legally and morally, there is simply no principled difference between that and describing a firm as all-female."

Bennie kept shaking her head. "This scumbag is lecturing me about morals? About laws?"

Judy sighed. "Arg."

Mary didn't know what to say. She had described the law firm that way herself and never thought twice about it. She knew that they hadn't discriminated against anybody, but she couldn't deny that Machiavelli was putting them in a terrible light.

"The law firm of Rosato & DiNunzio has only one male lawyer, named John Foxman, who was hired last year. But don't let that token fool you. Lest you doubt the veracity of our allegations, sitting at my right hand is Stephen McManus, who interviewed with Mr. Foxman when an opening for an associate was advertised. During that interview, John Foxman admitted that he often felt out of place as the sole male lawyer at the firm."

Roger eyed the screen. "Foxman is the one in the Complaint?"

"Exactly." Bennie shook her head, fuming. "The gift that keeps on giving."

Judy looked over, concerned.

Mary kept her own counsel but she was kicking herself, almost as much as the baby was kicking her. She should have known that Machiavelli wouldn't wait. She, Bennie, and Judy would hold their press conference, but they were already caught off guard, playing catch-up.

Machiavelli frowned. "Clearly, the principals of Rosato & DiNunzio have acted unlawfully and in violation of the Pennsylvania Human Relations Act, and we have filed this Complaint to vindicate the rights not only of these plaintiffs, but of men everywhere. We seek justice and the American ideal of equal treatment regardless of race, creed, religion, gender, national origin, and sexual preference. We'll be trying our case in the courts, not the media, so I won't be taking questions today." The reporters complained, but Machiavelli waved them into silence. "I urge you to continue to pay special attention to this case. I'm not going to show all the cards in my hand now, and surprises are in store. I'm betting that before we even get to court, you will understand the absolute truth of the allegations in this Complaint — and the reason that Rosato & DiNunzio should be out of business. Thank you."

Machiavelli finished by looking directly into the camera, his dark eyes boring into her through the lens, and Mary knew he was talking to her. She felt a shudder at hearing him threaten the firm so directly. Machiavelli was coming for them, and she didn't know if they could defeat him, even if they were represented by the Zen Master.

Roger ended the video, turning to them. "Breathe deeply, ladies," he said calmly.

"Hell no!" Bennie jumped to her feet. "He wants a press conference, I'll give him a press conference."

CHAPTER FIVE

Bennie charged off the elevator ahead of Mary and Judy, though Mary was getting used to lagging behind everybody, since it took forever to waddle anywhere. These days her belly button reached her destination before she did, followed by her stretch marks. Bennie was on a tear, having spent the cab ride back to the office ranting about Machiavelli, despite Judy's efforts to calm her and Mary's efforts not to fart.

"Marshall!" Bennie called as she approached the reception desk, but the receptionist was already on her feet and holding out a pink flurry of phone messages.

"Hi, guys. The media has been calling all morning. I told them about the press conference, and we're good to go."

"Thank you." Bennie grabbed the messages on the fly and headed down the hallway toward their offices, followed by Judy and Mary, who caught Marshall's eye with a wink.

Marshall stopped Mary before they left the reception area. "Mary, it's lunchtime, and you need to eat. I ordered you some vegetable soup and crackers, and it's in the conference room. I put your baby gifts in your office."

"Thanks so much," Mary said, meaning it. Marshall was a mother of three, so she had the pregnancy drill down. "Did you get lunch for Judy? She's eating for two — herself and Lao-Tzu."

"Namaste," Judy said with a smile.

Marshall chuckled. "Yes, I got you and Bennie the usual, and it's in the conference room. I think you have enough time to eat before it starts."

"Thanks," Judy said, and they started walking down the hallway after Bennie, who hurried ahead, barking orders.

"John, where are you? I need answers! And documents!"

"Here I am." John came out of his office with a handful of papers. "I figured out what happened with the plaintiffs. We got sixteen resumes in response to my ad, all the applicants were men. I interviewed three, one of which turned out to be a plaintiff. Mc-Manus. I think you were on trial at the time, that's why you didn't know. Here's your copies of the emails and resumes."

"Thanks." Bennie took the papers but kept moving. "Walk with me. I want to understand as much as possible about this fact situation. Obviously we're not telling them at the press conference, but I want to be up to speed."

John fell into step with Bennie. "Do you want me at the press conference?"

"Are you kidding?" Bennie didn't hide her annoyance. "You have to explain yourself, and we're going to meet now to prepare. Where's Anne?"

"Waiting for you inside," John answered, just as Bennie opened the door to the conference room and Mary and Judy filed in behind her, surprised at the sight. The room was back to normal except for a rolling rack of clothes, boxes of shoes, a professional grade makeup case, and a full-length mirror, leaning against the wall.

"Bennie, don't freak," Anne said, putting up her hand like a traffic cop. She had on a slim black dress which hugged her model-thin body, making her arms look like licorice sticks. Her long red hair had been brushed to perfection, and her makeup looked freshly done. "I know you're not going to like this, but you need to take my advice. Just this once."

"What's going on here?" Bennie stopped at the threshold of the conference room with John. Judy went directly to her lunch, which had been set out on the table, and Mary wobbled over to the clothes rack, which held an array of gorgeous dresses and suits with the price tags attached. They had been divided into three sections: BENNIE, JUDY, MARY.

"Just hear me out, Bennie," Anne said, urgently. "I know you don't care about clothes, but your messaging at the press conference has to be on point. Part of that is how you look. During lunch, I went shopping with a stylist friend of mine, and we pulled clothes for each of you, and a makeup artist I know lent us everything we need. I even have lip plumpers!"

"No." Bennie shook her head, incredulous. "That's absolutely out of the question. We need to prepare."

"I can make you up while you work, all of you. Just pick a dress and we'll get started."

"Get this stuff out of here." Bennie set the documents on the table.

"Bennie, listen. I watched Machiavelli's press conference, and it was perfection. He looked the part and so did the plaintiffs. They were appealing, put together, and credible."

"Oh please. The plaintiffs weren't credible because they didn't say anything."

"They didn't have to. They dressed the part and they acted the part. They scored without saying a word, and Machiavelli looked awesome, too. Respectable. Believable, responsible —"

"He's style, and we're substance. We always have been."

"Please, listen to me, I'm right." Anne took a step closer, her expression pleading. "This isn't an argument in court, it's a press conference, where the visual matters as much as the content. These reporters are going to take pictures of you, print them, and publish them. The photos of your press conference are going to be shown next to Machiavelli's —"

"We don't have time to argue this. We didn't get where we are on our looks."

Listening, Mary thought Anne was making sense. Why turn down a free makeover? Besides, one of the dresses was super cute, especially for maternity clothes. It was a navy-linen shift with a boatneck, in which she would look nautical but not like a battleship. But she would take a pass on the lip plumpers. Everything on her was plump enough.

Mary said, "Bennie, I think Anne might

be onto something. It's like Who Wore It Better, for lawyers."

"But we look fine, don't we?" Bennie strode to the mirror, and Mary could tell that even she wasn't completely happy with her reflection. Bennie's blonde hair had curled in the humidity, so tendrils coiled out of her topknot like broken springs. Her khaki suit was as wrinkled as a Venetian blind, and Mary was pretty sure she hadn't shaved her legs recently, but that was un-sayable.

"Sorry, but I agree with Bennie," Judy said, sitting at the table with her mouth full of cheese hoagie. "We are what we are. That is The Way of the Tao."

Mary looked over. "Did you really want to be a Buddhist nun?"

"Yes."

"How did I not know that?"

"Because people are eternally unknow-able."

"More Lao-Tzu?"

"No, my mother." Judy shrugged, chew-ing away. "Anyway we don't need to get all dressed up. Everybody already knows what we look like. We look like ourselves. I'm a case in point."

Mary hid her smile while Bennie, Anne, and John took in Judy's outfit, one of her wackiest ever. In fact, if Judy had a stylist, it would be spin art. She wore a banana-yellow T-shirt that said YOU SAY YOU WANT A WEAVOLUTION, which she had on with throwback painter's pants and vegan clogs, in green. Her pink hair stuck out like a fuzzy tennis ball, and from one earlobe hung a gray feather, which Mary hoped was a new earring and not from a passing pigeon.

Anne folded her arms. "Well, ladies? What's the verdict?"

"I vote yes," Mary answered.

"I vote no," Judy answered.

Bennie glanced sideways at Anne. "Only if you do it while we work. And no lip plumpers."

CHAPTER SIX

The press conference was about to start, and Bennie, Mary, Judy, Anne, and John settled on one side of the conference table, while reporters took seats on the other side of the table, spilling outside the room and opening notebooks, thumbing through cell phones, and taking pictures with their cell phones, cameras, and video cameras. Mary faced the throng with renewed self-confidence, since she had managed to keep her soup-and-crackers down and there was nothing like new clothes to boost a girl's mood. She had on a shiny pair of low-heeled black pumps, a fresh pair of contacts, and more makeup than most hookers, which wasn't necessarily a bad thing.

She glanced over at Bennie, who looked beautiful with only light makeup emphasizing her bright blue eyes and a bronzer on her lovely cheekbones. Her crazy curls had been flat-ironed into a classic French twist, and for the first time ever, she wore a suit that wasn't a Brooks Brothers khaki. Anne had talked her into a well-tailored red suit because it was a bold color, which made it butch enough for Bennie to feel in charge.

Sitting next to Mary was Judy, in a faux-Chanel suit of pinkish tweed, which looked fashion-forward with her magenta hair and edgy makeup. None of the reporters seemed to notice that she still had on her vegan clogs, since she refused to wear any of the new shoes because they were leather. Anne sat next to her, undoubtedly thrilled to be finished styling her colleagues while they studied documents, argued over case strategy, and rehearsed the press conference. John sat at the end of the line, holding his head high, which Mary knew was an act. He was still embarrassed that he had been mentioned in the Complaint, and most of the rehearsal was directed at him, since he would have to take questions about what he'd said during the job interview.

"Ladies and gentlemen," Bennie began, with a newly glossy smile. She had on nude lip gloss, since she wouldn't agree to actual lipstick, much less lipliner. "Thank you for coming. You know me and my partners well enough to know that we rarely speak to the press. We simply don't try our cases in the

63

media. But at the same time, we felt compelled to respond not only to the allegations raised in this meritless Complaint, but also to the entirely erroneous statements about us personally, made by opposing counsel Nick Machiavelli at his press conference today."

The reporters scribbled away, the photographers took pictures, and somebody in the back raised his hand. "Will you take questions later?"

"Of course, briefly." Bennie smiled again, as if she didn't mind being interrupted, which Mary knew she hated. In any event, they had already decided that they would take questions, anticipated what they would be asked, and developed answers for each one. "As you already know, Nick Machiavelli has today filed a complaint with the Pennsylvania Human Relations Commission on behalf of three individual plaintiffs, suing me and my partners personally under the Pennsylvania Human Relations Act, alleging that we failed to hire the three individuals because they were male. I'm not going to discuss the specifics of the allegations and I'm speaking for my partners today, Mary DiNunzio and Judy Carrier." Bennie gestured to Judy and Mary, who nodded, but stayed quiet, according to plan.

"We wanted to go on record to make clear that we deny these allegations, that they're completely untrue, and that we will prove as much before the Commission, and if need be, in the Court of Common Pleas. However, a categorical denial is not the reason we invited you to our offices today."

Mary's face twitched under her makeup. She knew what Bennie was going to say next because they had decided upon it together, but it was tough and aggressive. Judy had agreed even though it was against her religion, and Mary had gone along with it, too. But that didn't mean that she wasn't nervous. She sent up a prayer to St. Jude, Patron Saint of Lost Causes, and tried not to see that as symbolic.

Bennie tilted her chin upward. "What we want you to understand is that this litigation against us was filed in bad faith. It's not a lawsuit, it's a smear campaign. Behind the smear campaign is not these three individual plaintiffs. The person behind the smear campaign is Nick Machiavelli, and we have ample reason to believe that he manufactured this case." She paused when the reporters reacted with surprise and interest, obviously anticipating something juicy. "You may be wondering why he would do such a thing. The answer is, for personal revenge because we defeated him in a previous case — and for other personal reasons we will not detail today. But as he said, there'll be plenty of twists and turns as this litigation goes on, so stay tuned."

Instantly the reporters reacted, looking at each other, scribbling more hastily, or starting their cell-phone video cameras if they hadn't already. Judy stiffened in her chair, and Mary kept her face front and her lip-sticked smile plastered on, as Bennie continued.

"Unfortunately, the procedures under the Pennsylvania Human Relations Act do not provide for a counterclaim by defendants or a mechanism for dismissing a lawsuit brought in bad faith. However, we are putting Nick Machiavelli on notice. We will defeat him before the Human Relations Commission and if he continues to pursue this matter in Common Pleas Court, we will file a counterclaim against him for fees and damages." Bennie paused, eyeing the reporters directly. "And we will defeat him, and soundly."

Mary swallowed hard. She didn't know if Bennie was right that they would be able to prove that Nick had manufactured the case, but they were going to devote themselves to the case for the foreseeable future, or at

least until she gave birth to a child, whichever came first.

"Ladies and gentlemen, that's our statement, so I open it up to a few brief questions at this time."

The reporters all shouted at once, "Bennie, I have a question!" "Bennie, who's
counsel for the defense and why isn't he or
she here?" "So this is a vendetta?"

Bennie raised a hand to silence them.
"Counsel for the defense is Roger Vitez, and
he isn't here because we could handle it
ourselves. And no, this is not a vendetta,
not on our part. If anything, we're on the
receiving end of the vendetta, and if it was
anybody but us, I would say we were victims. But anybody who knows this firm
knows that we're no victims."

A few of the reporters chuckled, and a
woman nodded in approval. Somebody
from the back yelled out, "Bennie, any comment about the statement that John Foxman allegedly made to one of the plaintiffs?"

Bennie held up a hand again. "Yes, that's
an excellent question and needs to be addressed. So I'll turn it over to my associate
John Foxman, because he can speak for
himself." She gestured to John. "John,
would you like to take that question?"

Mary held her breath, knowing that it was

risky, even though they had discussed verbatim what he would say. She felt Judy nudge her under the table with her clog, which was kind of scratchy.

John cleared his throat, facing the reporter. "Yes, I can answer that succinctly. First, I do not believe that this firm or any of its partners discriminate against men. I do not believe they ever discriminated against me and I do not believe that they discriminated against the individual plaintiffs, as the Complaint alleges. I agree completely with Bennie that this lawsuit is a vendetta brought for personal reasons by opposing counsel Nick Machiavelli. I myself have personal knowledge of the facts that support our position, but I am not going to discuss that today."

John spoke firmly and confidently, his tone ringing true, and Mary could see the reporters reacting positively. She began to feel a glimmer of hope that this press conference had paid off, in addition to getting her a free dress and shoes. Getting out in front of the allegations was the right move, but she knew it was only the beginning of a long, difficult battle.

John continued, "That said, I did interview the plaintiff in question and I did make the statement that he alleged. However, in the

Complaint, the statement is taken completely out of context. As you can see, I'm the only male lawyer at this firm. And occasionally, yes, I do feel out of place. In fact, this morning we held a baby shower in this very room, and I felt out of place. *Way* out of place."

The reporters laughed, taking notes and snapping pictures of John, who forced a smile, and Mary gave him a lot of credit. This couldn't have been easy, but he was hitting a home run, just by being honest. She felt a sudden swell of pride for truth, justice, and the American way. Or maybe it was the hormones.

John heaved a final sigh. "So I think that's all I should say at the present time. As a trial lawyer, I hate to give the other side free discovery. But like Bennie, I felt compelled to respond to these allegations and explain them. Before I finish, I'd like to take a moment to apologize to my colleagues at the firm, whom I like and respect so very much. I'm sorry I spoke so imprudently, and I'm sorry I gave Nick Machiavelli ammunition to use against us."

Mary looked over in surprise and so did Bennie and Judy. They hadn't rehearsed any of this before the conference, and John was clearly speaking from the heart.

Bennie didn't hesitate. "John, thank you very much." She returned her attention to the reporters. "Any last questions before we get back to work?"

"Just one!" a female reporter yelled from the back. "John, if you like it so much here, why are you looking for a new job?"

"Wait, uh, well —" John didn't finish the sentence, turning red under his fair skin. Mary had no idea that John was looking for a job and she was pretty sure that nobody else knew either. John seemed completely flustered, so it must have been true.

Bennie rallied. "Thank you for your question," she called to the reporter, without missing a beat. "John's future employment isn't relevant to the allegations in this lawsuit, nor is it anyone's business but his."

"But did you know he had his resume out, Bennie?"

Bennie kept her smile firmly in place. "As you know, Rosato & DiNunzio was founded not as an all-female firm, but as a firm that represented those seeking justice and vindication for individual civil liberties. As such, we have no problems with anyone who seeks to change or even better their lot in life. And equally, we value the privacy of those that do so, as I assume you will too."

"John, why are you telling people that

'you'll never make partner at Rosato be-cause you're not a woman'?" The question came from the same reporter, a scruffy woman with spiky gelled hair, in the back. "Doesn't that support the Complaint? Or is that bad faith, too?"

John recoiled as if absorbing a blow. Mary froze, in stunned disbelief. Judy couldn't hide her frown, and Anne's eyes rounded with shock.

"That's enough for now." Bennie rose quickly, despite her new high heels. "We're not going to examine every single statement John may or may not have made, nor are we going to try the lawsuit in my confer-ence room."

"John, answer the question!" the scruffy reporter called out, and the others joined in, making a minor uproar. "Mr. Foxman, any comment?" "Is that true?" "Who'd you say that to?" "Mr. Foxman, look over here!"

Bennie ignored them all. "Ladies and gentlemen, thank you so much for coming. We appreciate your attention and we look forward to never seeing you again."

The reporters burst into laughter, closing their notebooks, pocketing their cell phones, shutting down the cameras, picking up their messenger bags, and getting ready to go. Mary, Judy, Anne, and John remained seated while Bennie did some glad-handing, then stopped the woman with the gelled spiky hair, who had asked the last question.

"Excuse me," Bennie said, touching the woman's arm. "What's your name? Who are you with?"

"I freelance," the reporter answered, hurrying ahead, bolting out of the conference room ahead of the others, then they left, and Bennie closed the door behind them. They were finally alone in the conference room, but nobody said anything. Mary sensed that partly they were waiting for the hubbub to die down on the other side of the door — and partly there was nothing to say. The press conference had been a resounding success until it turned into a disaster. Mary was still processing what she had just heard, and Judy looked as stunned as she was, now that they had let their game faces slip.

Bennie leaned against the back of the closed door. "Foxman!" she said, her blue eyes flashing with cold fury. "What the *hell*!"

CHAPTER SEVEN

The conference room went dead quiet, and Mary hadn't known she could feel worse, but she did. She was dumbfounded that John wanted to leave the firm and would bad-mouth them that way. Judy and Anne looked equally astonished. They had been utterly blindsided, and now reporters would run with the story that was new evidence against them, damaging their case. There could be no doubt that John had done it, because he looked guilt-stricken to Mary, and she should know because she was a guilt expert.

Bennie didn't rant and rave, but merely folded her arms, still leaning against the door. "You need to explain this to us, right now," she said, with controlled anger.

"I'm sorry." John rose hastily, as if about to address the court, which in a way, he was, and Judge Rosato wasn't having any.

"So that reporter's question was true? You

did make a statement that you 'would never make partner here because you're not a woman'?"

"Yes, that's true."

"Why didn't you tell us this before the press conference?"

"I didn't think it would come up," John answered, defensively.

"You let us get blindsided. You let us walk into it."

"How did I know the reporter would know?"

"People talk in this town. These reporters, they have sources, they cultivate them. That's their job. How naïve are you, Foxman?"

"I didn't see it coming."

"*You* didn't see it coming?" Bennie's temper flared, but she paused, composing herself. "Okay. Let's begin at the beginning. I want you to tell the facts, and all of the facts, so that we don't ever get surprised again. What gave rise to you making that comment?"

"So this is exactly what happened and why." John licked his dry lips. "You know the antitrust matter, *London Technologies*. If you remember, when you got the case, you assigned the case to Anne and me, and we met with the clients, Jim and Sanjay.

After the meeting, I asked you if I could be lead counsel because I'm an antitrust expert."

Bennie didn't bat an eye, and Mary wondered if she would ever be able to say that she was an expert in anything so easily. Except guilt, but that didn't count.

"But you said no." John swallowed visibly, his Adam's apple almost getting caught on his cutaway collar. "You made Anne lead counsel. Just about then, you made Judy partner, and I saw the writing on the wall. I didn't think you would promote me the way you do the others and I started to look around for another job."

"Let me make one thing crystal clear." Bennie glowered, but remained in control. "I made Anne lead counsel on *London Technologies* because she was senior to you, not because she was a woman."

John frowned. "But I've tried more antitrust cases than she has. She hasn't tried a single one."

Anne was about to say something, but Bennie waved her into silence. Mary knew Anne would be seething and didn't blame her. Anne was a superstar lawyer, slated to become the next partner at the firm. She'd earned it through talent and hard work, but she had lived a life of people underestimating her brains because of her looks, which were so gorgeous that she'd put herself through law school working as a catalog model. Still she'd become a great girlfriend to Mary and Judy, who had come to realize that hating on pretty girls was just plain mean.

Bennie continued, "That's not the point, Foxman, and it's not your decision. It's my client, and I make the decision. In addition, after we had our initial meeting with Jim and Sanjay, it was clear to me that they liked Anne. In fact, they told me as much, afterward."

"Only because of her looks," John shot back. "They were crushing on her, it was obvious."

Anne's mouth dropped open. "How dare you!"

John put up his hands, defensively. "Anne, I'm not saying that you intentionally used your looks, I'm saying that's part of your appeal. You know that, everybody knows it. You're hot. It helps. Appearances matter. That's why you bought those clothes. Not everything is merit-based, even in business, and when you got the case instead of me, I didn't think it was merit-based."

"It *was*, John!" Anne shot back, angering.

Bennie interjected, "Murphy, don't start
—"

Anne ignored Bennie, rising. "John, are you frigging kidding me? It doesn't matter if I tried an antitrust case. How many people have? They're massive and they almost never try! *London Technologies* isn't going to try either —"

"Murphy, let me deal." Bennie waved to get Anne's attention, but Mary knew it wouldn't help. Anne was a redhead, which is a blonde with poor impulse control.

"— and I can read the substantive law as well as you, because that's what any lawyer does in every case, and you may act like you're the 'brain behind the case' but believe it or not, I'm a *real live lawyer,* not Lawyer Barbie —"

"Murphy, let me —"

"— and as for Jim and Sanjay, maybe in the beginning they liked my looks, but I ignored that and they got over it. That happens all the time, and I deal with it, on my own, because nobody feels sorry for the pretty girl. Now Jim and Sanjay respect me for my work, and it's really sad that you don't! And while we're on the subject —"

"Murphy, let —"

"— John, I tell you, *your* problem is that you don't like taking orders from women!

77

You don't like it when I tell you what to do, even though I *am* lead counsel. You resist me. You don't listen. You come back at me, telling me that we don't need whatever I want. For example, in *London Tech,* when I didn't want to hire McManus, I told you to start over and get us a permanent associate. Instead, you ignored me and got a contract lawyer. If I were a man, you'd respect me. You'd do what I say when I say it, no question —"

"Murphy —"

"— and I don't even think you like it that the partners in this firm are female! *You're* the sexist, not us, and anyway, whatever you think, you have a helluva nerve bad-mouthing us around town! A *helluva nerve!*"

"Murphy, enough!" Bennie opened the conference-room door. "You made your point, but I think you should go. Anything we say is discoverable, and you don't need to be part of it. Thank you very much."

"Fine, I get it." Anne stalked toward the door, her glossy hair flying. "I'm out!"

Mary felt terrible, seeing Anne and John at odds, choosing opposite sides. She used to think that John liked it here, but she had been wrong. They had never turned on each other before, and it had always been Rosato & DiNunzio against the world. The fight forced her to accept the reality that their happy little law firm might be a thing of the past.

Bennie closed the door and returned her attention to John. "Let's get back to the facts. I'd like to know which statements you made with regard to your feelings that we discriminated against you."

John winced. "I didn't say *that,* and really, I don't even think that."

"But you said something like it?"

"Yes."

"What did you say exactly?" Bennie shot back, in cross-examination mode.

"I don't know, just, basically what the reporter said, that 'I don't think I'll make partner at Rosato because I'm not a woman.' " John grimaced. "But really I don't think that you discriminate *per se.*"

Bennie's eyes flared. "That's the definition of discrimination *per se.*"

"But I don't really think it, not *really,* I just said it, I should have thought before I spoke, I didn't know —"

"Enough." Bennie cut him off with a hand chop. "To whom did you say that?"

"The firms that interviewed me."

"Who? How many firms?"

John hesitated. "I have to think about that."

"Were there that *many*?"

"No, I just have to think. I don't remember them off the top of my head."

Listening, Mary felt a wave of sadness. She hated seeing John on the spot and she hated what he was saying. She glanced at Judy, who was biting her lip, her head tilted down. Mary knew she would be feeling responsible, since she was closest to him.

"Foxman, how could you not remember? You don't know where you applied?"

"Okay." Flustered, John raised a hand. "I know Hunter & Logue and Berger, Ginn. I'd have to think of the others. I sent the resume to a headhunter, and he's the one who put it out there."

"Which headhunter?"

"Dean Slovak."

"You contacted Dean or he contacted you?"

"He contacted me."

"Did he have a job opening in mind or he was just fishing?"

"He didn't say, but he called me after Judy made partner. It was my lowest point, and I just sent in the resume."

"When was this, exactly?"

"A few months ago. I have to check my calendar."

"Do you remember which firm or firms

you made the statement to?' "

"It was Hunter & Logue, I'm pretty sure."

"Did you say that at more than one firm?"

"I have to think about that, but I don't think so." John hesitated. "They asked why I wanted to leave, so I had to give the reason."

Bennie folded her arms. "Did you give all of them that reason?"

"No, only Hunter."

"And how do you know that?"

"Because I was most interested in Hunter. They needed to fill a position on a new antitrust matter, and that appealed to me. So we talked in more depth."

"With whom did you interview, do you remember? I know most of those guys."

"Sure, Mark Jacobowitz."

Bennie looked as if she were about to say something, then kept it to herself, but Mary knew how upset she would be inside. John's statement not only damaged their case, it embarrassed all of them. Even Mary hated to think that John would say that about her, around town. It wasn't true, and she knew tons of people in the legal community. Her reputation mattered, especially in Philly.

Bennie continued, "So Mark's the one you made the comment to. You're not sure if you said it to anybody else?"

"I don't think I did."

"Did you interview with anyone at Hunter besides Mark?"

"Yes, an associate."

"What was his name?"

"It was Mark's son. Bradley."

"Did you make the comment to Bradley, too?"

"Oops, yes, I forgot about him. I guess I felt comfortable with him."

Mary had no idea how they would mitigate the damage, and she was angry at the unfairness of the accusation. They hadn't discriminated against John because he was a man, and he wasn't senior enough to be a partner yet. Meanwhile, Hunter & Logue was an all-male firm, but nobody thought *that* was discriminatory. That was the status quo.

Bennie pursed her lips. "Did you take notes after any of these interviews?"

"No."

"Did you exchange emails in connection with any of these interviews?"

"Yes."

"I'd like to have copies of them."

"Sure thing," John said, his tone turning agreeable. "I also talked to Mark about the possibility of partnership in the next year. He said that was definitely something that they would consider."

"Did Hunter make you an offer?"

"Yes."

"And what did you do?"

"I declined."

"Why?"

John flushed slightly. "The pay was lower."

"Hmph," Bennie said, without elaboration. "Are you negotiating with them?"

"No, we were too far apart."

"Did anyone else make any offers?"

"I haven't heard back yet." John sighed, sensing his cross-examination was over. "Bennie, as I said before, I think I should resign."

"I wish you wouldn't."

"Why? I mean, how can I work here anymore?" John raised his hands in appeal, obviously at a loss.

"How can you not? If you leave, it will confirm the reporter's story, which we did not do in real time. And it leaves a huge, gaping hole in our *London Technologies* case. I don't know how we can stage that litigation without you." Bennie gazed at him evenly. "Bottom line, the best way to mitigate the damage to this firm is for you to work here and for us not to speak of this anymore. But it's your choice, and I leave it to you."

"I'd like to think about it."

"That is your right and privilege." Bennie opened the conference-room door. "Now if you'll give us some time in private."

"Again, I'm very sorry, to everyone," John said to Mary and Judy, then headed for the door.

Bennie let him out and closed the door behind him. "Well, well, well," she said, exhaling heavily. "We have an enemy in our midst."

Judy sighed, miserably. "He's not really our enemy, is he?"

"Yes, but no matter." Bennie's eyes glittered. "Let's take a page from Machiavelli's book. 'Keep your friends close and your enemies closer.' We can deal."

Mary looked up, worried sick. "What do we do now?"

"We review the documents and try to understand the facts of our own case." Bennie gestured at the credenza, where she had put the documents that John had given her. "In other words, we get to work."

"Arg, I am so sorry." Judy leaned back in her chair, as if pressed there by some unseen weight. "I can't believe he did this."

"Carrier, it's not your fault." Bennie slid her phone from her blazer pocket. "Let's call Lao-Tzu before he reads it online."

CHAPTER EIGHT

A copper sun dipped behind the flat roofs, satellite discs, and trolley wires that hung over South Philly like an urban canopy, and Mary braced herself before she went into her parents' house. She wished she could have gone straight home after the long afternoon at work, but her parents wanted to see her more often now that she was pregnant, which had upgraded her already lofty status as Amazing Daughter to that of Magical Grandchild Vessel.

Her parents, Vita and Matty DiNunzio, lived on Mercy Street, which was lined on either side by two-story redbrick rowhouses, differentiated by the color of their shutters (generally black), the railing on their front stoops (wrought-iron preferred), and the contents of their bay windows (Eagles, Phillies, or Flyers paraphernalia required, religious statuary optional, Virgin Mary always on point). Mary had grown up in this house, with its scrollwork D in the metal screen door, like all the other neighbors. When she was little, she'd thought it stood for "door" until she realized it stood for DiNunzio, DaTuno, and DeTizio, because back then, everybody was Italian-American. Nowadays the screen doors had changed, but the people were still the same. Which was the way of South Philly, if not the Tao.

"MARE, IS THAT YOU ONNA STOOP?" her father shouted through the screen door, because his hearing aid plugged his ear like a plastic cork, insulating him from all sound.

"Yes, Pop!" Mary opened the door and entered the long, rectangular house, which was so stuffed with people that it reminded her of a manicotti with too much ricotta filling.

Her father was watching the Phillies game with her husband, Anthony Rotunno, and her father's three best friends, The Tonys — Tony-From-Down-The-Block LoMonaco, Pigeon Tony Lucia, and Tony "Two Feet" Pensiera, whose nickname had a nickname, namely Feet. They were honorary uncles and hung out at the house, like an octogenarian street gang. Beyond the living room was the kitchen, which held her mother and her mother-in-law, Elvira, whom Mary secretly called El Virus. Most people would think that a kitchen with two women wasn't as full as a living room with five men, but these two women meant that the kitchen was not only dangerously over occupancy, but possibly thermonuclear. Mary's mother and El Virus were as different as old-school and no-school, but lately they'd been getting along unusually well, both counting down to the birth of their grandchild, coming soon from a uterus near you.

"Hey, honey!" Her husband Anthony came over, smiling his warm smile, his espresso-hued eyes meeting hers, telegraphing *I know you're beat but we'll get through this together,* then giving her a big hug.

"Hi, love you." Mary hugged him back, melting into the comfort of his arms and soft Oxford shirt. She knew he must've heard about the lawsuit against them, though she hadn't had a spare minute to text him, since they'd worked all afternoon preparing their Answer and discussing it with Roger on the phone. Luckily, her parents and The Tonys didn't go online, except Tony-From-Down-The-Block, who supplemented his Social Security playing PokerStars.com.

"MARE, HOW YA DOIN'? HOW YA

FEEL? COME AN' SIDDOWN!" Her father grabbed Mary and hugged her, and The Tonys clustered around her like a cloud of cigar smoke and Ben Gay fumes.

"Mare, you're getting bigger every day!" Feet patted her belly, and Mary didn't stop him. Everybody in the family touched her belly, and she figured it was preparing the baby for DiNunzio World, where you had to hug and kiss everybody anytime you left the room.

"Mary, it's so good to see you!" Tony-From-Down-The-Block took her right arm. "You feeling okay?"

"Maria, Maria!" Pigeon Tony took her other arm, leading her into the kitchen, where she was love-attacked by her mother.

"Maria, come and siddown!" Her mother tugged her into the kitchen and placed her bodily in a seat at the table, which was already set for dinner.

"Honey, you look so tired!" El Virus hustled over with a full plate of ravioli covered in tomato sauce, or "gravy" in South-Phillyspeak. "You gotta eat somethin' or you're gonna faint!"

"Mare!" El Virus picked up Mary's fork, stabbed a ravioli, and was just about to try to put it in Mary's mouth when Anthony intercepted the fork.

"Ma, stop, she can feed herself." Anthony set the fork down on Mary's plate.

"But Ant, look at her! She looks so tired!"

"She looks fine," Anthony said, patting Mary's arm.

Tony-From-Down-The-Block said, "I think she looks good."

Feet said, "I think she looks good, too."

"OF COURSE SHE DOES! SHE'S GORGEOUS!"

Mary smiled at her father, but let the others talk, having grown accustomed to everyone discussing her as if she weren't in the room, deciding what she should and shouldn't do, what she should and shouldn't eat, or whether she should or shouldn't work, exercise, or otherwise exist.

El Virus was saying, "Matty, are you *blind*? Take a good look at your daughter! Her face is white as a ghost!"

Anthony looked over at his mother. "Mom, she's not sick, she's pregnant."

"Right." Mary managed another smile, but sometimes pregnant felt like sick, though it would've been politically incorrect to say so.

El Virus waved him off, her gelled nails thickly red, like a manicured vulture. "Ant'n'y, you're a man, you don't know! I fainted all the time, carryin' you and your brother. She has to eat for her blood sugar!"

"Her blood sugar is fine." Anthony sat down as Mary's father and The Tonys settled into their seats and began passing the steaming platter of ravioli, which trailed an aroma of tomatoes, oregano, and fresh basil. Mary's mother hovered, waiting for Mary to need something before she sat down, dressed in her flowery housedress, with her arthritic fingers forming a gnarled ball at her waist and her gray hair teased to cover her bald spot.

"*Maria,* drink some water, you gotta drink."

"I will, Ma."

"Drink!"

"Look, see?" Mary raised the water glass and took a sip, like a drinking demonstration, and her mother smiled, leaning over and giving her a kiss on the cheek and a little back rub.

"Love you, *cara.*"

"Love you, too, Ma."

"So good you come home."

"I'm happy to." Mary kept her smile on, feeling guilty that she didn't mean it completely. Her mother loved her to the marrow, as did her father and The Tonys, and her family meant everything to her. But she'd had such a horrible day at work, with the firm being sued, the press conference that went sideways, and the fighting between John and Anne, that everything suddenly seemed like too much, on top of her pregnancy.

"Mare, you need to take it easy, you work too hard." El Virus pulled up a chair next to Mary, her Opium perfume as thick as tomato sauce. Mary tried not to breathe in, newly sensitive to smells, but the scent was her mother-in-law's trademark, along with her jet-black shag, bedazzled skinny jeans, and white tank top that read **World's Best Grandma**. It struck Mary that her mother-in-law dressed much younger, while her mother dressed much older, in the stop-time tradition of the DiNunzios.

Mary looked around, seeing the kitchen with new eyes. Everything was from another era; the dented spaghetti pot and coffee percolator had to be fifty years old, and her mother didn't own a garbage disposal or dishwasher, still doing the dishes by hand and collecting the "slop" in a metal bin in the sink. An old church calendar faded on the walls, with a washed-out Jesus Christ looking heavenward, or maybe rolling his eyes, undoubtedly wondering why her parents had no air conditioner but still used a fan, which whirred away on the kitchen counter, evenly distributing the humidity. The Mass cards tucked behind the switch-plate with dried palm were the only thing that ever changed here, growing in number as their relatives and friends passed away. Vita and Matty DiNunzio were getting older, and Mary felt the years closing in, along with everything else.

Tony-From-Down-The-Block tucked his napkin in his T-shirt collar like an adult bib, which Mary happened to know he had on with his adult diapers, so like a one-man Circle of Life. He said, "She should quit work. That's what I think. She shouldn't work while she's pregnant."

"Si, si, e vero." Pigeon Tony nodded, his bald head already deeply tanned since he spent so much time outside with his homing pigeons.

Feet pushed up his Mr. Potatohead glasses, clucking. "Mare, you gotta slow down. It's crazy, it's too much."

"SHE LIKES TA WORK. SHE'S GOT A BUSINESS TO RUN."

Feet frowned, his milky-brown eyes magnified by his bifocals. "But she can't work right up to the time the baby comes."

"Sure, I can, I'm fine." Mary glanced at Anthony, who was looking down at his plate as he ate.

El Virus pointed at Mary's food. "Mare, eat!"

Her mother, nodded, watching Mary. *"Maria, mangia."*

"I got it, Ma," Mary tried not to sound testy, picking up her fork. It seemed so Olive Garden that her mother actually said *mangia,* but some stereotypes rang true for a reason. She looked at her full plate, and her stomach rumbled. She knew she should eat, but the tomato sauce and Opium weren't mixing with the progesterone.

Feet frowned. "Mare, when are you gonna quit work?"

"When the doctor tells me to." Mary didn't want to have the discussion right now. She had been ducking this subject because it touched on a sore spot for her and Anthony. The subject made him feel terrible, since he didn't have a job. She wanted to keep working, and given their finances, she really didn't have a choice.

Feet persisted, "And then how much time you going to take off? Like a year, two years?"

"I don't think that long," Mary answered, keeping it vague, but she noticed her mother eyeing her, chewing slowly, and her father blinking behind his glasses. Both of them had to be wondering what Mary and Anthony had planned, but she didn't want to make any announcement right now, especially not with The Tonys here.

El Virus brightened. "Mary can go back to work right away. I'll babysit every day. It's no problem. I can't even wait! I already bought a playpen."

Mary's mother pursed her lips. "Elvira, I tol' you, I can take care a the baby. Every day, we'll come and sit."

"RIGHT! WE GOT YOU COVERED, MARE. ME AND YOUR MOTHER. I WONDER IF IT WILL BE A GIRL OR A BOY!"

Elvira glanced at Mary's mother, sideways. "Vita, don't hog the baby. We'll have a schedule. I'll sit on Monday, Wednesday, and Friday, and you guys sit on Tuesday and Thursday."

Mary's mother's eyes flared in indignation, so Mary stepped in. "Ladies, let's not worry about it now, we still have two months to go."

Feet interjected, "Mary, how are you going to swing this at work? You're going to stay home with the baby, right?"

Mary was about to answer, but Anthony stiffened, cutting her off. "No," he said coolly, "that's not what we're planning. Mary's going back to work as soon as she feels ready, probably in a few weeks, and I'm going to stay home with the baby."

Mary's mouth went dry. She wouldn't have gone there, but Anthony was on a roll, turning to his mother.

"Mom, I appreciate your offer, but we won't need a babysitter at all. I'm going to take care of the baby full-time." Anthony then faced Mary's mother, with a smile. "Vita, thank you so much for your offer to babysit, but I don't think we'll be needing you or Matty on a daily basis, either."

"What?" El Virus's mouth dropped open.

"Che?" Mary's mother asked, frowning.

"DID HE SAY HE'S GONNA BE THE BABYSITTER?"

The Tonys looked uniformly aghast. Feet set down his fork. "Ant, you're the *dad.*"

Tony-From-Down-The-Block shook his head. "Ant, you mean you're going to be, like, the mom?"

Pigeon Tony spoke rapid Italian, and again, Mary got the gist, which was, *Women are supposed to stay home with babies and men are supposed to go out and make money, the way God intended. Also they can have mistresses, but this might not be the time to bring that up.*

Mary didn't intend to argue with any of them. There was no point in trying to convince this very traditional group of men of anything remotely modern, like the fact that women should have the vote. Meanwhile, she could see her father getting with the program, his gaze softening. He slumped in his white T-shirt, and his eyebrows sloped down behind his glasses. He'd been a tile-setter his working life, but his blocky build had changed as he aged, his broad shoulders worn by time, like rocks. Even though he was uneducated, he was no dummy, and despite appearances, he was the more intuitive of her parents. Mary was a Daddy's girl, from way back.

Her father's soft gaze shifted to the Tonys. "GUYS, YOU'RE TOO OLD-FASHION. MEN CAN BE MOMS, TOO, NOWADAYS. IT'S THE NEW THING. IT'S OKAY. IT HAPPENS."

Feet nodded. "I know, I've heard of that. Hell, I got those guys across the street, they're gay and the one dad stays home with the baby and the other dad goes to work. If you got two dads, you gotta have a dad staying home. You got no choice."

Tony-From-Down-The-Block shrugged. "Whatever floats your boat."

El Virus turned to Anthony in bewilderment. "But honey, when do *we* get the baby?"

Mary's mother nodded, equally confused. *"Si, quando? Maria?"*

Mary had to derail this before the moms lost their minds. "Ma, Elvira, listen. Of course you'll get to see the baby. You'll come over our house, and we'll come over your house. You'll get to see the baby plenty. You just don't have to babysit every day."

Anthony added, "Exactly, it goes without saying that you'll see the baby. We want you to see the baby and we want you in the baby's life. But my staying home makes the most sense for Mary and me, and that's what we're going to do."

"Mmph." El Virus sucked her teeth. "I don't like the sound of this."

"Allora," Mary's mother said under her breath, and Mary knew her mother wasn't happy. *Allora* could mean *arg, sheesh,* or *we'll see about that,* and in this case, it meant all of the above.

"MARE, I HATE TO CHANGE THE SUBJECT BUT I GOTTA ASK. I HEARD SOME CRAZY NEWS FROM CAMARR ANNIE. SHE HEARD IT FROM CHICKEN JIMMY WHO HEARD IT FROM HIS SISTER DENISE WHO HEARD IT ON THE TV. FROM DENISE NAKANO, THE ONE YOU SAID IS JAPANESE NOT CHINESE."

97

"What?" Mary asked, worrying that dinner was about to go from bad to worse. Nobody in South Philly needed the Internet because they already had the Neighborhood.

"I HEARD THAT YOUR LAW FIRM IS GETTING SUED. IS THAT RIGHT? THAT CAN'T BE RIGHT, CAN IT?"

Mary cringed inwardly. "Yes, that's true. We got the papers today."

"HOLY GOD, WHAT THE HELL FOR?"

Mary picked at her ravioli. "We're being sued for reverse sex discrimination."

"HUH? WHAT ARE YOU TALKIN' ABOUT?" Her father's eyes flew open, cataracts edging his brown eyes like advancing stormclouds. "YOU CAN'T DO THAT, CAN YOU? THAT'S NOT LEGAL!"

"Mare, for real, some guy is suin' you because you're all girls?" Tony-From-Down-The-Block wiped his chin.

"Remember, we're not an all-women firm anymore. We have John Foxman, a male lawyer, and we also have Lou Jacobs, a male investigator."

Feet recoiled, blinking. "I can't get over this! That's not gentlemanly! What kinda man sues women? That's like hitting a woman! Who does such a thing?"

"Disgrazia!" Pigeon Tony frowned deeply, speaking Italian so quickly that Mary couldn't translate fast enough, though she got the gist again, which was *I will kill anybody who hurts you, Mary.*

"WHAT COURT WILL LET YOU GET SUED FOR THAT, MARE? THE JUDGE WILL THROW THE CASE OUT, WON'T HE?"

"Matty, stop askin' her questions." El Virus moved Mary's plate closer to her. "Mare, don't talk, eat!"

Her mother looked worried behind her glasses. *"Maria,* whatsa matter? You no like? You wan' some soup? Some crackers?"

"No, thanks, I'm fine, Ma," Mary said, stabbing a ravioli. "Pop, it's a ridiculous lawsuit, but we'll win. Don't worry. Nick Machiavelli's on the other side, so you know the whole thing's a sham."

"YOU'LL GET IT THROWN OUT. MACHIAVELLI IS A *CAVONE.*"

Feet nodded. "Sure she will. Mary's a great lawyer!"

Tony-From-Down-The-Block nodded, chewing. "You'll win, Mary. You always do. That phony's got nothin' on you."

"RIGHT." Her father's gaze, full of love, found Mary's across the table. "EVERY-THING'S GONNA BE ALL RIGHT,

99

HONEY."

"I know, Pop," Mary said, and for a second, she almost believed it was true.

CHAPTER NINE

After dinner was finally over, Mary and Anthony cruised in their Prius through the warren of streets that was South Philly. Mary began to relax, the fatigue of the day catching up with her. The car interior was dark and cool, she rested her head back on the headrest, content to let herself be driven. She always loved that Anthony knew the neighborhood as well as she did, and he could navigate the crazy matrix of one-way streets. Luckily there was almost no traffic, and the motion of the car lulled her into drowsiness.

"That went well," Anthony said after a moment, and Mary opened her eyes, realizing that she'd almost fallen asleep.

"What did?"

"You know, breaking the news that I'm going to be staying home with the baby."

"I was surprised that you did that," Mary said, realizing that it wasn't the best thing to say after the words left her lips.

"Somebody had to." Anthony looked over in the darkness, and Mary couldn't make out his features, but she knew from his tone of voice he was hurt.

"I didn't mean it to be critical."

"It sounded critical."

"It wasn't, I'm just tired." Mary felt it was the truest sentence she had spoken all day, and maybe even for the past seven months.

"Okay, whatever." Anthony fell silent, watching the light change from green to red. "I know it shouldn't bother me, but it does."

"What does?"

"You know, that I'm the one staying home."

Mary sighed inwardly. "Don't let the Tonys get to you. They're from a different place and time, you know that."

"I know, but still." Anthony hit the gas. "I'm only staying home because it makes the most sense for all of us."

"I know that, and I appreciate it."

"As soon as my book is finished, I'm hoping I can find a publisher."

"I know that, too."

"Then maybe we can get a nanny, or let our mothers do it, or whatever."

"Right, we'll see how it goes." Mary wished she could make it all right for him, but she couldn't. And part of the problem was how guilty she felt, because he had turned down a big teaching job at UCLA for her, so she didn't have to move away from Philadelphia.

"I mean, obviously, I'm excited about the baby and all, and I'll love being home with him. Or her."

"Of course you will."

"But it wasn't the plan. Obviously, it's not the plan."

"No, right." Mary bit her tongue. She had heard him say this before, but she never knew how to react. Truth to tell, it wasn't the plan for her either. She would've loved to have stayed home with the baby for more than a few weeks. She'd always envisioned herself as an at-home mother, at least for a time. But they got pregnant sooner than they'd expected, so they had to compromise. And like any good settlement, neither side was completely happy.

"I don't even know if I'll be good at it."

"Of course you will," Mary said, to soothe him. "You'll be a great dad."

"But will I be a great mom?"

"You're kidding, right?"

"Yes." Anthony chuckled.

"Seriously? Don't buy in. We don't have their ideas of what women do and men do.

Please don't let it make you crazy, or me."

"I won't."

"We're better than that. We're smarter than that."

"I know." Anthony paused. "But your parents get to me. I feel bad in front of them, ashamed."

"Why, honey?" Mary asked, hurt for him.

Anthony shrugged, his dark gaze looking out into the night. "Obviously, I wish I had been able to provide for you, so your father wouldn't worry or your mother."

"Aw, honey, don't be that way. They love you, and that's all that matters. They know you're amazing and great, and when you sell your book, things will change."

"But what if I don't sell it?"

"You will."

"But what if I *don't*?" Anthony repeated, and Mary knew the anxiety was deep-seated, for them both.

"Then you'll write another one, or another job offer will come up, and either way, we'll have each other and a beautiful little baby girl."

Anthony managed a smile, a welcome shadow in the dark car. "Hold on, I thought you said it was a boy. You said it felt like a boy."

"I changed my mind." Mary smiled back.

"At this point, I don't care if it's a girl or boy."

Anthony recoiled. "What? You want a girl."

"Not anymore. Either way, it'll get sued."

Anthony laughed.

"You still want a boy?"

"No."

"Liar."

"Truly, I'll take either. That's the kind of mom I am."

"Please, I've had enough gender politics for one day, with this litigation." Mary let her thoughts cycle back to the Answer, which they had spent the afternoon drafting. "I'll probably have to go in tomorrow to do some research on the case."

"But it's Saturday."

"I don't have a choice," Mary said, not wanting to fight. She and Anthony got along so beautifully, but the only thing they fought over was how much she worked, yet another role reversal.

"So Machiavelli's really suing the firm?"

"Yes, did you see the press conference?"

"I caught it online, and yours, too."

"Oh that must've been terrific." Mary shuddered. "Can we not talk about it? It was a debacle. The whole thing is a debacle."

"On the plus side, you looked pretty. So did Bennie. Less Amazonian than usual."

Mary smiled. "Anne made us up. Like my new dress?"

"How much did it cost?"

"The firm paid for it."

"Then I love it." Anthony sighed. "You really have to go in tomorrow? Can't you slack? It's been so long since we've had a lazy weekend. There's not that many more left before the baby comes."

"I can't, honey." Mary put her hand on his leg. "This lawsuit is too important. He named us as individual defendants, did you know that?"

"Wait, what?" Anthony braked at the light, and Mary could see his alarmed frown.

"He's suing us under a law that enables him to sue the three partners personally."

"Does that mean what I think it means? If you lose, we pay it? Personally?"

"Yes," Mary answered, kicking herself. She knew that Anthony worried about money, which she understood, but she was in no mood.

"How would we pay? How much? What damages are they asking?"

"It's unclear at this point."

"But they have to ask for damages in the Complaint, don't they?"

"No, it's not a complaint that you file in court, where damages are specified. It's an administrative complaint filed with the Pennsylvania Human Relations Commission."

"So how much can they get if they win? Like ten grand or fifty? Or one hundred grand?"

"It's hard to say, because we don't —"

"Can't you ballpark it?"

"No, because there's too many variables."

"What are you, a contractor?" Anthony scoffed. "Gimme a number. I have a right to know, don't I?"

"Okay, let me think." Mary had been calculating it in her head for most of the afternoon, though she, Judy, and Bennie kept coming up with different totals, since damages in a failure-to-hire case were notoriously hard to calculate. "It's three plaintiffs who say they weren't hired because they're men. Let's assume that we lose." Mary felt sick at the thought alone. "The way to make them whole is to award them what they would've earned if they had gotten the job for a reasonable period of years."

"Are you serious?"

"That's the theory." Mary hated getting into the weeds with him. She never should've said anything. "So if the going rate for an associate is seventy grand a year and they were wrongly denied that pay, then that's three plaintiffs at seventy grand a year, probably for five years and —"

"Are you *kidding* me? That's over a million dollars!" Anthony slammed on the brakes, harder than necessary.

"I know." Mary had to admit it sounded scary, to her too. "But I would only pay a third of it."

"So? Where are we going to get that kind of money? Especially now?"

"We're not going to lose, Anthony."

"But where will we get the money, if we did? You said yourself, you have to assume you lose, so where do we get that money?" Anthony threw up his hands. "We have a *killer* mortgage. I told you the house was a reach."

"We're doing fine with the mortgage." Mary held her tongue. The new house had been a bone of contention too, but she bought it with her savings, so she'd made the down payment. They would've been on easy street but for the fact that she'd gotten pregnant and gotten sued, not in that order.

"Mary, this is a *disaster.*" Anthony shook his head as he drove. "I didn't realize you're getting sued personally."

"I know, it's unusual. We think that's why Machiavelli chose to sue under the statute. In fact, he manufactured the whole case —"

"It doesn't matter how it began, it only matters how it ends!"

"Well, we don't know that yet, now do we?"

"No, but we know that," Anthony shot back, newly agitated. "We *cannot* get another loan to pay off any judgment against us."

"Okay, so we'll win."

"You better!"

"So maybe I should work tomorrow?" Mary asked dryly.

"I'll pack your lunch," Anthony shot back.

Suddenly Mary's phone rang, and she pulled it from her purse and checked the screen to see a FaceTime call from Machiavelli, which wasn't a complete surprise. It was his modus operandi to call her during their cases, like a kindergartener with his mother's phone.

She said to Anthony, "Guess who."

Anthony glanced over. "Him? You don't have to answer it."

"Yes, I do. You never know." Mary pressed the button to take the call, and Nick Machiavelli appeared on the screen. He was handsome in a vaguely seductive way, like Satan with a law degree. He wore his black hair slicked back, and his eyes were narrow slits, with dark brown irises that burned with intensity, even on the phone. His nose was strong, and his jawline was strong, if pugnacious. He dressed like a mobster who shopped at Neiman Marcus, and though he dated plenty of women, Mary could barely set her hatred aside to talk to him.

"Hey Mare, how was dinner?" Machiavelli asked, with a cocky smile.

"Why are you calling?" Mary didn't bother to hide her disdain. Machiavelli had his minions everywhere in the neighborhood, so he probably didn't have to guess that she'd been at her parents' house. She and Machiavelli were like the Good Witch and the Bad Witch of South Philly.

"How're your parents doing?"

"None of your business."

"How's Anthony?"

"Also not your concern."

"Tell him I said congratulations on the new baby."

Anthony flipped him the bird, though it was off-screen.

Mary was losing patience. "What are you calling about, Machiavelli? And you know I hate it when you FaceTime me."

"Which is why I do it." Machiavelli grinned. "Also it's fun. Work should be fun, Mare, don't you think?"

"Is this about the case? If so, get to the

point. If not, I'm hanging up."

"You guys ready to settle?" Machiavelli's smile evaporated, which reminded Mary that he never did anything without a purpose. Despite his joking around, he was deadly serious when he wanted something, and this time, he wanted to destroy her and her firm.

"No settlement, ever. And as you know, I'm a defendant in the suit you filed, not a lawyer, so you're not permitted to communicate with me directly. We hired a lawyer. He should have sent you a letter already."

"Roger Vitez, that hippie? He did, but I like you better."

"This is the last call I'm taking from you."

"Think about settling, Mare. Don't be stubborn. I know how you get."

"No, you don't."

"You guys are going down."

"Remains to be seen."

Machiavelli chuckled. "Isn't that from the Magic 8-Ball?"

"No, that would be, 'reply hazy, try again.' "

"It's going to get worse from here, Mare. Your press conference was a fiasco. I got you dead-to-rights. Your firm's been getting away with murder for too long. It's against the law to hire only women. We boys deserve a break today."

"Oh, please," Mary said, ending the call. She tried not to let it get to her, but she felt shaken. The stakes were high, and Machiavelli stopped at nothing.

"Babe?" Anthony said, softly.

"Yes?" Mary looked over.

Anthony smiled, grimly. "Beat his ass."

CHAPTER TEN

Mary rode upward in the elevator, late on her way into the office because she had stopped to get bagels and cream cheese for everybody. Even pregnant, she couldn't imagine working on the weekend without a food reward. She pulled up her maternity pants, trying to situate them comfortably on her belly. They were the only thing more annoying than maternity dresses, and she'd been horrified by this pair, ugly wide-legged jeans with a big swath of black elastic in the belly, as if someone had taken a black Sharpie around the equator.

The elevator doors opened, and she stepped into the office and trundled through the empty reception hall, breathing heavily. She felt like the Little Train That Could, huffing and puffing along, *I think I can I think I can,* but truth to tell, Mary had felt that way even before her pregnancy. She'd always had to give herself pep talks, telling herself she could do whatever it was that she was afraid of, and happily, she'd been right most of the time. This time, she worried she was up against her biggest challenge.

Her thoughts churning away, Mary walked down the hallway toward the conference room, where she knew the others would be waiting. For the first time ever, she had to admit that her stress levels were maxing out. Anthony had barely spoken to her before they fell asleep last night, and she'd left early enough so they only had time for a quick breakfast. She was as worried as he was about the possibility that they could lose the lawsuit, which could put them into personal bankruptcy. Not only that, but she was worried about whether this was the end of Rosato & DiNunzio. It seemed impossible, but the stakes couldn't be higher.

"Oh," Mary said, surprised as she arrived at the threshold of the conference room. She had expected Bennie and Judy, who were sitting at the conference table in T-shirts and jeans, but catty-corner to them was Roger Vitez, dressed like a Steve Jobs wannabe again, in what looked like a fresh black turtleneck and jeans, and he sat next to a younger, sandy-haired man in rimless glasses, who was dressed like a Vitez wannabe.

"Perfect timing, DiNunzio." Bennie flashed her a stiff smile, but didn't look especially happy, and Judy jumped up, came around the table, and reached for the bag.

"Let me take that."

"Aren't you nice?" Mary said, touched, as she entered the conference room.

"No, just hungry. What did you bring?"

"Lox and bagels."

"Nice, thanks. You're gonna be a great mom."

"I already am." Mary entered the room and sat down as Judy dug in the bag.

Bennie gestured to Vitez. "DiNunzio, you know Roger, and with him is an associate of his, Isaac Chevi."

"Hi Roger, Isaac. I didn't know you guys would be here."

Bennie interjected, "I only found out this morning."

Roger smiled his Zen smile. "I thought I might come by, since I'm allegedly your counsel."

"Okay," Mary said, not knowing what he meant. But then again, she was getting used to not knowing what he meant. She sat down in her chair while Judy distributed chubby lox and bagel sandwiches around the table, wrapped in waxed paper, but there were only three. "I'm sorry I didn't get enough food. I would have, if I had known."

Roger raised a hand. "No need. We're fine."

"Thanks, DiNunzio." Bennie pulled her sandwich over, glancing at Roger. "Why don't you tell Mary what you were just telling us?"

"Sure." Roger linked his fingers in front of him, the way he had before, and if he noticed that the air was beginning to reek of briny deli pickles, he didn't let it show. "Mary, I was just telling Bennie that I watched your press conference yesterday, with dismay. More than a little dismay."

Mary listened, trying to get used to the way he talked, which was odd. More than a little odd. Plus he wasn't the kind of guy you could interrupt, and she was big on interrupting. She and Judy interrupted each other constantly. Not only could they finish each other's sentences, they could start them, which was a girlfriend thing.

"It demonstrated fairly clearly that from here on, we need to alter the way we communicate with others, with respect to this case."

"You mean you want to change things?" Mary asked, trying to translate. "Because

116

we flunked the press conference?"

Judy looked over with a smile, her cheeks full of bagel. "Dude, we're trying not to think about it in such a binary fashion. Pass and fail. Thumbs-up or thumbs-down. It's not like that."

"Exactly," Roger said, pleased. "Isaac is an employee of my firm, and he speaks with my voice."

"That must hurt," Mary said, just to make him laugh, but he didn't. Judy did, so she hadn't completely gone over to the dark side.

"Isaac has degrees in marketing and psychology, and he deals with our firm's communications. It is my sincerest wish that from now on, any and all communications with regard to the litigation go through him, and he speaks for us all, with one voice."

Mary got the gist. "So he's a PR guy?"

Roger flinched. "Essentially."

Bennie frowned. "DiNunzio, to bring you up to speed, I was just telling Roger that I don't think we need a spokesperson. We know how to speak for ourselves."

"I agree," Mary said, for solidarity. And also she did agree.

Bennie raised her chin. "I haven't practiced law for decades to need a mouthpiece. I am a mouthpiece."

Roger's cool gaze slid sideways to Bennie. "Need I point out that your maiden voyage didn't go quite as expected?"

"We were sabotaged, and Isaac would've been in the same position. We didn't know the question was coming."

"Isaac?" Roger turned to Isaac. "Would you have a response to that that you might want to share?"

Isaac nodded, with a pat smile. "Bennie, this is in no way criticism of you or the way the conference went. Your point is well taken. However, as a matter of procedure, when we hold a meeting at any time with the press, everyone is required to sign in and identify themselves."

Isaac kept his tone calm and even, in almost the exact same cadence as Roger, and Mary had never heard anything like it, especially from a PR type or publicist. They all talked a mile a minute, which was a job requirement since everybody hung up on them.

Isaac was saying, "They're registered and they wear identifying badges during the event. In this way, we know exactly who is asking what questions, which is important information. If we had run the conference, we would know who the reporter was who asked those questions. Because clearly, she has some information that we need."

Bennie sighed. "Okay, good point, but still I don't think we need you."

Roger looked over at Bennie. "You don't like taking orders."

"No one ever gives me orders, so I don't know whether I like it or not."

Roger smiled, cocking his head. "And I'm betting that you don't like taking orders from a man."

"I have never done that either." Bennie smiled slyly, and Roger smiled back, and Mary wondered if this qualified as foreplay for lawyers. Meanwhile, Roger was barking up the wrong tree because Bennie was totally in love with her boyfriend, Declan, who might've been the exact opposite of Roger in every way. Namely, that he talked normal.

Roger leaned back in his chair. "In any event, you hired me to represent you, and Isaac is a part of my team. An essential part of my team. If you want me, he comes with."

"Oh fine," Bennie said irritably, and just then Mary heard a noise behind her and turned around to see John Foxman standing in the threshold of the conference room, dressed in a tie and a three-piece gray suit. His forehead was knit, and there were dark circles underneath his eyes, as if he hadn't slept well.

"Hi, everyone," John said uncomfortably. "I hope I'm not interrupting anything."

Bennie rose. "Foxman, this is Roger Vitez and Isaac Chevi." She gestured at John. "Gentlemen, this is John Foxman."

"Pleased to meet you," Roger said, though he didn't rise, and neither did Isaac.

"Sorry to interrupt, I want to get this over with, so I just thought I would come in." John squared his shoulders. "I reached a decision about whether I'm staying with the firm or going."

Mary sighed inwardly. She wasn't ready for this yet. She needed carbohydrates. Or not to be pregnant.

Judy set her sandwich aside. "John, seriously?"

John avoided her eye, turning to Bennie. "Bennie, this isn't easy, and I appreciate everything you've done for me. You know I think the world of you and this firm and —"

Bennie interrupted him, "What's your decision?"

"I've decided to resign. I don't think I can work here any longer."

"And why is that?" Bennie shot back.

Mary took it like a blow. She'd been sure that John was going to stay, after Bennie's

120

pitch last night. Judy looked equally upset, her lips parting and her attention glued to John, but she didn't say anything.

John sighed stiffly, his face a grim mask. "It's not tenable to stay here, in view of my statements and my view."

"Your view?"

"The fact is I made those statements, and they were the truth. I do feel out of place here, and even more so, since the Complaint was filed." John's expression softened. "I truly don't think you discriminated against me, however. And I do think you would have made me partner one day. But those are counterfactuals. Now that the lawsuit has been filed, I don't think I can stay."

Bennie frowned. "But what about the fact that this damages the case against us? We're parting ways, and the obvious conclusion after what happened is that the plaintiffs are correct on the facts. Or that you've been ousted."

"I can't control the implications of what I do, or what people infer. But I'll make it clear that this is my decision, not yours. I'll draft a statement that I'm resigning voluntarily and run it by you."

"Statement or no statement, the facts speak for themselves. The implication is clear. It could even look like retaliation."

Judy blurted out, "John, this is a mistake. The Complaint was just filed and everybody's upset. It's going to settle down. Why don't you give it a week or two? See how you feel then."

"I don't think so, Judy." John shook his head. "I'll feel the same way. It's a Band-Aid, and there's no reason to pull it off slowly."

Mary felt an overwhelming sadness descend over her. She could see that John had made up his mind, and he was jumping the gun. "John, Judy's right. Can't you just give it some time? I mean, I really loved getting to know you and working with you."

John smiled at Mary, softly. "I appreciate your saying that. I really enjoyed working with you, too. But I have to go and I don't want to delay."

Bennie interjected, "John, how long are you planning on staying? A month? Two weeks?"

John hesitated. "No, I'd like to leave right away. Today. I have an interview across town. I think the next two weeks are going to be really uncomfortable. There's no reason to put either side through that."

Judy gasped. "Either side? What are you talking about? Aren't we on the same side?"

"Of course we are," John answered

quickly. "I meant all parties."

Bennie rose, surprised. "But what about *London Technologies*? This is the worst possible time, in the middle of discovery. We have twelve depositions to take and sixteen to defend. There's even a dep to defend on Monday. How can you leave now? How is Anne going to handle that?"

"She'll be fine," John shot back, resentment edging his tone.

Bennie glowered. "And what about the client, Jim and Sanjay? *My* client. You have a responsibility to them, too. You're here today, gone tomorrow?"

"They prefer Anne anyway. They won't mind." John took a step toward Bennie, extending a hand, then stopped, seeming to catch himself. "Thank you for everything you've done for me, all of you. I wish you the best. I'll clean out my desk another time. I should go now."

Judy stood up, upset. "John, really? You're going to go, just like that?"

"Now?" Mary half-rose, not sure whether to hug him or let him go.

"Mary, don't get up," John said, waving her into her seat and flashing a sad smile at Judy as he headed toward the door. "Judy, sorry. I think I should just go now."

"Good-bye, John," Bennie called after him.

Roger broke the silence, clearing his throat primly. "Remain calm."

"Oh shut up!" Bennie's head snapped around, her face mottled with anger. "That he made the statement is bad enough. That he was interviewing with other firms is worse. That he's leaving now is a death blow. And we'll have to scramble to cover him on *London Technologies.* I have no idea how we'll staff that case."

Roger merely blinked. "I renew my recommendation that we initiate settlement negotiations."

"I told you no."

"I have your vote, but what about Mary and Judy? There are three partners here, not just one."

Bennie turned to Mary and Judy, momentarily chastened. "He's right. You guys get to say what you think. You have an equal vote. Do you want to settle with that jerk?"

"No settlement," Mary heard herself answering, her heart speaking for her. She knew how she felt, despite the personal risk. Anthony might not agree, but luckily, he wasn't here. "I love John, but he's wrong. He didn't deserve to be made partner yet, it was too soon. We don't discriminate against men here. We're in the right and we should fight."

Judy nodded gravely. "Roger, I understand your recommendation, and in other circumstances, I would agree. But we can't settle this. If you don't fight when you're right, when *do* you fight?"

Roger remained characteristically impassive. "I hear you three, for now. We can revisit the settlement question at any point. I am asking you to keep an open mind. We've been lawyers long enough to know that being 'in the right' " — he made air quotes with his nimble fingers — "doesn't guarantee a successful result, nor is it a very good reason to go forward in litigation. But for now, I'll accept your judgment, as I must."

"Good." Bennie rubbed her hands together, taking her seat. "Now, what we need to do is finalize the Answer —"

"— I was going to say that," Roger interrupted.

"— and go full steam ahead on the legal research we started —"

"— I was going to say that, too." Roger shot Bennie a look. "Who's running this case?"

"Who do you think?" Bennie shot back, with a cocky smile.

"Ha!" Roger laughed. "And I take it we agree on the need to utilize Isaac's services. We need him, now more than ever. John's departure raises questions we need to address in the media."

"Fine," Bennie said, reluctantly.

"Okay." Judy nodded.

"Uh, sure," Mary answered, but she was suddenly distracted. She didn't want to say so out loud, but she felt a warm dampness in her underwear, which, during a pregnancy, could mean trouble.

Roger smiled. "Excellent."

Isaac nodded. "Thank you for your confidence in me, ladies."

Mary rose, nervously. "Excuse me a minute. Bathroom run."

CHAPTER ELEVEN

Mary tried not to be nervous while her OB/GYN, Dr. Melissa Foster, examined her from somewhere behind the white tent covering her knees. Mary had texted Anthony, and he was on the way to the doctor's office, but Judy was with Mary now, holding her hand. Mary realized that a best friend was somebody who would hold your hand when you're in stirrups.

Mary glanced at Judy, who looked down at her with a reassuring smile, standing next to the examining table. She'd managed to exit the meeting gracefully, leaving behind a concerned Bennie, and Judy had hailed them both a cab and gotten them here in no time. Mary had gone to the bathroom and discovered that she was spotting, so she'd called the doctor and had been told to come right in.

Dr. Foster wasn't saying anything, and Mary fought the impulse to start chatting away, the way she always did. She abhorred silence the way Nature abhorred a vacuum and always found herself yapping at times that normal people stayed quiet, like when she was getting her hair cut, her nails done, or even during a massage. She had a pedicure once and talked nonstop at the pedicurist, who spoke only Korean, as it turned out. Mary was no different at the OB/GYN's office and she delivered some of her best lines when there was a speculum inside her. But not this time.

"Dr. Foster, is everything okay?" Mary asked, unable to stay quiet another minute.

"Give me another minute or two," Dr. Foster answered, which Mary knew was code for please stop asking questions.

Mary's gaze fell on Dr. Foster's framed diplomas, with their fancy gold seals, and that gave her some reassurance. Dr. Foster was one of the best OB/GYNs in the city, and Mary had been lucky to get into her practice. The doctor was in her early fifties, with an academic bent, since she taught at medical school. She was African-American and wore her hair short, and her features were fine-boned behind her glasses, with their heavy black frames. Little diamonds twinkled from her earlobes, and her frame was petite but superfit since she was a runner. Mary loved her kind but no-nonsense bedside manner. Dr. Foster was who you wanted if your pregnancy was in trouble, which Mary prayed wasn't the case.

She glanced around the room, trying to draw reassurance from the soft mint green of the walls, the colorful watercolor bouquet in a pale blue frame, and the flowery pink letters of the requisite inspirational sayings sign: I SET MY WORRIES ASIDE AND LET MY BODY DO ITS JOB. Mary looked away, because the sign wasn't helping. It only reminded her of her job, which was to be back at work, trying not to lose everything she and Anthony owned. She was still reeling from John's quitting and terrified that it would put a nail in the coffin of the lawsuit. Bennie had even called it a *death blow,* which wasn't the kind of panicky language she used. Mary had known that being sued was stressful, but she had never realized how completely stressful it could be, until it happened to her.

Suddenly there was a soft knock at the door, and Mary looked to the left to see Anthony enter the room, worriedly. "Hey, hubby, how are you?"

"The question is, how are *you.*" Anthony came over, kissed Mary on the forehead, and took her other hand, glancing at Judy and Dr. Foster. "Judy, thanks for bringing her. Hi, Dr. Foster."

"No worries," Judy answered.

"Anthony, hi," Dr. Foster said from behind the tent, which was at the opposite side of the room from the door. Mary realized the setup of the room was intentional, because nobody wanted to open a door onto whatever was on the other side of the white tent. The thought made her smile, but it went away.

"Okay." Dr. Foster got up from her rolling stool and smiled in a professional way, taking off her purple-plastic gloves. "I think everything's fine."

"Thank God!" Judy blurted out, even before Mary and Anthony, then realized she had talked out of turn. "Sorry."

"It's okay," Mary said, touched. "It's a relief, God knows."

Anthony looked at Dr. Foster, his dark eyes wet with the emotion he was trying to hold back. "But what was it then? Mary said she was 'spotting,' and I don't know, what exactly does that mean?"

"Spotting means there was some bleeding, and that's perfectly normal from time to time, especially in the first trimester —"

Mary interrupted, "But I'm in my third trimester."

"Yes, I know," Dr. Foster answered, patiently. "But I've examined you, and I'm not overly concerned. It does happen, and you need to come in and have me check it out when it does."

"But what causes it?"

"It's symptomatic of some conditions that luckily, you don't have."

"Like what?"

"Well, like placental abruption, which is caused when the placenta is detaching from the uterine wall. Or even preterm labor, but you are not in labor. You said you weren't feeling any contractions and you had no more nausea than usual."

"Right, and I haven't had any dizziness or anything like that."

"Got it." Dr. Foster cocked her head. "Are you under stress, Mary?"

Mary blinked, and Judy burst into laughter. Anthony didn't.

Mary answered, "Let's just say things are busy at work."

Dr. Foster smiled, more warmly. "I know, I hear you. Doctors always tell you to eliminate stress, and that's completely impossible in the modern world. You're a lawyer, and stress is part and parcel of your profession."

"That's exactly right," Mary said, without

elaborating. She didn't want to whine about being sued and she knew that Dr. Foster had a full waiting room, having squeezed her in on an emergency basis. "So what do I do about the spotting?"

"Nothing, just try to take it easier. Here, scoot down for me." Dr. Foster began closing up the stirrups and placing Mary's legs down under the sheet.

"Can I go back to work?"

"Yes, but no strenuous activities like racquetball."

"Good, I don't play racquetball."

"I do and it's going to be the death of me." Dr. Foster smiled. "Any other questions?"

Anthony looked over, frowning. "Dr. Foster, she was at work today. She should go home, right?"

"Maybe, just to relax, though it's not medically necessary."

Anthony shot Mary an *I-knew-it.* "But Doctor, when you say 'take it easier,' what do you mean? Should she cut down on her hours at work? Or work part-time?"

Judy squeezed Mary's hand. "Mare, if you have to, you could take it easier at work, like, take it down to three days a week. I'll watch your desk and pick up the slack, or you can work from home."

Dr. Foster shook her head. "There's no medical reason for Mary to do that unless she wants to." The doctor turned to Mary. "Do you want to?"

"No," Mary answered, avoiding Anthony's eye. "But on the other hand, I would never do anything that hurts the baby."

"Of course not. I wouldn't advise you to go back to work if I thought it would compromise the pregnancy or the baby." Dr. Foster put her hand on the doorknob. "But you're perfectly healthy, proceeding along right on track. Today was a blip on the screen, but that's it. Feel free to call if you have any other questions and of course if you have any further spotting. Okay?"

"Okay." Mary smiled, almost reassured. "Thanks so much."

"Dr. Foster, thanks," Anthony said, and Judy waved good-bye.

"Thanks from me, the aunt-to-be!"

Dr. Foster smiled. "See you at your next appointment, Mary. Just put your gown in the basket and leave when you're ready. Take care." She left the examining room, closing the door behind her.

"Okay," Mary said, heaving a heavy sigh, and Anthony bent over and gave her a kiss on the forehead.

"That was scary."

"I bet." Mary felt a wave of love for him, and concern. "I didn't mean to freak you out when I called."

"Not at all, I'm glad you told me."

"You didn't tell my parents, did you?"

"Are you nuts?" Anthony smiled crookedly.

"Okay, I won't go back to work, I'll go home with you."

"Yes, the car's in a lot. You check out, and I'll come pick you up."

"No, Anthony, I can go with you."

Judy touched Mary's arm. "Mare, Anthony's right. Let him get the car. You get dressed, and we'll meet him."

"Thanks for the assist." Anthony shot Mary a look. "Hear that, honey? Listen to reason."

"Or failing that, listen to me." Judy grinned.

"Ha." Anthony walked around the examining table, giving Judy a quick kiss on the cheek. "Thanks for taking her, Judy. You're the best aunt-to-be ever."

"I so am!" Judy grinned, and Anthony left the room, closing the door behind him.

Mary heaved another sigh. "I guess I should go home."

"You really should."

"I hate leaving you and Bennie in the lurch."

"You're not." Judy waved her off. "We have more than enough lawyers on the case. If anything, we have too many."

"But we have work to do on *London Technologies,* with John gone."

"We're not going to get it done today, and I already have a plan. The case is in the discovery phase now, so I'll team up with Anne, read the file, and review interrogatories and documents. I'll get up to speed, and she and I will take the depositions."

"But that's so much. What do I do? I want to help."

"You can, by defending the depositions. That will be easier. You don't even have to know the file."

"That's too easy," Mary said, feeling a wave of guilt. Defending depositions was much easier than taking them, since the objections were the same in every deposition, regardless of the subject matter of the case. The gist was to make sure the client didn't volunteer information or say something stupid.

"No, it's fine. Plus if you're defending the dep, the witness will have to come to us, so you don't have to travel. All you have to do is sit on your butt in the conference room.

It's the perfect division of labor."

Mary knew it made sense, even though it was the lighter load. She had a baby and she was thinking for two. "Okay, Anne said there was a dep to defend on Monday. I can do that."

"It may be too soon for you."

"No, I'm fine. We'll meet with Anne and she'll get us up to speed on the big picture. Meanwhile, I'll email her and get any passwords to the file, so I can read it at home today. I'm not that busy, I was already cutting back because of the baby."

"Okay, now, let me help you off the table." Judy took Mary's arm, and Mary slid off the white sheet to reveal her hospital gown, which was open in the back.

"Don't look at my butt."

"I've seen your butt."

"Not lately. My stretch marks look like a bear attack."

"Hush. You need help getting dressed?"

"No thanks." Mary smiled, touched again by her friend's thoughtfulness. Judy may have looked wacky to the outside world, with her magenta hair and fashion-challenged outfits, but she was one of the most reliable and levelheaded people Mary had ever known.

"Okay, I'll meet you in the waiting room."

Judy let herself out of the examining room, and Mary padded into the adjacent bathroom, where she dressed avoiding the mirror, her enemy for the past seven months. Whoever said pregnant people *glowed* needed glasses. Pregnant people *sweated.* Even in March.

She picked up her purse and left the examining room, trundling down the hallway and taking a left toward the billing and reception area, when she heard a hubbub coming from the reception area. She went through the glass door, only to be greeted by a reception room full of bewildered patients, a nervous Judy, and most of South Philly, in the form of Mary's mother, father, El Virus, and The Tonys, who surged forward as a vaguely hysterical group when they spotted Mary.

"Pop? Mom?" Mary recoiled, horrified. "How did you know I was here?"

"HONEY, YOU AWRIGHT? ANT'N'Y TOLD HIS NEIGHBOR HE WAS GONNA MEET YOU AT THE DOCTOR AND SHE CALLED CAMARR MILLIE WHO KNOWS COUSIN TOOTIE WITH THE EYE SO HE . . ."

CHAPTER TWELVE

Day turned to night at home, and Mary sat in her favorite chair by the window, which was called a chair-and-a-half since it was wider than normal. She and Anthony used to cuddle in it on Saturday nights and watch Netflix together, but now that she was pregnant, she needed the entire chair to herself. On her left was a box of saltines and on her right was a bag of popcorn, as if she had traded in her husband for carbohydrates. She had her feet up on the ottoman and her laptop open on her lap, though she had to type around her belly and her navel kept hitting the space bar.

She found her gaze wandering outside the window, watching her neighbors giving their dogs a last walk or coming home from restaurants or the movies. Her and Anthony's townhouse was in the Rittenhouse section of the city, a three-story brick colonial that was nevertheless a rowhome, although in a higher-rent district than South Philly. It had been their neighbors two doors down, the McIllhenys, who had spilled the beans about Mary's emergency visit to Dr. Foster, and it had taken Mary hours to persuade her parents that she and the baby were fine, so that they'd finally gone home.

She glanced at her laptop, trying to focus. She was supposed to be reading the *London Technologies* pleadings, but antitrust was one of the most technical, business-oriented areas of the law. She felt distracted by her worries about the baby, the lawsuit against her and the others, and John's departure. She hated that everything was exploding right now, when she should have been easing into the baby's arrival. She'd planned her caseload so carefully, scaling back the active files and not taking any new clients, but that had gone by the wayside. Life wasn't going well if contractions would be a relief.

Mary kept her eyes on the laptop screen and her worries to herself, especially about the pregnancy, because she didn't want to get Anthony started all over again. He had lectured her at lunch and again at dinner about trying to take it easy at work. He sat on the couch on his laptop, working on his book and ignoring the television, which was playing the new season of *The Crown,* their latest binge-watch. She didn't know when Netflix had become the background music to their marriage, but there were worse things.

Anthony stretched, checking his watch. "It's getting late, almost eleven. You wanna go up?"

"Sure," Mary said, though she hadn't gotten much done.

"Good." Anthony set the laptop aside, rose, and brushed down his jeans, flashing her a weary smile. "Can I get you anything?"

"How about a kiss?"

Anthony smiled, came over, and kissed her on the cheek, placing his hands on the soft arms of her chair. "How do you feel?"

"Fine," Mary answered, meaning it. "Absolutely normal, for a pregnant person."

"Tired?"

"A little."

"Crampy?"

"No."

"Bloated?"

"Very." Mary smiled, touched. Anthony was learning girl lingo, but he spoke it like a second language, which made sense. She had never been so aware of the differences between men and women before, maybe it was because of the pregnancy, or the lawsuit. Oddly, it felt like there were two separate sides, the way John had said, and she wondered if that notion was true or testosterone-induced. Mary didn't know, as testosterone was the only hormone she lacked.

Anthony smiled down at her, his gaze soft. "You're preoccupied."

"I was but it went away." Mary smiled, and Anthony kissed her again, this time on the lips, slowly. She felt a distinct tingle, and when he pulled away, she told him so.

"You felt a tingle?" Anthony frowned. "You mean a cramp?"

Mary smiled. "No, a tingle comes from somewhere different."

Anthony smiled back. "Somewhere off base?"

"Exactly. The forbidden zone."

"Or the promised land." Anthony laughed, and so did Mary.

"We shouldn't have sex, but at least I want to."

"It's the thought that counts." Anthony smiled. "We forgot to ask Dr. Foster when we could."

"Because we know the answer. Like, in 2082."

Anthony smiled. "When the kid leaves for college?"

"When the *last* kid leaves for college," Mary shot back, as her cell phone started ringing.

"Saved by the bell." Anthony chuckled.

"Or interrupted." Mary checked the screen, and it was Bennie calling, so she answered. "Bennie?"

"DiNunzio, did you hear?" Bennie's tone sounded urgent, and Mary knew something was very wrong.

"Hear what? What's the matter?"

"John's dead. He's been murdered."

CHAPTER THIRTEEN

Mary and Anthony parked as close as they could to John's apartment, which was in a townhouse in Old City. Night had fallen, but they could see the red-and-white lightbars flashing atop the lineup of police cruisers idling on his side of the street. Klieglights had been set up, and cops and official personnel hurried to and fro, making shifting silhouettes against the calcium-white backdrop. Sawhorses blocked the street from foot and car traffic, and a throng of spectators gathered behind the barricade, next to boxy news vans and reporters with their boom mikes and camera crews.

"Honey?" Anthony touched Mary's arm in the dark interior of the car. "You sure you feel okay to do this?"

"Yes, absolutely," Mary answered, meaning it, because the pregnancy was the last thing on her mind. She'd cried most of the way, shocked and heartbroken by John's murder. Her nose was congested, and her eyes stung. Bennie and Judy were going to meet her here. Anthony had been vaguely worried about her, but he understood that it was an emergency, so he had taken her. She had to find out what had happened because Bennie hadn't had any details when they spoke.

"Here, honey." Anthony opened her car door, helping her out of the car and closing the door.

"Thanks." Mary rose stiffly, taking his arm, and they walked toward the scene. Trying to compose herself, she straightened to see ahead, but she was too short and the crowd blocked her view. John's street was narrow and one-way, typical of those in the oldest part of town, and it took only a few barricades set lengthwise to block it completely. From the other side of the sawhorses came the official hubbub of shouted orders, hurrying personnel, and rumbling engines. The crowd clustered talking, smoking, and taking pictures with their cell phones, rubbernecking on a cool spring night. It killed Mary to think that they were being entertained by such a tragedy.

"This is awful," Anthony said, as they walked. "It's just so sad. I always liked him."

"I know. He liked you too." Mary felt her

throat thicken.

"I wonder what happened."

"It's like, I want to know, but I also don't." Mary suppressed the tears. "I don't know what got into him lately, but it wasn't like him. He really was such a good person. He took care of his brother, you know."

"I remember, you told me that."

"Right." Mary realized she had told him more than once, since the news came in. "His parents are gone, and I don't even know what other family he has. An aunt and uncle maybe. I think he's from Minnesota originally. Judy would know better."

"You said that, too." Anthony patted her hand, and they passed the funky boutiques and indie restaurants sandwiched between colonial rowhouses converted to apartments.

Mary felt a wave of dread, walking along. "Judy is going to take this hardest of all. They were friends. She brought him on."

"We'll help her through it. She can stay with us, this weekend. For as long as she wants."

"Thanks, I don't want her to have to go home alone." Mary swallowed hard as they approached the end of the block, where a cop with a glowing orange flashlight was directing a line of traffic away from the scene. She felt queasier the closer they got, but she made herself go forward. "It's just so horrible, I keep hoping it's not true."

"Of course you do, honey." Anthony put his arm around her as they walked.

"Maybe there's been some mistake," Mary said, knowing it wasn't possible, and Anthony didn't reply. Suddenly they spotted Bennie and Judy heading down the cross street toward the crowd.

"Bennie!" Anthony shouted, waving his free hand.

Bennie and Judy turned toward Anthony's voice, then cut diagonally to the corner, making fleeting shadows in the headlights of passing cars. They hurried toward Mary, and Mary found herself letting go of Anthony and surging toward them, no longer able to hold back the tears.

"Mary!" Judy began to sob, collapsing in Mary's arms. "John's dead! It's not possible! Who killed him? Who would've killed him?"

"Honey, I'm so sorry." Mary clung teary to her best friend. "I'm so sorry."

"What happened?" Judy wailed. "What happened?"

"I don't know, we'll find out."

"I don't get it, it doesn't make any sense!" Judy sobbed, her body wracked as Mary held her tight.

"We'll find out, we'll see. I'm so sorry," Mary repeated, hugging Judy and meeting Bennie's flinty eyes over Judy's shoulder. Bennie greeted Anthony, and Judy's tears began to subside. Bennie handed Judy a flurry of tissues, and Judy started mopping up her eyes, then blowing her nose.

"I just can't believe it," Judy said, her nose bubbling. "I just can't."

"I know, neither can I."

"He was such a good guy, and a good lawyer, too. I know he's been acting weird lately, but that wasn't really him."

"I know."

"He was so good to his brother, William. He took care of him all by himself. His only other family is his aunt and uncle, they live outside Minneapolis. They're older and they rarely come east. Somebody will have to tell them and William."

"I know." Mary took Judy's arm. "Honey, you don't have to go see. I'll wait here with you. Anthony and Bennie can go."

"I want to!" Judy cried, blowing her nose again.

"They're not gonna let us through the barricade anyway," Mary said, trying to convince her. She'd come here wanting to see as much as possible, as she would have on any murder case before, but now that

147

she was here, she realized how different John's murder was from any other. This wasn't a case, this was *John.*

Judy shook her head, stuffing her Kleenex in her pocket. "I want to go. They'll let us pass."

Bennie turned, heading toward the scene. "You're damn right they will. Also Anne and Lou are on the way. We didn't wait."

"How did Anne take the news?"

"Not well."

"Poor thing." Mary felt a wave of sympathy, knowing that Anne's grief would be complicated, given that she had worked closely with John and they had parted on bad terms. Mary had never experienced complicated grief. She had lost her first husband, and her grief had been uncomplicated, which had been unbearable enough.

"I wasn't able to find out anything new since we spoke. All I know is that John was found murdered inside his apartment. I don't know how he was killed, time of death, or who found him. I don't know if they have any suspects." Bennie's gaze stayed riveted on the action, and Mary could see her assessing critically what was going on. Bennie had practiced criminal law for decades, specializing in murder cases, and she had defaulted to professional mode.

"Did you call anybody in the Homicide Division? You know a few detectives, don't you?"

"I'm not exactly beloved here. We're defense lawyers, did you forget?" Bennie's mouth went tight. "They must know where he worked, that's easily discoverable. Besides, we're probably among the last people who saw him alive."

"Oh, of course. So the police will want to interview us." Mary realized she might end the night at the Roundhouse, Philly's police administration headquarters. Judy was wiping her eyes, and Mary assumed she and Bennie had already discussed this, so Mary was the one playing catch-up. When she'd left the house, she had been too upset about John's murder to consider the implications.

"I called Roger, and he's en route, but he won't be here for a while. I caught him on his way to D.C."

"Yo, Mare!" came a shout, and they looked over to see Lou, signaling that he'd meet them across the street.

"Let's go," Bennie said, and they crossed to meet him, gathering at the periphery of the noisy crowd. Spectators were craning their necks to try to see what was going on, and an acrid cloud of smoke wafted into Mary's face. One of the onlookers held a beer bottle, and a female anchorperson from TV was getting ready for a video shoot, a paper towel tucked in her collar so she didn't get makeup on her dress.

"Ladies, I'm so sorry about John," Lou said, hugging Mary and Judy briefly. "This is a cryin' shame, just a cryin' shame."

Bennie turned to him. "I don't even know what happened. Nobody would tell me anything. Can you call anybody?"

"I tried, but I don't know anything." Lou stood on tiptoe, scanning the other side of the barricade. "Yo, I see one of the cops I used to know over there."

Bennie nodded. "Go see what you can find out. I'm going to see if I can talk us past this barricade."

"Good luck." Lou waded into the crowd, heading to the left, and Bennie charged to the right with Judy on her heels, followed by Mary and Anthony.

"Lady with a baby," Mary called out, but nobody even turned around, so they wedged their way to the front of the crowd. She could see the townhouse, which she knew since she had been there. The front door hung open, and John had a two-bedroom apartment on the second floor, living above his landlord. The black van from the Medical Examiner's Office sat parked in front, and mobile crime techs in booties and gloves came and went from the house.

Finally Bennie got the attention of one of the cops and tried to fast-talk them through the barricade. "Officer, we worked with the victim, John Foxman. I'm his boss, and we need to get through."

"Sorry, lady." The cop shook his head, but it was too dark for Mary to see much of his expression. "I got orders. Nobody gets through."

"But we're close —"

"Close but no cigars. Stay back."

"But we're his friends, we're coworkers —"

"Gimme a break, lady." The cop moved on, shifting sideways, and just then Mary saw a familiar redhead in the crowd. It was Anne, making her way toward the front of the barricade.

"Anne, Anne!" Mary called out, waving, and Anne turned, waving back. Anne threaded her way through the crowd to them, her face a mask of sorrow, and mascara smudged under her lovely eyes. She reached Judy first and threw open her arms, beginning to cry.

"Judy, he's . . . gone?" Anne asked, between sobs. "Can he really be gone? I feel so awful! I was so mean to him!"

"It's okay," Judy said, tearing up again, and Mary came over, giving a stricken Anne a warm hug.

"You weren't mean to him, Anne. We had a fight, and we all were a part of it, not just you."

"Oh no." Anne shook her head, hugging Mary back. "I just never thought anything like this could ever happen. I feel so terrible."

"I know, it's horrible." Mary patted Anne's back, and she seemed to rally, wiping her eyes and streaking her mascara even more.

"What do we know about how it happened?" Anne asked, trying to compose herself. "Do we know anything?"

"Not yet, unless Lou does. Here he comes." Mary squinted over her shoulder to see Lou making his way back to them, and he hugged Anne when he got there.

"I'm so sorry about John, honey."

"Lou, it's so awful, I was *so* awful to him."

"No, no, don't think about that now. You guys were buddies, and he knew it. Now listen, I tried to get information." Lou released Anne from his embrace, and Bennie pressed closer.

"Lou, what did you find out?" she asked, urgent.

"So I talked to my buddy, Oscar. He

152

knows me from way back, like when I worked security at Blackstone, back in the day, and I used to go fishing with his cousin and —"

"Lou, please," Bennie interrupted, impatient.

"He doesn't know anything. I got *bupkis.*"

"Anybody see or hear anything?"

"Don't know. I know they got uniforms canvassing."

"Time of death?"

"Oscar doesn't know but he was called in an hour ago."

Bennie checked her phone. "So, eleven thirty. Who found the body?"

"He doesn't know that either."

Bennie frowned in thought. "Somebody had to see or hear something. This is a city neighborhood on a Saturday night. Apartments cheek by jowl, restaurants, galleries, foot traffic."

"But it's late, and it's Philly. You know the joke. I was asleep already."

"How about street cameras? Did they start looking for them yet?" Bennie squinted at the traffic light in the darkness. "I can't see a damn thing, but there has to be video."

Suddenly the spectators erupted in chatter and motion. People held up their cell phones, reporters with microphones surged to the barricade, and photographers hoisted still cameras, their motor drives clicking away. Mary and the others turned to see what was going on.

At the sight, Mary's hand flew to her mouth. Uniformed assistants from the Medical Examiner's Office were coming down the front steps, carrying a stainless-steel gurney that held a black-vinyl body bag.

"Oh no!" Judy cried out, covering her face, and Anne emitted a horrified gasp. Anthony held on to the three women as best he could, and only Bennie and Lou remained stoic, watching as the assistants loaded the gurney into the back of the van, then closed its doors.

"I got the bag shot!" said a gleeful photographer.

Lou gave the photographer a dirty look, and Anne burst into new tears. Judy did the same, and Mary tried to comfort them, with Anthony's help. Bennie kept her gaze on the scene, her expression grim.

And in the next moment, she ducked under the barricade.

CHAPTER FOURTEEN

Anthony drove with Mary in the passenger seat and Bennie and Judy in the backseat. Anne and Lou had gone home, leaving Mary and the others snaking through the city streets in the darkness. Mary didn't know what Bennie had done after she went through the barricade, but somehow it had resulted in their leaving hurriedly for the Roundhouse, the police administration building. Mary wasn't sure it was a great idea, and Anthony probably felt the same way, though she hadn't had a chance to ask him. But like most wives, she could read her husband's mind.

Mary cleared her throat. "So Bennie, why did you go through the barricade?"

"I still don't get why you didn't follow me. I thought you guys would follow me."

"We tried, but they wouldn't let us."

"I was hoping we could get into the house."

"But that's not police procedure. It's a crime scene. They don't let anybody through the perimeter."

"I know, but I wanted to give it a try, together, as a group."

"You mean like *storm* the house?"

"No, talk our way in," Bennie shot back. "Like we always do."

"So what did you say?"

"I grabbed the first cop I saw, and told him I was a lawyer and needed to see the detectives on the case, so he took me to them."

"And *that* got you through?" Mary asked, incredulous.

"He thought I was an assistant district attorney."

"You told him you were an ADA?" Mary would've laughed on any other night. Judy stayed quiet in the backseat.

"No, but I implied it, or rather, he inferred from the circumstances."

"What circumstances?"

"DiNunzio, you've worked enough murder cases to know. A lawyer who arrives at a crime scene in the middle of the night? Every cop in the world assumes that's an ADA. All I had to do was act important, and I can do that in my sleep. In fact, I do."

Mary suppressed a smile.

"So then he took me to the detectives in charge, and they were young guys I don't know. Detectives Krakoff and Marks. I told them we were willing to give them a statement, so they said fine."

"Why did you do that?" Mary asked, confounded. They all felt miserable tonight, shocked over John's murder, and maybe Bennie had lost her mind. It really was true that everybody grieved differently.

"It's obvious, isn't it? I want to get into the Roundhouse and nose around. I want details."

Mary didn't know if she could handle the details of John's murder, but she didn't say so. "But why tonight? Couldn't we have waited until they asked us to come in, instead of provoking it?"

"Nothing benefits from delay, DiNunzio. It's always better to get the jump. And you know in any murder investigation, facts can develop early on. Besides, I want to talk to them before they know enough to ask us better questions. Once they figure out about the lawsuit and the statements John made, this could get sticky."

"I don't know if we should be going in unrepresented."

"We're lawyers. We know how to handle a

police interview, we've defended plenty of them."

"What about Roger? We told him we would play nice."

"I called him earlier, but this is a murder case, not a reverse-discrimination case. He's not our lawyer for all things and all times." Bennie snorted. "If you want, I'll text him where we're going. I'm not about to carry him on a sedan chair."

"Don't we want his PR guy, too? Isaac?"

"I don't, but if you do, I'm fine with their coming. We know how to handle the press in a murder case. Basically, don't feed them. And don't flip them the bird, even if you want to." Bennie paused. "Look, DiNunzio, I just realized, I should've thought of your condition." Her tone softened. "You must be beat and you should probably go home. Why don't you drop me off? I can do my own snooping."

"No, that's okay," Mary said, with a twinge of regret. She felt bad for saying anything, and secretly, she didn't want to miss out. Anthony looked over, his mouth tight, so Mary added, "I actually feel fine. I'm not even tired. I don't want to go home."

"Carrier," Bennie said, again softly. "You can go home too. I know this is roughest on you. You guys were pals."

"Thanks but no," Judy said, her voice thick. "I don't want to go home, either. I wouldn't sleep anyway."

Bennie asked, "Are you sure?"

"Yes," Mary answered, firmly. "I'm just trying to understand why you're doing what you're doing. What you hope to accomplish."

Bennie fell silent a moment, and Mary wasn't sure Bennie had heard the question. Mary glanced back, but Bennie's face was turned away, and Mary couldn't see her expression. The only lighting in the backseat was intermittent, from the streetlights.

"Bennie?" Mary repeated. "Are you okay?"

"DiNunzio." Bennie turned to face her, and Mary could see Bennie's eyes glistening with raw emotion. "I'm doing what I'm doing because somebody killed one of my associates. One of *our* associates, a young man who joined our firm and worked hard for us. I'm doing it because he mattered to me. His life mattered to me. And so does his murder." Bennie wiped her eye quickly, catching a tear before it fell. Her fingers were trembling, which was something Mary had never seen before, but Bennie kept talking, the words coming out with a force of their own. "I'm pretty good at murder cases. I've been doing them for years, and so have you. So I'm not going to sit on my thumbs and let two rookie detectives screw this up, or miss something, or forget even a single detail. I'm going to be all over them from day one. From now. Until they find who committed this murder. That's why I went through the barricade. I heard you say Foxman has no family here, but you were wrong. *We* were his family. And even though we had a family fight, that doesn't mean we're not family anymore. That's why we're doing this. For him."

Mary felt a lump in her throat as Bennie turned her head quickly away, looking out the window. Silence fell in the car, and Mary realized how wrong she had been back at the crime scene. She had thought Bennie had been defaulting to professional mode on John's street. Instead Bennie had been keeping her emotions within, channeling them into action to find John's killer. Mary felt touched at Bennie's devotion and loyalty, but she couldn't say so right now. She tried to hold back her tears, and for some reason, she didn't look over at Anthony. She knew he felt the same way she did, because she was his wife.

Mary looked out the window as they

passed the gritty industrial area around the concrete cloverleafs to I-95, interspersed with boxy warehouses and factories converted to funky apartment buildings. In the distance, the Ben Franklin Bridge glowed a ghostly blue in the dark night. They made their way through the streets cruising in light traffic through the grid of one-way streets. They went west on Market Street past the United States Courthouse, a modern monolith that anchored the corner of Seventh and Chestnut Streets, then turned onto Seventh, catching sight of the round concrete buildings that gave the Roundhouse its name.

Anthony shifted into the left lane, heading for the Roundhouse's parking lot, and as soon as they got to the entrance, Mary could see the crowd of media collecting in front of the building with their klieglights, video cameras, and the same crowd of reporters from the crime scene. Their white news vans with tall microwave towers overflowed the press section of the lot, but Anthony found an empty space and parked, cutting the ignition.

Mary braced herself, eyeing the noisy throng of press. "So we just go through and say 'no comment.' "

"Yes," Bennie answered firmly. "No fear,

161

DiNunzio. We've done this a million times. Just put your head down and keep walking."

Anthony interjected, "Don't worry, Bennie. If they want to get to Mary, they're going to have to go through me."

"That's the spirit." Bennie rallied. "Everybody good to go?"

"Not yet," Judy answered hesitantly, then she fell abruptly silent.

"What is it, Carrier?"

Judy didn't answer Bennie, and Mary turned completely around, which wasn't easy, considering the size of her belly.

"Judy, what?"

Judy bit her lip. "There's something I have to tell you. You should know it before the police find out."

CHAPTER FIFTEEN

Mary didn't understand why Judy was stopping them before they went into the Roundhouse. Her best friend's face was visible in the ambient light, and Judy looked stricken, her agonized expression incongruous with her pink hair and the quirky, multicolored poncho.

"Honey, what's the matter?" Mary asked, concerned.

"Um, well." Judy looked down at her hands, fumbling with a ball of soggy tissues. "There's something you guys should know before we go in. I've been keeping it from you. I should've told you before now but, well, uh, I didn't. I didn't know how you would react."

Mary frowned, pained. "Honey, you can tell me anything. I won't react any way. You know that, I love you."

Bennie looked over at Judy. "Carrier, just tell us," she said, her tone uncharacteristically gentle.

Judy heaved a sigh that shuddered as she exhaled, then lifted her gaze, which was teary, glistening in the light. "John and I, well, we weren't just friends. We were dating."

Mary blinked, hiding her shock. She felt surprised that Judy would keep it from her, but this wasn't the time or the place for that, and Judy's heartbroken demeanor made complete sense. Judy was taking John's murder so hard because she had been seeing him.

Bennie frowned. "Wait. You were dating Foxman? An associate?"

"Yes." Judy sniffled.

"You can't do that."

"I knew you wouldn't like it. That's why I didn't tell you."

"That doesn't make it right, that only makes it secret."

Mary flared her eyes, interjecting, "Bennie, really? Now?"

Bennie sighed. "Sorry, Carrier."

"I'm sorry." Judy nodded, miserably.

Bennie added, "But I hate surprises, and now we have to deal with this. We're blindsided."

Mary interjected again, "Bennie?"

Bennie pursed her lips. "Carrier, how long

164

did you two date for?"

"We've been dating for, almost, eight months." Judy's wet gaze met Mary's directly. "Since you found out you were pregnant, Mary. After your case with Simon and his daughter. It started with a friendship, then I started seeing him in a new light. I guess I always crushed on him, but we're so different, like, he's so straight, but anyway, we got together. I'm sorry I didn't tell you, I wanted to, so many times."

"It's all right." Mary managed a reassuring smile, though she felt bewildered. "You could've told me, but it's okay that you didn't. What really matters is that I'm very sorry that you lost him. I knew you were friends, but I didn't know you were, well, closer."

"We are, I mean, we really were." Judy dabbed her eye with the soggy Kleenex. "I should have told you, but you were so busy with the pregnancy and I didn't want to take the focus off of you, and we weren't sure when we wanted people to know in the office. We were keeping it to ourselves until we knew it was working out." Judy turned to face Bennie. "I didn't think you would approve. I was a partner and he was an associate, but if you remember, you kinda sprung partnership on me, when you

165

thought the firm was breaking up. Anyway, I didn't know how you would feel about an office romance, especially since I was technically his boss. I didn't tell you. I didn't tell anybody."

"Understood," Bennie said quietly, without rancor. "I'm so sorry for your loss."

"I'm sorry I didn't tell you guys." Judy sniffled, and Mary could see she was fighting to remain in control.

"It's okay, honey, don't worry about it." Mary couldn't reach Judy to touch her, but in the next moment, Bennie did, surprisingly, patting Judy's hand.

"Carrier, that's the last thing you should be worried about. But it's good that we know that before we go into the police interviews."

"Wait, there's more." Judy sniffled, half chuckling. "Arg, I know, it sounds like those dumb commercials. 'Wait there's more!' "

"What more?" Bennie asked, calmly.

Mary glanced at Anthony, who was listening, his head cocked.

Judy swallowed hard. "I was there tonight, at John's."

Mary recoiled, unable to process the information fast enough. Her first thought was that it wasn't a good thing.

"What time?" Bennie kept her hand on Judy's.

"I guess until about nine o'clock, and we had a big fight." Judy raked her fingers through her hair, shaking her head. "It's just so sad, and so awful, I don't even know where to start, I mean, I can't believe he's gone."

"Carrier, begin at the beginning." Bennie's tone strengthened. "Tell me the chronology of your day. We were together in the morning, then you took Mary to the doctor."

"Right." Judy nodded, sniffling anew.

"What time did you leave the doctor?"

"Anthony picked Mary up at around two o'clock."

"What did you do then?"

"I went to John's."

"How did you get there?"

"I took a cab."

"Why did you go there?"

Judy sniffled, wiping her eyes again. "We were in a fight from the night before, when the Complaint came in from Machiavelli. I was so surprised and shocked, really. I didn't know John had said any of those things about us and I didn't even know he was looking for a job. He kept it from me, and we had a big fight about it, on Friday night, and uh we —" Judy's eyes welled up, and Bennie squeezed Judy's hand.

"Stay with me. We need to figure this out and we need to figure it out right now."

"Okay, okay," Judy said, trying to recover.

"All you have to do is answer my questions. Let's back up to Friday night. What time did you go to his house Friday night?"

"After work, at seven o'clock."

"And what happened?"

"I told him I was really mad at him about the Complaint and the things he said, and also at the press conference, because that was such a mess and I didn't know that he had even been interviewing for a job. He hadn't told me." Judy hesitated. "And well, he, uh, said he was interviewing because he didn't think we could work at the same firm if he was an associate and I was his boss, and he wasn't going to tell me until he had an offer he wanted, so that's why he didn't tell me, but anyway we had a big fight."

"What time did you leave his apartment?"

"I left around one in the morning. We fought, like, all night. It was horrible, and now I feel horrible —"

"Was there shouting?"

"Yes." Judy blew her nose. "Me, mostly. You could've guessed that."

"Okay, let's return to Saturday. So you go to his apartment at two o'clock." Bennie paused. "Wait a minute. Didn't he have a job interview? I remember he said that, and he was dressed for it."

"Yes, but it was over by two."

"Do you know who it was with?"

"No." Judy shook her head, distraught. "I didn't know he was doing any of that. I feel so terrible that he said such bad things about us, and I can't believe that he really felt that way, and that's what we were fighting about, back and forth."

"Okay, so you were at his apartment from two o'clock today. What did you do there?"

"We tried to work it out and we talked, and we fought, and we ordered in, but we couldn't work it out, and I was so angry at him and he was angry at me for being angry at him and anyway, so, well, uh, we broke up."

Listening, Mary felt a wave of profound sympathy for her best friend, who must've been suffering so deeply. Judy was one of the most sensitive creatures on the planet, despite her happy-go-lucky exterior, and Mary's heart went out to her.

Bennie asked, "Was there more yelling?"

"Yes."

"Do you think any neighbors heard it?"

"No, I don't know, maybe, does it matter?" Judy sniffled. "His landlord lives downstairs, they're an older couple. I don't think they're home this weekend. They cruise all the time, and John feeds their cat." Judy's eyes welled up again. "Now he's gone, I don't know what's going to happen, he was so good at taking care of everything, and he was William's guardian. I don't know what William's going to do now, or who's going to tell him. He doesn't have anybody but John. The aunt and uncle haven't been east in years."

Bennie patted Judy's hand again. "The police notify next of kin, so let's stay on point. Do you know his landlord?"

"But I don't want the police to tell William. They're strangers."

"I'm sure the aunt and uncle will then, but talk to me. Do you know the landlord?"

"Yes, I've met him a few times."

"But you didn't see him today or his wife?"

"No."

"So you broke up today and you left the apartment at nine o'clock tonight, is that right?"

"About that, I think, give or take."

"How much give and how much take?"

"About twenty minutes."

"How do you know that?"

"I don't know, I don't remember, I was so

exhausted and I think I looked at my phone because I just kept thinking about calling Mary." Judy looked at Mary, her eyes welling. "I wanted to come over and tell you everything, that John and I were seeing each other and that we just broke up, but I didn't call you. It was late and I knew that you needed to rest after the doctor's appointment, and I didn't want to upset you or stress you, so I just decided to go home."

Mary groaned. "Aw, honey, I'm so sorry. You know, you can always call me and —"

Bennie interrupted, "Carrier, is that what you did next? You went straight home?"

"Yes, well, not straight home."

Bennie frowned. "Where did you go?"

"Let me think, I was really upset and I didn't know what to do" — Judy's words ran together with emotion — "and I went to this pocket park because it was such a nice night and I just wanted to calm down, but then I knew I had to get home because the dog had to go out, so I got a cab and went home."

"What time did you get the cab?"

"I don't know."

"Was it a Yellow cab or what?"

"Yes, a Yellow."

"How long did you spend in the park?"

"About an hour, I think."

"Do you know or are you guessing?"

"Both." Judy dabbed her eyes.

"Were there other people in the park, that you saw?"

"Yes, a few."

"Did you talk to any of them?"

"No."

"Where's the park located?"

"Around the block. Does it matter?"

"Then you went home?"

"Yes."

"What did you do when you got home?"

"I walked the dog. I didn't take him that day, because he was so bad the day before."

"Did you see any of your neighbors when you were walking the dog?"

"No."

"And then what happened?"

"I went to bed and I couldn't sleep, I was so upset and I thought about calling him, like, so many times, I just kept lying in bed staring at my phone." Judy's eyes spilled over with tears, and she began to sob again. "And now . . . I keep thinking what if, what if . . . *what if* I had called, that was probably when the killer was there, and I could have stopped it . . . or interrupted it and if I did then John would still be alive m—"

Bennie squeezed her hand. "Carrier, we need to sort this out. So then what happened?"

"So you called" — Judy squeezed the Kleenex to her nose, stifling her sobs — "and you told me that the reporter called you and told you that John was dead and I totally freaked out and got a cab to go to his apartment. That's when I saw you on the street, so I got out of the cab and we walked the last block together, then we saw Mary and Anthony, and I just can't believe this is happening, I just can't, it's so horrible and I feel so terrible —"

"Okay." Bennie patted Judy's hand in a final way. "I don't think you should be going into any police interview."

"Why, I want to —"

"Carrier, that wouldn't be smart. We know that the police were called to the scene around eleven thirty, so time of death was before then. The medical examiner can't always fix time of death with certainty, usually there is a window, maybe an hour, maybe two." Bennie squeezed Judy's hand. "Do you understand what I'm telling you? You could have been in the apartment around the time of death, as far as we know."

"So what are you saying, Bennie?" Judy's eyes flared, wetly.

"I'm saying that you could be a suspect."

"Don't be ridiculous!" Judy recoiled,

aghast, but Mary was in agreement, though she didn't interrupt Bennie.

"Carrier. You were there at the time, so that's opportunity. We don't know how he was killed, so we can't speculate about that, but you have motive."

"What motive? Why would I kill John? That's *crazy!*"

"Think like a lawyer, not like yourself. You were seeing each other for eight months and you were fighting. You could have been overheard by anyone. Neighbors, anybody with an open window."

"But I would never kill anybody, much less John! I *loved* him!" Judy's voice broke with agony.

"Think about it from the police perspective. They don't know that, they don't know you. You get in a fight, maybe you lash out, violently. That's motive."

Mary interjected, "Even the lawsuit can be motive. John's statements in the Complaint, and what happened at the press conference — they'll find out that we weren't happy with him. Our fight was in public. Judy, the police could think that you went over to talk to him about the lawsuit, you got in a fight, and you killed him."

"But I would never!"

Bennie turned to Mary. "DiNunzio, where

were you at the time of death?"

"I was home with Anthony." Mary realized that Bennie was checking if she had an alibi, which, thank God, she did. "Where were you, Bennie?"

"I was at a Town Watch meeting from eight o'clock on. That's where I was when I got the call. Eight witnesses can attest to that." Bennie returned her attention to Judy, who was trying to regain her composure. "Carrier, you're the only one of us without an alibi. You can't walk into that interview unrepresented. It's too risky. And we can't represent you because we're fact witnesses."

Mary chimed in, "Judy, she's right, you should let Anthony take you to our house. You shouldn't be alone this weekend. I'll go with Bennie, we'll give our statements, and find out everything we can about what happened to John."

Bennie nodded, tense. "That's what I was thinking. The cops don't expect the entire firm to show up. Two is a good showing. It'll take time until the cops discover you guys were dating. Hopefully they — or we — find the killer before you become a suspect."

Judy sagged, lost in her poncho. "Okay, I get it."

"I'm in." Mary grabbed her purse and

turned to Anthony. "Thanks so much, babe."

"Sure thing." Anthony pursed his lips. "You really feel up to this?"

"I'll be fine," Mary answered, meaning it. "It won't take long."

"Let's do this." Bennie reached for the door handle.

CHAPTER SIXTEEN

Mary and Bennie rode up in the elevator of the Roundhouse, having run the gauntlet of press. Mary hadn't been here as many times as Bennie, so it was unfamiliar, and she felt vaguely nervous. There was a lot at stake, and they had to get as much information possible without giving any, which would be a neat trick. She smoothed down her jacket, trying to look professional in her maternity jeans, which was mission impossible for girls.

The elevator doors rattled open, and Bennie stepped off into a narrow, grimy hallway. "Man, this place never gets any prettier, does it?"

"No," Mary answered, following Bennie around a hall that curved to the right, following the shape of the building. The walls were scuffed, the fluorescent light flickered, and the brown tile felt gritty underfoot, with some of the tiles cracked and broken. The

Roundhouse had been built in the sixties, when its space-age design looked modern, and it was way overdue for a renovation. Politicians had promised to build a new police headquarters uptown, but that had yet to materialize. Welcome to Philadelphia. And every other major American city.

Mary and Bennie went down the hall, passing a lineup of battered gray file cabinets on the left, and on the right, a dimly lit bathroom with its urinals on full view, since its door was propped open by a plastic trash tub. Mary's nose twitched at the odor but she tried not to breathe, and they reached the end of the hallway and a door with a window of bulletproof glass, under the sign, **Homicide Division**. Bennie pushed the buzzer, the door buzzed open, and they let themselves in.

Bennie took the lead, ignoring the low railing that enclosed the waiting area and beelining to the front desk, while Mary followed, glancing around the waiting area, which was small, dirty, and unoccupied. Black-plastic chairs lined the walls on either side under a slew of Wanted For Murder posters, arranged like a nightmare portrait gallery. They were the most lethal fugitives in the jurisdiction, men and women of all shapes, sizes, and ethnicities, their facial expressions defiant, angry, or affectless. Mary wondered if one of them had killed John, which made her shudder.

Bennie identified them to the desk officer, who was young, tall, and African-American, while Mary checked out the squad room, which was empty except for one detective on the phone. She used to expect that a homicide squad room would be bustling on a Saturday night, just like on TV and the movies, but the opposite was true in reality. More murders were committed on the weekend and at night, so the detectives were out on "jobs" at those times. In fact, the Homicide Division had unofficial sweatshirts that read Our Day Begins When Yours Ends.

Meanwhile, the squad room was even crappier than the last time Mary was here. It was long and skinny, one continuous line of connected rooms, with the far wall curved like the building itself and its long panel of windows barely covered by broken blinds. The desks that filled the room were mismatched and shoved in together, and old gray, brown, and black file cabinets lined the wall. The computers were ancient with big boxy monitors, the floor looked grimy, and the dropped ceiling showed water damage, with brownish stains marking its white tile in shapes like the continents of the world.

"DiNunzio," Bennie said, over her shoulder. "Officer Lloyd needs to see your ID."

"Of course." Mary got her ID from her wallet and showed it to him, and Officer Lloyd reacted immediately when his gaze dropped to her pregnant belly.

"Oh, sorry, I didn't realize." Officer Lloyd rose and came around the desk. "I'm not gonna let you wait in the waiting room. Let me show you to the interview room. You can wait for Detectives Krakoff and Marks in there."

"Thanks," Mary said, pleased, since her pregnancy hadn't been good for anything except a baby, until now.

They walked with Officer Lloyd through the narrow pathway that led to the three interview rooms on the right, and he unlocked the middle room, a windowless box the size of a prison cell, containing four mismatched chairs and a typing table with a tan Smith-Corona typewriter and a stack of Miranda waivers. Officer Lloyd gestured them inside. "Ladies, please. I'll let them know you're here as soon as they get back."

They thanked him, sitting down in the hard chairs, and after he had gone, Bennie leaned over. "DiNunzio, you think I was too hard on Carrier? About dating Foxman?"

Suddenly a young detective walked by the open doorway, followed by an older, beefy detective in a tan suit and loosened tie. The older one paused when he spotted Mary, and Mary did a double-take. It was Detective Thomas Azzic, who had worked with her on one of her first murder cases. His blond hair had grayed and thinned, and his aviator glasses had acquired a bifocal window, but his big grin was the same.

"Is that *Mary DiNunzio?* As I live and breathe?" Detective Azzic entered the room. "All grown up and *with child*?"

"Hi, how are you, Detective Azzic?" Mary rose, smiling back, and Detective Azzic helped her to her feet and gave her a great big hug.

"Please, call me Tom. It's so good to see you! It's been forever! You were just a young lawyer back then!"

"I know, I could barely drive!" Mary laughed, and Detective Azzic joined her, glancing at Bennie.

"Hey, the famous Bennie Rosato. Good to meet you."

"Good to meet you too." Bennie smiled in a professional way.

Mary said, "I'm Bennie's partner now. Got my name on the door and everything."

"Whoa, legit. Congrats." Detective Azzic beamed, then turned to Bennie. "You've got quite a partner here."

"I absolutely agree."

Detective Azzic returned his warm gaze to Mary. "So when did you get married?" He hesitated for a panicky moment. "Wait, er, you're married right?"

"Of course, you know me."

"I know, nice Catholic girl like you. Your mother would kill you." Detective Azzic gestured to his partner, who came up behind. "Hey, Mary, Bennie this is my partner, Francisco Becerra. Francisco, her family is awesome. You should meet her mother. She made me peppers and eggs once. Oh my God, it was *amazing*."

Detective Becerra looked confused. "A frittata."

"What?" Detective Azzic scoffed. "Don't embarrass yourself. A frittata isn't *peppers and eggs.* It was delicious. And the coffee, it was perked, in a percolator. So what are you doing here, Mary? You got a client?"

"No actually, it's very sad. One of our coworkers was murdered tonight, an associate named John Foxman."

"Oh, no. I'm so sorry." Detective Azzic's face fell, pained. "The name's Foxman? I heard about that case. Krakoff and Marks caught it."

"We know. Bennie met them at the scene." Mary saw an opening, since Detective Azzic was one of the friendliest detectives in the division, warm and talkative, even blabby. "You see, John, the victim, didn't have any family in town, and we knew him pretty well, so we thought we would come in, let you all know what we know, and find out anything we could."

"Good idea. I don't think they're back yet."

"They're not. We're waiting for them, but we don't even know how it happened. Can you tell us?"

Detective Azzic frowned. "Yes, but it has to stay confidential. You saw the press outside."

"Of course, we'd never say anything."

"Nothing's official yet, but they figure your friend was killed in the course of a burglary. Best they can tell, he interrupted the burglar."

"Oh no." Mary heard herself moan.

"It happens all the time. More often than you think."

"How do they know that's what happened?"

"His electronics were gone and there were signs of a struggle."

Mary fell silent for a moment, imagining the horrifying scenario.

Bennie didn't miss a beat. "How was he killed, do you know?"

"Blow to the head."

"With what, do you know? Did they find what was used?"

"I don't know."

"So I assume there was forced entry?"

"Yes."

"Poor John." Mary shuddered to think of him fighting for his life, struggling to survive, and in the end, being killed so brutally and cruelly. John was so brilliant, possessing a magnificent legal intellect. She felt tears come to her eyes, but willed them away.

"Mary, you okay?" Detective Azzic touched her arm, his gaze sympathetic. "Why don't you sit back down?"

"Thanks." Mary sank into a chair.

Bennie remained standing. "Do you know if they have any suspects?"

"Not yet. It's way early."

"So nobody saw anybody running away or anything like that?"

"Not that I know of."

"Do you know what time he was killed?"

"We got the call around eleven thirty. I think time of death was shortly before."

"Do you know who found him?"

"Don't know."

"So any witnesses?"

"Not that I heard of, but like I say, it's early. Something will turn up, in that neighborhood. It's busy on a night like tonight. It's way too soon in the investigation to speculate."

"Are there a lot of burglaries in that part of Old City? I wouldn't have thought so."

"It doesn't happen often, but it happens." Detective Azzic shot Mary a comforting glance. "Don't worry, we'll lock up whoever did this to your friend. I'll keep an eye on the case, personally."

"Thank you so much," Mary said, meaning it.

"Yes, thanks," Bennie added.

"See you later." Detective Azzic turned around as two more detectives came up behind him. "Oh, here we go. Here are Detectives Jason Krakoff and Jonathan Marks."

Bennie straightened. "Good to see you again, Detectives."

Mary introduced herself, shaking their hands, though she took an instant dislike to Detective Krakoff. He had a stiff formality despite his youth, and his eyes were ice blue and set close together, with a long nose. His chin was fashionably grizzly, his dark hair scissored into neat layers, and his eyebrows more well-groomed than hers. Mary hadn't plucked her eyebrows or shaved her legs in forever. Basically, she was a hair factory.

Detective Azzic edged back. "Jason, you know Bennie Rosato, and her partner Mary is an old friend of mine. Your vic was a lawyer in their firm."

"Right, I know."

Detective Azzic placed a hand on Detective Krakoff's shoulder. "Jason, I just briefed them on what you know so far. You can fill in the details."

"You briefed them?" Detective Krakoff lifted an eyebrow, his expression impassive.

"Yes, but they know it's confidential. I'll leave you to it, but take good care of them. Mary's one of my favorite people on the earth. If you don't treat her right, her mom's coming after me with a wooden spoon."

Mary laughed.

Detective Krakoff nodded. "We'll take it from here, Tom."

"Sure." Detective Azzic went to the threshold. "Good-bye Bennie. Mare, give my best to your family."

"Will do," Mary called after him, and Detectives Krakoff and Marks sat down opposite from Mary and Bennie.

Bennie shifted forward. "Detectives, John Foxman was a brilliant young lawyer and we all liked him very much. We want to see whoever killed him brought to justice. Do you have any suspects?"

"We're not at liberty to discuss that."

"Understood, and you have our word that we would keep it confidential. We've handled a great number of murder cases. We never talk to the press or anybody else, for that matter."

"Nevertheless, it's police business." Detective Krakoff crossed his long legs.

"You may not know that Foxman had no family in town, only an aunt and uncle who live in Minneapolis. We're essentially the only family he has in Philadelphia and —"

"You're not family, though."

"But we have an interest in knowing some basic information, like for example, if you have any suspects or witnesses."

Detective Krakoff frowned. "It's standard procedure not to disclose official police business during a murder investigation. We have already notified the victim's aunt and uncle as next of kin."

"Oh, how did you get their contact information?"

"Also police business."

Bennie pursed her lips. "We understand

that he was killed during a burglary, from a blow to the head. Do you know what he was struck with? Was it a gun? Did you recover it?"

"I regret that you were given that information. I'll take you at your word when you say you won't disclose it to the press."

"Of course we won't," Bennie shot back, becoming irritable. "It's obvious you don't trust us, and I'm telling you that you can. Details of a police investigation are not discussed with the general public, but we certainly stand in different shoes than a stranger on the street. We'd like to know your findings so far."

"That's not how we work our cases."

"I'm not asking you anything that won't be in the newspaper tomorrow, if not the next day."

"Then you can read it there. But you won't hear anything more from me tonight than you have already heard."

"Is it true that he was killed during the course of the burglary, from a blow to a head? Detective Azzic told us that much, so can you confirm?"

"Yes," Detective Krakoff answered, without elaboration.

"Who called 911? Who found the body?"

"That I won't divulge."

"But at that hour of the night, it had to be a witness, since his landlord was away. Did somebody see something through a window? Or hear something?"

"Ms. Rosato, I don't know how many ways I can say this. I'm not going to discuss details of the case with you."

Mary interjected, "Detective Krakoff, what my partner is trying to say is that we loved John. He mattered to us, and we're upset by this. We're heartbroken. We just want to know what you know. We may not technically be family, but we think of ourselves as family."

Detective Krakoff blinked, obviously unmoved. "I understand, and I will brief you as the investigation proceeds, to the extent that it's consistent with police procedures."

"But can't you tell us anything more, just to give us some hope?" Mary kept talking, hoping to convince him. "We know that the uniformed officers were canvassing when we left, and there's a lot of people in that neighborhood. Anybody could've seen or heard anybody going into John's apartment, and if there were signs of a struggle, I would hope that the uniformed officers or you would have someone identify the witness —"

"Excuse me. As I said, we will divulge any such information as is appropriate." Detective Krakoff slipped a pen and skinny notebook from inside his jacket. "Ms. Rosato, when we spoke earlier outside of the victim's house, you had some information that may help us. If you do, we'd like to know that now, in the early stages."

"Certainly. John Foxman was an associate at my office. He worked for us for about four years. His parents are dead, he's unmarried and the guardian of a brother with cerebral palsy, William Foxman, who resides in a group home in the suburbs. I can get you the address if you wish."

"I would appreciate that." Detective Krakoff made a note. "Now, it's my understanding that Foxman was referred to in a lawsuit that was recently filed against your law firm for reverse discrimination. Is that correct?"

"Yes," Bennie answered lightly.

"We saw video footage of a press conference that took place yesterday, in that regard. He intended to leave the firm. Can you tell us about that?"

"It's self-explanatory, isn't it?" Bennie shrugged. "He was looking for another job and was going to leave the firm. That was fine with us, even though we were surprised to learn it at the press conference. We employ people, not imprison them."

Detective Krakoff made another note, and Mary hid her nervousness. They weren't going to get any more information and they were entering a danger zone.

"Did the victim have any enemies, that you know of?"

"Not that we know of."

Mary knew this line of questioning could end up close to Judy. Bennie couldn't reveal the fact that Judy was dating John, nor could she lie outright to the police.

Detective Krakoff made a note on his pad. "How about friends of his? Did he have a group of friends?"

"We assume so, but we don't know."

"How about a girlfriend?"

Suddenly Mary jolted in her chair, her hand flying to her belly. "Oh, yikes. *That* doesn't feel good."

Detective Krakoff looked over. "Pardon me?"

"Ouch!" Mary grimaced. "That felt *weird.* It felt like a contraction, but it could have been a kick. Probably it's just Braxton-Hicks, but you never know."

Bennie's eyes flared with credible concern. "DiNunzio, do you need to see a doctor? Do you want me to get an ambulance?"

"Oh no. You mean, the baby's coming?"

Detective Krakoff grimaced in alarm, and Mary nodded in bogus pain.

"I hope not, I doubt it, I'm only seven months, but you never know. I think I need to go home and lie down. Sorry, Bennie, I hope you don't mind if we go."

"Not at all." Bennie rose, picking up their purses. "We can't take any chances, especially after you were already rushed to the doctor today."

"I agree, you're reading my mind." Mary rose, her hand on her belly, hamming it up. "Detectives, sorry, but I had a medical emergency earlier, well, you don't need the details, but my doctor said I had to take it easy. And this feels like a contraction."

Bennie took Mary's arm. "Detectives, I'm taking Mary home. It's been a long, hard day. She needs to rest."

"Of course." Detective Marks nodded, agitated. "Do you have a ride?"

"The car is outside." Mary took her purse from Bennie. "Ooh, that hurt! You never know, and I don't want to have a baby right here. Maybe we could do this another time, Detectives?"

"Anytime, yes." Detective Krakoff nodded, vaguely flustered.

"Bennie, let's go." Mary headed out of the interview room, rubbing her belly.

"Good-bye, Detectives!" Bennie called behind her. "We'll be in touch."

CHAPTER SEVENTEEN

Mary let herself into her house, setting down her purse in the entrance hall and following the soft light emanating from the living room, where she wasn't surprised to see Anthony asleep on the couch with Judy's golden retriever curled up on his stocking feet. In contrast, Judy was awake in the chair-and-a-half by the window, looking exhausted and numb.

"Mare, how did it go?" Judy started to get up, but Mary waved her back down.

"Stay put, I'm coming over." Mary crossed to the chair and kicked off her flats, so her feet could swell to Fred-Flintstone proportions.

"You must be starving. You want a slice? I can heat it up for you." Judy gestured to the coffee table, which held a cardboard box of pizza, a few bottles of water and soda, and a Greek salad that released the aroma of feta cheese and onions despite its plastic clam-shell.

"No thanks, I'm fine." Mary picked up a bottle of water, twisting off the cap and taking a slug. She wanted to stay hydrated, but she didn't feel like eating.

"Are you okay? You must be so tired. I'm sorry to put you through this."

"You're not putting me through it, honey." Mary drank more water. "Can we both fit in that chair?"

"You mean, all three of us? Totally." Judy managed a smile, removing one of the pillows and shifting over to make room for Mary, who squeezed in beside her.

"Cuddly."

"Right?"

"We need it."

"We sure do." Judy dabbed at her eyes, which were bloodshot and swollen. "So what did you find out? They're not saying anything on the news, just that he was a lawyer and he was murdered."

"We got the basic facts, but do you want to hear them?"

"Yes." Judy nodded, sniffling. "I cried all the tears I can cry, at least for now."

"They don't have any suspects yet and they won't tell us if they have any witnesses." Mary met her best friend's gaze directly and softened her voice to ease the blow. "They think he interrupted a burglar. His electronics were gone, and he was killed by a blow to the head."

"Oh no." Judy moaned, her eyes glistening. "That's terrible. That's *terrible.*"

"That's all we know. We don't know anything else, not even who found him or anything like that. We talked to the detectives on the case and we got as much information as we could, for now."

"No suspects?"

"No, it's too soon."

"No witnesses?"

"They won't say."

"They don't even know what time he died?"

"If they do, they're not telling us." Mary knew that John's body would already be at the Medical Examiner's Office and his autopsy would be scheduled for tomorrow. It usually took a few days to process and release a body, but this wasn't the time to review those details with Judy. Mary wanted to shift the topic from the gruesome details. "The only bright spot is that I ran into Detective Azzic, who I used to know. He told us what we know and he might be a way to find out more in the future. But that's it for tonight."

"That's it?"

"That's it. We tried." Mary patted her leg. "You know how Bennie is. She cross-examined them."

"Like she did me, about seeing John."

"Right." Mary flashed on Bennie's question, back in the interview room before the detectives had entered. "She feels bad about that, she told me."

"She did?"

"Yes," Mary answered, though it was only partly true. Judy needed the comfort tonight, and Bennie had felt bad about giving Judy a hard time. Plus, a white lie was only a venial sin.

"I know why she said it, I get it. I knew she'd feel that way, that's why I didn't tell her. I know it didn't make it right, but it wasn't like that, it was . . ." Judy's sentence trailed off, and her gaze wandered over to the couch, where Anthony and the dog were sleeping. "It's just so sad, that's all, and in any event, it's the definition of a moot point. John's gone, so whether he was an associate and I was a partner doesn't matter at all."

"I'm so sorry, honey," Mary said, though she had said it before, many times. She remembered that when she was grieving her first husband, she hadn't understood why people said *I'm sorry,* since it wasn't their fault. But now, she understood. It really meant, *I'm sorry this happened to you,* and that moment of empathy made us human.

"He was such a sweet guy. I tried to call William's cell, but there was no answer. They have to turn their cell phones off at night in the group home."

"How well do you know William?"

"Pretty well. John would go out there, mostly every Sunday, and I went with him lots of times. William saw me more often than his aunt and uncle. His aunt is their mom's older sister, Susan Hodge. Her husband's name is Mel."

"Do you know them?"

"No, never met them. John wasn't that close to them, and I bet they don't even know about me." Judy's gaze stayed on the couch. "I'm guessing the police were able to reach the Hodges, since they're next of kin. John was so orderly, he probably has them as the emergency contact for him and for William. So they probably reached William. I guess I'll leave it to them to tell him, right? They're family."

"Right," Mary said, though her definition of family was changing as she'd gotten older. She had grown closer to Judy and further away from her own twin sister, Angie. Even though Mary had been raised in a family where blood was as thick as tomato sauce, she felt as if Judy were her sister. And she was starting to understand that family was something you weren't born with, but chose.

"I really am sorry I didn't tell you about John and me."

"Don't worry, I understand." Mary patted Judy's leg again. "I know you love me."

"I do, I really do, and I knew you wouldn't tell Bennie. It's just that, it was like we wanted to keep it to ourselves, like, our thing. You know, John and I are so different, *were* so different, and I just didn't know how it would be, out in the open. We're not the likeliest couple. The preppie and the goofball."

"You're not a goofball."

"Well, whatever." Judy's gaze returned to the couch. "It's like we were incubating, you know? I told him that once. I said, 'Let's see if we just grow on our own, see what hatches.' He was fine with that, he didn't want anybody to know, but honestly, his reason for keeping it secret didn't have to do with what Bennie would think or anybody else."

"Then why?"

"He was more private, naturally. That's why I'm not *totally* shocked that he didn't tell me he wanted to leave the firm, or that he felt the way he felt about why he didn't make partner, or even that he was interviewing. He was a big processor, like, he *brooded*. He would've told me when he was ready, when he had it sorted. He kept himself to himself."

"That's a perfect description of John."

"Isn't it?" Judy dabbed her eyes. "I was crazy about him, I really was. We're so different, but it was yin and yang, you know?"

"I bet." Mary had wondered about that. "So opposites attract?"

"Not exactly, but close, but I think in some ways we had the same take on life, and deep inside, we were alike. Like even though I'm more confessional and never shut up about my emotions, he felt things very deeply. He was a private guy, but that didn't mean he didn't have emotions. It just meant he didn't talk about them."

"I understand." Mary nodded, thinking when she had mistaken Bennie's businesslike manner at the crime scene for professionalism, when it was really just a cover. "You and me are so yappy, we don't always get it when people aren't."

"Exactly." Judy's mouth set in a forlorn line, the corners turning down. "John and I were happy, really happy. I couldn't have been happier. I think he was too, even though he was less vocal about it, but we were in love, we said it, I said it first, of course, because you know how I am, but he said it later, at a Phillies game of all places." Judy almost smiled at the memory, her gaze still in the middle distance. "He loved baseball and we went all the time. He was so excited about the season. It just started."

"*You* went to a baseball game?" Mary asked, incredulous. Judy always said she avoided anything with a sportsball and rules you couldn't break.

"Yes, *me.*" Judy's eyes flared happily. "I got the hat and everything. I even ate a hot dog. Me, a vegetarian."

Mary smiled. "Did you like it?"

"Of course, I'm not crazy, and it was so fun to go, especially because John always buys the program and writes down the hits and runs, whatever, I don't even know why, but he did it. He has a record of every baseball game he ever went to."

"I've seen those guys at the game, writing stuff down. I can't believe he was one of those guys."

"He said it made it more fun but I used to tease him because he never really smiled when he did it, he just became *absorbed,* and anyway, this one time, I forget which game, one of the players hit a home run, and the cannon went off and the scoreboard went crazy, and he was so happy, he hugged me and he said, 'God, I love you.' "

"That's so cute."

"He was cute, he really could be." Judy gestured at the couch, and tears brimmed in her bloodshot blue eyes. "You see Anthony over there, with the dog?"

"Yes." Mary didn't know where she was going.

"It's just so nice to be in this house, with your sweetheart of a husband and a great dog, in a really nice, quiet room. And now you're going to have a baby, and I've been sitting here, and I have to tell you this is all I really wanted in my life." Judy's eyes filled, and she gestured around the room. "What you have here. What's in your living room. And not that I'm jealous of you, I would never be, and you know that, but I want these things, this is all I really want, this happiness, this quiet, this *peace.* A family of my own. And I almost had it, this time."

Mary's heart went out to Judy all over again, understanding the depth of what her best friend had lost. Not only John, but the possibility of what could be, their future.

"I've had great boyfriends in the past, like Frank, he was great, but he wasn't the right one. I didn't have it with him, but I had it with John. I know I did, and I would've loved to have been married to him. I could see it happening. We would've been so happy together, we were really happy." Judy sniffled. "We really were, and now he's gone. Really gone, for good."

"Oh boy." Mary put her arm around Judy, and Judy rested her head on Mary's shoulder, wiping her eyes with the soggy Kleenex.

"It just really sucks."

"I know." Mary hugged her closer, and Judy shifted in the seat, straightening up.

"Oops, I almost forgot. I have something for you." Judy bent over on the far side of the chair, reached down for something on the floor, and straightened up with a gift in her hand, wrapped in wrapping paper covered with daisies. "Open your present."

"My present?" Mary had almost forgotten. "From the baby shower?"

"Yes." Judy rallied, with a crooked grin.

"You are so nice. You want to do this now?"

"Are you too tired?"

"No, but it's a sad time."

"All the more reason." Judy smiled bravely. "That's The Way of the Tao."

"Are you serious?"

"Yes. The Tao is full of paradoxes. The

Sage would tell you that there is no better time to open a gift than in a time of sadness."

"In other words, cheer up?"

Judy smiled. "Exactly. Maybe it's not so paradoxical?"

"Whatever, just don't join the cult."

"It's not a cult, it's a world religion."

"I know, I'm just kidding. Meanwhile, were you really going to become a Buddhist nun?"

"I thought about it."

"You never told me."

"Because you think it's a cult." Judy smiled.

"And they have nuns?"

"Yes, and priests too. But no guilt."

"Too bad." Mary smiled back, unwrapping her gift, quietly, so as not to wake Anthony. Ordinarily, she would've shared it with him, but no matter how good the marriage, a girl still needed alone time with her best friend, especially on a night as sad as this one.

"I hope you like it. I'm having present anxiety."

"Don't be silly." Mary took the wrapping off and set it aside, revealing a flat rectangular white box. She shook it, prolonging the moment. "What's in here?"

"Edible undies."

"Don't be disgusting."

"Why stop now?" Judy grinned, with a final sniffle, and Mary took the lid off the box, then moved aside some hot pink tissue paper to find one of the most beautiful baby blankets she had ever seen. The design of the fabric was absolutely miraculous, a weave of fuzzy threads in a warm pink alternating with cornflower-blue threads, which together formed a sweetly fluffy cloud of babyness.

"Oh my God, did you *make* this, on your loom?" Mary took the blanket out of the box, marveling at how soft and light it felt in her fingers.

"Yes, it's my first big project. I mixed the two colors since we don't know whether you're having a boy or girl."

"That's a great idea!"

"Do you like it?"

"I love it! Thank you so much. How long did it take to make?"

"Forever. Do you feel guilty yet?"

"Yes." Mary felt a wave of happiness wash over her, followed by a wave of sadness, as if she were in an emotional wave pool at a nightmare amusement park. "This is really lovely of you to do, and I really appreciate it. I'm so sorry about John."

"I know honey. I'm sorry too." Judy sighed heavily, and Mary felt a final wave, this time of exhaustion. Maybe it was the release, nestled into the safety and security of her home, her best friend, her husband, and a golden retriever with worse gas than her own.

"Boy, am I tired." Mary pulled up the blanket to her chin. "I could fall asleep right here."

"Why don't you, honey?"

"I can't, I shouldn't." Mary closed her eyes, and weariness numbed her to the bone. She had never known exhaustion like the kind that came with pregnancy, which could make her almost crazy with tiredness at times, but she had so much to do before bed. She had to empty the dishwasher, make sure Judy had fresh sheets, and put towels in the guest bathroom and find a tube of toothpaste that wasn't folded in an accordion . . .

But in the next minute, she had fallen asleep.

Chapter Eighteen

Sunday morning dawned clear and sunny, and Mary sat at the conference table, trying not to think about the fact that John wasn't alive to see this lovely day, but was instead lying on a stainless-steel table in the morgue, maybe being autopsied right now. Judy sat to her right, sad and solemn, her shoulders sloping downward in her cheery yellow T-shirt. She had tried to call William, but there had been no answer. Anne was placing a greaseboard on a large easel, so she could bring them up to speed on *London Technologies.* In truth, none of them felt like coming into the office this morning, but they'd had no choice because there was a deposition tomorrow. Bennie had come in, too, and she was in her office with Roger, working on their reverse-discrimination case.

Mary felt worried that Judy was in legal jeopardy, because sooner or later, Detectives Krakoff and Marks would find out that she had been at John's apartment the day he was murdered. They had discussed it with Bennie and had sent Lou out canvassing today on John's street, to see if anybody had seen or heard anything.

Mary shifted away from a beam of sunlight streaming through the window, which hurt her itchy eyes. They were just about to get started, now that she had updated Anne on the few details of John's murder, and Judy had revealed to Anne that she'd been dating John. Anne had been as surprised as anyone else, but they talked it over and tried to start work.

"Okay, let's begin." Anne stood in front of the easel in a trim white sleeveless dress with her thick red hair in a bouncy ponytail, like the prettiest kindergarten teacher ever. "Mary, just so you know, I did try to get the deposition tomorrow postponed given the circumstances, but I couldn't. The other side refused. I could ask the judge for a postponement and I think he would grant it, but I don't want to ask him. I pick my battles."

"I get it."

"Besides, I don't want to back up the deposition schedule, which is heavy, and I printed it out so you could put it in your calendars." Anne handed them both a deposition schedule. "Of course, we've already taken depositions of some of the middle-management types, building the case from the bottom up, so when we depose the big guns, we'll have the facts at our disposal. So the best is yet to come."

"Or the hardest."

"That too." Anne smiled, still perky. "I emailed you both a copy of the Complaint and their Answer. You probably didn't get a chance to read them."

"We tried," Mary answered, speaking for them both.

"I understand, no worries. It's a massive Complaint, 134 pages, and their Answer is almost as long." Anne plucked two thick packets off a stack of paper and gave one to Mary and the other to Judy. "I had copies made in case you want to follow along. I'll take you through the basics and then Mary, I'll tell you about the witness whose deposition you'll be defending tomorrow."

"Great, thanks." Mary flipped through her copy of the Complaint, trying to remember what she had read, but so much had changed since then. Judy didn't open her copy, but Mary knew that she didn't have to, because she was smart enough to follow along. Even at half speed, Judy was smarter than anybody Mary had ever met.

"First, let me say, the good news is this case is a sure winner. We have the facts, we have the law, and as you'll see, we have hard evidence of bad intent by the defendants. Our goal is a great settlement. We'd win at trial but that costs too much for these guys. That's why the Complaint is so detailed. We put it all out there, setting up a great settlement."

"And the bad news?"

"The bad news is it's going to be super-hard to run this case without John. But we have to try. We can do it if we pull together. Maybe." Anne cleared her throat. "Now, London Technologies is our client, and we filed suit on its behalf in the Eastern District of Pennsylvania against two defendants, Express Management Systems, or EXMS, and Home Hacks, Inc. We alleged that they violated Section 1 of the Sherman Act, which as you know is the antimonopoly provision of the federal antitrust law. We also allege violations of Pennsylvania law, which we'll get into later. I'll explain more about the parties later, but suffice it to say that this is a battle between David and Goliath, with us as David — and this time, there are two Goliaths."

"We love the underdog, don't we?" Mary

smiled, trying to be supportive to Anne, who was rallying to explain a complicated lawsuit at the worst moment in their collective professional lives.

"The parties in this lawsuit are competitors in the data integration business. Specifically, they develop, manufacture, and sell software that integrates data for furniture dealerships all around the country. Now, you ask, what is data integration software?" Anne cocked her head, and her ponytail bounced. "Hold on, I'll tell you."

Mary sipped her coffee, pretending it was caffeinated. She'd spent most of her pregnancy pretending water was wine. Neither of these things was working, and only Jesus Christ could turn water into alcohol.

"Data is simply business information and data integration software allows a furniture dealership to use and analyze that information. They use data integration software for every aspect of their business, including personnel, payroll, accounting, inventory" — Anne counted off on her manicured fingernails — "pending and completed sales, financing, service, and importantly, customer information, such as secured identification and financial information, likes and dislikes, and purchase history."

Mary tried to stay focused because she

was the one defending the deposition to-morrow. She didn't have to know every detail, but she had to know more than she knew now, which was nothing. Basically, she had to be able to hum a few bars.

Judy barely listened, but nobody blamed her.

"Let me explain briefly about the data integration market, which is the defined market for this lawsuit." Anne uncapped her marker, turned to the greaseboard, and drew a big circle on the left, in which she wrote, DATA INTEGRATORS. "Okay, so here you see this circle is data integrators."

"I got that part," Mary chirped, trying to make Judy laugh, but it didn't work.

"In this lawsuit, EXMS is the data integra-tor. That means they store and manage the information given to them in a database." Anne drew a circle on the right and wrote APPLICATION PROVIDERS inside it, then drew an arrow from the Data Integra-tors circle to the Application Providers circle. "You may be wondering, what is an application provider? In our litigation, the other defendant, Home Hacks, is an ap-plication provider. Think of them like an app for your phone. They're the friendly interface that connects to the dealerships. EXMS provides standardized data to Home

Hacks. Follow me?"

"It this gonna be on the test?" Mary asked, and this time Judy smiled, so she felt rewarded.

"Very funny." Anne was already drawing a third circle at the bottom of the grease-board, so that the three circles formed a triangle balancing on its end. "This circle is the dealership. What connects the Application Providers to the dealerships? They perform services for the dealerships, and as I said, they're like their app."

Mary listened, with an eye on Judy.

"Now, for the final and most important part of the market." Anne drew an arrow from DEALERSHIP to DATA INTEGRA-TORS, completing the third leg of the upside-down triangle. "What does the furniture dealership give to the data integrator, which is the crux of this litigation? It gives them the all-important, extremely valuable, raw business data. In other words, the dealership gives its raw business data to the data integrator and the data integrator puts it into its database, using its proprietary software."

Mary pulled over a legal pad so she could take notes, trying not to be intimidated by the buzzwords. Anybody who thought Anne was dumb because she was pretty was dead wrong.

"Express Management Services, or EXMS, is a publicly traded Pennsylvania company with headquarters in Delaware, which employs three hundred people and owns a dominant market share, and it has done so for the past ten years, which is the relevant time period."

Mary made a note, noticing that Judy had begun reading the Complaint, her head down.

"Home Hacks, Inc., is a Pennsylvania company with headquarters in King of Prussia. They're privately held and owned by a consortium of businesses from Pennsylvania and New York. They employ two hundred seventy-five people and also own a dominant market share."

Mary made a note.

"We're the plaintiff, London Technologies, and we're teeny-tiny as compared to the defendants. Jim Hummel and Sanjay Amravati are the owners and got the idea for the company on a trip to London, so they named it London Technologies. They're also a Pennsylvania company and their headquarters used to be Jim's garage in Narberth, if you can believe that." Anne smiled with corporate pride. "But now they have an office in the city, employing twenty-five people. London Technologies owns only about 7 percent of the market share, but as we know, in theory, the law is the great equalizer. So we're going against the big boys, and when you find out what they did wrong, you'll be as stoked as I am about this case."

Mary noticed that Judy was still reading the Complaint, not even looking up at Anne, who continued speaking.

"Let me tell you how big Goliath is. They control approximately 91 percent of the data integration software market in the chain furniture stores, if you measure using what is known as 'rooftops,' that is, dealerships. And when you measure it by the dollar value of merchandise sold per year, the market dominance is even more pronounced, with a combined market share exceeding 94 percent."

Mary tried to take notes, and Judy kept reading the Complaint.

"Also the defendants own almost identical market shares in their separate markets, because they planned it that way and they executed their plan. They have colluded to drive out competition, even though it's a *per se* violation of the monopoly laws."

"How did they get away with that?" Mary

asked, surprised. Judy kept reading, seeming not to hear.

"They both had about 25 percent market share in their markets and it was very competitive, with roughly nine data integration software manufacturers and ten application providers slugging it out in the chain furniture market, nationwide. EXMS and Home Hacks gave consideration to merging, but when that didn't happen, they formed a written agreement called the Access Memo. They actually agreed that they would no longer compete against each other, but would combine forces, driving out all competition. They even made statements to various people at trade associations. They don't realize it's illegal or if they do, they don't care."

"I understand," Mary said, trying not to be distracted by Judy, who was studying the Complaint as if she were memorizing it, which seemed odd. Anne glanced over at Judy, but didn't say anything.

"To make a long story short, since that agreement, the collusion between the defendants has resulted in their dominating the market." Anne folded her skinny arms. "Then along came London Technologies with a completely different business model. The defendants decided to try and drive

216

them out of business. I'll detail how later, but suffice it to say, that's when they came to us."

Mary nodded at Anne. Oblivious, Judy turned the page of the Complaint.

"By the way, you're probably wondering about the procedural history of the litigation. We made a settlement demand early on, but they countered too low. After I took the first deposition, they came back with a slightly higher amount but it was still ridiculous. Since then there have been no other settlement negotiations, and we're going full speed ahead, hoping for settlement because litigation is so big and expensive."

"Of course." Mary glanced over at Judy. "That doesn't surprise you, does it, Judy?"

"Excuse me?" Judy looked up from the Complaint, completely preoccupied.

"Nothing."

Judy returned to reading, and Anne cleared her throat again, continuing her lecture.

"Jim and Sanjay had a hell of a time trying to find anybody else to represent them at all. The consortia that own the defendants are a variety of different businesses, most of which are located in the Delaware Valley area, and that means that other firms represent their related companies or their subsidiaries, which conflicts out most big law firms from representing London Technologies." Anne made a sad-emoji face at Mary. "What this means is that we were the last resort for London Technologies. They're counting on us. If we let them down, they go under. If we lose, they go under. No pressure, right?"

"Not at all." Mary managed a smile. Judy turned the page, but was no longer reading the Complaint, only turning the pages.

"But let me explain to you what Jim and Sanjay innovated as a business, which threatens the defendants." Anne pointed to the greaseboard triangle. "What Jim and Sanjay figured out is that when you look at this market, the furniture dealership does not need both a data integrator and an application provider. Jim and Sanjay realized that the dealership could provide the information *directly* to the data integrator, bypassing the application provider and thereby eliminate the onerous fees that the application provider was charging. So they wrote software that did that and licensed it to dealerships to enable them to deal with a data integrator directly, thus cutting out the middleman, Home Hacks."

Mary nodded, understanding. Judy was still turning the pages, as if she were trying to get to the end.

"Then some friends of Jim and Sanjay started talking about a startup that would compete with EXMS, using the same no-middleman, buy-direct no-frills business model. It would be cheaper for the dealerships, who could pass the savings on to consumers. And that's the point of the antitrust law, to open new markets, foster innovation, and increase competition, which ultimately benefits the consumer."

"Right."

"But as soon as they did this, both defendants were alarmed because it threatened their business model, even if it resulted in cheaper prices to the dealerships. It cut into their ability to charge excessive fees and control the market." Anne frowned. "So the defendants, via EXMS, refused to accept data from the dealerships that was not integrated by Home Hacks. At the same time, they demanded their dealerships sign exclusive dealing contracts, promising that they would deal only with Home Hacks. And they just refused to deal with dealerships that were attempting to buy or use software from London Technologies. As you know, that's unlawful *per se.*"

"As it should be," Mary said, meaning it. Judy was still reading.

"Worse, when the dealerships got angry

with EXMS over this and demanded their data back, EXMS refused to give it back, claiming that EXMS owned the dealerships' raw data, which was improper. Essentially, they held the data hostage. We alleged in the Complaint that these exclusive dealing arrangements and business practices were patently anticompetitive. We have three different counts under Section I of the Sherman Act, and here's where we get to the nitty-gritty. Ready for the hard part?"

"Yes." Mary looked over at Judy, who had reached the last page of the Complaint, which showed the signatures of the filing attorneys. Bennie's was at the top, Anne's second, and finally John's. Judy's gaze was riveted to John's signature, and her lips trembled as she fought for emotional control.

Anne fell silent, her lovely features softening in sympathy.

Mary asked gently, "Judy?"

Judy looked up after a moment, her eyes glistening. "Anne, John drafted this Complaint, didn't he?"

"Yes. I didn't change a word, and neither did Bennie. It couldn't be improved upon, so we didn't try."

"I could tell." Judy placed a hand on the Complaint, facedown. "I never knew an antitrust Complaint could be so elegant, but this one is. He had a beautiful legal mind. Truly."

Anne nodded sadly. "I agree."

"I know he got testy with you, and said some mean things, but he didn't mean them. That wasn't him. He was just upset."

"I know that." Anne's lower lip puckered. "And I'm sorry I said what I said, too."

Suddenly Bennie stuck her head in the doorway, urgent. "Ladies, we have action."

"What?" Mary asked, alarmed.

"The police want to see Judy."

CHAPTER NINETEEN

"What do we do now?" Mary asked, nervous, as Bennie, Roger, and Isaac the PR guy entered the conference room. Judy looked stricken, her palm still resting on top of John's signature. Anne sank into a chair in front of her *London Technologies* greaseboard, which receded into the background, literally and figuratively. There was nothing more important, or more terrifying, to everyone than the fact that Judy could be suspected of John's murder.

Bennie took the lead, standing at the head of the table. "Don't worry, Carrier. We got this, and we know what to do —"

Roger stepped partially in front of Bennie, physically upstaging her. "Judy. Let me tell you what I would advise, at this point —"

Bennie stepped forward. "I was going to let you —"

"*Let* me?" Roger smiled, but it wasn't friendly, and the time for joking had passed.

His expression was intent and his focus total. He straightened, looking even taller and slimmer in his lightweight charcoal sportcoat, which he had on over a gray-cashmere turtleneck and skinny jeans. "Here's where we are now. Judy, you have to go to the Roundhouse. There is no question about that."

"I know," Judy said nervously.

"You're not going in unrepresented. That would be foolish. So the question is, who will represent you?" Roger spoke calmly and conversationally, which Mary would have expected from a Zen Master, but his demeanor soothed her and she listened carefully while he continued.

"I have a recommendation for your representation today, Judy. Please keep an open mind. What I'm going to suggest is unorthodox. Ultimately, this will be your choice. You are not a suspect in John's murder, but you are a potential suspect. As such, you have the right to choose your attorney."

"Okay." Judy nodded, and Mary put her hand over Judy's.

Roger paused thoughtfully. "The conventional choice would be to hire the biggest, baddest, defense counsel in the city, with the most experience in murder cases."

Bennie interjected, "That was my first

thought, I admit. Go in, guns blazing, and back them down."

Roger ignored her. "But I have persuaded Bennie that that would send the wrong message to the police and to the press. It raises the stakes, ups the ante, and a variety of other clichés I'll allow you to supply. It also suggests that we're taking this investigation too seriously. Which in turn implies that Judy may be guilty, which is absurd."

"Of course it is," Bennie interjected again.

"Judy, your second choice would be to have Bennie represent you. She has the requisite experience in murder cases. In my view, she's not disqualified as a fact witness for these purposes. She had no idea that you were at John's yesterday afternoon, nor did she know that you had an intimate relationship with him. She may have knowledge as a witness of prior conversations between you and John about the discrimination lawsuit, which took place in her presence, but they're not determinative." Roger held up an index finger. "However, I counsel against choosing Bennie. It raises the same problem as outside defense counsel. She's too high-profile. She's the big gun. This is merely an investigatory interview. That's how we want to keep it. We need to downplay, not amplify. Do you follow me, Judy?"

"You want to minimize the drama."

"Exactly." Roger smiled, pleased. "That leaves my recommendation, which is that Mary represent you."

"Mary?" Judy asked, surprised.

"Me?" Mary added, equally surprised.

Roger raised his index finger again. "Mary is the perfect choice. She has significant experience with murder cases, so she knows what she's doing —"

"I do?" Mary blurted out. "I mean, I do, but this is Judy we're talking about. This is my *best friend.* You're putting *her* life in *my* hands."

"Who better?" Roger asked, again calmly. "Let me explain. Mary strikes the perfect note. She's not as high-profile as Bennie or outside counsel, which is consistent with downplaying the investigation. In fact, she's your friend, so she looks as if she's along for the ride, not necessarily as counsel."

"That's true," Judy said, cocking her head.

Mary could see why it made sense for her to represent Judy, but she didn't feel a hundred-percent confident about it. Then again, she never felt a hundred-percent confident about anything.

Isaac interjected, "If I might add that, with Mary, the optics are excellent."

"Isaac, are you nuts?" Mary almost started

laughing. "Have you *seen* my *optics* lately? I'm retaining more water than a swimming pool. I'm a fishbowl with feet."

Isaac smiled. "That's what I like about your optics. You're pregnant, *very* pregnant. Imagine the photos of the two of you, you and Judy, side by side, entering the Roundhouse" — Isaac put his hands up in a U-shape, like a Hollywood director — "two women, one very pregnant, alone against the world? It makes a vulnerable image, online and on TV. People *like* pregnant women. They want to protect them, not prosecute them."

"So we're pimping out my pregnancy?"

"I heard you did it at the police station last night and it worked."

"True," Mary had to admit.

"You need to look like victims, not victimizers."

Bennie cringed. "Isaac, we're strong women. We're not victims."

Isaac frowned. "You're crime victims, Bennie. No matter how strong you are, you're victims of crime, and you have to play that to the hilt."

Mary ignored Isaac and looked over at Judy, rallying. "Okay, let's do it. I'd love to represent you, if you want me to."

"Aw." Judy smiled, obviously touched.

"I'd love you to. I know you can do it and I feel better with you being there."

"Done!" Mary hugged Judy over her photogenic belly. "So folks, I know the defense-lawyer drill. Go there, say nothing, right? Don't give them any information at all?"

"Correct," Roger and Bennie answered in unison.

Bennie added, "I called Lou but he's still canvassing the neighbors, so there's no new news. A lot of the neighbors aren't home because it's such a nice day. Maybe we'll get lucky later. DiNunzio, you can anticipate what the detectives already know, can't you?"

"Yes, like we talked about." Mary found her emotional footing. "They probably have surveillance film from some camera somewhere, showing Judy on John's street, coming and going. So let's assume they can place her there around the time of death." Mary was thinking aloud. "And maybe somebody heard them fight."

"Exactly." Bennie nodded, satisfied. "I don't think they'll know anything that will surprise you, so stick to the script. Act cooperative even though you're not cooperating. DiNunzio, let her state her innocence and don't let her answer a single question.

Or confirm or deny anything."

Isaac interjected, "Don't speak to the press, except to say that we'll have a comment later. Don't frown or appear angry. That won't play well."

Roger nodded, pressing his hands together at his chest. "And remain calm."

"Calm, me?" Mary rolled her eyes. "I'm Italian-American, have you heard?"

"That's merely a label, Mary. Don't label yourself. Say to yourself, 'Be here now.' Do you understand?"

"No." Mary smiled, jerking his chain. "Where am I now? Am I here or there? Or is it neither here nor there?"

Roger ignored her, closing his eyes lightly. "Visualize this with me. Sit in the interview with Judy. Try to breathe deeply. Find a space of conscious mindfulness. Say to yourself, 'Go inside to serve outside.' "

"Whatever, let's go!" Bennie clapped her hands loudly, startling Roger. "Once more, into the breach!"

CHAPTER TWENTY

Mary and Judy sat in the interview room opposite Detectives Krakoff and Marks, and Detective Marks had taken notes while Detective Krakoff had conducted the questioning. Mary thought it had gone well, since Judy had refused to answer any questions, remaining composed even when they'd Mirandized her "out of an abundance of caution." Mary wasn't fooled. This was custodial interrogation, and they were narrowing their suspicions on her best friend, which meant that Mary morphed into a bulldog. A *pregnant* bulldog, at that.

"So Ms. Carrier." Detective Krakoff crossed his legs in his dark suit, dressed oddly formally. "Are you refusing to cooperate with us?"

Mary interjected, for Judy, "Not at all, Detective Krakoff. Don't try and bully her. She's already made her statement."

"So Ms. DiNunzio, you're here in an official capacity, as her lawyer?"

"Yes, in case she needs one."

"And from now on, should we desire to communicate with her, we should do so through you?"

"I can't imagine why you would want to, given what she's already told you, but yes."

Judy's mouth set firmly. "Detective, as I said, I don't know anything about John's murder. I have no idea who killed him. I have no facts whatsoever that would further your investigation."

Mary interjected again, "If we knew anything helpful to the police, we would tell you immediately. All of us are devastated over John's murder, and we want you to find his killer and bring him to justice. That's exactly why I came here last night with our law firm's founding partner, Bennie Rosato."

Detective Krakoff returned his attention to Judy. "Ms. Carrier, did you have a romantic relationship to the victim?"

Mary interjected, "She's not going to answer that. You and I both know that no putative defendant would, in the circumstances."

"What circumstances? We haven't charged her. She's not a suspect. She's not even a person of interest."

"You *Mirandized* her," Mary shot back. "Detective Krakoff, why don't you tell us the information you have so far, so we understand why you called us down here? After all, last night, you refused to give me or Bennie any information or answer any of our questions."

Detective Krakoff smiled slightly. "By the way, how are you feeling, Ms. DiNunzio? I would hate for you to have another contraction that would cut short the interview."

"I feel much better, thanks." Mary arranged her face into an expressionless mask, though it wasn't easy since she had labeled herself Italian-American, before she'd found out that labels were bad.

"Glad to hear that." Detective Krakoff faced Judy again, his mouth a firm line. "Ms. Carrier, I'll lay my cards on the table. Our investigation is in the preliminary stages, but we have already developed facts supporting a theory that you committed this murder. We believe it is in your interest to consider making a deal and we are prepared to offer —"

Mary interrupted, "Detective Krakoff, none of this makes any sense. I was told that John was killed in the course of a burglary."

"No, that's incorrect."

231

"But that was what Detective Azzic told me last night."

"He was mistaken."

"He heard it directly from you."

"He did." Detective Krakoff didn't blink. "But I didn't confirm or deny to you last night, if you recall. Before your contractions, that is."

Mary let it go. "Why did you tell him that, if it wasn't true?"

"We may have believed that initially, given the signs of struggle and the disappearance of the victim's electronics. But there was no sign of forced entry, so that didn't square."

"I see." Mary found herself wondering instead if Detective Krakoff had misled Detective Azzic, playing close to the vest with his investigation, which seemed likelier. If so, Detective Krakoff was no pushover.

"As I was saying, I don't have the authority to offer your client a deal, but we can informally explore —"

Mary interrupted again, "And as I was saying, I'd like to hear the facts that you found. That was the question I asked you, and I reiterate that my client is completely innocent of John's murder. Otherwise we'll just end the interview." Mary fake-reached for her purse. "We were at work today and we have a major case to prepare for."

"Fine." Detective Krakoff pursed his thin lips. "The medical examiner has performed his autopsy and placed the time of death as between nine o'clock and eleven o'clock last night. We know, Ms. Carrier, that you were the victim's girlfriend and that you were at his apartment at that time last night, engaged in a quarrel."

Mary controlled her expression, though she felt fear bolt through her. "What evidence do you have for that?"

"The next-door neighbor heard arguing in the apartment for much of Friday night and into Saturday, up to and including the relevant time period. She was able to identify Ms. Carrier's voice as the one she heard, and she identified her as the victim's girlfriend."

Mary felt her heart sink, but didn't let it show.

"Emergency dispatch received a call from another neighbor at nine fifteen concerning arguing in the apartment. She lives across the back and she saw Ms. Carrier and the victim arguing in the apartment, though it was too far to hear them. She worried because she has a personal history of domestic abuse by an ex-boyfriend. She said she felt 'triggered' " — Detective Krakoff made air quotes — "and suspected it may have been a domestic dispute. She identified the woman in the apartment as Ms. Carrier. In addition, there was a dog barking constantly in the victim's backyard on Friday night, which annoyed her. She works at home, a website designer."

Mary took mental notes, since he was filling in the gaps in her information. So the detectives had an eyewitness and an earwitness, which was substantial evidence.

"Although emergency dispatch got the call at nine fifteen, an officer was not dispatched to the scene until later. As you may have heard, there was a double homicide in the Northeast last night, which drew uniformed resources. So it wasn't until 11:16 P.M. that a patrol officer went to the domicile and discovered the victim, who was deceased."

Mary kept her game face on, and so did Judy.

"The facts lead us to believe that the victim was killed by someone he knew, someone he felt free admitting to his apartment, or even had her own key, like a girlfriend." Detective Krakoff glanced at Judy. "The medical examiner confirmed that the victim was killed by blunt force trauma to the back of the head. There was a heavy Luxor lamp on his desk, and the killer used its base. We believe it was opportunistic. Somebody lost her temper, like a girl-friend in a fit of anger." Detective Krakoff eyed Judy hard. "That's why we brought you in for the interview."

Mary bore down, setting her emotions aside. "Detective, my client had nothing to do with any of that, even assuming that scenario, which I might add, involves a great amount of speculation."

"Ms. DiNunzio, these are facts, not speculation. We find the facts and we follow where they lead, and in this case, they lead to your client." Detective Krakoff spread his palms. "As I mentioned to you, we have seen the videotape of the press conference. We know about the reverse-discrimination lawsuit that was filed against your firm. It quotes the victim stating a position contrary to the interests of the firm's partners, of which Ms. Carrier is one. We believe that the fight that night concerned the victim's statements in the Complaint and at the press conference. I think we can prove that, if we have to."

Mary said nothing but told herself to stay the course, since she had answers to the questions. It wasn't a great picture for the defense, but it was hardly airtight on the part of any prosecution.

"I know you haven't spoken with the assistant district attorney yet, and I'm talking out of school, but I bet that he'd make Ms. Carrier a reasonable deal. She could plead out and get fifteen years."

Mary masked her fear. It terrified her to think of Judy spending even a moment in prison. She felt herself break a sweat, not daring to look over at Judy. "My client has nothing to confess. She's completely innocent, as she told you."

"What about the videotape of her on the victim's street?"

"The fact that you think you captured her on film doesn't prove that it was her. Plus Old City is a busy neighborhood, especially on a Saturday night. There's tourists, restaurants, bars, and clubs. It could've been anybody on the videotape, including a burglar whom John may have admitted, mistakenly." Mary kept going, wanting to make him doubt his own conclusion, so they didn't bring any charges against Judy. "Are there traffic cameras on both ends of the street? I don't recall that there's an intersection at the other end."

"We're checking into the other video cameras."

"Then you jumped the gun, obviously. If you don't have a camera at that end of the street, that leaves open the possibility that the killer could've come in by the other end of the street. There's a myriad of other possibilities."

"Like what?" Detective Krakoff's eyes narrowed.

"There are other ways to access John's apartment, Detective. In fact, I've been there myself, and I happen to know there's a fire escape right outside the living-room window, in the back of the house." Mary sensed she touched a nerve when Detective Krakoff's brow furrowed just the slightest bit, a micro expression that gave him away. "John's apartment is only on the second floor, and the house backs onto a narrow backstreet where residents park their cars. If I'm not mistaken, John parks there himself. Anybody could've entered through the back and not used the front door at all."

"And what about the dog?"

"I don't recall the last time a dog convicted anybody." Mary reached for her purse. "That's all, we'll go. You don't have enough to charge her because she didn't do anything wrong. Judy Carrier is a partner in our law firm, which is one of the best in the city. She's a skilled appellate lawyer and one of the most prominent members of the Philadelphia Bar Association. You can't seriously think she would murder someone, much less an associate at our firm."

"Come on, Ms. Carrier is hardly the conventional lawyer." Detective Krakoff's eyes strayed to Judy's pink hair.

"How dare you," Judy said, taken aback.

Mary felt anger flicker in her chest. "If you think that her *hairstyle* is going to convince any jury she's a *murderer,* you're out of your mind. You should be trying to find the real killer, not coming after my partner based on some tenuous connection with a reverse-discrimination lawsuit. We don't *kill* people who sue us, Detective Krakoff. We beat them in court."

"Hold on one minute." Detective Krakoff reached his hand into his jacket pocket and extracted a pair of purple latex gloves, which he proceeded to put on, with some difficulty.

Mary didn't know where this was going. "What are you doing, Detective? Am I dilating?"

Detective Marks burst into surprised laughter, then silenced quickly.

"Bear with me a moment." Detective Krakoff reached into his jacket pocket and pulled out a brown-paper evidence bag. "Ms. Carrier, before you leave, I'd like to show you an important piece of evidence. We found it in the victim's apartment. We'd like to know if it belongs to you."

"Fine." Mary glanced at Judy, who seemed intrigued, so they stayed put. If Detective Krakoff had evidence against Judy, they needed to know it now rather than later.

"Give me another moment, please." Detective Krakoff dug into the bag with one hand, making much of the process, as if he were intentionally keeping them in suspense.

Mary snorted. "Detective, we don't have time for whatever game this is."

"Here we go." Detective Krakoff produced a small black-velvet box from the evidence bag, and in one fluid motion, he held it in front of Judy and opened the lid, as if he were presenting it to her. It was a ring box, and inside was a sparkling diamond engagement ring.

Judy gasped, her hand flying to her mouth. "Oh my God!"

"How dare you pull such a stunt?" Mary jumped to her feet. She grabbed Judy's arm and hoisted her out of the chair, snagging her purse on the fly.

Judy burst into tears, losing control. "Oh my God, Detective, where did you get that ring?" she blurted out, heartbroken. "Where did you find that? Was that in his apartment?"

"Is this your engagement ring, Ms. Carrier?" Detective Krakoff stood up with a triumphant smile, holding the beautiful ring box in his outstretched hand. "I have the receipt for it, if you want to see that, too. He bought it three weeks ago."

"That's it!" Mary flung the door open and pulled Judy outside.

"He was going to propose to you, wasn't he?" Detective Krakoff called after them, following them out of the interview room. "You were his girlfriend, weren't you? I take it that's a 'yes'?"

Mary hurried a sobbing Judy out of the squad room and down the hallway, hustling for the elevator.

But even she knew it was too late.

CHAPTER TWENTY-ONE

Mary hustled Judy past the crowd of reporters, which had increased since earlier this morning. She assumed that they were at the Roundhouse for the double homicide in the Northeast, John's murder, and any other sordid news crumbs they could get, but Judy's outburst drew them like flies.

"Yo, what's going on?" "Any comment?" The reporters shouted questions and raised video cameras and cell phones, recording audio and video. "Is that Judith Carrier?" "Ms. Carrier, what's the problem, any comment?" "Is this about the Foxman murder?"

"No comment!" Mary shouted over her shoulder, putting her arm around Judy, who was trying to regain control, wiping her eyes. They hustled together through the parking lot to the street, and Mary looked for a cab with reporters chasing them.

"Mary, why is Judy Carrier here?" "Where is Bennie Rosato?" "What's going on with the Foxman murder?" "Do they have any suspects?"

"I told you we'd make a statement later!" Mary shouted back, spotting a cab coming toward them, so she flagged him down frantically.

"Come on, Mary!" "What's going on?" "This has to be about the Foxman murder?" "Do they have any leads?" "You're not suspects, are you?"

Mary stiffened. She couldn't leave that question unanswered. She had to think on her feet. She turned to the reporters. "Hold on, I have a comment."

"They must have a lead, don't they?" "What's going on?" "What's your comment?"

Mary waved them into silence. "Folks, we don't know any more than you do. We met with the detectives and we hope they will find whoever killed our friend and associate, John Foxman. You can see for yourself the toll this is taking on us. We pray that the police will bring the killer to justice."

"Ms. Carrier, any comment?" "Any comment?" "Any leads, Ms. Carrier?"

"She has no comment," Mary answered for Judy, just as the cab arrived and parked at the curb. She flung open the door, stowed Judy inside, and jumped in, closing the door. "Driver, head toward Center City, thanks."

"Got it, lady," the driver called over his shoulder, hitting the gas, and the cab lurched into traffic heading toward the expressway.

Mary turned to Judy, who was still distraught, her eyes bloodshot and her skin mottled with emotion. "Honey, I'm so sorry. I didn't see that coming."

"You couldn't have." Judy sniffled, wiping her cheeks, leaving pinkish streaks. "I can't believe he bought a *ring.* He was going to *propose,* Mary. I was this close, *this close* to everything I ever wanted . . ." Judy started to cry again, and Mary gave her a hug, rubbing her back.

"I know, honey, and I'm so sorry."

"He was going to propose . . . all that time we were fighting." Judy sobbed. "He was going to . . . propose."

"We'll get through this somehow." Mary kept rubbing her back, sensing that the revelation of the engagement ring had struck Judy like a blow, a double whammy after the shock of John's death.

Judy's phone started ringing in her pocket, and she let go of Mary, her eyes brimming with tears. "That's probably Bennie." Judy took her phone out of her pocket. "Oh, it's

William's group home. I better get it." She took the call, sniffling quickly. "Hello, this is Judy Carrier . . . Of course, yes, hi, Mike . . . Oh, my . . . Hold on, let me put you on speaker so my friend can hear." Judy pressed the button. "Mike, yes, so can you explain what's happening?"

"Sure, Judy. This is Mike Shanahan, the supervisor at Glenn Meade. You remember, we've met a few times, when you and John came to see William."

"Of course, Mike." Judy gave a final sniffle.

"You have my deepest condolences over the loss of John. He was so young, and this is a terrible tragedy."

"Thank you. I've been trying to call William but there hasn't been any answer. Are the Hodges there? You know, William and John's aunt and uncle? Susan and Mel Hodge?"

"No, that's what I'm calling about. We have a problem. You see, when John was murdered, the police notified the Hodges. They called me and told me the bad news and said they wanted to tell William themselves. They were going to fly out this weekend and were due to arrive today. Unfortunately, Susan Hodge fell on the escalator at Minneapolis airport and may have broken her ankle. Mel is with her. They're at a hospital in Minneapolis now."

"Oh no." Judy frowned.

"So they won't be able to fly in to see William today. Since you know him pretty well, maybe you should be the one to tell him that John passed. I can do it, but it might be better coming from you."

"So he doesn't know . . . anything?" Judy grimaced, wiping her eyes.

"No, and he's expecting John and you today for your Sunday visit. You know, you guys usually come in the afternoon."

"Right, of course." Judy sighed heavily. "I think he should hear it from me, too."

"That's why I called you. William had your number. John had given it to him."

"Okay." Judy bucked up. "I'll tell him today."

"Thanks." Mike sounded relieved, even to Mary. "What time will you be here?"

"Around three."

"Okay. See you then. Good-bye."

"Good-bye." Judy hung up, her watery gaze connecting with Mary. "You heard it. I have to go out there. It's in Devon."

"I'm so sorry you have to deal with this."

"It's okay. John would want William to hear it from me. He never liked Shanahan, and it's the right thing to do." Judy straightened up, and Mary could see a change in her demeanor, like a renewed sense of purpose.

"I'll go with you."

"No, don't even think about it." Judy got a Kleenex out of her pocket and blew her nose. "You have work to do. Go back to the office and immerse yourself in *London Technologies.*"

"No, thanks." Mary found a smile. "I've had enough data integration for one day. I'm going with you."

"But you have a deposition to defend tomorrow."

"I'll be fine. I know enough to hum a few bars."

"Plus you're pregnant."

"I am? Who knew?"

"Do you feel up to it?"

"Sure, if I eat so I can throw up." Mary leaned forward and said to the cabbie, "Driver, change of plans. We're heading to Devon."

"You got it," the driver said, switching to the left lane, toward the expressway ramp to the western suburbs.

Judy wiped her eyes, regaining her composure. "John was all William had. I don't even know what will happen to him now."

"Will the aunt and uncle become his

guardian?"

"I don't know. That's the kind of thing you provide for in a will." Judy frowned, rubbing her forehead. "I don't know where my brain is. I remembered John told me there's a trust that provides for William. So I'm sure John had a will. That would be like him."

Mary thought a minute. "What about a funeral? I'm getting the impression that the aunt and uncle are out of the picture, aren't you? Somebody has to plan a funeral."

"Oh man, I guess I do." Judy inhaled deeply, straightening in the backseat of the cab.

"I can help you do that too, honey." Mary felt a wrench in her chest that she sensed would never go away. She remembered planning her first husband's funeral. Her parents had offered to help, but in the end, she had done it alone, as her final act of love. Suddenly Mary's phone started ringing, interrupting her reverie. "This must be Bennie." She checked the screen and answered the call. "Hey, Bennie."

"DiNunzio, we just saw you on TV. Judy looks so upset. Did something happen?"

"Yes, I can explain later. We're heading out to the suburbs to meet John's brother, William. Judy has to tell him the bad news about John."

"Oh, my. Did you learn anything from the police?"

"Yes." Mary gave her the rundown over the new details of John's murder, leaving out the part about the engagement ring. Judy didn't need to relive that moment, especially now that she had regained her equilibrium.

"Good job," Bennie said, after Mary had finished. "Hold on, Isaac wants to speak with you."

"Fine," Mary said, suppressing her annoyance. Judy turned her head away, looking out the window with a heavy sigh.

Isaac came on the line. "Mary, Judy?" he said, bubbling over. "You guys did terrific! You couldn't have done better!"

"I owe it all to my pregnancy," Mary said dryly.

"Your statement was short and sweet, and those tears from Judy, wow! They could *not* have been more *perfect.* You two were the very picture of —"

"Thanks, Isaac, bye now." Mary hung up, abruptly.

Judy turned from the window with a shaky smile. "Thanks."

"My pleasure," Mary said, smiling back.

Suddenly, Mary's phone started ringing

again, with the unusual ring of a FaceTime call, and she looked down to see Machiavelli was calling. She showed Judy the screen. "The hits just keep on coming, don't they?"

Judy's eyes widened. "You should take it."

"Why?"

"He's suing us. You never know."

"Okay." Mary took the call, and Machiavelli popped onto the screen, dressed in a gray suit with a white polo shirt. His hair was slicked back, and his narrow eyes glittered darkly. He was wearing his fake-earnest face, but Mary didn't know why.

"Mare, you looked damn good on TV. I think you're even sexier pregnant, you know that?"

"What do you want? I told you not to call."

"I went to early Mass. I didn't see you."

Mary suppressed an eye roll. They lived in the same parish, and the thought of him sitting in her church made her blood boil. "Why are you calling?"

"I wanted to pay my respects about John Foxman. My condolences. I lit a candle for him. So did my mom."

Listening, Judy shrugged, but Mary wasn't fooled. "Thank you," she said, coldly. "Now why did you really call?"

"Is Judy still with you? Tell her I'm sorry."

"I'm hanging up."

"I'm giving you another chance to settle, considering. This must be tough, after Foxman's murder. You got your hands full. Judy's crying at the Roundhouse. You're stressed out *and* you're havin' a baby. You don't need this hanging over your head."

"We're not settling. Didn't Roger tell you that?"

"Yes, but I'm talking to you now. Come on, I'm not gonna negotiate against myself. Gimme a number."

"No, now I have to go —"

"Mare, you're not thinking. My case against you just got stronger. You know that, don't you?"

"How? Why?" Mary grimaced, disgusted. Judy recoiled, off-screen.

"Mare, think. Foxman's statements, his *admissions,* are already on the record. They're going to come into evidence in my case against you guys. They're not hearsay anymore. And, now you won't have a chance to rehabilitate or cross-examine him."

"That's so sick! That's ghoulish!" Mary recoiled. She hadn't even begun to think about how John's murder affected their reverse-discrimination case.

"Whatever, be real, Mare. It makes my case more credible than ever, even sympathetic. The main witness against you ends up murdered? You know I'm gonna use that. I have an *obligation* to my clients to use that. I'm going to turn that frown upside down —"

"You are so revolting! Never ever call me again!" Mary hung up, and Judy looked appalled.

"He's *ruthless.*"

"That's what I've been trying to tell you." Mary shuddered. "Sorry I took the call. I should've known better."

"We can't settle, no way." Judy shook her head, newly determined. "I'll turn his frown right-side up. With my *fist.*"

"Attagirl," Mary said, forcing a smile.

Chapter Twenty-Two

Mary and Judy got dropped off at the entrance of Glenn Meade, and they walked along a paved asphalt path that led to William's house, which was on the southern edge of the campus. Oak trees lined the path, shedding dappled sunlight on the manicured lawns, and Mary marveled as they walked along. Glenn Meade wasn't a single group home like the one she had seen, but a large, clustered development of modern, redbrick apartment buildings, modified to accommodate some 125 residents and connected by paved asphalt paths. The campus was fifty-five acres and surrounded by woods that had been made handicap accessible with more paved asphalt paths.

"This place is incredible," Mary said as they walked along.

"I know, it's wonderful. John used to feel

really good that William was in such a nice place."

Mary spotted a sign that read **Duck Pond,** which blew her mind. "I've been to plenty of group homes, and this is the nicest. It must cost a fortune. Who pays, can I ask?"

"Yes, but it's a sad story." Judy frowned. "William has cerebral palsy, caused by a birth injury. The obstetrician who delivered him was drunk at the time. He was an alcoholic."

"Oh no," Mary said, appalled. "I never knew that. John kept it to himself, even when we worked together."

"That would be John. That's why I was so surprised by the ring." Judy looked away as they walked along, and Mary couldn't imagine how hard this was for her, to have just lost John and now to have to tell his brother the awful news.

"I'm so sorry about all of this, honey."

"Thanks, but anyway, let me answer your question. What happened was that William's mother's regular obstetrician was out of town when she went into labor, so his partner covered for him, but he was so drunk that he couldn't even function at the delivery." Judy's lips curled in disgust. "If it hadn't been for a nurse who stepped in, William would've died. John's mother might have, too."

"Oh no." Mary shuddered, her hand going involuntarily to her belly.

"Oops, I didn't mean to freak you out." Judy grimaced as they walked along. "I'm sorry, I don't know what I was thinking —"

"No, it's okay." Mary knew it was unlikely that anything would go wrong with her delivery, but that didn't mean she didn't worry. Constantly.

"The hospital knew the obstetrician was an alcoholic, but they covered it up. Their negligence was so clear that John's family sued when William was a year old and they got a great settlement. That's what funded William's trust, and it should care for him for the rest of his life, at Glenn Meade." Judy shook her head. "I love all medical mal lawyers now. They may have cheesy commercials, but they're doing God's work. Doctors make mistakes just like everybody else and they have to be held to account."

"Right." Mary felt the same way. "Lawyer jokes are real funny until somebody leaves a sponge in your mom."

"Exactly." Judy nodded. "William's forty-two and he's lived here for about twenty years. He loves it. There's only six residents in his apartment. He gets along with them all, and they have roughly the same level of intellectual disability."

"What is his level of intellectual disability?" Mary knew from her special-education practice that there were different levels of functioning for people with cerebral palsy, and she had been successful in mainstreaming many of her younger clients.

"He functions intellectually on about a fourth-grade level. It's not always easy to understand him, and his hands are spastic, like knotted, and he can't feed or bathe himself. Still, he can work his laptop using voice-recognition software and he's on Facebook and Instagram, too. John helped him set up the pages." Judy smiled sadly, but it passed. "He opens his iPhone with his knuckle and has voice-recognition software on it too, and Siri."

"God bless voice recognition." Mary had seen the same thing with her young clients who had special needs.

"I know, it's opened up a whole new world for people with CP. John got him an Alexa, and it recognizes his voice and commands, and he uses that to turn on the lights and TV and play his playlist from his phone."

"What's his personality like? Is he like John?"

"John always used to say, 'William is the

nice one and I'm the mean one.' But that wasn't true. John wasn't mean." Judy smiled, sadly.

"No, he wasn't." Mary felt for her.

"He took such incredible care of William. He came out here all the time to visit him and they would just hang. He was picky about the way they took care of William. And you know John, he didn't suffer fools."

Mary smiled. "Now that sounds like him."

"The guy we talked to on the phone, Mike Shanahan? He started about six months ago. John thought he wasn't as attentive as he should be, but anyway, William is happy here and he's a total sweetheart, you'll see. He's friendly, outgoing, and he loves people. And music, hip-hop mostly." Judy smiled again, shakily. "It drives John crazy — it *drove* John crazy. John downloaded Mahler for him, but William wanted Jay-Z."

"How are you gonna tell him about John?" Mary dreaded the task at hand, for Judy's sake.

"I don't know." Judy looked pained. "We'll take him out. John and I used to take him down to the duck pond. We haven't been there in a while, it was too cold. He likes it there, and we watch the ducks or sing. He likes to sing."

"Do you want to take him home with us,

until the funeral? I can make room for him, too."

"No, thanks. I'll ask him, but he won't want to go. His support system is here. He'll go to the funeral, so I'll come back and take him out for that." Judy's lip trembled. "I'll tell him out at the duck pond. It's going to be so hard for him."

"You want me there, or you want me to wait back at his house?"

"No, of course, come with us. He likes to meet new people. He's going to be devastated."

"Maybe Mike can get him therapy or grief counseling? Do they have that here?"

"Good idea, I'll ask him." Judy sighed. "The problem is that Mike can be chilly. Like he's professional, but he's a cold fish."

"That's not a good personality for this job."

"That's what John always said." Judy looked up as they reached a sign that read POPLAR HOUSE, in front of a squarish red-brick apartment building, given a homey feel by multicolored pots with plants outside of its glass front door. "Oh, here we are. Follow me."

Mary fell in behind Judy as she knocked briefly, then entered a large sunny common area. Three men were sitting in wheelchairs, which faced opposite a large-screen television playing a baseball game. The man on the end had to be William, because he looked like John and as soon as he spotted Judy, his eyes came alive with animation behind his horn-rimmed glasses.

"Jud'!" William called out, beaming.

"William, hi! Hi, everybody!" Judy beelined to William and gave him a hug, and William tried to hug her back, raising his clenched hands slightly, though his skinny forearms remained mostly rigid at his sides, as if he were pinned by the elbows. "William, this is my friend Mary."

"Hi!" William grinned up at her, raising his arms slightly, and Mary gave him a hug.

"William, I'm so happy to meet you. I heard such nice things about you from Judy."

William nodded excitedly, still beaming, though his facial muscles were so drawn back that that it looked almost painful. He had on a plaid shirt and baggy jeans with black sneakers, his feet resting askew in the stainless-steel footrests of his wheelchair, which had a tall padded back. Around his neck was a pair of Dr. Dre headphones, and a smartphone was clamped to his wheelchair arm. He had darker, curlier hair than John, but his blue eyes reminded Mary of his brother's, piercing, wide-set, and connecting with her intently. William was trying to tell Mary something, struggling to form the words, and spittle appeared in the corners of his mouth.

Mary put her hand on his, bending over. "What is it, William?"

William smiled hard, and his lips quivered with the effort of speech, then it burst forth: "You have a . . . baby in there!"

Mary laughed, too. "Right, I do! I have a baby, right in here." She rubbed her tummy, and William kept grinning, though a new look in his eyes made Mary think he was curious. On impulse, she asked, "Do you want to touch my belly? The baby is inside."

"Yes!" William nodded with excitement, his head jittery and his neck tilted to the side, frozen in that position. He tried to reach his hand out, with its knobby clenched fist, but Mary leaned over and her belly made up the extra distance.

"Here we go, William. Can you feel that?"

William brushed it gently with his knuckles. "Ha!"

"What do you think?"

"It's a boy!" William burst into merry laughter, and so did Mary, since she hadn't seen that coming. As they were laughing, a tall, middle-aged man came over with a professional smile. He was well-built in a white polo shirt with the Glenn Meade logo, khaki Dockers, and sneakers.

"Judy, hi, glad you could make it today."

"Hi, Mike." Judy gestured to Mary. "This is my friend Mary DiNunzio."

"From the phone? Nice to see you." Mike extended a beefy hand, and Mary shook it.

"You too, thanks."

"Sorry about William, his excitement gets the best of him." Mike frowned down at William. "William, you're not supposed to touch pregnant ladies. It's rude and —"

"No, it's okay," Mary interrupted. "I invited him to and I have no problem with it, actually. Total strangers on the bus touch my belly. I'm like a walking Blarney Stone."

Mike blinked. "My wife tells me it's not politically correct."

"I'm Italian-American, and even though that's only a label, we like to be touched." Mary smiled down at William, who was still grinning, so Mike's rebuke hadn't fazed him. "William, you can pat my belly anytime."

William looked at the door, raising his chin slightly. "Where's John?"

"I'm taking you out today, with Mary," Judy answered quickly, walking around the back of the wheelchair and taking the handles. "Let's go see the ducks."

"Okay! Can we feed them?"

"Yes, I have change for the machine."

Mike went to the door, opening it. "Judy, we packed him a water bottle and strawberry yogurt for a snack, if you want to give him that. It's in his bag on the back of the chair."

"Thanks, see you soon." Judy pushed William through the door in his wheelchair, with Mary following.

"Bye, Mike!" William called out over his shoulder, and Mary didn't think he was that hard to understand, after she got used to him.

Judy rolled William into the sunshine, checking in the large black bag that hung on the back of his wheelchair. "William, do you want your prescription sunglasses? They're in your bag."

"No. I like the sun." William grinned, still blinking against the brightness.

"So how have you been?"

"Good." William smiled, and a soft breeze ruffled the curls in his hair. Now that they were outside where it was quieter, Mary could hear hip-hop music playing through the headphones resting around his neck.

Judy rolled him past yellow crocuses blooming beside the asphalt path. "William, look, flowers. Everything is blooming, and spring is here. No more winter."

"I don't like winter. It's *cold*!" William smiled, still blinking. He leaned forward in the wheelchair, his excitement plain.

"I don't like it either. I like spring."

Mary fell into step beside William's wheel-chair. "I like summer."

"Me too!" William looked up at Mary, delighted. "I can go fast! Judy, make me go fast!"

The path led gently downhill, and Judy leaned over to William. "Here we go down the hill! Hold on tight, William!"

"Whee!" William cheered, though he was in no danger, strapped into the wheelchair by belts at his waist and chest.

"Don't fall out!"

"I won't!" William laughed, thrilled, as Judy wheeled him downhill. The path led behind the back of Poplar House, and ahead lay a grove of tall evergreens and underneath a verdant blanket of kelly-green ferns and hosta. Beyond was a large pond dotted with grayish-brown mallards and ringed at regular intervals with weathered cedar benches. The sight would have been idyllic, but for the fact that Mary knew Judy was going to tell William the worst news of his life there.

William grinned up at Mary, breathless.

"Are you Judy's friend?"

"Yes." Mary found herself wishing that they could walk slower, just to prolong William's last moments of happiness. "I've known her for a long time."

"How long?"

"I have to think about that a minute." Mary caught Judy's eye, and they both smiled. "I don't even remember. A long, *long* time."

Judy chuckled. "I don't remember, either. William, can you believe that? I've known Mary for so long I don't even remember how long? Isn't that silly?"

"Ha!" William laughed. "I have friends. Tom and Jason and Big Bill."

"You have a lot of friends." Judy smiled. "You're a friendly guy."

"I know them a long time."

"You've lived here a long time. Everybody likes you." Judy leaned down to William as they walked. "Remember what I told you about the name of your house?"

"What?" William raised his head, squinting.

"It's called Poplar House but I said you should call it . . . ?"

"*Popular* House! Ha!" William laughed again.

"And do you remember why?"

"Because I'm *popular*!"

"That's right! You're *very* popular."

"John is *my* best friend." William smiled, looking happily around as they traveled down the gentle hill.

Judy swallowed hard, and Mary felt her chest tighten. They reached level ground, heading toward the duck pond, and Mary could see grayish-brown mallards floating around on the glassy surface.

"Ducks!" William shouted happily.

"Ducks, here we come!" Judy glanced over at Mary, as they approached a cedar bench. "Mary, why don't you wait for us here? I'll take John to feed the ducks. We don't want to scare them with too many people. Is that okay?"

"That's a great idea," Mary answered, keeping her tone light. On impulse, she patted William's hand, clenched tightly atop the padded armrest of his wheelchair. "William, I'll see you when you get back. I'll wait here."

"Okay, bye!" William's attention was already drawn to the ducks, and Mary met Judy's eye, feeling her pain.

Judy turned away and traveled ahead, pushing William toward the lovely scene, and Mary found herself standing still, watching them go, hearing Judy chatter and

William giggling as they walked along.

Mary sank into the bench, trying to imagine how he would bear the news that John was gone, and she felt new rage at whoever had killed John. The killer had taken John's life — and William's lifeline. They were the true victims, this tiny, lopsided Foxman family, formerly only two members, now only one.

Mary watched as Judy and William reached the pond. William kept pointing to the ducks, but Judy leaned over talking to him, then sat down on the cedar bench and turned his wheelchair around, so that he was facing her. Judy leaned over, her face close to William's as she spoke, and though Mary couldn't hear her words, she witnessed their impact.

William cried out in pain, then hunched over crying, his spiny back and clenched fists shaking with sobs, and Judy enveloped him in a weepy embrace of her own.

And that was when Mary made a vow.

To find out who killed John.

CHAPTER TWENTY-THREE

The afternoon sun stalled in the hazy sky over South Philly, and Mercy Street was typically sleepy on Sunday, with nobody out except for a few neighbors in plastic chairs on the sidewalk, which had all the charm of a concrete beach. Mary stood with Judy at the front door to her parents' house, hesitating before they went inside. Mary wouldn't have come home for Sunday dinner but for the fact that Judy had begged her to, after the heartbreaking afternoon with William. Mary had called her parents on the way to town, and they'd been delighted to have her home. Mary had texted Anthony that Judy needed some girlfriend-time, which he understood. Plus he'd had enough carbohydrates for the week.

Mary put her hand on the doorknob, eyeing her best friend, who looked heartbroken and exhausted. Her eyes were puffy from crying, and even her happy pink hair had dulled. "Judy, are you sure you want to go in? This is your last chance to come to your senses."

"Totally, I want to. You know I love your parents, and they're exactly what I need tonight."

Mary could hear the sound of the Phillies game coming from the TV inside, at maximum decibel levels. "Did you remember that my father shouts when he talks?"

"That's how I know he loves me. When he screams."

"My mother's going to hug and kiss you. And fill you with carbohydrates in mass quantities."

"Yes, I want her to feed me. Literally, with a spoon. I want her to feed me, hold me, rock me, and maybe even burp me."

"MARE, JUDY? IS THAT YOU? COME IN ALREADY! WHAT'RE YOU WAITIN' FOR?"

"Coming, Mr. D!" Judy sidestepped Mary and her belly, opening the screen door. "Mr. D, I need a hug!"

"JUDY, COME 'ERE, DOLL! IT'S BEEN TOO LONG!" Mary's father bear-hugged Judy, and Mary entered the living room, loving that her parents adored her best friend. From day one, they had made the tall, countercultural Northern Californian an honorary DiNunzio, even though Judy stood out in this family like a lighthouse among tugboats.

"JUDY, WHAT'S A MATTER, HONEY? IT'S ALL GONNA BE AWRIGHT. WE'LL MAKE IT ALL BETTER."

"Mr. D, I missed you!" Judy burst into tears, and Mary's father held her tighter.

"DON'T WORRY, DOLL. IT'S GONNA BE AWRIGHT. EVERYTHING'S GONNA BE AWRIGHT."

"Jud', Jud, *che cosa, cara*!" Mary's mother scurried from the kitchen on her black orthopedic shoes, drying her hands on a cloth dish towel, her flowered housedress flying. She threw her short arms around Judy, who melted into her embrace, too.

"Mrs. D, it's so terrible, everything is so terrible!" Judy clung to Mary's mother, who stroked her back and soothed her in Italian, which Judy didn't understand at all, but it didn't matter. In time, Mary's parents calmed Judy down, guided her into the kitchen, and placed her in a chair at the table, which had been set for Sunday dinner.

"JUDY, DRINK SOME WATER. YOU'LL EAT, YOU'LL FEEL BETTER, YOU'LL SEE." Mary's father eased into his chair, and Mary's mother hovered over

Judy, clutching her arthritic hands in front of her.

"Thanks, guys." Mary put an arm around her mother and kissed her fragrant hair cloud, which smelled of old-school Aqua Net and fresh tomato sauce. "Judy needs some love, Ma."

"*Si, si,* Jud', *di'* me."

Mary sat down, comforted to hear her mother say *di' me,* her favorite Italian expression, which meant *tell me.* She had grown up in a family that loved to talk, but it also loved to listen, and for that, she was so grateful. Judy was closer to Mary's family than her own, and Mary was thrilled to lend Judy her parents' listening ear, even if it did have a hearing aid.

Judy sniffled, wiping her nose with a napkin, then launched into the story, catching Mary's parents up on the facts that John had been murdered, that she had been dating him, that the police had found the engagement ring, and that they had just come from delivering the bad news to William, which was when Mary's father had teared up behind his bifocals.

Mary's mother had listened to every word, as she managed to serve dinner, which was a plate of steaming ravioli with slow cooked tomato sauce and broccoli rabe glistening with olive oil, garlicky enough to leave an aftertaste for days, until it finally left Mary's body via her pores. Judy wolfed down her meal as she finished the story, which did Mary's heart good. If Judy was eating, sooner or later, world order would be restored. But what preoccupied Mary was John's killer.

"MARE, YOU UPSET, TOO, AREN'T YA?"

"Yes, I am." Mary pushed her plate away, since she had eaten for three. "I can't imagine who would kill John. I want to touch base with Lou and see if he found out anything. I called him and Bennie, but I haven't heard back yet."

Judy looked over, miserably. "They would've called us if they found anything."

Mary knew it was true as soon as Judy said it. "So what do we do tomorrow? Just business as usual, with all this going on?"

Judy nodded sadly. "We have to, we have no other choice. You have a deposition to defend in *London Technologies.* The show must go on — until I get arrested."

"JUDY, JESUS, GOD! DON'T SAY THAT! THEY CAN'T DO THAT! YOU DIDN'T KILL NOBODY! YOU NEVER WOULD!"

"*Che, che?*" Mary's mother asked irritably,

just as some car commercials started blaring on the TV in the living room, making it harder for her to hear.

"Ma, I got it, don't worry." Mary rose, went to the living room, and picked up the remote, about to turn off the TV when the screen changed with a teaser for the evening news, but the lead story showed a picture of Nick Machiavelli. LAWYER CLAIMS KNOWLEDGE OF SUSPECTS IN SLAYING OF CENTER CITY ATTORNEY, read a banner under the screen.

"Judy, come in here quick!" Mary shouted, appalled, and Judy hurried into the living room, followed by Mary's mother and father, who stood in a shocked circle around the television.

A female anchorperson was saying, "Our lead story tonight involves bombshell allegations by Center City attorney Nick Machiavelli in connection with the murder of fellow Center City attorney, John Foxman. We take you now to Attorney Machiavelli's offices, where he is speaking live with our reporter . . ."

Mary froze as Machiavelli appeared on the screen, interviewed in his office, behind his ornately carved desk. He was leaning forward earnestly, his hair slick as an oil spill and his manicured fingers linked in

271

front of him. He gave the appearance of being honest and believable, unless you knew better, which Mary did.

"The police claim they have no suspects in the murder of John Foxman, but they're covering up the truth. I'm calling on them now to expose the conspiracy that I believe exists behind John Foxman's murder. Because it is my opinion that he was killed by the partners of the law firm of Rosato & DiNunzio."

"What?" Mary said, astonished.

"Did he say *conspiracy*?" Judy's eyes flew open.

"HE SAID YOU DID IT!"

"Deo!" Mary's mother said, frightened.

The reporter frowned, though he held the microphone under Machiavelli's face. "But to be fair, Mr. Machiavelli, the authorities reported today that they have no suspects, so what are the facts on which you are basing your opinion?"

Machiavelli lifted an eyebrow. "It's obvious, isn't it? They took Mary DiNunzio, Judy Carrier, and Bennie Rosato into the Roundhouse for questioning this weekend. Those are the three partners that I am trying to bring to justice because they discriminated against my clients. And John Foxman's statements that those three women discriminated against *him* formed an important part of my proof against them. He was going to be my best witness — and now he's dead."

Mary gasped. "I can't believe he's doing this. This must be what he meant on the phone, before. But this is defamation. This is *slander.*"

"No, it's not." Judy shook her head, looking grave. "It not defamation if it's a statement of opinion, and he's couching it in those terms. Defamation arises when it's a misstatement of fact that damages somebody's reputation. For example, it's defamation to say 'he was drunk in the operating room,' but it's not defamation to say, 'I believe he's a drunk.' And, truth is an absolute defense. The statements of fact, like the fact that we were called in to the police station, or that John said he believed he was discriminated against, are true. It's not defamation, but he's killing us and the firm."

"MARE, HE'S NOT GONNA GET AWAY WITH THIS! I'M TELLIN' THE BOYS! HE CAN'T TALK ABOUT YOU THAT WAY! I ALWAYS HATED HIM AND HIS SPACONE FAMILY!"

"*Va, fanculo!*" Mary's mother shook her fist at the television, and Mary didn't

273

translate the Italian, which was self-explanatory.

Machiavelli continued, "So ask yourself? Who stands to gain the most if John Foxman, the key witness against them, ends up dead? Murdered?"

The reporter shook her head. "But these are only allegations, isn't that correct?"

"That's up to your viewers." Machiavelli turned to the camera and looked into it directly. "Everybody out there can make up their own minds. The main witness against Mary DiNunzio, Judy Carrier, and Bennie Rosato was found murdered. He was the *only* male lawyer who worked at this all-female law firm, and he had already come forward to say that he was leaving them because he felt that he would not make partner there, as a man. How far will these lawyers go to protect themselves and their corrupt law firm? Do we have to spell it out?"

Suddenly Machiavelli held up a video on his phone, showing uniformed police officers leaving the building that held Rosato & DiNunzio, carrying several cardboard boxes and a large desktop computer. "If the partners weren't suspects, why would police be raiding their office today, taking John Foxman's office computer and files? I have the footage right here, you can see for your-self!"

"When did *that* happen?" Mary asked, horrified.

Judy recoiled. "When we were with William. Oh no, I hope they didn't search my office too. And what about my apartment? Do you think they searched *my* apartment? My *laptop*?"

"God, I hope not." Mary's mind raced. Things were happening so fast, she could barely keep up. "I don't think they have enough for a search warrant against you yet, or Bennie or me. They can seize John's property as part of the investigation, but not yours."

On the TV, the reporter turned, shaken, to the camera. "This is a live interview, and certainly, these views do not necessarily represent the views of our station, management, or anyone in its —"

Mary pressed Off on the TV remote, plunging them into stunned silence. Until her and Judy's cell phones started ringing like crazy.

CHAPTER TWENTY-FOUR

Mary hurried off the elevator with Judy, waddling as fast as she could with a bellyful of baby and ravioli. The lights were on in the reception area, and they hurried past the reception desk and down the hall, but their steps slowed as they passed John's office, where Judy's face fell into crestfallen lines. John's large desktop computer was gone, his typically neat bookshelves had been searched, and his desk drawers hung open, with some of the files missing. Black smudges of fingerprint dust marred the tan file cabinets, the surface of his cherrywood desk, and even the doorknob.

Judy stopped, stunned. "I can't believe that they took his stuff, just like that."

Mary put an arm around her. "Don't let it get to you, honey. It's standard operating procedure. But they don't have enough to search you yet. And we'll do our damnedest to make sure they never do."

"Thanks." Judy let Mary guide her toward the conference room, where Bennie, Anne, Roger, and Isaac were sitting around a table covered with *London Technologies* documents, empty pizza boxes, and styrofoam coffee cups. The combined odors of caffeine and anchovies hung in the air, making Mary feel almost sick to her stomach. Or it could've been the circumstances.

"So they showed up with a search warrant?" Mary gestured at John's office.

Bennie nodded. "I would've called you but didn't since you were with John's brother."

"There was no mention about searching Judy's office or ours, was there?"

"No, they don't have enough, and they knew they'd have to have their ducks in a row before they come at us."

"Do you *believe* Machiavelli is going after us this way?" Mary eased into a chair. "I tell you, this is what he does. He even called me and Judy this morning, pressuring us to settle. He said he was going to use John's murder against us."

Judy sat down, next to Mary. "I have to admit, that TV interview scared the crap out of me. He spoke directly to the camera, pressuring the police to arrest me. To investigate all of us. He's peddling that conspiracy theory like it's real. We could all end up in jail."

Mary shuddered. "I thought my parents were going to have a heart attack. They never heard my name on TV that way. He accused me of being a murderer. He accused *all* of us of being murderers."

Anne looked grave, turning to Mary and Judy. "He's ruining our reputation. Jim and Sanjay called and they're nervous."

Bennie's eyes flashed with cold anger. "We're going to fight back, that's what we're going to do. I will *not* lose Jim and Sanjay. I will *not* lose any other business."

"What's going on? Have you lost other clients already? I think mine are running scared, too." Mary's clients had been calling on her cell nonstop, so she'd put her phone on silent.

"Yes, we didn't get Nutrex. You know, that independent stock brokerage that we put on the dog-and-pony show for?"

"What happened?" Mary asked, aghast. Nutrex wanted to bring a massive securities fraud action against the big-time stock brokerages and they had interviewed the top firms in Philly, including Rosato & DiNunzio, two weeks ago.

"They passed on us. No explanation. I got

an email from the general counsel. Not even a call."

"But he told you that we were a shoo-in, didn't he?"

"Yes, but now that we're being accused of *murdering* one of *our own,* they're not hiring us." Bennie's eyes glittered with resentment. "Do you know how much *business* that would've been?"

"So what do we do? How can we fight this? He's ruining our reputation and he's putting Judy in jeopardy. He's putting all of us in jeopardy." Mary noticed suddenly that Roger had remained silent and still while they were yapping away, like the calm eye of a lawyer hurricane. "Roger, what do you think?"

"I think we have a worthy adversary." Roger smiled calmly, linking his fingers on the table behind a half-finished garden salad.

"So what do you think? What do we do? Hold a press conference? Counter what he said? We have to react."

"No." Roger shook his head. "We don't have to react."

"Why not?" Mary shot back.

"Nick Machiavelli is doing what he does. In other words, he's performing in a way that's consistent with who he is. Whether it's because he is a genuine ancestor of Prince Niccolò Machiavelli, he epitomizes Machiavelli's ethos."

"Does this matter?" Mary felt her patience wearing thin. They had all been accused of murder on national television, and even worse, somebody had killed John and broken William's heart. And Judy's.

"Yes, Mary, it does matter. Machiavelli's way is, 'The end justifies the means.' If we understand his way, then we can predict his next move."

"Okay, now we're talking. How do we take him down?" Mary rolled her chair closer to the conference table, or as close as she could get. The baby was remarkably quiet, so maybe it didn't mind anchovies as much as its mother.

"We do not 'take him down.' " Roger made air quotes. "We do not counter, fight back, or engage."

"We don't?" Mary felt deflated.

"No. I have already had this conversation with Bennie, and she agrees. I hope you and Judy will see it my way, as well." Roger cleared his throat primly. "Given Machiavelli's way, as we just discussed, he will continue to ratchet up his attacks on the firm. We can predict that with absolute certainty, now that we understand his ethos."

"And we're going to take it lying down?"

"I don't know how to deal with that statement, so I won't." Roger's eyelids fluttered, apparently involuntarily. "We do not meet his energy with coequal, oppositional energy. It would be counterproductive over the long term. We wait and issue a brief written statement to the effect that we are mourning the loss of our friend and colleague John Foxman and remain one hundred percent behind efforts by the authorities to bring his killer to justice."

"And we'll deny the allegations of murder and conspiracy, won't we?"

"No, we're not even going to refer to those allegations." Roger glanced at Bennie, who nodded in grudging acceptance, so he continued. "We are going to defuse the situation. We are going to *not* react to him in a way that he expects. It will defang him. It will disarm him. It will take the sting out of his accusations. It will isolate him. It will show him for who he is, a bully, spouting lies."

"In other words, we're not adding fuel to the fire." Mary got it, though it wasn't her instinct. "But I hate letting such personal accusations stand. It's outrageous."

Judy remained silent, as did Isaac, though Mary guessed that Isaac was already up to speed with the game plan.

Roger nodded slowly. "Mary, I understand your position. I hope I have your consent to do things my way. As I told you when you interviewed me, we have different energies. My way to think about this is that we set our path and follow it. Cleave to it, and in the end, we will find ourselves where we need to be."

"Haikus aside, does that mean we win?"

"In the long run, yes." Roger smiled, just the slightest. "So do I have your consent? I'd like you and Judy to be on board, since Bennie has already said yes."

"Okay," Mary answered, trying to make peace.

"I agree, Roger," Judy said quietly.

"Thank you. Isaac and I will draft the statement and will show it to you before we issue it tomorrow. In the meantime, to the extent the press cycle returns to the story, they will rerun *ad infinitum* the footage of Mary and Judy outside the Roundhouse. Given our silence, they will have no other choice. That will inure to our benefit."

"That's true," Mary said, brightening.

"Excellent." Roger looked up suddenly, as Lou entered the conference room, looking uncharacteristically disheveled. His steely-gray hair was out of place, and his navy-blue sportcoat was wrinkled, though he still looked natty with his loosened tie and khaki pants.

"Folks, I'm getting too old for this. I been knockin' on doors all day. I feel like I used to when I was a beat cop, back in the day." Lou rolled out the chair next to Mary and flopped down. "And then on the way home, I hear Machiavelli on the radio in the car. He's got some nerve, doesn't he? I want to punch that kid in the face."

Bennie made a hurry-up motion. "Lou, how did it go? I'm dying to know what you found out. Next time, make sure you charge your phone, so we don't have to wait all day to hear from you."

"I tried to find a pay phone." Lou shrugged, defensively. "I looked everywhere. First I got one that had no receiver, then I got one that had no dial. It's a disgrace! I never understand why these knuckleheads break —"

"Lou, what did you learn?" Bennie asked, urgent.

"Okay, relax." Lou grabbed a Coke from the table, popped the tab, and took a slug. "Let me tell it right. First off, so Mary told me that the cops told her and Judy that they had two witnesses. One was John's next-door neighbor, who heard them fighting and puts her there the night of the murder."

Judy looked over. "Right, she lives to the left of John's house. Her name is Linda Stallworthy."

"Right. Linda. I talked to her." Lou nodded. "The other witness they had was a lady out the back, who saw through the window. She was an eyewitness but she didn't hear anything. She saw Judy and John fighting in the apartment. She's the website designer, remember?"

"Right." Bennie nodded. "Did you talk to her, too?"

"Yes, pretty girl but too skinny, in her thirties. Barbara Mulcahy."

"And what did she say?" Bennie asked, defaulting instantly to cross-examination mode.

"Don't rush me." Lou put up a wrinkled hand. "The headline is this. They both identify Judy positively. The next-door neighbor, Linda, she likes you, Judy. She said you've been seeing John for a while, so she's going to confirm that for the cops, but she also said you never fought before, that it was very unusual for you to fight. She told me that she told the cops that too, but I guess they didn't tell you that."

"No, they didn't. We never fought, really."
Judy swallowed hard, and Mary patted her
hand.

Bennie asked, "Lou, what did Barbara
Mulcahy say? The one who saw through the
back window."

"She confirms what the cop said too, that
she was worried about Judy's safety during
the fight. Not that John took a swing or
anything, on account of she had an abusive
ex. She didn't hear anything but she saw it.
So there's nothing new there." Lou took
another slug of Coke. "Barbara stopped
watching the window after you left, but you
know what time you left. She just knows
that she looked back at the window and you
weren't there."

"Did she see John?"

"No." Lou frowned, his concern folding
into the deep lines of his tanned face. "So,
that could mean that the killer had already
come and gone, unless you can see him on
the floor from the window. I don't know the
angle of the window."

Judy grimaced. "I don't think you can,
but I'm not sure."

Lou eyed her with sympathy. "Sorry,
honey. This can't be easy for you."

Mary rubbed Judy's back. "She's doing
amazing, poor thing."

Lou took another slug of Coke. "So I talked to eight other neighbors, three on the same side of the street as John and four on the opposite. Hold on a second, I wrote it down. The addresses." He tugged an old red notebook from his jacket pocket, flipped it open, and read silently to himself.

Bennie looked at him like he was nuts. "Lou, wanna let us in on it?"

"Nah. Waste a time." Lou flipped the notebook closed. "It was just the details, like house numbers and names. I'll type it up for you later. Bottom line, none of them saw anything, none of them heard anything. None of them could identify Judy from a picture. One of 'em had hair the same color pink. They're yuppies, they're never home, they got a bunch of wacky artsy jobs. I got nothin' from them."

Bennie nodded. "What about surveillance cameras? Did you find any other cameras?"

"No." Lou shook his head, buckling his lower lip. "There's no camera at the other intersection because there's no traffic light there, only a stop sign. I stopped in at six restaurants and an art gallery on that three-block strip. No cameras, so far. I'll draw ya a map later and show you exactly who I talked to and where." Lou sighed. "Now, one of the managers in the Mexican restaurant on that block was out today and will be back tomorrow, so I'll follow up. And I'll call up some of my guys on the force and ask them where are any other cameras they know of. Then I'll follow up."

Mary knew it was a tough break. "Okay, that sucks, but let's stay with my original theory, which is, unfortunately, proving a negative. We can't show yet that somebody else came from the opposite direction. But the police can't show that there was nobody else but Judy. So we have to keep hammering that it had to have been someone who came in after she left the apartment." Mary glanced at Judy, who was on edge. "I just can't figure out why anybody would want to kill John. Can you?"

"No, not at all."

"He got along with the neighbors?"

"He hardly knew them. He was private. You know how he was."

"Was he ever burglarized before?"

"Not that I know of."

"Never mugged or anything?"

"No." Judy raked her fingers through her hair. "I just can't believe they suspect me of killing him. This is a *nightmare.*"

"Honey, don't worry, they need a lot more than they have to meet reasonable doubt."

"That's true," Bennie added. "It's not

enough to charge you, Carrier."

"What more do they need?" Judy raked her hands through her hair again. "I should know, but I can't even think. It's been a horrible day." She looked over at Roger, almost apologetically. "And I'm trying, but I don't feel very centered right now."

Roger's expression softened. "That's completely understandable, Judy. I have some thoughts that may help you with your loss, which I can let you have at a more appropriate time. As you know, there is much in the teachings about passing on to the next stage."

"Yes, in Buddhism, too." Judy sighed. "But I have more immediate worries, like the police."

"Of course. I'm not a criminal lawyer, so this is beyond my ken."

Bennie leaned forward. "Carrier, before they can charge you, they need physical evidence, for starters. Trace evidence, like DNA, hair, fibers, fingerprints, maybe blood."

Judy bit her lip. "But my blood, hair and prints will be all over his apartment, and sooner or later, the cops are going to call me back in. I'm going to have to give samples. I don't have a right to refuse that."

Mary's thoughts raced. "But not on the

murder weapon, right? The detectives told us that they think John was killed using the base of a lamp. Did you touch the base of the lamp?"

Judy's forehead remained tense. "I doubt it. I know the lamp they mean. It's a chrome desk lamp. It has a big heavy base, and one of those metal arms that has a joint, like an elbow."

Mary could visualize it. "He called it a Luxor lamp."

Judy rallied. "I might have touched the top, like, the knob you turn it on with, but I doubt that I touched the base."

Bennie nodded. "So if it's the murder weapon, it will have the killer's trace evidence on it, not yours. That's a major problem for them."

Mary breathed a relieved sigh. "Good. So that will slow them down."

Bennie rested her chin on her hand. "I'd like to get inside his apartment and examine the scene."

Lou turned to her. "They were about to release the scene when I left. They were waiting for the okay."

Bennie blinked, surprised. "They released the scene already? Isn't that soon?"

"Yep, that's the way they do it now. They get in and get out. With budget cutbacks by the city, they don't have the manpower to hold the scene the way they used to."

Judy shrugged. "I have a key to John's apartment, at home."

Mary looked over. "Do you feel up for it, if we go?"

"What do you think?" Judy answered, without elaborating.

CHAPTER TWENTY-FIVE

Mary lingered at the threshold with Judy, trying to get her emotional bearings while Bennie and Lou entered John's living room, poked around, and started taking pictures with their cell phones, since Lou had charged his phone in the car. Mary couldn't bring herself to take photos because being here made it so real that John had been brutally murdered. It was harder to take, having spent the afternoon with William, and she realized she was learning more about John in death than she had in life, which gave her a guilty wrench.

Judy stood rooted to the threshold, fighting for emotional control, and Mary knew why, reaching for Judy's hand. The exact spot where John had been murdered was straight ahead in the living area, in a direct line from the door. Dark blood soaked a grayish-wool rug, making a grotesquely vast pool, maybe as wide as three feet. The blood wasn't even completely dry, so some patches were darker than others, and blood sprayed out in droplets and long lines, radiating like lethal sunrays. A sickening metallic odor tainted the air, and Mary prayed that she was the only one who could detect it, because of her pregnancy.

Mary squeezed Judy's hand. "I'm sorry, honey."

"This is horrible," Judy said, hushed.

"Do you want to wait outside?"

"No, thanks. I'll stay here, but you should go in and look around."

"You sure?"

"Yes, please, go ahead," Judy answered, eyes brimming.

"Okay, hang in." Mary gave Judy's hand a final squeeze, set her emotions aside, and analyzed it as a crime scene. The living room was shaped like a large box, with an eat-in kitchen on the left, and on the right, a sitting area that held a black-leather couch facing a black entertainment center against the wall. There were no windows in the living room, so it was somewhat dark, and the only light at this point was from an old-fashioned crystal fixture mounted on the ceiling. Directly ahead on the far wall of the living room were two open doors that led to two rooms, one on the left and one on the right.

Judy pointed from the doorway. "His bedroom is on the right and his office is on the left. The bathroom's just off the bedroom. There's only the one."

"Thanks." Mary made her way through the living room, among the debris. The furniture showed heartbreaking signs of a struggle; seat cushions were scattered, a black-ceramic lamp was lying on the rug, and the other end table had been upended, scattering coasters, pens, legal papers, and the remote control to the floor. Novels and law books had fallen from bookshelves in the entertainment center, and framed photographs lay willy-nilly on the rug.

Mary picked one up, hating to leave them on the floor. It was John's parents on their wedding day, and they made an attractive couple, both of them with glasses and sandy-blonde hair, looking intelligent, well-heeled, and vaguely preppy, like John. Another photo was lying face down, and Mary picked it up, turning it over. It was a childhood snapshot of William sitting in a red Radio Flyer, his knotted fists in his lap, and he was being pulled by John. John couldn't have been more than six years old, grinning ear-to-ear in Ninja turtle pajamas.

"Mary, let me see," Judy said, finally coming over.

"They're so cute." Mary handed her the photos, and Judy looked lovingly at the one of John and William.

"Aw, do you think it's okay if I keep these?"

"I'm sure it is." Mary looked around, and everywhere were the signs of the police investigation; a fresh blue bootie used by crime techs lay curled up on the floor, large sections had been cut out of the blood-stained rug to be analyzed, and black smudges of fingerprint dust marred the surfaces in the living room and kitchen.

Bennie and Lou came over, joining Mary and Judy, and the four of them formed a forlorn group around the bloodstain. Bennie shook her head. "Oh, man. What we really want is John back. What we'll settle for is justice. I say it every time, I think it every time. Justice is only a consolation prize, and even so, it's still the best one going."

Lou hung his head, the wrinkles of his face deepening with sadness. "Ain't that the truth. Judy, we're real sorry."

"Thanks." Judy held the photos to her chest. "So what are you guys thinking? I'm not much help yet. It's hard to get my brain in gear."

Bennie patted her shoulder. "Okay, let's get busy. Carrier, where would the lamp usually be, the one that the killer used?"

Judy pointed. "It used to be right here, on the end table on the right side of the couch. John used to work on the couch with his laptop, or read. He liked the focused light, and the lamp had a shade that faced down."

Bennie nodded. "So it's clear the way this happened. There's no sign of any forced entry, so John must've let somebody in, somebody he knew or at least wasn't threatened by. They started talking on the couch, maybe sitting down together, this way." She gestured to the couch and its matching chair, catty-corner. "The killer picks up the lamp and attacks John, who fights back. These chairs are too heavy to be knocked over, but everything else gets knocked over."

Lou nodded, listening. "But the killer killed him with the base. He might've taken the lamp outta the base first. It lifts right out of the center, like, it swivels. He prolly threw it aside. You thinkin' what I'm thinkin'?"

Bennie half-smiled. "If so, the killer's prints will not only be on the base, but also on the arm of the lamp and maybe even the shade. Judy, do you remember touching the arm or the shade?"

Judy brightened a little. "No, I don't think I did. The shade gets hot when you use the lamp. You're supposed to use a low wattage bulb, but John always used a higher wattage so he could see better. And this was his side of the couch, not mine. I may never have touched that lamp."

"Okay, that's good. Score one for us." Bennie walked to the bedroom, taking pictures with her cell phone. "I assume you guys had your argument in here and that's how Barbara Mulcahy saw you through the window."

"Right. We were in the living room too, but on Saturday night, we were in the back bedroom."

"Let me see." Mary slowed her step as she entered the bedroom. She felt uncomfortable as if she were intruding on John's privacy, especially when she caught sight of his beloved black Mont Blanc pen on the dresser, which he always used to sign pleadings. It was next to a pump bottle of eyeglass cleaner and a special gray cloth, and she suppressed a twinge of sadness, remembering that she used to tease him about cleaning his glasses so much. And next to that on the dresser sat a sales receipt on top of an unopened box of Bose headphones that he was undoubtedly going to give to William.

Lou and Bennie crossed to the window, taking pictures, and Mary forced herself to focus. There was a queen-size bed with a blue comforter and a wooden headboard flush against the wall on the right, and the dresser and a closet with a sliding door on the left. Between the two was a double panel window, covered only on the bottom by one of those top-down shades that roll from the top down, not the bottom up.

Lou lowered his cell phone, frowning at the shade. "I have these shades too. They let in the light at the top, but they block the view from the neighbors."

Bennie took another cell-phone photo of the shades. "Exactly, so how does Barbara Mulcahy see anything? Carrier, did John open the shades every morning, so they roll all the way down?"

Judy appeared at the threshold. "No, not generally. We left them that way. It's the southern exposure, and we liked the light coming in at the top. We left them just the way they are now."

Mary went to the side of the window. "So Judy, is this how you remember them that night?"

"I don't remember them that way, but that's probably how they were."

"Lou, here." Bennie dug in her bag,

297

produced a tape measure, and handed it to Lou. "Get me the dimensions of the window and measure how much of it is covered by the shade. I want to be able to reproduce this exactly. When you're finished, we'll roll the shade down all the way and see how far Mulcahy's window is from this window, as well as the angle."

"Okay." Lou started measuring and making notes on his cell phone, and Bennie turned to Mary and Judy.

"Ladies, this is also good for us. It makes me question how much Mulcahy could actually see of the apartment. I'm assuming her apartment is on the second floor, roughly level with this floor. There's not a lot of three-story buildings on these blocks. If she's on the second floor, she can't see anything through the lower half of the window."

Mary sensed Bennie was right. "So maybe she sees what's going on only when they stand up. Judy, does that sound right, on Saturday night?"

"Yes." Judy nodded sadly. "Sometimes he was standing up and sometimes I was or we both were."

Lou clucked, as he measured. "So that answers one question. She definitely couldn't have seen John with the killer in the living room, or anybody in the living room, not through the window at this angle."

"I agree."

"Okay, done. Ready to roll down the shade." Lou pocketed the tape measure, rolled down the shade, and they all gathered at the window, with Mary in front, since she was the shortest.

"Mulcahy's not home now," she said, looking into the darkness. Across the way was the back of another block of row houses, and they were all two stories. Nobody was home in the house directly behind this one, on either side. Each house had a small backyard, fenced in by wooden privacy fences or cyclone fencing, and one or two were paved for private parking spaces. Otherwise cars were parked lengthwise on both sides, probably illegally.

Mary looked around for a streetlight or any other kind of light, but there weren't any. "I'm surprised there's no lights back here, not even one."

Bennie frowned. "It's a private drive, so the city doesn't light it. There may be lights on motion detectors down there, but we won't know until we walk it."

Mary's thoughts raced. "This is more good news for us, isn't it? It supports the theory I told the police, that the killer could've entered the apartment in the back and not been seen."

"You're right." Bennie smiled, and Mary looked out the window to the left to see the black-iron lattice of the fire escape going from John's office and down the back of the house.

"Look! The fire escape is right there, off the office window."

"Understood." Bennie nodded with approval. "It's a completely alternative theory. Somebody enters the apartment through the fire escape, an intruder or burglar. He could have surprised John in the living room, while John was working. The killer sneaks up behind him, they struggle, he kills John with the lamp base and steals the laptop and phone, if that's what the police meant by electronics. We have yet to find that out, by the way. We need to know what was actually taken. We'll have to get his phone records, too."

Mary nodded, grimly. "It's a good theory, assuming the office window isn't locked."

Judy's face had gone pale. "It won't be. We never locked these windows. John loved fresh air. He worked in his office all the time with the window open."

"Let's go see." Mary left the bedroom,

followed by everybody else, and she entered the office, switching on the light. An overhead fixture came on, revealing a room slightly smaller than the bedroom, with a computer workstation covered with legal files and papers on the right side, and on the left, two gray file cabinets and a bookshelf full of old law school textbooks.

"Please God, give us a break." Mary beelined for the window, which had no shade on it, unlike the bedroom. She checked the window lock and almost cheered. "It's unlocked!"

"Whew." Bennie heaved a relieved sigh.

"Hold on, lemme take some pictures." Lou snapped photos of the window, and Bennie did the same.

"Let's see the fire escape." Mary opened the window, letting in the cool night air. The fire escape was directly outside the window, and its landing was only about two feet lower than the windowsill.

Bennie leaned outside the window. "The fire escape's right here. Anybody could've climbed in through this window. Anybody."

Mary nodded. "Anybody who wasn't pregnant."

Bennie smiled. "I have to tell you, that the killer is a burglar makes sense to me. That must be why the police went there initially."

"What's your reasoning?" Mary asked, intrigued.

"It gives a motive for the crime, and it's a motive that makes sense. This neighborhood is mixed, and there's transients. John is a successful lawyer, and there's people passing through who don't have jobs. They could see where he is, they could even follow him home. And one day, they decide to come back." Bennie gestured out the window. "You could even see John sitting here, working at his desk. You know he has a laptop, and some money, and a second-floor climb is easy. Please, I know somebody who was burglarized using a fire escape, and they lived in a fourth-floor walk-up."

Mary mulled it over. "But if they saw John here, then why try to burglarize the apartment when he was home? The detective's theory was that John surprised the burglar when he came home, but we know that didn't happen because we know Judy had just left, relatively, so John wasn't out."

Bennie shrugged. "Maybe the burglar thought John wasn't home, but he was, or maybe he just didn't care. With the typical burglary, you'd expect ransacking of the apartment, like drawers overturned and such, but this was interrupted, botched. The burglar was surprised to find John and kills him impulsively because he doesn't want to get caught. He doesn't have time to look for any other valuables, so he grabs the laptop and John's phone. We don't know if he took his wallet and watch. Nor do we know if he leaves by the back entrance, but that's most likely. We have to find out if there's any cameras out back."

"Will do." Lou nodded, gravely. "It does explain the motive. I can't see any other reason why anybody would kill John. And I will look at cameras on the back. I focused on witnesses because I wanted to get people when the recollections were fresh. I'll follow up with that tomorrow. It'll be easier in the daylight."

"Hold on a second." Bennie dug in her bag and produced a flashlight, and Mary marveled at the stuff the woman carried around, since she didn't bother with makeup bags or blotting papers.

Lou looked over. "Bennie, you going out there?"

"Yes, to test our theory." Bennie switched on the flashlight. "You coming with me or are you too old?"

"How dare you." Lou smiled as Bennie climbed out the window and onto the fire escape, shining the flashlight on the landing so Lou could climb out, which he did, slowly with a theatrical groan.

Mary watched them go down the stairs outside the building, feeling a rush of happiness, for the first time in a long time. They had lucked out, and her theory was actually a credible one, which might save Judy from being charged with murder.

Mary turned around, excitedly, until she saw that Judy had sunk onto a chair at John's desk, her head in her hands. "Oh no, honey."

"I'm okay." Judy straightened up, rubbing her face, and Mary came over, putting a hand on her shoulder.

"I'm sorry, I didn't mean to be so thoughtless."

"You aren't, you're not. It's just hard to get excited about knowing how he was killed. I just can't see it academically, like any other murder case." Judy's eyes brimmed, but she held back her tears.

"I totally get that. Really, I'm sorry."

"I mean, I knew it wasn't me who did it, but I can't stand to think that some burglar, some *thug,* snuck up behind him and killed him. Somebody who wasn't fit to clean his shoes. Somebody who would kill another human being for a *laptop.*" Judy's lips quivered, but she stayed in control. "And I know this is weird to say but I just keep thinking, where did the police find the engagement ring? How? Was it in his dresser? His closet? Did they search *everything*?"

"I don't know."

"You know what's worse? What if after we had the fight, he took out the engagement ring from wherever it was? Or maybe he even had it while we were fighting. Maybe he was going to propose this weekend, but then I gave him such a hard time, and we broke up, and he didn't —"

"You can't go down that what-if trail again."

"I can't help it, or what if he takes the ring out and he's sitting on the couch with it? After all, we had just had a fight. Maybe he felt bad, maybe he was even crying. I know I was." Judy shook her head, broken and bewildered. "And if he had the ring in his hand, maybe that's what was happening when the burglar snuck up behind him."

"No, that's not what happened. If it were, the burglar would've stolen the ring, too."

"Maybe he didn't see it? Maybe it rolled under the chair or the couch, and the police found it, but the burglar didn't. It's possible. The burglar would've been in a hurry, but the police weren't."

"Oh, honey." Mary gave her a hug, catching sight of the papers on John's workstation. She blinked twice when she saw the form on top, which sat inside an open manila folder thick with correspondence.

DEPT. OF HUMAN SERVICES, Complaint, read the caption, and it was the draft of an official form that John had filled out, in his handwriting. In the box for Complainant, John had written, *John Foxman, Esq., as Guardian for William R. Foxman,* and under Respondent, John had written, *Michael Shanahan, Supervisor, Poplar House, Glenn Meade, Devon, Pennsylvania.*

"Judy, did you know that John was complaining about Mike Shanahan to the state?"

"Really?" Judy asked, rising.

"Look." Mary scanned the form. In the block where the description of the complaint was supposed to be supplied, John had written in light pencil:

I am filing the complaint regarding ~~negligent treatment of~~ my brother, who has cerebral palsy and is a longtime resident of Glenn Meade. I am reporting negligence and neglect by Michael Shanahan, supervisor of Poplar House. It takes a caretaker about half an hour to feed my brother, because he has tongue thrust and that makes it difficult for him to swallow, ~~which~~

306

is typical of many adults and children with cerebral palsy. Mr. Shanahan is a new supervisor at my brother's group home and in the past two weeks, he has been complaining to me that my brother is "taking too long at mealtimes" and this is "throwing off" the schedule ~~of the house~~. Mr. Shanahan has suggested to me that my brother be put on a feeding tube, but this is ~~absolutely ridiculous. It is~~ not for my brother's welfare, but for the convenience of Mr. Shanahan. My brother opposes this, and his consent is necessary, and so is mine. None of this was a problem before Mr. Shanahan became supervisor. ~~Because~~ Mr. Shanahan and I have not been able to resolve this informally, so I am

Mary looked over at Judy. "Did you know about this?"

"Only generally. He told me that he had issues with Shanahan, but not the details. I didn't know he was going to file a complaint."

"Do you think Shanahan knew John was going to file a complaint?"

"I doubt it." Judy frowned. "If John didn't tell me, I doubt he would tell Shanahan."

"What effect would this complaint have, do you know? Could it get Shanahan fired?"

"I don't know. You know disability law better than I do." Judy met Mary's eye, as a realization dawned on her. "What, are you thinking that Shanahan had something to do with John's death?"

"It's possible, isn't it?"

Judy recoiled. "That would be an extreme reaction, don't you think?"

"Maybe," Mary said, reconsidering. "but I don't know Shanahan at all. Do you?"

"No."

Mary shrugged. "Maybe we need to learn more about him. I would feel better if I ran it down, wouldn't you?"

"You know, this suggests that John and Shanahan had been talking about it. Some of the talks could have been face-to-face and maybe some would be in email."

"So there should be some emails between the two of them. We should be able to recover John's emails, even though we don't have his laptop or his phone. If he used his work email, we could get them off the firm server. Did he have personal email as well?"

"Yes, Gmail. JGFoxman@gmail."

Mary felt stumped. "It takes a subpoena to access somebody else's Gmail, and they're not easy to get."

"John might have made copies of the emails. That would be like him." Judy

308

started looking around the desk. "Knowing him, there's a William file here, somewhere. I know he had the records for William, like birth certificate and the trust document."

"Here's the hard question — do you think that John told William that he was going to file a complaint about Shanahan's treatment? Because if John did that, that could even mean that William was in jeopardy."

"I don't know for sure." Judy frowned, concerned.

"Take a guess. You knew them both."

"I'm sure that they would've talked about the problem with the eating and swallowing, but I don't know if John would've told William he was filing a complaint. On the other hand, he could have. John always wanted William to know that he was looking out for him. They were close."

"So you'll have to ask William."

"Right. I'll do it when I see him. It's easier than over the phone." Judy grimaced. "This worries me."

"Me, too." Mary's gaze fell on the file cabinet. "Okay, let's get on it. I'll search the cabinet and you search the desk."

"Okay," Judy said, starting to dig.

CHAPTER TWENTY-SIX

It wasn't until two o'clock in the morning that Mary finally slipped into bed, having stayed up to decompress with Judy in the guest bedroom, flopping around with her gaseous golden retriever, talking about John, William, and theories of the murder. They had searched John's file cabinet in his apartment, but they hadn't been able to find a William file or emails from John to Mike Shanahan, so they'd resolved to look at the office at work tomorrow. Mary had emailed Lou to run a background check on Shanahan and see if he could turn up anything interesting about him. She wasn't about to leave any stone unturned.

Mary pulled the sheet up to her chin carefully, so as not to wake Anthony, whose back was to her. Oddly, she didn't feel as tired as she had last night or most of the pregnancy. Her brain crackled with activity, and she breathed deeply, trying to settle down because she knew she had to get up early. She had to review the *London Technologies* file so she could prepare to defend the deposition. She didn't mind flying by the seat of her pants, but she didn't even know the name of the deponent, which would be an all-time career low.

"Mary, do you really think I'm asleep?" Anthony asked quietly, his tone unmistakably unhappy.

"Oh sorry, yes, I thought you would be. We tried to be quiet."

"You didn't wake me, I've just been awake, wondering when you were coming home." Anthony turned over on his side, facing her, and Mary could see the silhouette of his head and shoulder in the light flowing through the curtains.

"Well, I mean it was a long night, I spoke with you before Judy and I went to see William —"

"I know but —"

"— and I spoke with you saying we were going to my parents, and I texted you saying we were going to the crime scene —"

"My point isn't that you didn't tell me where you're going. My point is that I don't know what you're doing." Anthony's tone sounded bewildered and slightly critical, in the darkness.

"There's a lot going on, we're trying to figure out who killed John, make sure Judy doesn't get charged, deal with Machiavelli and —"

"Babe, you're not understanding me. You went to the doctor yesterday, you are having issues. She told you to take it easy. Did you forget you're pregnant?"

"Of course not," Mary shot back, becoming irritated. "How can I possibly forget I am pregnant? The fact that I'm pregnant is every single waking second of my life. I smell weird things, I feel nauseated, I throw up. Don't tell me that I forget I'm pregnant."

"You're not acting like you're pregnant. You're not doing what the doctor said. You're running around as if you're not pregnant at all."

"No I'm not," Mary started to say, angrily, but then she realized that Anthony might be right. "You know, I stand corrected. Today might be the first day that I really didn't think about my pregnancy first, above everything. I didn't feel my symptoms as much. I was hardly nauseated. I just didn't think about it for once."

"I know, and that's what's bothering me."

"Is it bothering you?" Mary asked, more sharply than she had expected. Suddenly it occurred to her, with a flash of insight, what was going on. "You know, as soon as I learned I was pregnant, I changed everything. I thought about the baby first, all the time. I ate differently, I made sure I was hydrated, I ate yogurt to build the baby's bones, and I don't drink anything but decaf. I don't even have a Diet Coke. I've changed everything because I'm carrying a baby."

"Since when do you have a problem with that?"

"I didn't think I did, but maybe I do." Mary heard the words coming out of her mouth, surprising even herself. "Because I can tell you that today I felt terrific. I didn't think about the baby first today. I thought about John, who was brutally murdered by some thug or God knows who. I thought about William, his brother who has cerebral palsy, who was devastated that he lost his brother, leaving him alone in the world. I thought —"

"Honey, where is this coming from?"

"— about Judy, who thought she was going to get married, but now has lost John and all of her dreams. And I even thought about litigation, *London Technologies,* a client who came to us to save their business and is wondering if we're a cabal of murderesses, like *witches.* I have to defend a deposition tomorrow, and you know what, I feel good about that. I like the idea of being a lawyer again. I like putting a client's interests ahead of my own and fighting for them —"

"Okay, but I think you're overreacting —"

"— so excuse me, if just for one single day in seven months, I didn't think about the baby first. I thought about *me*. And for the first time in a long time, I felt like *myself*." Mary stopped talking abruptly, having realized how strongly she felt. Now that the words were out of her mouth, she wasn't about to disown them.

"So, babe, what are you saying?"

"I was pretty clear, don't you think? I said a lot of things." Mary tried to suppress a flicker of irritability. "I have a lot on my mind and there's a lot going on, and I really don't need to come home and have you tell me that I'm a bad mother, when I'm not even a mother yet."

"Wow. Seriously?"

"Yes, seriously." Mary let herself reply angrily, which was something she ordinarily didn't do. She couldn't remember the last time she felt this cranky, not at Anthony. They hardly ever fought, truly. But she'd never been through anything like this before.

"You sound like you resent the fact that

you're pregnant."

"No I don't," Mary replied, reflexively. "Or maybe I do. I didn't think I did, but I do when you tell me that I'm a bad person for doing what I need to do for myself and for everyone around me."

"But not for the baby, honey. You're not doing what's best for the baby."

"Yes I am!" Mary said, taken aback. "The doctor didn't say I had to sit still all day long and stare out the window. And besides, what am I supposed to do? Anthony, you tell me. Did you *see* Machiavelli on TV today? He called me a *murderer.* He's telling the world that I killed John. I have clients calling me about it and I didn't have a spare second to return one of those calls. I'm avoiding my email because it will be more of the same. So you tell me, what would the doctor say I'm supposed to do, a pregnant person accused of a colleague's murder? Maligned in public, freaking out my parents? Really, these are extraordinary circumstances."

Anthony sighed slowly, his breath shuddering from his lips, and Mary could even feel it on her face. Her nasal superpowers told her that he had his favorite late-night snack, a glass of red wine, roasted peppers, and black olives. Somehow the image of

Anthony eating his snack by himself softened Mary's heart.

"Look, Anthony, I'm sorry. I didn't mean to pop off."

"Babe, I'm sorry too. I wasn't trying to criticize you."

"But you did."

"No, I didn't."

Mary knew she should let it go, but she couldn't. "You told me I'm running around too much."

"But you are," Anthony shot back, without hesitation. Or rancor. "It's just the truth. I have to be able to tell you the truth."

Mary considered it. "You're right, you do. But I have to be able to tell you the truth too, and I think I just laid a truth bomb on you."

"You sure did." Anthony chuckled slightly, and Mary's anger began to ebb away.

"Maybe I just feel like I need more breathing room now. We're obviously in a crisis at work."

"O-kay," Anthony said slowly. "But you're also in a crisis here. Not with me, but with your home life. With the baby."

"I would never do anything to hurt the baby, you know that."

"But I'm worried what you're doing could hurt the baby, or you."

"And if I don't do it, it hurts me." Mary felt as if she were thinking clearly for the first time in seven months. "I'm doing everything I said. I cut back my cases. I'm going to stay home when the baby comes. But I just can't ignore what's happening around me. John, Judy, now William. Machiavelli. *London Technologies.*"

"So what do you do? What do we do?"

"Trust me to sort it out and handle it the way I see fit." Mary thought hard, trying to wrestle with it in her own mind. "You don't know what it's like to be pregnant. It's really, in some ways, strange. My body is doing things I never thought it could do, it's completely out of my control. It's hijacked, in a way."

"Hijacked?"

"Honestly, yes. I don't own my own body anymore. It's obeying its own rules and rhythms. The baby's calling the tune."

Anthony groaned. "That's a negative view, honey."

"Well, it's true," Mary told him, torn. "And I'm not negative about the pregnancy, not really. I'm excited about it, but these other things are also true, so it's a mixed bag. And just now, with so much happening, I have to be able to deal. I want to come home and not get grief."

"You're not getting grief, you're getting truth."

"I'm getting both," Mary said, though she knew that he was partly right. But so was she, which might have been why marriage wasn't easy.

"All right," Anthony said, his tone newly final. "I won't give you grief or truth anymore. I'll let you do what you're doing, your own way."

"Thank you."

"But I want you to remember what I'm telling you tonight. Because you aren't who you used to be. You're pregnant now, and anything can happen."

"Nothing is going to happen."

"Mary, you were rushed to the doctor yesterday —"

"I wasn't *rushed.*"

"Honey, come on."

"I wasn't *rushed,*" Mary repeated. "I was sitting in a meeting and I had to leave the meeting."

"All I'm saying is, you don't want anything to happen to the baby and neither do I. Because that would be unthinkable, and you would never forgive yourself."

"Nothing is going to happen to the baby." Mary felt nervous even saying so, as if she were jinxing something. Herself. Her pregnancy. Maybe even the baby.

"Okay, good night." Anthony leaned over, kissed her quickly, and lay back down, throwing an arm over her. "Love you."

"Love you, too." Mary looked at the ceiling, knowing she'd never get to sleep.

Chapter Twenty-Seven

Mary and Judy stepped off the elevator the next morning, ready for the day, or as ready as they would ever be. Mary hadn't been able to sleep after the conversation with Anthony, then had finally given up and read through the *London Technologies* file, so she was prepared to defend the deposition, at one o'clock. Judy hadn't been able to sleep either, so she had been up early, too, calling funeral homes to arrange a memorial service for John.

"Mary, Judy, hurry!" Marshall called from the reception desk, with a frown. "I was just about to text you guys."

"What's up?" Mary hurried/waddled to the desk, and Marshall leaned over, keeping her voice low.

"Jim and Sanjay from *London Technologies* are in the conference room."

"Why?" Mary asked, taken aback.

"I don't know, but everybody just went in.

You'd better go." Marshall handed Mary and Judy thick packets of phone messages. "Also these are for you, mostly the press but some clients. They say they've been trying to reach you but they haven't been able to."

"Thanks." Mary and Judy took the messages, then Mary said, "Marshall, I need you to do something. I want you to go through John's email on the firm server and search under the name Michael Shanahan, a supervisor at Glenn Meade, the group home where his brother William lives. Print all of them for me. I'm looking for anything about Shanahan's care of William or a complaint about William's care that John was intending to file with the DHS."

"Okay." Marshall made a note.

"And look through his desk and file cabinets, too. We need to know what the cops took, if anything. I'm looking for a file of his personal papers, like anything relating to his guardianship of William."

"I got it."

"Where's Lou?"

"He came in but he went out again. He said to tell you he's on it."

"Thanks." Mary and Judy took off, hustled down the hallway, and reached the conference room, where Bennie and Anne looked up, smiling in a professional way.

"Mary, Judy, perfect timing!" Bennie said lightly, from the head of the table.

Anne gestured at the clients. "Hi, please, meet Jim and Sanjay."

Mary and Judy shook hands as Anne introduced the two men taking their seats. Jim was a tall, lanky forty-year-old, with hipster glasses, a scruffy haircut, and an unstructured black jacket and jeans. Sanjay was in the same cool-guy outfit, but handsome, with thick dark hair and melting brown eyes, generally crushworthy if Mary had been in the mood, which she wasn't.

Mary flashed them a smile meant to inspire confidence, which was her job. Unfortunately, she could see the men alternately staring at her belly or trying not to stare at her belly, even though she had worn a navy blazer over her maternity dress. There were a lot of things they didn't teach in law school, and lawyering while pregnant was one of them. Most male clients wouldn't generally feel protected by a lawyer whose belly had a mind of its own.

Bennie sipped coffee from her I CAN SMELL FEAR mug, speaking to the client side of the table. "Gentlemen, I'm so glad you came in this morning. This gives you a chance to meet your new team, after the tragedy of John Foxman's murder." Her expression fell into grave lines, and Mary knew that much of her feelings were genuine. "We are devastated, as I know you must be."

"Absolutely," Jim said, frowning. "You have our sympathies. It's a terrible tragedy. I spoke to him on the phone last week."

"Yes, deepest sympathies." Sanjay nodded.

"Thank you." Bennie straightened at the head of the conference table. "However, we know that the show must go on. As I emailed you, we briefly considered postponing Steve's deposition a day or two, but the defendants refused, and we chose not to go to the judge. Mary and Judy have stepped in to take John's place, so we have a full-court press on this litigation. Anne has briefed them both, and Mary's fully prepared to defend Steve's deposition today. We have a discovery schedule to follow and we intend to keep the defendant's feet to the fire."

Suddenly Mary's cell phone started ringing, and she hurried to silence it, slipping it from her purse. She glanced at the screen and recognized the number of the caller with a nervous jolt. It was the Homicide

Division and it had to be Detective Kra-koff.

"We agree." Jim frowned, his hand playing with the label around his water bottle. "And please don't think we're jerks. We know it had to be challenging to work this weekend, especially for you, Anne. You and John worked together really well on this case."

"Thank you," Anne said quietly, though Mary's thoughts strayed far from the conference room. She was thinking about Detective Krakoff and she guessed that he wanted Judy to come in to give blood, DNA, and hair samples. Mary knew that the samples would ultimately support Judy's story, but it was never good when detectives wanted more evidence, suggesting that Judy was morphing into a person of interest, if not a suspect.

"But here's the problem." Jim broke eye-contact, still playing with the label. "We saw on the news that you three were under suspicion of John's murder —"

"No, that's not true at all," Bennie interrupted, firmly. "We are not suspected of John's murder. We are not even persons of interest."

Mary kept her mouth shut, though she felt like a total fraud, listening to Bennie state that they were not persons of interest, given that she had just gotten a phone call from Detective Krakoff. But she kept her mouth shut, since she couldn't be exactly sure that's what the detective wanted. Even so, it felt like a material omission at best, and at worst, a venial sin.

Jim continued, "Bennie, that's not what it said on the news. I was home when that lawyer was interviewed yesterday. My wife saw it, and then we went online and saw the video of John at the press conference. There's a lot we didn't know, a lot that has been going on behind the scenes at the firm."

Mary knew Jim was talking about Machiavelli, which made her furious. Machiavelli was the one who had set these awful events in motion, by filing a revenge lawsuit, and it had dove-tailed with the circumstances of John's murder to point an accusatory finger at Judy. Meanwhile, Anne went white behind her perfect makeup, and Judy stared at her hands.

Jim continued, "Bennie, I'm not gonna lie, I got calls last night from our employees and friends, and so did Sanjay." Jim glanced at Sanjay, who nodded in unhappy agreement. "We came today to meet with you face-to-face. We are very concerned and we never thought we would be in this position.

What's going on here? And what effect will it have on this litigation?" Jim gestured to his phone, lying faceup on the table. "People are already tweeting about it. The story is all over the tech sector in Philly, maybe nationally. It puts us in an impossible position. We're going to be real with you — we're considering ending the representation."

Bennie raised a calming hand. "Gentlemen, we hope you won't do that, and there is no reason to. There is nothing to worry about and it won't have any effect on this litigation. You're tech entrepreneurs, and nobody knows better than you that social media and the Internet are rife with inaccuracies. Your colleagues in the tech sector know that, too. Nobody will believe the ranting of a random lawyer who gave that interview. His name is Nick Machiavelli and he lost to us in past cases, so he's seizing upon this tragedy to smear us. As I say, we are absolutely not suspects."

Mary kept a poker face, though she had never felt so uncomfortable. Her thoughts started to churn, figuring out her next move. She hadn't heard back from Lou about the background check on Mike Shanahan because it was too early. But she still had a move or two if she had to take Judy down to the Roundhouse to give samples.

Jim pursed his lips, still frowning. "But we saw you, you've been to the Roundhouse. All three of you. We saw Mary and Judy on TV."

"Yes, of course we've been there. We care very much about John. We met with the police several times to press them to find his killer and help their investigation in any way that we can." Bennie spoke urgently, leaning forward. "They have no suspects at the present time, they don't even have a person of interest. Confidentially, we believe the murderer was a burglar, who came in through the fire escape at John's apartment."

Mary breathed easier, knowing that Bennie was on solid ground about the burglar, and she hadn't had a chance to tell Bennie her theory about Mike Shanahan.

Jim frowned. "But we read the press release that you put out, online. It doesn't even deny that you did it."

"No it doesn't, because we chose not to dignify these comments with a response."

Jim glanced at Sanjay. "That seems ineffective, don't you think? Sanjay and I would've put out a strong denial if somebody had said that about *us*. I mean, you're being accused of murder and you're lawyers? What are we supposed to think when you don't even deny it? We thought you were suspects."

Mary felt the visceral force of the argument. Every instinct in her told her that they should've responded, and she felt angry at herself that she had let herself get talked out of it by the Zen Master. It might have backed the detectives down preemptively and now Mary wouldn't feel comfortable stating it in a press release, especially if Detective Krakoff was going to ask Judy for samples.

"It's just a style difference," Bennie answered lightly. "You have read that President Richard Nixon stated, 'I am not a crook.' It went down in history as a statement that everybody remembered, because to deny something so absurd gives it credibility that it would otherwise not have." Bennie allowed herself a tight smile. "So we're glad you came in and we appreciate your honesty. We understand that you feel that you may be in a difficult position, but you are not." Bennie's tone strengthened, with a new firmness. "The best course is to ignore mindless chatter, as we will. If you need a denial from us, then here — 'We did not kill John Foxman.' But you will not hear me say so in public, and frankly, I will never say that again. I find it personally offensive and I know my partners feel the same way."

Jim blinked. "We didn't mean to offend you."

"Understood." Bennie eased back into her chair. "Now, gentlemen. We are more than prepared to go forward and prosecute this litigation. We are prepared to go forward and win. If you would like us to remain your counsel, we will happily do so. If you would like to retain other counsel, we will send them your file. It's your choice."

Mary swallowed hard, realizing once again that Bennie was a fearless leader. Maybe Mary would feel the same way someday, but until then, she'd have to settle for being a fearful leader.

Jim exchanged glances with Sanjay, who nodded. "Bennie, we think the firm has done an excellent job so far. We're going to stick with you."

"Thank you so much." Bennie smiled, still tightly. "An excellent decision with which to start the day."

Anne grinned, her relief obvious. "I'm so glad, guys. I promise we will get through this together. We are in the right in this lawsuit, and I know that we can prove it. We're stronger than ever before. All of us are completely on board and ready to fight for you."

"I agree," Mary joined in, because they needed to hear it from her, too. "You should have absolute confidence, going forward."

Judy nodded. "You have our full attention, and we're devoting ourselves to this case. It's what John would've wanted. His funeral service is tomorrow, by the way. I made the arrangements."

"Well done, Carrier," Bennie said, and just then, Mary noticed her phone screen light up with a text alert. It was from Lou and read:

Check your email. I got something on Shanahan.

CHAPTER TWENTY-EIGHT

Mary and Judy made it through the gauntlet of press outside the Roundhouse, rode upstairs in the grimy elevator, and got out in the lobby, where Mary put a steadying arm on her best friend's shoulder. "The key thing is, don't worry."

"How can I not?" Judy grimaced.

"Because you're innocent and you're in excellent hands." Mary flashed her a smile that was intended to be reassuring, though it took effort. "Detective Krakoff said you could go to the lab directly. Just give them your samples and obviously don't say anything."

"Of course not."

"I'll come get you when I'm finished. I won't be long. Don't go back into the squad room on any account." Mary gave her a brief hug. "See you in about twenty minutes."

"Bye." Judy rallied, turning away and

striding down the hall toward the lab, and Mary went down the hall in the opposite direction, getting buzzed into a bustling squad room full of detectives. She was shown to Detective Krakoff, who took her into an interview room, where they could talk privately.

"So is Ms. Carrier giving her samples?" he asked, sitting down.

"Yes." Mary sat opposite him, her phone in her lap, and she didn't hide her contempt for what happened the last time. "That was quite a stunt you pulled with the engagement ring."

"It was no stunt."

"Yes, it was, and it was unprofessional." Mary met his eye directly. "I've worked my share of murder cases and I know detectives here. I don't know a single one who would've pulled crap like that."

"I got the answer I wanted." Detective Krakoff blinked, his expression impassive. "Ms. Carrier was the victim's girlfriend."

"That engagement ring doesn't prove that. You don't know who John bought it for, nor do you know if he was seeing any number of people. You don't even really know if it belonged to him. He could even have been holding it for someone, a friend of his who intended to propose to his girlfriend."

"That's highly unlikely." Detective Krakoff lifted a groomed eyebrow.

"But it's certainly possible, and you can't eliminate any of those possibilities, which is another term for reasonable doubt." Mary wanted to shift the conversation. "In any event, you said on the phone that Judy Carrier has become a person of interest."

"Yes, she has."

"Why?"

"For all the reasons I told you at the interview. She was the girlfriend, and they were fighting up to and including the time when the victim was killed."

"But she's not yet a suspect."

"No, a person of interest."

"Then why do you want the samples?"

"We're investigating. That's our job."

Mary let it go. "I advised her to give them because she has to legally, but they will be completely consistent with her innocence. In fact, we went to John's apartment last night and examined the scene."

"Oh?" Detective Krakoff look genuinely surprised, which was what Mary had hoped for.

"I have two theories about who killed John Foxman, which I'd like to share with you. The first was the one I mentioned to you, that a burglar entered through the fire escape. The window was unlocked, and the climb is easy enough. In fact it was your first thought, and sometimes the short answer is the easy one."

Detective Krakoff didn't say anything, but Mary didn't need him to. She had come here for a reason. The difference between a person of interest and a suspect was a critical one, and she still had a chance to give the police information that would challenge their initial assumptions and findings. She had a credible alternative in Mike Shanahan, but she also wanted to throw as much as possible on the wall to make Detective Krakoff suspect anybody other than Judy.

"But the second theory, and one I wanted to share with you, involves facts you may not know."

"Like what?" Detective Krakoff asked, skeptically.

"John Foxman was the guardian of his brother William, who has cerebral palsy and lives at a group home, Poplar House at Glenn Meade in Devon. The supervisor there is Michael Shanahan, and Shanahan has only been there for six months."

Detective Krakoff slipped his hand inside his breast pocket and pulled out a pen and his skinny notepad, flipping open the cover.

Mary spelled Shanahan for him, but she

was going to save the best for last. "John and Shanahan have had a contentious relationship over the past six months."

"How do you know that? Did the victim tell you or Judy Carrier that, prior?"

"We found some papers on his desk, a draft complaint." Mary dug in her purse, extracted a manila envelope, and handed it to Detective Krakoff. "Here are copies of the relevant documents, and you can look them over later."

"You took these from the scene?"

"Yes. It was released early, so why not?"

"Where were they?"

"On his desk in the office."

Detective Krakoff made a note. "How did you know they were there?"

"We didn't."

"How did you find them?"

"We looked." Mary didn't say, *by accident* because it didn't sound as good. "They support everything I'm telling you. Briefly put, it takes a long time to feed William because he has difficulty swallowing, and Shanahan wanted to put William on a feeding tube, which John felt was out of expedience rather than in William's best interest."

Detective Krakoff started taking notes, which encouraged Mary, so she continued.

"John intended to file a complaint with

the Department of Human Services regarding mistreatment of his brother by Shanahan. A copy of the draft is in the envelope. There's no doubt that the filing of such complaint and any subsequent investigation would've gotten Mr. Shanahan fired from his job at Glenn Meade. It might have even prevented him from getting a job elsewhere."

"So you're accusing Shanahan of murder?" Detective Krakoff looked up.

"I'm trying to cooperate with you in your investigation. I think these facts are very concerning, and they provide a motive for Shanahan killing John. I think that John may have told Shanahan that he intended to file a complaint, and Shanahan may have come to John on Saturday to discuss it. John would have let him in to talk, then there could have been a fight, and Shanahan was the one who killed him." Mary kept going because he was taking notes. "And I don't know if John discussed the fact that he was going to file a complaint with William, but if he did, then William could be in jeopardy or even danger. If Shanahan really is the killer, then he might go as far as killing William too, to silence him."

Detective Krakoff pursed his lips. "Have you met Shanahan?"

"Yes."

"Did you confront him with this?"

"No, it's new information to me. I'm asking you to follow up with him, as part of your investigation of John's murder."

"How do you know that the victim told Shanahan that he was going to file the complaint?"

"Because I know John. He was a prudent and fair-minded lawyer. He would have talked it out and tried to settle it with Shanahan before he filed. If he couldn't do that, then he would've told Shanahan he was going to file because that's what any good lawyer would do. I believe John told Shanahan and I bet if you asked Shanahan, he would not be completely surprised." Mary kept her purpose in mind. "Detective Krakoff, Shanahan is somebody that you need to be investigating. I know that you guys decide who you 'like' and who you don't, then confirmation bias sets in and before you know it, the wrong person has been suspected of murder, even charged. I will not stand by and let that happen to Judy Carrier, who is completely innocent."

"So you think Shanahan killed John to keep his job at a group home in the suburbs?" Detective Krakoff leaned backwards. "That's a stretch, don't you think?"

"I did at first, so I asked Lou Jacobs, a former cop and our firm's investigator, to do some legwork for me. Lou found out that Shanahan has a history of violence."

Detective Krakoff's dark eyes flared briefly open. "How so? A criminal record?"

"No, but Shanahan has had three protection from abuse, or PFA, applications filed against him by his now ex-wife, named Jody Shanahan. She alleges that he assaulted her and has anger-management issues. These three incidents took place within the past two years, though she filed for divorce six months ago, which is approximately when Shanahan took the job at Glenn Meade." Mary gestured at the envelope. "A copy of the court docket is included in the packet I just gave you."

"So was he charged?" Detective Krakoff set the notebook aside and opened the manila envelope.

"No, because his ex-wife dropped the application after she filed it, each time. That's why Glenn Meade didn't pick it up on a reference check before he was hired. We ran a basic computer background check, and he has no criminal record, so you may not have his fingerprints on file or in any database." As Mary spoke, Detective Krakoff took the papers out of the envelope and started reading, so she kept going. "I strongly suggest that you investigate Shanahan and get some samples from him. It may very well be his fingerprints and other trace evidence that you find on the base of that lamp. Because I know it will not be Judy Carrier's. And you'll know that too, as soon as the lab analyzes the samples they're taking now."

Detective Krakoff turned to the docket sheets that Lou had printed off the computer. They hadn't been hard to find, since court records were searchable by party.

Mary picked up her bag. "Detective Krakoff, the only thing I ask is that you give me prior notice before you go visit Shanahan."

Detective Krakoff looked up sharply. "I don't notify defense counsel of the steps I take in an investigation."

"I'm asking out of concern for the safety of John's brother, William."

"The reason doesn't matter. It's not procedure."

"Please, reconsider, for William's sake." Mary spoke from the heart, still raw at the memory of William's sweetness, as well as his pain. "I'm assuming that Glenn Meade doesn't know about these allegations against Shanahan or they wouldn't have hired him. Shanahan will probably lose his job when this comes to light, whether from you or me. Now that I know that Shanahan may be violent, I'm concerned that he may retaliate against William for my coming to you, even if he hadn't been told before about the complaint, by John. Either way, I don't want William in harm's way because we're about to expose Shanahan."

"I still don't see the need to notify you." Detective Krakoff's attention returned to the papers.

"But you wouldn't have this information if I hadn't given it to you. I came in a spirit of cooperation, hoping we could coordinate our approach and —"

"How many ways do I have to say it? Police business is confidential."

"But, obviously, I won't reveal anything. I'm worried about William's safety."

"I'm not informing you of what I do."

"But he's an innocent person, whose brother was just murdered. He's alone in the world. Vulnerable."

"Not my problem," Detective Krakoff said without looking up.

"You know, I wanted to give you a second chance after that stunt you pulled with the ring. I was hoping you could be trusted." Mary rose to go. "But since you can't, let me give it to you straight. If anything happens to William because you talked to

Shanahan without telling me, then I will hold you personally responsible and sue you *blind.*"

Detective Krakoff snorted. "You don't scare me, Mary."

"That's because you see what I look like, not what I can *do.* I may have a bellyful of baby, but I'm one of the best lawyers in the city." Mary crossed to the door. "And if William gets hurt, you're going to find out what I'm capable of. It will cost you your house, your car, your pension, and every last penny you have."

"And how is that exactly?" Detective Krakoff looked up, his expression amused.

"I just recorded everything you said." Mary showed him her phone. "Imagine how callous and awful you'll sound to a jury, or judge, or even your boss, if something happens to William."

Detective Krakoff fell quiet.

And Mary turned away, smiling.

Ten minutes later, Mary and Judy were hurrying to the glass exit doors of the Roundhouse, bracing themselves for the throng of media. The story of the triple homicide in the Northeast had blown up, with one suspect in custody and a citywide manhunt for another under way, and the Police Commissioner had been giving periodic updates from a makeshift lectern in front of the entrance, which was Philly's idea of a classy press conference.

Mary and Judy hustled out of the building and past the reporters, keeping their faces down to avoid being recognized. They stepped off the curb behind the empty lectern, and just then Mary heard a female reporter shout, "Hey, Mary DiNunzio! Judy Carrier! Why are you back? You're suspects in the murder of John Foxman, aren't you? Where's Bennie Rosato? Any comment? Any comment?"

The other reporters joined in, calling out questions. "Any comment, Mary?" "Are you suspects in the Foxman murder?" "What's going on?" "Give us a comment!"

"No comment!" Mary hurried away as fast as she could, and Judy bolted ahead of her toward the street, breaking into a jog and flagging down a cab at the parking lot entrance. The cab lurched to a stop, and Judy opened the door, climbing in and sliding aside for Mary, who waddled like a duck on steroids.

"Mary, when are you going to make a statement?" shouted the same female reporter, dogging her steps. "What about Judy and Bennie? Are you going to confess? Are you trying to get a deal? What's going on with the Foxman murder?"

Other reporters called out, "Any comment, Mary?" "Are both of you suspects?" "Come on, just one comment!"

Mary glanced back to see the female reporter who had started the questioning, startled to recognize her as the scruffy woman with the gelled spiky hair, who had been at the press conference.

"Come on, Mary!" "How about a comment? Just one comment?"

"No comment!" Mary ducked into the cab, raised her phone quickly, and snapped a picture as they took off.

CHAPTER TWENTY-NINE

Mary and Judy got off the elevator, passed the Rosato & DiNunzio sign, and hustled down the hallway toward their offices, surprised to find Bennie, Anne, and Lou talking with Roger in front of the conference room.

"Hi, Roger," Mary and Judy said, in unison.

"Hello. Sorry to have missed you both." Roger hoisted a trim leather messenger bag onto his shoulder. "How are you?"

"We've been better," Mary answered, since Judy had been subdued in the cab, nervous that she had given the samples and obsessing over her fingerpads, which now bore telltale black ink from the fingerprinting process.

"I'm officially a person of interest," Judy answered quietly.

"But I told Detective Krakoff about Shanahan," Mary interjected quickly, trying to buck up Judy's sagging spirits. "Meanwhile, what's going on here? Is something the matter?"

"Yes, Machiavelli's upping the ante." Bennie frowned. "Roger got a letter from our case investigator at the Pennsylvania Human Relations Commission. They want to interview the three of us as soon as possible."

"So soon?" Mary didn't get it. "We didn't even answer the Complaint yet."

"Machiavelli's been lobbying them. He's accused them of dragging their feet in the investigation. He just sent them a letter to that effect, copying Roger."

"Are you kidding?" Mary asked, astounded. "It's been, like, two days! This is ridiculous!"

"I know, and of course he's pushing the fact that John has been murdered. He even suggested to the Human Relations Commission that they coordinate their investigation with the police, given that 'we may be suspects' in his murder." Bennie made air quotes. "He claims that John's statement in the Complaint could be proof that we had a motive to kill John, so he wouldn't testify against us."

"Geez, he stops at nothing!" Mary gritted her teeth. "He has no decency whatsoever!"

"They want to interview us separately and they want the first interview on Wednesday. DiNunzio, why don't you take it? I'm on trial, and Judy needs some time. That's only one day after John's memorial service."

"I'll go, I want to. I'll give them an earful!"

Roger put up his hand like a traffic cop. "There's no reason to get bent out of shape."

"I've been bent out of shape for seven months," Mary shot back. "And you don't know Machiavelli like I do. This is just the kind of stuff he does. He presses forward on all fronts. He never lets up. He's seriously demented. He's got no family, no friends. He never married or had kids. His job, his firm, his *ego,* is all he's about and he hates to lose."

"I understand," Roger said, calmly. "I know how to deal with him."

"Oh really?" Mary tried to check her tone, but she felt angry. "Did Bennie tell you that we almost got fired this morning because our denial wasn't strong enough in the press release?"

Roger blinked, his mouth a grim line. "Yes, and we've discussed that. Allow me to remind you that we agreed that I will conduct this litigation as I see fit."

"Yes, we did, but I know more about Machiavelli than anybody here and you don't seem to be listening to me."

"I am, but I'm staying the course. I have reminded Bennie of her agreement to let me do so. I would ask you to do the same." Roger hesitated. "Mary, I understand your emotion, but it's misdirected. You're not angry at me, you're angry at Machiavelli."

"I'm angry at you both," Mary said, though she wondered if Roger were right. "We're getting whipsawed, don't you see that? Machiavelli will use John's murder against us in the reverse-discrimination case, and I bet if he has his way, the police will use the reverse-discrimination case in the murder case, maybe even against Judy."

Roger shook his head. "You're getting carried away. The police think Judy's motive is a lover's quarrel."

"Two motives are better than one, and they were fighting about the reverse-discrimination complaint." Mary glanced over at Judy, who looked upset, so she let it go. "Look, Machiavelli will go lower than you can ever think. You guys have been working on the reverse-discrimination complaint, haven't you? Have you seen any connection between the three plaintiffs and Machiavelli?"

"None," Roger answered, patiently.

"We tried," Bennie chimed in, her expression resigned. "Machiavelli is their lawyer, but as far as we can tell, that's the only connection. The three plaintiffs never worked for him or never met him."

Mary wasn't buying it. "I *know* he's behind it. I *know* he manufactured that lawsuit."

Bennie waved her off. "Let it go, DiNunzio. We don't need it anyway. We have our hands full."

Roger nodded. "More than full."

Mary couldn't let it go. "I want to see those resumes, and any of the documents on the reverse-discrimination case. Will you email them to me? I just can't believe there's no connection. Machiavelli will stop at nothing, *nothing.* Let me give you another example." Mary slipped her hand in her pocket and showed them her phone, with its photo of the reporter. "Do you recognize this woman with the spiky hair? She was at our press conference here. Just now, she was also outside of the Roundhouse, asking us questions. She said she was a freelancer, does anybody remember?"

Bennie leaned over, squinting at the phone. "I do."

Anne nodded. "She's the one. That's

definitely her."

Mary felt validated, which only made her angrier. "That's what I thought, and you know what else? I bet she's not an independent freelancer. I bet that Machiavelli hired her."

"You think so?" Bennie asked, skeptical. "You think she's a proxy, too? And the plaintiffs?"

Roger smiled slightly. "Mary, that does seem somewhat paranoid."

"No it isn't." Mary had been thinking it over in the cab. "It's too coincidental that she's everywhere we go. Her questions aren't typical reporter questions, they're shouted accusations."

"Really?" Bennie cocked her head.

"Yes, think about it. We know he uses the press. He gets himself on camera. She's just a proxy for him, and there's probably others." Mary showed Lou the picture. "Lou, can you find out who this woman is? Do you have any way to do that?"

"Let me see, Mare." Lou took the phone from Mary's hands, squinting at the photo through his bifocals. "I could give it a shot. If she came to our press conference, she would have to sign in and show ID at the security desk."

"Unless she used a fake name, but please

check." Mary took her phone back. "And you know what else I want to know, Lou? How did she know that the police called us to the Roundhouse? Does Machiavelli have somebody leaking police information to him?"

Anne interjected, "If she freelances, she could have been there already. Maybe it's not about us."

Lou folded his arms. "I'll look into it, Mare. How did it go at the Roundhouse, about Shanahan?"

"Good, and thanks for the information. I suggested to Detective Krakoff that he look into Shanahan, and he agreed." Mary turned to Bennie and the others, filling them in on John's draft complaint with DHS and Shanahan's abusive history.

Bennie's blue eyes narrowed. "So you think this Shanahan is the killer? Not a burglar?"

"I think it's certainly possible, and we're concerned that William could be in jeopardy, if John told him that he was going to file a complaint against Shanahan."

"That would be risky for Shanahan," Bennie said, dubious.

"I agree, but we don't want to take any chances. William is more vulnerable now than ever, alone and without a legal guardian. If Shanahan wanted to hurt William, now would be the time. Shanahan might want to make the whole problem go away, with William. And if Shanahan wanted to press the feeding tube issue, he might try that now too."

"Agree." Judy nodded, worriedly. "I'm going to the group home to get William now. I want him with me before the police start investigating Shanahan, and the funeral's tomorrow anyway. I have to get him a suit and shoes, and I'm also going to call John's aunt and uncle, the Hodges, and talk about temporary guardianship, so Shanahan doesn't try to preempt me on the feeding tube. I wanted to apply for it myself, but I'd have to disclose that I'm under suspicion of John's murder, and no court will award me guardianship of William in those circumstances."

"Right." Bennie checked her watch. "Okay, I gotta get to work."

"So do I." Roger nodded. "Unless Mary would rather I stay?"

"No, thanks, Roger." Mary felt a guilty twinge. "Sorry I snapped, but I want to go on record as having new doubts that your way is going to work with Machiavelli."

"I hear you." Roger smiled, starting to go. "I'll keep an open mind if you will."

"It's a deal," Mary said, but she didn't mean it.

"Good-bye." Roger headed out, and after he was gone, Mary finally exhaled.

"Bennie, are you really going to stay with The Way of the Guru? It's not working. We're getting *handled* by Machiavelli."

"Let's stay the course. We gave Roger our word, and we have to stand by that." Bennie turned to Judy, placing a hand on her shoulder. "How are you holding up, Carrier?"

"For a person of interest, pretty good."

"So go get William, then. You've got me worried about him now."

CHAPTER THIRTY

Mary settled in at the deposition next to her client, Alex Chen, Director of Marketing at London Technologies. He was about her age and easily the most attractive deponent she'd ever defended, not that that mattered, since she didn't want to reverse-sexually harass. Alex was tall, well-built, and officially edgy in a leather motorcycle jacket, which he had on with skinny jeans and a crisp white tailored shirt, no tie. His hair was longish, with hip sideburns, and he had a dazzling smile, which was probably a job requirement in a marketing director.

The court reporter sat at his stenography machine, and opposing counsel, Marcus Benedict, sat across the table, an older preppy from Barret & Tottenham, one of the white-shoe firms that used to be completely populated by old preppies that had outlived their usefulness, like a legal appendix. Benedict still dressed in a three-piece suit and had horn-rimmed glasses, though not the ironic kind. His laptop sat open in front of him, but he had written his questions on a legal pad and was taking Chen through them in a methodical, chronological fashion, which worked for Mary. Her laptop was open and she was typing away, multitasking. Lou had told her that the female reporter was named Amanda Sussman, and Mary couldn't wait to start digging and see if Sussman was connected to Machiavelli.

"Mr. Chen, please state your name and place of birth for the record."

"Alexander Thomas Chen. New York, New York."

"And what is your date of birth?"

"July 3, 1991."

"And where did you attend college?"

"Penn State."

"Did you graduate?"

"Yes."

"When did you graduate?"

Mary tuned out through the endless preliminaries, went online, and typed "Amanda Sussman." A clean, modern website popped onto the page, with a posed picture that Mary recognized as the female reporter dogging her steps. In the web photo, Sussman looked more corporate than scruffy and was smiling in a stock-photo sort of way. She was probably in her early twenties, had short brown hair, and wore a light blue turtleneck that matched her eyes as well as the font color of her website.

"Mr. Chen, where were you first employed upon graduating from Penn State?"

"I worked at a startup called LockIn."

"And what was your position there?"

"I was an assistant in the marketing department."

Mary read the bio on Sussman's "About Amanda" page.

Amanda Sussman is a freelance writer who specializes in blogging, web content, and print content. She has a legal background and worked as a paralegal for two years. She also has a background in graphic design and has crafted webpages for companies in a variety of industries and she also blogs for B2C and B2B businesses. She can write anything, from features to brochureware, and she can help your company create promotional materials to help expand your customer base.

"Mr. Chen, now that we've been through your academic and employment history, we come to London Technologies. How long have you been marketing director at London Technologies?"

"Four years."

"And who held that position before you?"

"No one."

Benedict blinked behind his bifocals. "So is it fair to say you were the first marketing director?"

"Yes."

"And why is that?"

"I don't understand the question," Alex answered, and Mary glanced over, proud of him. She had prepared him for his deposition over sandwiches in her office, and he was sophisticated enough to know the basic drill, which was *answer only the question asked, don't volunteer,* and *if you don't understand the question, say so.*

"Mr. Chen, why was there no marketing director before you?"

"If you know," Mary interjected, which was her favorite interruption. It always served as a reminder to the witness to stick to the facts, and not be helpful or even show off, because the person on the other side of the table was an enemy.

"I don't know," Chen answered.

Mary returned her attention to the website, since she knew the deposition wouldn't be important until later. The website read:

Amanda's articles and pieces concern a variety of topics, including fast-breaking news stories, business and CEO profiles, and developments in law, real estate, personal finance, and retail in the Philadelphia area. Her specialty is helping people and businesses become major influencers in the Delaware Valley and beyond. Click here if you want to see her portfolio of articles.

Benedict consulted his notes. "What are your duties as marketing director for London Technologies?"

"To help market the company."

"Mr. Chen, can you elaborate?"

"Briefly, my job was to oversee our direct mail, and advertising to sell our data integration software to furniture retailers."

"Was one of your duties also to attend trade shows?"

"Yes."

"Where are they located?"

"They move around the country."

"How often are they held?"

"Three times a year."

Mary half-listened, knowing they were getting closer to why Chen had been called as a witness. In the meantime, she clicked to see the type of article Sussman wrote and skimmed the titles: "5 Common Pleas Court Judges You Need to Avoid, If Possible"; "The Biggest Mob Case You're Not Watching, or Joey Merlino Strikes Again"; "10 Restaurants Near Family Court That Are Cheaper Than Filing Costs"; and "Around the Roundhouse — An Insider's Guide to Philly's Police HQ." Mary made a mental note of the last one, but was wondering if there was a list of clients anywhere on the website.

"Now Mr. Chen, was one of your duties also to attend trade association conferences?"

"Yes."

"How many trade associations does London Technologies belong to?"

"Just one."

"And that is?"

"Home Furnishings Group, or HFG."

"How often do you attend those conferences?"

"Twice a year."

Mary noticed a link on the website for "Amanda's Clients," clicked, and skimmed the list which varied from restaurants, boutiques and bars, with corporate at the bottom. EDWARD BLACKEMORE & ASSOCI-

ATES, THE GUPTA GROUP, NATHAN & RAD-
DATZ, LLC. Mary recognized them as small
law firms, but there was no mention of Machiavelli. Then she realized if Machiavelli
had hired Sussman, he would've made it
confidential, so it probably wouldn't be on
the website. She felt momentarily stumped,
then got an idea.

"Mr. Chen, where are the conferences located?"

"The October conference moves around
the country, but the April conference is in
High Point, North Carolina."

Benedict turned a page of his notes. "Let's
discuss the first HFG conference you attended. Do you recall when that was?"

"Yes."

Listening, Mary felt proud of Chen again.
Anybody else would've supplied the more
complete answer, but he was proving to be
a professionally badass witness. Meanwhile,
she navigated to "Contact Amanda" on
Sussman's website and clicked. An email
form popped onto the screen, and Mary
typed:

Dear Amanda, It was great seeing you at
the Roundhouse today! Rosato & DiNunzio could use an enterprising freelancer
like you! Why don't you ditch Nick Ma-

chiavelli and come work for the good guys? Either way, we've got your number. Regards, Mary DiNunzio.

Mary added a CC to Machiavelli, then hit Send.

"Mr. Chen, when was the first HFG conference you attended?"

"In October, 2015."

"And where did it take place?"

"At Lake Harmony in the Poconos, at Harmony Spa & Conference Center."

"Did you attend alone?"

"No."

"With whom did you attend?"

"I went with Jim and Sanjay."

"And by Jim and Sanjay, do you mean the owners of London Technologies?"

"Yes."

"How long did the conference last?"

"Two days."

"Mr. Chen, did there come a time after a breakout session, when you spoke with Jeremy Dietl, president of Home Hacks, one of the defendants in this matter?"

"Yes."

"And how did that come about?"

"At the end of the breakout session, we ran into one another at the coffee station set up outside the main room."

"And did you have a conversation with Mr. Dietl at that time?"

Chen frowned. "It wasn't a conversation. It was a threat."

Mary smiled inwardly, but said nothing. She hadn't had to rehearse Chen for that line earlier, because he was dying to get it on the record. Dietl's statement was a critical proof of their case, showing that EXMS and Home Hacks intended to put London Technologies out of business.

"Was anyone else present for that, er, discussion?"

"No."

Benedict consulted his notes. "Before we go forward, how many people were at that breakout session, would you say?"

"If you know," Mary interjected, just to remind Chen that they were entering enemy territory.

"I happen to know it was about 120."

Benedict nodded, pursing his lips, which wrinkled deeply at the corners. "How is it that you came to be speaking alone with Mr. Dietl, in the crowd of 120 people? *If you know.*"

"I was looking for green tea and so was he. It wasn't on the regular coffee setup, only on the one that was out-of-the-way."

"How long was your conversation, er,

discussion with Mr. Dietl?"

"Approximately two minutes."

"And what was its substance?"

"You mean what was the threat he made to me?"

"Yes, your words."

Chen straightened in his chair. "Mr. Dietl said, and I quote, 'If you keep undercutting us in the subscription market, we'll disable the logins of any dealer who works with you. We'll cut you off at the knees.' "

Mary kept on her professional mask, though she was cheering inwardly. Chen's testimony had the absolute ring of truth, and he would be a great witness if the case ever went to trial.

Benedict's eyelids fluttered behind his bifocals. "Mr. Chen, do you remember that he said those words exactly?"

"Yes I do."

"How do you remember that, though it occurred so many years ago?"

"You never forget being threatened."

Benedict consulted his notes. "Why do you characterize that as a threat?"

"Because it is. Obviously."

Mary relaxed in her chair, since Chen was even more aggressive than she would've been, which was perfect.

"Mr. Chen, what did you mean by 'disable the logins'?'"

"I didn't say it, Dietl did."

"What did he mean by that? If you know."

"I know *exactly* what he meant by that, because it is what EXMS and Home Hacks started to do to dealers we were working with, the very next week. Dealers who had pushed their data to Home Hacks and EXMS were locked out of their *own information.*" Chen spoke faster, and the court reporter's fingers flew. "Suddenly, out of the blue, their logins had been disabled. They couldn't get into their own accounts. It was corporate bullying, designed to punish dealers who were contracting with London Technologies from competing in the data integration workplace."

Mary let Chen talk, because he was only revealing how strong he would be as a witness, which could help settlement. Meanwhile, she kept an eye on her email screen, though she hardly expected Amanda Sussman to write her back. In fact, if Amanda didn't answer Mary's email, it made it more likely that she was working for Machiavelli.

"Mr. Chen, how was it 'corporate bullying'?"

"EXMS and Home Hacks were both threatened by our business model because we were empowering dealers to keep, organize, and integrate their own data at one-sixth of the cost. EXMS and Home Hacks charged dealers who subscribe $300 a month, and we charge $65. We're cheaper, better, and fairer, and Home Hacks knew their days of price gouging were over. Gouging is corporate bullying."

Benedict cocked his head. "Are you saying that London Technologies was attempting to drive Home Hacks out of business?"

"Not at all."

Mary let them talk, though it was wasting time, which was the downside of a witness like Alex Chen, getting overzealous. If it didn't end soon, she'd have to intervene.

"Mr. Chen, how is it an antitrust violation when London Technologies is being driven out of business but not when Home Hacks is being driven out of business?"

"If Home Hacks hadn't been so grossly overcharging for its service, then it never would have had its business model jeopardized." Chen frowned, in derision. "Furthermore, we could never put Home Hacks out of business. Home Hacks and EXMS have the lion's share of the market, and we're minuscule in comparison. The only business who will be driven out of the market is London Technologies. That's why we brought this lawsuit and —"

Mary interjected, "Excuse me, I think you answered his question."

"Oh, right," Chen said, nodding.

Benedict kept asking follow-up questions, trying to shake Chen's testimony, but Chen stuck to his guns and there were no more speeches. Mary listened to him pound away at Benedict and gleefully imagined what her email to Amanda Sussman had set in motion. Sussman and Machiavelli were probably on the phone right now, and Machiavelli would probably fire Amanda, now that her cover had been blown.

Mary smiled, inwardly. It was a victory, but she knew it would be short-lived because Machiavelli wouldn't stop.

Unless she stopped him.

CHAPTER THIRTY-ONE

Mary sat at her desk, eyeing the papers in frustration. Alex Chen's deposition had ended an hour ago, but she had been in her office since then with the door closed, on a tear. On her desk in front of her, in three separate piles, were the resumes for the plaintiffs in the reverse-discrimination lawsuit against them, in addition to notes that John had taken during the interview and writing samples they had submitted. She had read everything, but kept coming up empty. She couldn't find any connection between the three plaintiffs and Machiavelli, which confirmed what Bennie and Roger had concluded. But she just couldn't let it go. She would've staked her life that the plaintiffs were proxies of Machiavelli and that he had manufactured the lawsuit. And her theory was that they must have worked for Machiavelli, either during their summers at law school or even as interns. But no dice.

Mary sipped some bottled water, trying to think what she could have missed. The waning sun streamed in the window behind her, its tarnished rays falling on the quilt that hung on her wall. Its pinks, blues, and pale greens were usually so soothing, but it was a wedding quilt with a pattern of interlocking rings, which reminded her uneasily of Anthony. He would probably have preferred her to be home, but she couldn't leave just yet. She had texted him that she would be late, needing the time to figure out what was going on with Machiavelli and how he was connected to the three plaintiffs.

Mary picked up Michael Battle's resume, skimming it for the umpteenth time. He worked in general litigation in the legal department at Wheels-up, a private jet sharing service in Wayne. He'd graduated with honors from Villanova Law School and F & M, having graduated magna cum laude. His prior work experience was in the summer associate program at Wolf Block, a large, respected firm in the city, having nothing to do with Machiavelli. Battle's personal interests were "hiking in Nepal," so she doubted he had ever encountered Machiavelli on a trip. Nor was there any other geographic connection, since Battle had grown up in upper Darby, a middle-class suburb of Philadelphia.

Mary set down the resume and picked up Graham Madden's. Madden worked in general litigation at Hamptons Holdings, LLC, a financial services company in Southampton, N.Y. He had gone to Harvard undergrad and Penn Law, where he was a Legal Writing Instructor. He had grown up in Hempstead, on Long Island, and worked summers at small firms in New York. Mary couldn't imagine Machiavelli having any entrée there. Madden's interest was "surfing in Montauk," so there was no connection to Machiavelli.

Mary sighed to herself, picking up the last resume, Steve McManus, the applicant John had interviewed. McManus wasn't from Philly, having grown up in Chicagoland, and had worked summers at Mayer Platt Brown, one of the best law firms in Chicago. His personal interest was robotics, and he worked in general litigation at AI-Intelligence, a robotics company in Cheltenham, with a headquarters in Oak Park. McManus graduated from Temple Law School with honors and the University of Michigan with a degree in engineering.

Mary set the papers down and eyed her laptop screen, but didn't bother to search online again. She had searched on Philly and Pennsylvania Bar Associations meetings, as well as Chicago and New York, trying to see if there were any board memberships in common, or even cocktail parties, CLE conferences, or other meetings, but nothing had panned out. She had taken a stab at geographical similarity, but there was none. Machiavelli lived in a townhouse in South Philly, Battle lived in an apartment in Wayne, Madden lived in Brooklyn, and McManus lived in an apartment in Cherry Hill.

Mary eyed the laptop screen as it went black, racking her brain. She had even looked on the applicants' social media, but there was no connection to Machiavelli, and she supposed that there could be a random way they could have met, like a train or a plane, but she had no way of knowing. And she had to admit to herself that she didn't know why the plaintiffs would agree to front for Machiavelli, unless he was paying them a fortune, but they didn't seem to need the money.

Her gaze fell on the notes that John had written during his interview of Steve McManus. John had taken about a paragraph's worth, handwritten on a legal pad, and it wrenched her chest to see his characteristically neat handwriting. He had noted "careful, logical thinker," "would impress clients," "ease with math and numbers, could be a plus on London Technologies," and "serious-minded." None of it gave Mary any clues as to how McManus could be connected to Machiavelli, and it made her sad all over again to think that John was gone.

Her office felt a shade darker and a bit cooler, and the sun had dropped behind the buildings. Her phone was lying up on her desk, and she pressed the screen to see that it was 6:13. Judy would be winding up her long, sad day, going to pick up William and buy him a suit for the funeral.

Mary felt her mood spiral downward, not only frustration at not being able to connect Machiavelli to the plaintiffs, but that so much was up in the air about John's murder. She feared that Judy was still under suspicion, even though the lead on Shanahan was a good one. She picked up the phone and speed-dialed Judy, who picked up after a moment. "Honey, how are you?"

"Hanging in," Judy answered, her tone cheery, so Mary guessed that William was within earshot.

"Did you get William?"

"Yes."

"Good. How's he doing?"

"He's sad, but he's okay."

"Did Shanahan say anything to you?"

"No."

"Have the police been out there?"

"No. Listen, I'm at the Loew's hotel. I realized I can't come back to your house with William."

"Why not?"

"Your steps are a problem with his wheelchair. Same with my apartment. I should've thought about it before. The hotel has handicap access and a bathroom he can use, too."

"Oh, right." Mary realized again that the world needed to do better to accommodate the handicapped. Progress was being made, but not nearly fast enough. "Do you want me to come help you?"

"No, and I stopped by your house and got the dog, too. The hotel is dog-friendly."

"How did you get into my house?"

"I have a key, remember? So we're going to check in and chill."

"Order room service," Mary said, trying to cheer her up, but she knew it was useless. "Isn't there anything left I can help you with? Did you make the arrangements for the funeral service?"

"I think I got it in control, and Marshall helped. I sent out an email about the memorial service to his friends. His aunt and uncle are flying in tonight and I'm going to book them a room too. And I made a phone call to make sure, and John was, well, um, *taken care of* today."

"Oh." Mary knew that Judy meant that John's body had been cremated. Her heart went out to her best friend, who had to be in agony right now. "You sure you don't need help?"

"I'm fine. You know, I'm rethinking our theory about Shanahan." Judy lowered her voice. "It's hard to believe he did it."

"You mean killed John? Why?"

"Seeing him out there today, he was helping everybody get dinner ready. And he really did seem genuinely sad for William. Maybe Shanahan's not the nicest guy, and he may have anger issues, but is he a *murderer*?"

"Just because he's nice sometimes doesn't mean he's not a murderer."

"And I don't know if it's enough motive. Even if John had filed that complaint with DHS, Shanahan wouldn't have been severely penalized. There's no jail time, there's not even a fine. He'd just get fired."

"So? Losing your job matters, and he'd be blackballed in the business."

"I know," Judy sounded uncertain. "But as a motive for *murder*?"

"We don't know what else Shanahan has to hide. Maybe there's more in his past. Other crimes, maybe under an alias, anything. It could be anything. Killing John would have headed off any investigation into him."

"I just feel like we're missing something. Anyway I can't talk now. Meet me there at nine fifteen tomorrow morning, would you? The service is at ten o'clock. Love you."

"Sure. Love you too. Call if you need anything."

"Will do, bye." Judy hung up, and Mary pressed End, setting the phone down and mulling it over. She wondered if Judy was right that Shanahan wasn't John's killer. Maybe it *had* been a burglar. Or maybe they were missing something, because Mary had to acknowledge to herself that as soon as Judy had said those words, they had struck a chord.

I'm missing something.

Mary eyed the computer screen without really seeing anything. She felt unsettled and uneasy at her very core, like a gut instinct that she was ignoring. Maybe she was missing something, but the only thing that she could see that they would be missing was Machiavelli.

Which was when it struck her.

"DiNunzio, did you hear me?"

Startled, Mary looked up to see Bennie standing in the threshold to her office, a grim look on her face. Her heavy briefcase and purse hung from shoulder straps, and stray blonde curls escaped her topknot. The blue of her eyes seemed diluted, and the lines in her face more prominent than Mary had seen before.

"Oh, hi, Bennie. I didn't see you there." Mary set down her phone. "That was Judy, and she has William."

"Good." Bennie motioned Mary up. "DiNunzio, come on. Time to go. I'll walk you out."

"I can't go yet. I want to keep looking for a connection between the plaintiffs and Machiavelli."

"There isn't one, except that he's their lawyer." Bennie's dry lips made a flat line. "Anne and Lou have gone home. You and I are the last ones here."

"Bennie, can you sit down for a minute? I just got an idea I want to try it out on you."

"Okay." Bennie set her bags on the floor and eased into the chair opposite Mary's desk. "What idea?"

"What if *Machiavelli* killed John?"

Bennie recoiled, frowning. "What are you talking about?"

"Let me just think out loud with you. I think that Machiavelli has been trying to destroy this law firm. And so far, he's certainly hurting our reputation. We didn't get Nutrex and we almost lost London Technologies."

"O-kay," Bennie said slowly.

"We know that Machiavelli is behind the reverse-discrimination complaint because he's the opposing counsel, whether or not I can prove that he manufactured the lawsuit. And by the way, I *know* he manufactured it. I can feel it in my *bones.*"

Bennie eyed the papers on Mary's desk. "I couldn't find any connection between the plaintiffs and him. Could you?"

"No, but I *know* it exists." Mary heard the strength of her own voice, though she knew she couldn't prove it, but she went with it anyway. Because maybe it was time to start believing in herself. "But let me return to the point. Machiavelli files a reverse-discrimination suit with a statement by John, and next thing that happens is John turns up murdered, which puts us in the hot seat. Judy becomes a suspect. We become suspects in conspiracy to murder. In case anybody misses the point, he accuses us on television."

"I think he exploited the tragedy."

"Unless he *created* the tragedy." Mary found herself speaking faster, convinced of her own words even as they left her lips. "Isn't it at least possible that Machiavelli killed John? Think about it. We know Machiavelli can be violent. Impulsive. Remember, after that last case with him, I went to see him in his office and he tried to kiss me?"

Bennie glowered. "Yes, I do, the bastard. But murder? Maybe you really are getting paranoid."

"No, I'm not. Why is it not possible?"

"The question isn't whether it's possible. The question is whether it's probable."

"You're dismissing it like it's out of the question." Mary threw up her hands. "What makes it so improbable?"

"For one thing, you have to look at who would benefit from John's murder. It doesn't benefit Machiavelli to have John dead. If John were still alive, Machiavelli could've called him as a witness when the reverse-discrimination case went to trial. That would be very compelling testimony on the plaintiffs' behalf. John made admissions against us. But without John on the witness stand, it's hearsay."

"But we're not going to trial yet. We're only before the Human Relations Commission, and they don't follow the rules of evidence. Machiavelli's got John's statements in the record, and it all comes in, admissions and all. Machiavelli even called me and Judy about settlement, remember I told you that? He said he thought his case was stronger now."

"Right."

"I emailed that freelancer, Amanda Sussman, who was bothering us, calling her out, so I bet she disappears. But there'll be more reporters tomorrow, probably some legitimate and some not. We barely recovered from the reverse-discrimination lawsuit before we got hit with a murder case, with *us as suspects.*" Mary got more excited the more she thought about it. "How many Nutrexes will we lose? Who isn't hiring us because of these rumors? This is the kind of thing that can bring us down completely. Not just that we discriminate against men, but that we *kill them?*"

Bennie almost laughed out loud. "DiNunzio, I think you've got derangement syndrome. Machiavelli is a massive jerk, but I don't know if he's capable of cold-blooded murder."

"What if he hired somebody to kill John? Maybe he told him to make it look like a burglary. Anybody can see the fire escape from the alley, and John's address is public record. It wouldn't be a hard murder to plan, to do us in." Mary thought a minute. "Do you know where Lou is?"

"He told me he was going back to John's to look for more street cameras. There were no lights or motion detectors, so I don't know how much you could see from the fire escape anyway."

"Let me text him, see if he got anything." Mary picked up her phone, scrolled to the text function and sent Lou a text: **Having any luck? Lately I'm thinking it's Machiavelli but Bennie says I'm crazy. For a change.**

Bennie rose. "DiNunzio, I think you need to go home. We have a big day tomorrow, a tough one. Declan won't be able to come in for the service. He's on trial in York."

"But Bennie, don't you think I could be right? Maybe we're missing something. Maybe we're missing the forest for the trees. Machiavelli could be behind everything, all of it —"

"He's not the Wizard of Oz. This is not a discussion for now." Bennie picked up her purse and messenger bag. "You need to go home and so do I. Sadly, I have to draft a eulogy for John. It's time for us to think about him."

"I am," Mary shot back. "This is about finding his killer. And what if it really is Machiavelli?" Suddenly her text alert sounded, and she picked up the phone and read the text, from Lou. **So far, no luck. Will keep you posted. BTW you're crazy.**

"Was it Lou?"

"Yes, and he says no luck yet."

"Come on, let's go." Bennie sighed. "We have to bury our dead."

CHAPTER THIRTY-TWO

Mary sat with Anthony, Anne, Marshall, and Lou, listening to Bennie's eulogy next to her father, her mother, and The Tonys. Up ahead, Judy sat in the front row with her arm around the back of William's wheelchair, next to John's aunt and uncle, Susan and Mel Hodge, their gray heads downcast. The memorial service was held at the William J. Lowell Funeral Home, a large converted brownstone in Society Hill, the most historic section of the city.

A hundred mourners, including fellow lawyers, friends from law school, and even clients like Jim and Sanjay from London Technologies filled the large, rectangular room, which had authentic colonial wainscoting painted a creamy white, high plaster ceilings with refined crown molding, and polished-bronze sconces between tall windows with bubbled glass. Somebody had commented to Mary that John would've loved the setting, but that gave her no comfort. John should have been alive, not in a bronze urn set on a flowery table at the front of the room.

From the lectern, Bennie was saying, ". . . John was loved by all of his friends, and so many of you came here today, even from his law school days . . ."

Mary tried to face front and listen, though it was hard to look at the urn, and her gaze strayed to her hands, folded around her belly in her lap, in a black maternity dress. She felt the baby kick, and it struck her as heartbreaking that she was carrying new life in the same moment that she was mourning the death of someone who was too young to die, much less so brutally.

". . . and John was so valued by his clients as well, and I see many of you here, to honor him today, despite your busy schedules . . ."

Mary had thought about John's murder all last night, wondering whether Machiavelli, Shanahan, or a burglar had killed him. She sensed it was Machiavelli, but when she'd told Anthony her new theory over dinner, he'd thought she was as crazy as Bennie and Lou did. She hadn't been surprised to find that the media in front of the funeral home did not include Amanda Sussman, confirming that Sussman must've been working for Machiavelli. Anyway, she had been too tired to think about it anymore by bedtime and had cried all the tears she could cry until she had seen Judy this morning, grief-stricken even as she comforted William, who wept openly through the pastor's words at the beginning of the service.

". . . The temptation is to say something profound about life and death at times like this, but my experience with death has taught me, if anything, that death is a terrible teacher. We don't learn from each other in death, we learn from each other in life, and we love each other in the living years. Death is loss, and what it leaves us is each other, sharing the loss, missing John, and holding each other as we go forward without him . . ."

Mary heard Judy hiccup in the front row, beginning to sob, her pink head bowing like a drooping petunia, and it was all Mary could do not to go comfort her. Judy sagged against William, the two of them sharing their broken hearts, though the two halves could never become one whole, Mary knew. When she had lost her first husband, her parents had been beside themselves, but together their family could not mend the pieces of their hearts, and their lives, which lay shattered. Only time had accomplished that, and it had taken awhile.

". . . I had not met John's brother, William, until today, but I have certainly heard about him, and so had anybody who knew John. John adored William and was completely devoted to him, and now I understand why. And I'm delighted to see the resemblance between the two brothers, for they have the same smile, the same curly hair, and even the same glasses . . ."

William laughed, then it trailed into a sob, his curved back shaking uncontrollably in his new suit, and Judy put her arm around him, holding him close, as Bennie continued, summing up.

". . . And ladies and gentlemen, friends and neighbors, and most especially John's family and Judy, let these be my last words today, and the end of this memorial service. John lived a life that we could all be proud of, every single day. He held himself to the highest standard in his professional and in his personal life. He stood up for what he believed, no matter what the cost. No matter who disagreed with him, either."

Mary felt the words resonate in her chest, thinking back to what John had told them all, about how out of place he had felt at the firm. It hadn't been easy for him to say or for them to hear, but it was honest. Mary gave Bennie credit for seeing that as a strength in John, even though it had rocked the firm.

"John Foxman was one of the finest lawyers I have ever met and one of the finest young men. Let's live our lives the way he did, and honor him. Deepest condolences to his brother, William, his aunt, Susan, and uncle, Mel Hodge, and to all of his friends and colleagues here today. Thank you very much."

Bennie stepped away to the sound of renewed sniffling, then went to check on Judy and William. Mary wiped her eyes as the pastor returned to the front of the room, said some concluding words and a final benediction, then finally gave the bronze urn holding John's remains to William and ended the memorial service, dismissing everyone.

Mary felt so numb and sad through the long, painful slog of saying good-bye to John's friends and clients, including Jim and Sanjay, then she had to make sure her parents and The Tonys were okay. They all looked teary-eyed and frail in unaccustomed black, and Mary and Anthony ushered them and The Tonys out of the emptying funeral home behind Marshall, Lou, Judy, William, and John's Aunt Susan and Uncle Mel, a forlorn group heading for a private lunch reception at a nearby restaurant.

The front door of the funeral home stood open, letting in a bright shaft of sunlight, and Mary held Anthony's hand, taking up the back of the line. Mourners filed outside, and she and Anthony had almost reached the threshold when shouting broke out outside, out on the street. Mary turned to Anthony, alarmed. "Did you hear that?"

"Yes?" Anthony craned his neck over the crowd. "Oh no!"

Suddenly the mourners shifted forward, and the shouting became a chant, "Justice for John! Justice for John! Justice for John!"

Mary stepped out of the funeral home, horrified to see what was going on. Mourners were being confronted by a flock of angry protesters, chanting and pumping homemade signs that read, #JUSTICE FOR JOHN! ROSATO & DINUNZIO CRYING HYPOCRITE TEARS! ROSATO & DINUNZIO — KILLER LAW FIRM!

Mary recoiled in shock. She never would have expected that there would be protesters at the funeral. She hadn't heard that any of John's friends were organizing on his behalf and there would be no reason to. She scanned their angry faces, but none of them seemed like the types of persons who John would have been friends with. His friends were lawyers and businesspeople his own age, and these protesters were younger and on the fringe. Suddenly she realized they weren't real protesters at all, but they must have been sent by Machiavelli. He must have paid them to disrupt the funeral, and the depth of his depravity enraged her.

Funeral home attendants rushed to make way for mourners to pass, but the protesters outnumbered them, blocking their path, pumping signs, and chanting, "Justice for John! Justice for John! Justice for John!" The reporters filmed the mob scene with cell phones and video cameras. Traffic on the street slowed to a stop, and drivers rubbernecked at the scene.

Suddenly the protesters targeted Judy, surging toward her and jostling William in his wheelchair. William cried out in fear and curled into a ball, frantically protecting the urn in his lap. Protesters shouted at Judy, as if William weren't even there, "You killed John! You killed John! Justice for John! Justice for John!"

"No, get back!" Judy flailed, trying to wave them away from William.

"Judy! Pop!" Mary hurried to help, but Anthony blocked her.

"No, it's not safe for you. I got this. Stay here." Anthony rushed forward with Bennie, Lou, Anne, Marshall, and the funeral attendants. They reached Judy and William and tried to push back the protesters, who kept chanting.

"Justice for John! Justice for John! Justice for John!"

A group of mourners including Jim and Sanjay were able to slip away, but Mary saw with horror that the older people were getting shoved around in the melee. Pigeon Tony got swallowed up by the crowd, and Feet's Mr. Potatohead glasses popped off. John's Uncle Mel threw his arms around his wife, Susan, hobbling in her black boot from her broken ankle, and Mary's mother tried to help her, she was only four feet eleven inches tall.

Mary couldn't stand by another second. She rushed off the step, pushed into the crowd, and hurried to her mother, gathering her in her arms as they were jostled left and right by the protesters, shouting their slogan.

"Justice for John! Justice for John! Justice for John!"

"Leave us alone!" Mary shouted at a female protester, hugging her mother close. "You work for Machiavelli, don't you? He sent you, didn't he? You should be ashamed of yourself!"

"Justice for John!" the female protester shouted back, mechanically. "Justice for John! Justice for John!"

"John, who?" Mary shot back, spitting mad. "Do you even know his last name? What is it?"

"Justice for John!" the female protester replied, on autopilot. "Justice for John! Justice for John!"

"You're a killer!" A male protester rushed to confront Mary. "You don't want the truth to come out! You're in the lawyer conspiracy!"

"Get out of here!" Mary yelled back, and the male protester was about to grab Mary's arm when Anthony flew out of nowhere, grabbed his arm, and punched him in the face.

"Keep your hands off my wife!" Anthony's face contorted with anger, and behind him Bennie, Lou, Marshall, Anne, and the funeral attendants had succeeded in hustling Judy, William, The Tonys, and the Hodges away from the protesters and down the sidewalk.

"Babe, follow them!" Anthony took her right arm, and her father scooped up her mother, a bloody cut over his eye.

"Pop!" Mary gasped, horrified. "Are you hurt?"

"GO, MARE! GO!"

Mary took off with Anthony and her parents, and the funeral attendants formed a protective shell around them, getting them down the sidewalk and keeping the protesters at bay. A police cruiser raced to the scene, and two uniformed cops leapt out. The police contained the protesters, with the press behind filming away.

"Justice for John! Justice for John!" the protesters chanted, until the sirens swallowed their hollow cries.

CHAPTER THIRTY-THREE

The restaurant was a few blocks from the funeral home, and the shaken circle of family and friends went there together, on foot and by wheelchair. The trip seemed to settle everybody down, and by the time they reached the restaurant, they were shown to a lovely private dining room, where a long banquet table had been set with arugula-and-goat-cheese salads and abundant antipasto platters of cold cuts and cheeses.

Mary's parents, The Tonys, the Hodges, and Judy sat down with William on the end in his wheelchair while Mary, Anthony, Bennie, Anne, Lou, and Marshall hovered over them, making sure they were okay. The Hodges sat close to each other, their lined faces masks of grief and sadness. They were otherwise an attractive and refined couple with gold wire-rimmed glasses and fluffy gray hair, and they looked well-heeled in dark wool suits. Feet had found his Mr. Potatohead glasses, but he seemed upset, and Pigeon Tony and Tony-From-Down-The-Block hadn't bounced back yet, since they hadn't even touched the salami-and-pepperoni antipasto.

Bennie asked the waiters to keep water, wine, and beer coming, and Mary got her father a whiskey and a Band-Aid, which she and her mother used to cover the cut on his forehead. Luckily, it wasn't serious, so Mary's blood pressure returned to normal, and Anthony put a hand on her shoulder.

"Mary, please sit down. You need to get off your feet."

"I will in a minute." Mary patted his arm, noticing the redness on his hand from punching the protester. "How's your hand, honey? I can't believe you hit that guy."

"I can't either." Anthony forced a smile, pulling out her chair. "Honey, please sit."

"Thanks." Mary sat down, eyed her father. "Pop, you sure you're okay?"

"I'M FINE, DOLL."

Mary still felt so angry. "That was Machiavelli's doing. Every time we think he's hit rock bottom, he gets lower. So it's not just the press he's sending after us, it's protesters. It's an outrage."

"I KNEW IT WASN'T JOHN'S REAL FRIENDS BECAUSE THEY WERE IN-

SIDE WITH US. I'M JUST SO EFFIN MAD AT THAT BASTARD — OH, SORRY, EXCUSE ME." Mary's father glanced at the Hodges, but Mel waved him off with a polite smile.

"Matty, I've heard worse. We might be Minnesota nice, but I served in Vietnam. Now, who *were* those protesters? Why do they think Judy killed John? What conspiracy are they even talking about?"

Judy's face reddened. "It's so awful, it's a fraud."

William looked up at Judy, his head jittery. "Judy? Was that *real*?"

"No, not at all." Judy frowned, patting his clenched fist. "They're lying."

Mary could see Judy was upset, so she took over. "William, it's not real, and Mel and Susan, those people don't really care about John. They don't even know John. They were sent there by a lawyer named Nick Machiavelli. He must have paid them to make a scene, for the cameras."

"Really?" Mel's hooded eyes widened behind his trifocals. "Why would he do such a thing, at John's memorial service?"

"Because he wants to make us look bad. He's got a thing against us and our firm. He's suing us, accusing us of John's murder, and now he's out of control, practically waging war against us."

"HE TRIED TO PICK A FIGHT AND HE GOT ONE. HE ACCUSED MARY OF MURDER ON TV. I SAW IT WITH MY OWN EYES. WE'RE NOT GONNA TAKE THAT LYIN' DOWN. WE GOT A FAMILY NAME, AND IT STANDS FOR GOOD, NOT LIKE HIS."

Feet snorted. "Hell, no. We're not letting him get away with this. He picked on the wrong guys."

Tony-From-Down-The-Block sipped his beer. "We're already tryin' to get him back from what he said about Mary. We've been diggin' into him, big-time. Tryin' to get the dirt."

"You have?" Mary asked, looking over in surprise. Between them, The Tonys and her father knew almost everyone in South Philly and they could have turned up something useful. Or something ridiculous.

Bennie frowned at Mary. "DiNunzio, we shouldn't talk about this now. I'm sure William and the Hodges would rather relax and eat something. Machiavelli and his proxies don't deserve another moment of our time."

Mel interjected, "It's okay, Bennie, I'd like to know what's going on. We'd rather not make small talk. We've thought of nothing *but* who could have murdered John. It's shocking that this man is accusing Judy, or any of you, of being his killer."

Susan nodded, her expression drained. "I go over and over it in my mind, asking myself how anybody could have done that to him. He was such an intelligent, gentle soul, like my sister. Bennie, do the police have any suspects? You're not truly a suspect, are you? Or Judy?"

"Let me fill you in, briefly," Bennie answered, then brought William, Mel, and Susan up-to-date on everything, ending with her theory of the burglar. Mary didn't correct her to add Shanahan because that would upset William, nor did she say anything about her suspicion that Machiavelli was behind John's murder because she didn't have any proof. Mary knew from her own experience that speculating wouldn't help William and the Hodges bear their burden. No one but a crime victim could understand what another crime victim went through, to endure not only a murder, but its aftermath.

Mary turned to Bennie. "Those protesters were the last straw, as far as I'm concerned. Machiavelli's playing by his own rules, and we're playing by Roger's rules of Zen. And it's resulting in what happened today. They ambushed us. I think we need to fire Roger."

"I would normally agree with you, but we can't fire him now. Your interview's tomorrow with the Human Relations Commission. You can't go in unrepresented." Bennie's phone rang in her pocket, but she ignored it. "That's probably Roger calling."

"Then we find somebody else overnight, it's not impossible. Or we postpone. Because this isn't working. We're so civilized, we don't fight back. We have to let them know that we're onto them and that we won't take it."

"BENNIE, I GOTTA BACK MARY UP, NOT 'CAUSE SHE'S MY KID. MACHIAVELLI, HE DON'T PLAY FAIR. YOU ACT ALL NICEY-NICE AND HE'S GONNA TAKE ADVANTAGE."

Judy blinked, dubious. "Mary, I agree with you but it's not practical. Not with your interview tomorrow."

Mel shook his head, the deep lines in his forehead buckling. "Ladies, I don't know much about the law, but I know about war. You have to fight fire with fire."

"I'M WITH YOU, MEL. THIS IS HOW THIS MACHIAVELLI FAMILY ACTS. BELIEVE ME, I DONE SOME ASKIN' AROUND ABOUT THEM. EVERYBODY IN THE NEIGHBORHOOD'S GOT A

STORY ABOUT THEM. THEY CHEAT PEOPLE, THEY STIFF PEOPLE, THEY GOT NO RESPECT."

Bennie's phone kept ringing, so she slid it out of her pocket and checked the screen. "It's Sanjay, not Roger. We should take this."

Anne rose. "Let's step away."

Mary and Judy stood up. "Excuse us, everybody," Mary said, touching Anthony on the shoulder, and they crossed to the wall, huddling around the cell phone, which they put on speaker.

Bennie said into the phone, "Hello, Sanjay, yes we're fine, thanks."

"Good." Sanjay sounded relieved. "We were concerned for your safety. The crowd was out of control. It looked as if the older people got in harm's way."

"Fortunately, they're fine now, Sanjay. Thank you for asking. We have you on speaker and we're safe and sound at the restaurant."

"Oh, okay." Sanjay's tone hardened. "I'm glad to hear that you're all safe, but Jim and I have decided to let you go as counsel. Our mind is made up."

Mary's heart sank on an already terrible day. "Sanjay, no —"

Anne sagged against the wall. "Sanjay, can I ask why?"

396

"Anne, I know you worked hard on the case, but we just cannot be involved in this public relations nightmare for another minute. You may not have had a chance to look online yet, but the videos and stills are a disaster. We're in some of the pictures. My wife freaked. Everybody's calling us to see if we're okay. We have to explain that we're caught up in a fight with people attacking our lawyers. We have to draw the line."

Mary cringed. "Sanjay, I defended Alex Chen's deposition and it went beautifully. The case is in place, and we are going forward with the deposition schedule. We are fully prepared to continue this representation. We're not responsible for what happened today. We are as appalled by it as you are."

Bennie interjected, "Yes, and think about it, Sanjay. Where else will you get replacement counsel so quickly? So many of the other firms were conflicted out. That was why you came to us, and we're doing great —"

Sanjay interrupted, "Bennie, please don't make this harder than it already is. We have decided. We may not even continue the suit. We doubt we could find anybody else to take it on a contingency. We don't have the money to stage this litigation otherwise. We might have to abandon it, if push comes to shove."

Bennie pursed her lips. "But we can get this thing settled, you have to hang in until trial. So just stay with us and —"

Sanjay interrupted again, "We can't. Business is ruthless. Nobody knows it better than the little guy. David doesn't beat Goliath, not in real life. We're snake-bit, and with John's murder . . ." his voice trailed off, ". . . we'll let you know what happens next and where you should send the file, if we pursue it further."

Bennie paused. "Okay. I hear you. Thank you very much, Sanjay. We're always here for you, wishing you the best. And thank you for coming to John's service. Good-bye, and take care."

"You too." Sanjay ended the call, and Bennie slid the phone into her pocket, exhaling tightly.

"Oh, man. He fired us, and I don't blame him. Do you guys?"

"No," Mary admitted, though it drove her crazy. "So they lose, we lose, and Machiavelli wins."

Anne moaned. "No more London Technologies? The whole case is gone, just like that?"

"It happens, Murphy." Bennie made a sympathetic face at Anne, who shook her head.

"All that work, down the drain. It was *such* a good case. They were in the right. They deserved to win and they would have. We would have had an awesome settlement, I know it. We were almost *there.*"

"I bet." Judy looked at Anne, her lower lip buckling. "I'm sorry. I know you worked really hard on it, and it sucks that this happened today, of all days. John would be so upset."

"Okay, enough." Bennie ushered them away from the wall. "We can't let this distract us from what really matters. Please, go sit down." She gestured to the table, and they retook their seats, then she raised her wineglass. "Everyone, excuse that interruption, but I say, let's toast to John."

"L'chaim," Lou said sadly, raising a wineglass, joined by Anne and Marshall.

"Yes, to John." Judy helped William raise a water glass, both of them holding back new tears.

"To John, a wonderful nephew." Mel hoisted a wineglass, and so did Susan, her eyes glistening.

"TO JOHN!" Mary's father raised his whiskey, and her mother and Anthony raised wineglasses.

"To John." Mary sipped water, her emotions whirling. One look at Judy, William, and the Hodges told her how agonized they were feeling, and now they'd been cheated of a peaceful memorial service that could have provided some healing. Somewhere, Machiavelli was laughing. Mary felt like the bad guys were winning.

Her father rubbed her back. "MARE, YOU GOTTA FIGHT SOUTH PHILLY WITH SOUTH PHILLY. HE THINKS HE'S A BIG MUCKETY-MUCK, JUST 'CAUSE HE'S GOT HIS OWN LAW FIRM? WELL, SO DO YOUSE."

Mary's mother nodded in approval. *"Si, e vero."*

"Thanks." Mary forced a smile. The baby hadn't kicked in a while, giving her a break.

"We sure do." Bennie patted Judy on the shoulder. "We have each other. We're partners, and we're going to mourn John, then get it together and fight back. I already have some ideas."

"Me, too," Mary said, since a plan was hatching in the back of her mind. Meanwhile, the waiters entered the dining room with trays of salmon filet and broccoli, then started serving the Hodges, The Tonys, Anthony, Marshall, and William, as Judy

400

began to cut his food to feed him.

"HE'S ON HIS HIGH HORSE ON AC-COUNT OF HE HAS SO MUCH MONEY AND BUSINESSES, TOO. I WAS ASKIN' AROUN' AND JOEY ONE EYE TOLE ME THAT MACHIAVELLI HAS INVESTMENTS ALL OVER. EVEN IN THE HAM TINS."

"The ham tins?" Mary asked, ignoring the meal placed in front of her, for the time being.

"YEAH. IT'S A FANCY PLACE IN NEW YORK. THEY GOT BEACHES AND HORSE SHOWS."

"You mean the Hamptons?"

"YEAH, THAT'S IT."

"Are you sure about that?"

"YES, JOEY ONE EYE TOLE ME. EVER HEARD OF THE PLACE?"

"I've heard of the Hamptons, but I mean the business. Are you saying that Machiavelli has a business in the Hamptons?" Mary felt something gnawing at the edges of her memory.

"YEAH, LIKE FINANCIAL SERVICES OR SOMETHIN'. HE OWNS IT."

Suddenly it came to her. "Was the name of the company Hampton Holdings?"

"YEAH, I THINK THAT'S IT. WHY?"

Mary felt a bolt of excitement. "One of

401

the plaintiffs from the reverse-discrimination lawsuit worked there during the summers. I think it was Graham Madden."

Bennie looked over. "You mean the lawsuit against us? One of those plaintiffs used to work for a company of Machiavelli's?"

Judy came alive. "For real?"

"Yes." Mary reached for her phone, rallying. "I can show you the resume. I was searching to see if the plaintiffs had worked for him at his law firm. I didn't know Machiavelli owned businesses other than his law firm so I didn't see the connection."

Anne blinked. "He owns companies, in addition to his law firm? Who does that? Is that a thing?"

Bennie nodded. "Sure. I don't own any other businesses, but Declan does, and I have other friends who do. Mostly business lawyers, not litigators. They buy shares of companies or form consortia to buy them, like any other investments."

Judy straightened in her seat. "So Machiavelli *did* manufacture the lawsuit against us."

"I knew it!" Mary searched her email, found the email from Bennie, and opened the attachment, enlarging the screen to see Madden's resume, with its reference to

Hampton Holdings, LLC. She held up the phone. "It's right here. Madden worked for Hampton Holdings in the summers before law school."

Bennie and Judy exchanged looks. Bennie said, "So Machiavelli meets this kid when he's in college, then the kid goes to law school, and Machiavelli puts him up to suing us?" She frowned. "But why would the kid do that?"

Judy's blue eyes came to life. "He would if Machiavelli *put him through* law school. He'd owe him."

"Right!" Mary felt the puzzle pieces fall into place. "Madden does well in school, then one day, Machiavelli asks him a favor. He says, Apply to Rosato & DiNunzio for a job, and when you get turned down, sue them. It's evil, and it *works*. I bet the other plaintiffs worked for Machiavelli's other businesses. Pop, what were they, do you remember?"

"NO, UH, IF YOU SAY THE NAME, I MIGHT. I WROTE IT DOWN. IT'S AT HOME."

Mary opened the attachment of Michael Battle's resume, skimming to his employment experience. "How about Wheels-Up, an aviation insurance company in Wayne?"

"UH, YEAH, THAT'S ONE." Her father

nodded.

Mary's heart beat faster. She opened the attachment of Stephen McManus's resume, reading his work experience. "How about AI-Intelligence, some kind of robotics company? It's in the Chicago area."

"YEAH I THINK THAT'S ONE, TOO."

"Were there others?"

"YEAH, BUT I FORGET."

"Who told you this again?"

"JOEY ONE EYE. YOU DON'T KNOW HIM. YOUR MOTHER'S CAMARR JOSIE KNEW HIM FROM HER OLD PARISH BEFORE SHE MOVED AND —"

"How does he know all this about Machiavelli?"

"HE USED TO DO SOME BOOKKEEPIN' FOR MACHIAVELLI, EARLY ON BEFORE HE GOT TO BE A BIG SHOT."

Bennie interjected, "If this man was an accountant, he has a fiduciary duty to keep it to himself. It's confidential information."

"BENNIE, DON'T WORRY. JOEY ONE EYE'S NOT A REAL ACCOUNTANT. HE WAS GOOD WITH NUMBERS IN SCHOOL AND MACHIAVELLI USED HIM BECAUSE HE'S A CHEAP BASTARD. JOEY ONE EYE GOT PISSED AFTER MACHIAVELLI STIFFED HIM

'CAUSE HE COULDN'T WORK NO MORE."

Mary asked, "Because he lost his eye?"

"NO HE DIDN'T LOSE HIS EYE. HE'S GOT TWO EYES."

Mary let it go. South Philly nicknames were their own language. "So Pop, do you remember any of the other companies?"

"NO, SORRY, MARE." Her father turned to Feet, who had discovered the pepperoni on the antipasto platter. "FEET, YOU WERE THERE. YOU REMEMBER ANY OF THE OTHER COMPANIES MACHIAVELLI OWNS?"

Feet frowned, chewing away. "I think there were two more. One was Katonah Industries. That was in New York, too. I remember because I thought of cats and I miss my cat, Jilly. He died."

"Sorry, Feet." Mary made a note in her phone. "Do you remember the other company name?"

Feet kept chewing. "Oh, yeah. Florence Financial. I remember it because I dated a girl named Florence, back in the day. Met her at a mixer. Nice girl."

Mary was making a note in her phone when she noticed Anne leaning over the table, toward Feet.

"Excuse me, Feet?" Anne said, puzzled.

"Did you say Florence Financial?"

"Yeah."

"And Machiavelli owns it?"

"Yeah."

Mary looked up. "Why do you ask, Anne? Does that name mean anything to you?"

Anne's mouth dropped open. "Florence Financial is one of the companies in the consortium that owns Home Hacks."

Bennie looked shocked. "You mean Home Hacks, one of the defendants in *London Technologies*? Machiavelli has a connection to that case."

"Evidently, he does," Mary said, astonished.

Anne nodded excitedly. "He must. I remember from the Certificate of Incorporation for Home Hacks, which I had to get for the Complaint. I saw the name Florence Financial on the list of the consortia that owned the parent company, but I didn't need to know the details about the parent company to file a Complaint against its subsidiary, Home Hacks. We weren't suing the parent."

Judy looked over in disbelief. "So Machiavelli owns Home Hacks, which we're suing on behalf of London Technologies."

Bennie interjected, "Correction, which we *were* suing before Sanjay fired us, just now."

"Even so." Judy's eyes narrowed in thought. "So what are the implications? What's Machiavelli up to?"

"I think I know," Mary answered, when it hit her.

Chapter Thirty-Four

"Let me break it down for you," Mary said, standing in front of the easel with the diagram about the data integration business. She, Bennie, Judy, and Anne had come back to the firm after the luncheon, for an emergency meeting with Roger and Isaac. Anthony had taken her parents and The Tonys home, and the Hodges had taken William back to the hotel, leaving Mary remarkably energized, having figured out Machiavelli's scheme. Lou had gone back to the scene to keep investigating and he'd promised her that he'd keep an open mind about Machiavelli's being the culprit. She knew in her heart that Machiavelli was guilty of John's murder, but she couldn't prove that yet.

Mary pointed to London Technologies on the diagram. "Allow me to remind you that London Technologies developed data integration software that enabled furniture manufacturers to store and organize their own data. It's a bit player in the data integration market, which was dominated by the defendants Express Management Services and Home Hacks."

Anne smiled, nodding. "You get an A plus."

"Thank you." Mary smiled back. "Home Hacks is a data application provider, in other words, it takes data from the furniture retailer or wholesaler, organizes it, and stores it with Express Management Services. Together they formed the Goliaths in the integration data market. Right, Anne?"

"Exactly."

"But essentially, Home Hacks is a middleman in the market and they gouge their customers for subscriptions for the service. If you remember, London Technologies' software would eliminate them, destroying their business, which we know they weren't happy about."

Roger cocked his head. "How do we know that? Other than common sense?"

"We know that because the president of Home Hacks threatened Alex Chen, the marketing director for London Technologies, at a trade association meeting. He told Chen that he would put them out of business. I defended the deposition, and Alex is rock-solid on his testimony."

"Okay." Roger made a note.

"Alex Chen also testified that Home Hacks took measures against London Technologies to stop them, like the exclusive dealing contracts and so forth, which are anticompetitive business practices unlawful under the Sherman Act. So we know that Home Hacks was attempting to retaliate for being put out of business. In other words, it had it out for London Technologies. That's why we filed suit on their behalf."

Roger kept taking notes.

"At the luncheon, we learned that Nick Machiavelli owns a company named Florence Financial, which is part of a consortium that owns Home Hacks. So we came back and did our research." Mary gestured at an array of documents on the conference table, which they had found online and printed so they could study them. "We did as much digging as we could to learn the company's value and management. We also wanted to know who are the other owners of Home Hacks, in other words, who makes up the consortium. It wasn't easy to find because Home Hacks is a privately held company and they play close to the vest. Business articles place their valuation at approximately $16 million."

"So it's lucrative." Roger's eyebrows lifted.

"Very. There appear to be only two other investors in the consortium, both corporations. One is called the Roma Holdings, LLC, and the other is called The Milano Group."

"They're all Italian cities."

"Yes, now, *you* get an A plus," Mary said, trying to play nice with him, since she couldn't fire him. "We know that Machiavelli owns Florence Financial, and I'm assuming that he owns the other two companies."

"Is his name on the other corporate registrations?"

"No, they're owned by two other corporations, and we didn't recognize the name of the corporate agents who signed the forms."

Bennie interjected, "They're probably shell companies, owned by other shell companies. We'll task Lou with that, ASAP. But right now, we have the only connection we need, which is with Home Hacks."

Roger frowned slightly. "So why does Machiavelli use Italian city names, if he's trying to play it close to the vest, as you say? It's not hard to see that pattern. And why own Home Hacks outright, through one company, and use shell companies for the other two companies?"

Bennie sipped her coffee. "We don't have all the answers. Maybe when they were incorporated matters or maybe for tax purposes, or tax shenanigans, but we don't need to know that now."

"I think I know how to find out, and I will." Mary didn't elaborate, since Roger wouldn't think that Joey One Eye was as reliable as Dun & Bradstreet. Though Joey One Eye was probably more so. "And of course, the gravamen of the London Technologies Complaint was that both EXMS and Home Hacks conspired to maintain a monopoly on the market together and they jointly required dealerships to deal with them exclusively. The point is, the conduct of the two defendants was so coordinated in the market that we strongly suspect that *both* entities are owned by Machiavelli — not just Home Hacks, but EXMS."

Roger's eyes flared. "Really."

"Yes, we researched the corporate registration of EXMS, but that's a privately held company too, owned by another entity, or shell company. It will take more sophisticated digging to pierce those corporate veils, but we're working on that assumption for now."

Isaac frowned in confusion. "But Mary, what does this have to do with anything? I don't know why any of it matters."

"Okay." Mary straightened. "What we think happened is that about six months ago, we filed suit on behalf of London Technologies and the Complaint was drafted by John. John was an antitrust expert and he regarded himself that way. He let it be known generally. The clients liked Anne, but she had to fight the notion in the beginning that he was the brains in the case."

Anne reddened. "True. Not to speak ill of John, because I never would. But he was definitely regarded as the MVP on the team. He was right, what he said. I was the pretty one, he was the smart one. He took the lead, and in the beginning, I let him."

Mary could hear the guilt in Anne's voice. "In any event, John drafted the initial discovery and signed and sent it himself, without Anne or Bennie's signature. The defendants would have seen John as the prime mover in the litigation."

Judy cleared her throat. "He drafted a beautifully written Complaint and he would be seen as a serious legal threat by any defendant."

"Like Machiavelli," Mary supplied, finishing her best friend's thought.

Roger nodded. "I'm catching on. So Machiavelli owns Home Hacks, which is under threat by John Foxman. Is that your point, Mary?"

"Yes, bluntly put." Mary felt her chest tighten, at the depravity of the scheme. "Machiavelli sees his company Home Hacks as being threatened by our client London Technologies, which is represented by MVP John Foxman. So what Machiavelli does is contact three kids that he probably put through law school — Michael Battle, Graham Madden, and Steve McManus. You recognize those names, of course."

"The plaintiffs in the reverse-discrimination lawsuit."

"Yes, and we have learned that they have worked for other businesses that Machiavelli owns around the country, before they went to law school. We posit that he puts them through law school, calls in a favor, and they apply with us and are rejected. The only one who gets an interview is Steve McManus, and he's personable enough to get John Foxman talking. In other words, Machiavelli targets John and sends in McManus, who gets John to say that he feels out of place here, discriminated against because he's a man."

Roger lifted an eyebrow, but didn't interrupt her.

"As we all know, John's statements form the crux of the Complaint against us before the Pennsylvania Human Relations Commission. Machiavelli knows that as soon as the Complaint becomes public, John will be compromised and will either be fired or will quit. Either way, he will be off the *London Technologies* case, leaving it in the lurch at the worst possible time and us struggling to staff it. Which is exactly what happened." Mary inhaled slowly, letting the words sink in, and their import. Roger looked grave, as did everyone around the table, and Judy looked heartbroken. "Bottom line, the reverse-discrimination lawsuit was manufactured by Machiavelli in order to eliminate John on *London Technologies.* And thereby save Home Hacks."

"But can't London Technologies hire another lawyer?"

"It's doubtful, and they might have to abandon the suit. They couldn't get representation before because Express Management Services and Home Hacks are big enough to spread their legal work around and conflict out the best firms from suing them."

Roger frowned. "I abhor the use of litigation that way. It's gamesmanship, not justice."

"I agree," Mary said, meaning it, though it was the least of Machiavelli's crimes. "When John didn't quit initially, Machiavelli tried other things to compromise him and the firm, like writing to the Human Relations Commission and telling them they better step it up. Or calling us murderers on TV and sending protesters to John's funeral."

"But with John gone, why did he need to do that?"

"Because he wanted us out of the case completely, by that point. He wanted us fired, so he sent the protesters to the funeral, provoking us, knowing that Sanjay and Jim would be there. Any client would have fired us, after that." Mary braced herself. "What really matters the most is what this all means, and I think I have convinced everybody by now, that it was Machiavelli who killed John himself, or who had John killed." Mary paused, making sure she didn't continue speaking until Judy had absorbed the words' emotional impact. "We've seen that Machiavelli has no limits to what he will do to accomplish his ends, and now that we know that his was much greater than getting revenge on us. It was to bring the reverse-discrimination suit, which was a smear to make us look bad, in order to get us fired on the much bigger fish, the anti-trust litigation against at least one of his multimillion-dollar companies, if not two multimillion-dollar companies."

Bennie turned to Roger, her expression grave. "I'm completely on board with Mary, now. I think Machiavelli is behind John's murder, not a burglar or Shanahan. To me, this answers the question that was always lurking in the back of my mind, which is, why now? Why would Machiavelli come at us now? The answer has become clear, now that we discovered he's an owner of Home Hacks, if not EXMS. It's much stronger motivation than either of those, and in fact, his plan worked like a charm. We've been fired by London Technologies, and they are left with no choice, in practical terms, but to abandon the lawsuit against Home Hacks and EXMS, i.e., Machiavelli."

Anne shook her head, sadly. "The lawsuit goes away, and now he'll drive them out of business. His companies will continue to dominate the data integration market, gouging the dealers with no upper limit, now that there is no competition. Machiavelli has a major cash cow and he'll do anything to protect it. To him, John was a casualty, like collateral damage in a war."

Judy cleared her throat, clearly struggling

to maintain emotional control. "And we're going after him. We're going to bring him to justice, for John."

Roger leaned back in the chair, his frown deep. "Well, this is just terrible," he said, his tone hushed. "This is much more than I ever thought would happen, when I agreed to represent you."

"I bet," Mary said, understanding. "We never thought we were in this situation, but we are, and we have to stand up for John. We've come up with a plan, and we need your help."

"Absolutely. How can I help?"

"Our plan begins when you and I go into that interview tomorrow at the Human Relations Commission."

Roger frowned slightly. "You want to talk about John's murder at the Pennsylvania Human Relations Commission?"

"No, it's just the first stage of the plan. You'll never guess what we're going to do."

"Yes, I do," Roger said, resuming his dry tone. "You've learned there's a bad-faith underpinning to the Complaint, so you want to saddle up and go into your interview, guns and documents blazing." He gestured at the corporate registrations on the table. "You want to prove Machiavelli's behind these three plaintiffs, rant and rave,

418

pound the desk, and demand that the Commission drops the Complaint and then —"

"No," Mary interrupted him. "That's what you'd *think* we'd do, but you're wrong. We have a new plan, as a team. This time, *we* are the Zen Master."

Bennie nodded. "We don't want Machiavelli to know that we're onto him. So we came up with an unorthodox strategy, for us."

Anne chimed in, "And we think it will bring Machiavelli to justice in the end."

Judy smiled, for the first time. "Roger, remember, you can be a warrior, but a humble warrior."

Roger smiled back, shifting forward. "Okay, lay it on me, ladies."

CHAPTER THIRTY-FIVE

Mary had just finished filling Roger in on their plan when Lou appeared in the threshold of the conference room, wearing a grin that she knew meant he had good news. "Lou, what?" she asked, feeling her heart lift. "Do you have anything?"

"Hi, everybody, Roger, Isaac." Lou entered the conference room, taking off his jacket and putting it around the back of his chair, then loosening his tie. "Daddy has brought home the bacon, kiddos. What's that expression? It's always darkest before the dawn?"

"Come on, give," Bennie said, impatient.

Anne shifted forward in her seat. "Lou, don't make us wait, not today."

"I second that emotion," Judy said quietly, and Mary heard the sadness in her tone.

Lou must have too, because his victorious smile faded as he rolled out a chair and sat down, with a characteristic grunt. "I found a camera and I got some video. It's right on the money. Wait'll you see."

"Get out." Mary rolled her chair closer to him. "Does it show Machiavelli? We think he killed John, or had him killed."

"Oh Jeez, why?" Lou recoiled, his hooded eyes flaring.

"We found out that he owns the defendant in the *London Technologies* case and we think he murdered John to get him out of the case."

"That's terrible. I wouldn't put it past him."

"So what does the film show? Does it show him?"

"It could, you'll see for yourself."

"Oh my, really?" Judy grimaced. "I don't know if I want to see it. Okay, maybe I do."

Anne asked, "How did you get it, Lou?"

"And where was the camera?" Bennie leaned over the table, as did Roger and Isaac, while Lou pulled his phone out of his back pocket, and started scrolling, then handed it to Mary in exasperation.

"Mare, do it for me, will ya? I left my reading glasses in the car. Damn it!"

"What am I looking for?" Mary took the phone, not surprised to see the icons on the home screen magnified to the max.

"Go to my email. I got a video clip I sent

to myself. You'll see the angle ain't great. The only camera I could find, and believe me, I knocked on the door of every bar, restaurant, gallery, and tattoo place in the area."

"Hang on." Mary scrolled to Lou's email, opened the most recent one, and clicked the video attachment, waiting for it to upload.

Lou leaned over. "You can't see much, especially not on the phone. We gotta send this to our guy, the one that does the trial exhibits for us. He prolly can blow it up and give us more detail."

"I'm sure he can," Anne said, leaning over the table.

Bennie interjected, "Lou, I asked you where the camera was. Where was the camera?"

"Okay, the angle is on a diagonal across the street from the little street that goes behind the apartments like John's, where the yards are and the residents park." Lou motioned with his hands, but that didn't help explain anything. "And the angle is good but it's, like, very sharp, like *acute* because the camera was underneath a little roof that had a light above the front door."

"The front door of what?" Bennie asked, exasperated.

"A massage parlor."

Bennie recoiled. "Really?"

Roger smiled. "Did you go in, Lou?"

"Only to ask about the camera," Lou answered, mock-huffy. "I'd rather fish."

"Okay, gang, showtime." Mary held the phone up so everybody could see it, and the video began to play.

They all fell silent as a grainy, black-and-white picture came onto the screen, showing tiny, shadowy silhouettes walking back and forth in front of the backstreet behind John's apartment. The bottom of the screen read ENTRANCE MAIN and under that was the date and 21:03:00, a military clock changing numbers, in seconds.

Mary squinted at the video, feeling a bolt of excitement. "So that's the relevant time period, right? That means three minutes after nine o'clock?"

"Yes," Lou answered, pursing his lips.

Mary stayed glued to the video, and she could see lights on in several of the apartments if only because they were gray rectangles set lengthwise.

Bennie asked, "Which apartment is John's?"

"This one." Lou pointed at the window in the middle.

"Let me see if I can enlarge that." Mary

swiped over the middle window on the phone screen, and the view enlarged. The focus worsened, but the outline of a fire escape appeared, its heavy iron elements thin and spidery. "That's John's fire escape."

"Right." Lou's tone turned tense, and everyone fell silent again.

Mary held her breath, watching the video and realizing that what they were about to see was Machiavelli, or his thug, after having killed John. The very thought made her sick to her stomach, and she glanced at Judy.

"I'm fine," Judy said, anticipating Mary's question.

Mary watched as in the next moment, a small, shadowy silhouette appeared in John's office window, backlit by the lights in John's apartment. "Is that him?"

"Yes," Lou pointed at the darkness. "By the way, there's no motion-detector lights out back. I checked again today."

Mary and the others lapsed into a tense silence as in the next few moments, the silhouette got large, closer to the window, clearly visible in outline. The killer's face was in the camera's view, but it was completely obscured by darkness, and Mary prayed for better detail, but it was too grainy. Together, they all watched as the shadow did something at the window, presumably opened it, lifting one arm up while the other held something the same size as a laptop, and then climbed outside, lowered the window, and vanished into the darkness around the fire escape. A few moments later the shadow reappeared on the backstreet behind the row of houses, then took a right turn and left the camera view.

Mary groaned. "Ugh, you can't tell if it's him or whoever he sent. It's not enough proof, is it?"

Bennie shook her head. "No, not unless we can get it enlarged or enhance the image. It's not enough to charge him or even question him."

"This is awful, this is just so awful." Judy's voice sounded choked, and Mary reached for her hand and held it tight. The numbers changed at the bottom of the video screen, and Mary realized this was when John lay on his living room floor, bleeding to death. She felt tears come to her eyes, wishing she could turn the numbers back, make them rewind to zero so that John was still alive, William and the Hodges were happy again, and Judy had a future with a man she had finally found, after so long.

Bennie broke the silence. "Lou, when does he come in the apartment?"

"He doesn't, according to this video. I

watched the whole video. He doesn't enter by the window, he only leaves by it. He musta entered by the front door."

"So what does that tell us?" Bennie asked, thinking aloud. "It tells us that John knew who he was and let him in, or at least John wasn't afraid of him. But after the killer kills John, he leaves by the back."

"It doesn't tell us much." Mary hit Stop, and the screen froze in grainy stillness. "You could say that it tells us that the act was impulsive, that he's panicky and he leaves by the back. But it doesn't really tell us that, logically. There could've been a lot of people on the street and he wanted to avoid detection. He knew he'd just killed John, so he leaves by the back. Even a professional would've done that. If he'd put on a suit, John would've let him in. He could've even said he'd been sent by Machiavelli to talk about the reverse-discrimination case, for that matter. Because the killer knew he would kill John, so John wouldn't be alive to testify."

"Poor John." Judy withdrew her hand from Mary's, wiping her eyes.

Bennie sighed, and everyone went stone silent, their expressions uniformly grave as Mary looked around the table. Judy dabbed at her eyes with a napkin and straightened her shoulders, turning to Lou.

"Lou, that was good work. Thank you."

"I'm happy to help, honey." Lou patted her hand, and something about seeing his lined wrinkled hand, with its age spots, resting on top of Judy's small girlish hand with its funky pink nails, touched Mary's heart.

She sighed. "I wish the focus could have been better."

"It's okay." Bennie shrugged. "It establishes that the killer left on the fire escape. It corroborates what we already know, and it does fix the time of the murder."

Mary looked over. "Bennie, don't you think it exonerates Judy somewhat? In terms of timing, she was gone, and why would she leave by the fire escape? That makes no sense. She had a key and she could go back and forth out the front door."

"Right," Judy chimed in, brightening. "Doesn't this mean I'm off the hook?"

Bennie looked less certain. "No, you can't tell it's *not* Carrier by this video, and there's too much give on the time of death. She could react the same way the real killer did, go out the back to avoid detection."

Mary remained unconvinced. "I would still argue that it does, when we give the cops the tape. We have to give them the tape, don't we?"

"Lemme think." Bennie looked at Lou. "Do you think they had it already? What do they say at the massage parlor? Had the police been there?"

"Yes, but I know the cops don't have the tape. The manager told me that the police came by and asked about cameras, but the manager wasn't in so nobody would let them in the back. I don't know if they're going back, but I wouldn't feel comfortable sitting on this." Lou patted Judy's hand again. "They are not going to let you off the hook until they like somebody better."

Mary's thoughts were racing. "But wait, on second thought, that puts me in a difficult ethical position, as Judy's lawyer. This is our work product, and I don't have an ethical or legal obligation to turn over work product that would inculpate my client. On the contrary, I have an obligation *not* to."

Bennie nodded. "You're right."

Lou frowned in disapproval. "Maybe we take our time in turning it over? Can we do that?"

Mary looked at Lou. "Let's table it for now. Judy's right, you did a great job. Maybe our guy can get something out of it and we can see more of the face. We also have to check if there are any cameras on the front of the house or the street, because that will show somebody entering."

Lou pocketed his phone. "I can double-check and maybe it'll have a better view."

"Maybe," Bennie said, hopeful.

"Honey, what's going on?" Mary had finally gotten home, only to find Anthony's roller-bag in the entrance hall and him standing there, ready to leave, phone in hand.

"I was just about to call you." Anthony kissed her quickly on the cheek, excited. He was dressed in a sport jacket and jeans, with his fancy raincoat draped over one arm. "I have to go to Boston."

"Boston, why?"

"You know the professor I told you about, the one in the history department at Harvard? I've been trying to get an interview with him for weeks, for my book."

"Yes, right," Mary said vaguely, too tired to remember right now.

"He said he could meet with me tomorrow, and there's a lecture we should attend together, the day after that. So I have to go to Boston for two days. I got a hotel and I'm on the next flight." Anthony touched her cheek, with a smile. "Do you mind? I think you'll be okay, won't you?"

"Sure, I'll be fine." Mary smiled, happy to

see him so happy. "I just have work, I'll be fine."

"Great, thanks. You have to promise me you'll take it easy, though." Anthony passed her to the door.

"I'll take it easy."

"Don't be crazy." Anthony shot her a warning look, opening the door. "Remember what the doctor said."

"Okay, okay."

"I love you." Anthony picked up his rollerbag. "Good-bye."

"Good-bye, and I love you, too."

"And I love you, little baby," Anthony said to Mary's belly, then he was gone.

CHAPTER THIRTY-SIX

The Pennsylvania Human Relations Commission was housed in a generic, modern office building at Eighth and Arch Streets in Center City, with a façade of indeterminate tan stone and slitted windows more common to a prison than a building with a PennDot driver licensing center on the main floor. Upstairs, the agency's offices were similarly institutional, with nondescript wooden furniture and spare padded chairs throughout. Mary and Roger were shown into a windowless conference room that held a long conference table with chairs, a speakerphone, and some stray pencils. The walls were freshly painted white, and the only decorations were color portraits of Pennsylvania's governor and lieutenant governor, next to an American flag and the cobalt-blue flag of the Commonwealth of Pennsylvania, both of which listed to the right, like beech trees in a strong wind.

Mary sat next to Roger, trying not to be nervous as they waited for the case investigator to come in. She had on a fresh white-silk T-shirt underneath a lightweight wool dress, which was her prettiest maternity outfit, an oxymoron. Roger looked like his normal hip self in a tailored gray suit with a patterned gray and white tie, and Mary got a whiff of his aftershave, which smelled like sandalwood and world peace.

"Mary, let me do the talking," Roger said quietly, looking over.

"That's why you make the big bucks."

Roger smiled. "Except that it was your legal strategy."

"I learned from the master." Mary smiled back. She'd warmed to Roger since he'd agreed with their plan, but it was nevertheless risky enough to worry her. Theory was one thing and practice another, and Mary had tossed and turned last night. The baby wasn't kicking yet, so at least one of them was sleeping in.

The door to the conference room opened, and a compact African-American woman entered, who looked in her fifties. Silver strands shone through the short curls of her hair, she had on oversized dark glasses with gold hoops and a navy-blue suit. She entered the room holding a red accordion file and a silvery laptop and shut the door behind her with a warm, broad smile. "Folks, I'm so sorry to keep you waiting. My name is Vanessa Walker and I'm the investigator on this matter. You must be Roger Vitez and Mary DiNunzio."

"Yes, please call me Roger," he said, extending a hand, and Mary rose and did the same. They sat down, with Vanessa on the opposite side of the table, setting a file aside and opening her laptop, before she began to speak.

"I'm pleased to meet you both, and thank you for coming in today." Vanessa regarded them in a professional way, pushing up her glasses with a manicured nail. "Oh, and you have my condolences on the murder of John Foxman."

"Thank you," Roger and Mary said, together.

"Let me tell you how I like to do things. You both know that the Human Relations Commission is the state's body that enforces the antidiscrimination laws in the Commonwealth. As soon as the Complaint is filed, we begin our investigation, and we have fast-tracked this one, since it's in the news so much lately."

Roger nodded, and so did Mary, though neither of them interrupted her.

"I like to keep things informal, so we will be interviewing the principals in the firm of Rosato & DiNunzio in the days to come." Vanessa hit a few keys on her laptop, then turned to Mary with another warm smile. "Congrats on your baby, by the way."

"Thank you," Mary said, happily surprised. "She's quiet this morning. Or he is."

"Enjoy it while you can," Vanessa shot back, and they all laughed. "Okay, let's get to brass tacks. As you know, the Complaint filed by Messrs. Battle, McManus, and Madden alleges that your law firm failed to hire them because of their gender. What I'd like to do is explore with you the decisions not to hire those plaintiffs. I'll ask you informally, and you can answer equally informally. These proceedings are not under oath, but of course, we expect you to tell the truth. Is there anything you want to say before you begin?"

"Yes," Mary answered. They had a plan to put into effect, and it started now. "I'm happy to be here today and answer any questions you have. However, I want to state first, so you hear it from me, that we did not discriminate against these plaintiffs on the basis of their gender. We would never do such a thing and we have always stood at the forefront of equality at our firm. And as a factual matter, I didn't make the decision to hire or not to hire these plaintiffs."

"So you're not the decision-maker?" Vanessa started typing away.

"No, I'm one of the partners and I was the first one available for an interview, so here we are. But I didn't interview any of the complainants. I didn't even know one interviewed and I wasn't aware of them at all, until the Complaint arrived at our offices the other day."

"Okay, thank you very much." Vanessa started typing away, but continued speaking. "Then we can explore hiring practices in general at your firm."

"I'm happy to do that."

Roger cleared his throat. "Vanessa, before we do, I'd like to discuss something with you, also informally. I know you have a mediation program here and settlement is favored by the Commission, where appropriate."

"Yes, that's quite right." Vanessa stopped typing. "Is settlement something you want to explore, even before the interview?"

"Yes, as a matter of fact, it is. First, if I may, I'd like to clarify a few points."

"Go ahead." Vanessa leaned away from the laptop, linking her hands in front of her.

"I've reviewed the file, and correct me if

I'm wrong, but Messrs. Battle, Madden, and McManus are currently employed. Is that correct?"

"Yes." Vanessa nodded pleasantly.

"A typical defendant, in a matter like this, might look at a Complaint from plaintiffs in that posture as failing for lack of damages. By that I mean to say, even assuming that the Rosato & DiNunzio firm failed to hire them because of their gender, which we deny, they incurred no monetary damages as a result of that failure to hire."

"That's true." Vanessa's eyes narrowed. "However, we at the Commission would generally not deny investigation of a Complaint because it may not have resulted in monetary damages."

"Of course, nor would I expect you to, as a citizen." Roger spread his hands, palms up, his tone reasonable and calm.

"So why do you bring up the damages question, if you don't think the Complaint should be denied because of its deficiency?"

"Because it makes this case unique."

"That's true too. The case is also unique for its allegations, since we don't get many reverse-discrimination cases."

"Quite right. I could find very few in my research." Roger straightened in his chair. "But the damages question got us thinking about how we can settle this case. Settlement is typically a monetary amount, a compromise determined by what the plaintiff lost as a result of the unlawful act."

"So what are you prepared to offer?" Vanessa turned to Mary. "Or what are *you* prepared to offer, as a principal of the firm? If you don't mind answering directly."

"In our view, since the plaintiffs haven't incurred any financial damages, they don't need to be made whole financially. We decided to make a wonderful settlement offer to these plaintiffs."

"Which is?" Vanessa asked, impatient.

"We'd like to offer all three of them jobs at Rosato and DiNunzio."

"What?" Vanessa's eyes flared in surprise.

"We'd like to hire them, as associates. Their records are excellent, and we need to hire qualified associates. We don't discriminate against men and we would like the opportunity to prove as much."

"Really?" Vanessa shifted forward, cocking her head with interest.

"It's a win-win situation," Mary said, with conviction, since it had been her idea. She hadn't turned Zen, but she had taken a page from the real Niccolò Machiavelli's book. His most famous saying was, *Keep your friends close and your enemies closer.*

"So you would offer them a job, full-time?"

"Yes, absolutely. In addition, if they felt some minor sum was justified for legal fees they have paid, we would reimburse them, as a sweetener." Mary masked her annoyance at having to pay Machiavelli's legal fees, but if it did him in, it would be her pleasure. "Bottom line, we would love to have them work for us and we hope that will settle this case."

"Well, this is certainly unorthodox." Vanessa smiled, surprised. "Most defendants never want to set eyes on the Complainant who sued them, ever again. The *last* thing they want is them on the premises."

"I'm sure, but that's not how we operate. The Complaint wasn't filed that long ago, so it's not as if we accumulated bad will, and certainly, we have a better perspective on life, after the loss we suffered as a firm."

"I can see how that would be so." Vanessa's expression brightened. "I must say, I didn't expect this at all. I expected something on the order of righteous indignation."

"Oh, I could do that," Mary said, with a smile.

Roger laughed. "Believe me, she could."

Vanessa smiled back. "My, my, this is a

game-changer."

"I would think so." Mary wanted to hammer the point home. "After all, we pay associates extremely well, and it's what these three men wanted when they applied. It's more than reasonable as a settlement offer, don't you agree?"

"I must say, it's impressive."

"Will you recommend that they settle?"

"I have to discuss that with them before I discuss it with you. Regardless of any recommendation of mine, they are free to make any decision they wish. But I will certainly discuss this with plaintiff's counsel, and it will be up to them to decide what they want to do."

"Of course." Mary put on her game face, gambling that Machiavelli wouldn't out-Machiavelli them and instruct the three plaintiffs to accept the job offer, since she didn't think he would do that, or they would accede. What she gained was a possible settlement of the reverse-discrimination case, having called his bluff by their offer. If Machiavelli refused such a reasonable settlement offer, the Commission would never go his way. Plus Mary got the added benefit of not revealing she was onto Machiavelli, not only with respect to his manufacturing the reverse-discrimination suit, but his owning

Home Hacks in the *London Technologies* case. Because what she really wanted was to get Machiavelli on *murder.*

Vanessa returned to her laptop. "Mary, let's complete the interview, just in case."

"Of course," Mary said, but she was already thinking about stage two of their plan.

Which went into effect right now.

CHAPTER THIRTY-SEVEN

After the interview, Mary and Bennie went to the Roundhouse, having called for a meeting with Detectives Krakoff and Marks, who listened and took notes while the two women explained how the reverse-discrimination case was manufactured by Machiavelli in order to eliminate John on the *London Technologies* case, and ultimately, why they believed that Machiavelli was responsible for John's murder, whether he had killed him himself or hired someone to do it. They had decided not to mention the surveillance videotape while Judy's legal fate was still in jeopardy, and it wasn't a clear enough image of Machiavelli anyway, so it wasn't their strongest evidence.

Mary handed Detective Krakoff the corporate registration for Home Hacks, ending her argument. "So that's it, in a nutshell. We think you need to investigate Machiavelli for this murder."

Bennie straightened her chair. "So Detectives, what do you say?"

"Thanks for coming in, ladies." Detective Krakoff closed his pad, sliding the pen in the spiral on one end.

Mary didn't hide her impatience. "What does that mean? Are you going to investigate Machiavelli?"

"Mary, we've been through this. I'm not about to divulge police business to you."

Bennie interjected, "Detective, we would keep this absolutely confidential."

Detective Krakoff frowned, eyeing Bennie. "Excuse me, but you weren't here the more recent time that your partner Mary came in. You were here only the first time, when she had those dreadful labor pains. I'm not going to ask you if you took her to the doctor —"

"What does that have to do with anything?" Bennie shot back. "This isn't about us, it's about John Foxman."

"Mary was in here the other day, telling me that Mike Shanahan was a likely suspect in the murder and that we should investigate him." Detective Krakoff turned to Mary. "Mary, I don't know what game you're playing."

"I can explain," Mary said, defensive. "I told you about Shanahan because I thought

442

that he was a real possibility. But now I have new information —"

"Or you were promoting any suspect you could to deflect attention away from your client Judy Carrier."

"That's not what's going on," Mary shot back. "Machiavelli is the one you need to be looking at. And of course Judy isn't guilty, not in the least. Somewhere in your heart, you have to know that. It's absurd to suspect her."

Bennie threw up her hands. "Detective, you know that in any investigation, new facts arise. We came to you as soon as we got this information. We didn't want to waste any time. We assume you don't either. So are you going to investigate Machiavelli?"

Detective Krakoff pocketed his steno pad. "As I said, you're not immediate family, so you're not entitled to that information."

Mary got an idea. "You know, John's brother is in town, and so are his next of kin, his aunt and uncle. They're going through hell right now, so I would like very much not to bring them in. But if I got a letter from them, or some kind of phone authorization, would you talk to us then?"

Bennie nodded, eagerly. "Yes, we could get a letter from them authorizing us as their attorneys. We could speak with you as counsel."

Detective Krakoff hesitated. "Is William in town?"

"Yes, why?"

"Where is he?" A concerned frown crossed Detective Krakoff's face.

"He's at the hotel with the Hodges, his aunt and uncle. They're elderly, she has a broken ankle, and William's in a wheelchair. Obviously, it would be so difficult and upsetting to bring them in. Couldn't you just play ball with us?"

"When is William going back to Glenn Meade?"

"I don't know, I haven't had a chance to check. Probably later today." Mary hadn't discussed it with Judy and she still didn't want to admit to Detective Krakoff that Judy had been John's girlfriend.

Detective Krakoff paused, pursing his lips. Mary asked, "What is it? Why do you ask?"

"I will share limited information with you. But it must remain confidential."

"Yes, totally," Mary said quickly.

"Of course, please do." Bennie nodded.

Detective Krakoff said, "Shanahan has disappeared."

"What?" Mary asked, shocked.

Bennie blinked. "How do you know?"

"We followed up on your lead, Mary. We

went to Glenn Meade this morning to talk to Shanahan. He didn't come to work. They called his cell, and there was no answer. We went to his apartment. His car's gone, so are his clothes. He said nothing to the landlord or neighbors about where he was going."

"But why would he go?" Mary's thoughts raced. "I swear to you, it was Machiavelli that killed John, not Shanahan. I'm sure of it."

Bennie forward. "We still think it's Machiavelli, and the fact that Shanahan has gone missing doesn't change that. Even if he didn't do it, he could have been worried he'd be accused, given the Complaint. Or he simply could have felt the situation was too hot to stick around, given his past."

Mary nodded, glad of the support. "So Detective, what happens now? Will you follow up with Machiavelli?"

"We're looking for Shanahan. The timing of his disappearance isn't coincidental, to us." Detective Krakoff frowned. "I divulged the information for a reason. It would be best for William if he didn't return to Glenn Meade until we locate Shanahan, out of an abundance of caution. I have concern for William's safety there, should Shanahan seek to contact him. Glenn Meade has no security measures to speak of."

"I agree, I don't want to take any chances with William's safety."

"So you see, I'm a nice guy after all." Detective Krakoff smiled, but Mary felt so frustrated that her case against Machiavelli was slipping away, when they'd come so far.

"Detective, I do appreciate your concern for William, but I truly don't think Shanahan did it. Machiavelli did. We're talking about millions and millions of dollars in one company, if not the two companies." Mary gestured at the corporate papers on the typing table. "And they're sure producers in the future because he monopolized the market. Machiavelli would kill to keep those businesses and hurt our firm in the bargain. It's more than enough for motive."

Detective Krakoff cocked his head skeptically. "You're telling me that this Machiavelli is a successful lawyer in town?"

"Yes."

"With his own law firm and major investments? Major businesses? Data integration and what not?"

"Yes, but that doesn't tell you anything. He doesn't have to look like a murderer to be one. He can look like an upstanding citizen."

"But you admit you have a history with him."

"Yes, but it certainly doesn't affect my motives in coming to you with this."

"I'm not saying it does. I'm saying if you have bad blood, you might not be as objective as you think."

"No, I see this clearly, I really do." Mary could tell she wasn't getting anywhere.

"She does," Bennie interjected. "We all do. We're all on the same page. Machiavelli is the one you need to be following up on. Or do both. Knock yourself out. It doesn't have to be one or the other."

"Okay. I've heard you. Thanks." Detective Krakoff's tone turned final. "We do have to go, now. We have to get back to work."

Bennie rose. "Fair enough. Thank you."

"Yes, thanks," Mary said, getting up. She hadn't come this far to quit now.

They would have to find another way.

"Now what do we do?" Mary said under her breath, as they hurried from the Roundhouse, ignoring the press. Reporters shouted questions at them and filmed them leaving, but they knew the drill and kept their heads down, plowing ahead. Amanda Sussman wasn't among them, so Mary mentally confirmed her small victory, a bright spot in an otherwise terrible morning.

"We do what we planned." Bennie charged through the parking lot toward the curb, and Mary struggled to keep up, breaking a sweat in the sun.

"But they're not going to follow up with Machiavelli."

"We can't deal with that now. We have to do the next step." Bennie checked her phone on the fly. "We're right on time. Judy and Anne will meet us there."

"But this is a setback."

"So what else is new?" Bennie powered ahead.

"We have to figure out a way to go after Machiavelli without the cops."

"We'll figure it out."

Mary put her hand on her belly, instinctively, as she chugged along. The baby hadn't kicked during the meeting with the police, which was probably a good thing, considering that her fake labor pains had come back to haunt her.

"DiNunzio, can you walk faster?"

"No, can you walk slower?"

"I have to get us a cab."

"Oh, okay. I have to make a human being."

"You had to go there?" Bennie rolled her eyes, but she slowed down, and Mary reached the curb a step behind her, on a street congested with noonday traffic to the Expressway.

"It's Machiavelli, I'm telling you, I know it in my bones. We have to bring him down this time, once and for all."

"We will. For John."

"Right. For John."

Bennie flagged down a cab. "I have good cab karma with you. I hope you're pregnant forever."

"Thanks," Mary said, burping.

CHAPTER THIRTY-EIGHT

Bennie, Mary, Judy, and Anne filed into the glass-walled conference room at London Technologies, where Sanjay and Jim looked up, startled. "Good morning, gentlemen," Bennie said, closing the glass door behind them, as a young receptionist stuck her head inside.

"I'm so sorry, Sanjay," she said. "They saw you from the door. I couldn't stop them."

"It's okay, Linda." Sanjay waved her off, and the receptionist disappeared, leaving the four women to face Sanjay and Jim.

Bennie took the lead. "Sanjay, Jim, I hate to barge in, but this is an emergency."

Mary added, "If you give us a chance, we can explain everything."

Judy chimed in, "It's not just about your case against Home Hacks and EXMS anymore."

Bennie nodded, standing tall. "And it isn't

just about us working for you either. If you decide you still want to fire us at the end of this argument, then so be it. But hear us out, please."

Sanjay pursed his lips, glancing at Jim, who nodded. Then Sanjay said, "Okay, fine. Say whatever you have to say."

"Thank you." Bennie remained standing as Mary, Judy, and Anne sat down, since she always said she thought better on her feet, then she launched into a full explanation of everything they had learned, namely that Home Hacks was owned by Machiavelli, that they suspected that he also owned EXMS through shell companies, and that he had filed the reverse-discrimination lawsuit and ultimately killed John in order to cause London Technologies to abandon its meritorious suit against his companies.

Mary footnoted Bennie's argument by showing them the corporate registrations, and Anne reminded Sanjay and Jim how integral John had been in the litigation. Sanjay and Jim confirmed that they had thought of John as the expert early on, but asked why the women hadn't gone to the police, and Judy explained about William, Shanahan, and the fact that they had all agreed that Machiavelli was responsible for John's murder. By the end of the argument, Bennie had seated herself, the other women had fallen quiet, and Jim and Sanjay looked stricken.

"My God," Sanjay said, in hushed tones. "It's so awful to think that somehow John's murder was connected to our case."

Jim had gone white in the face. "It sickens me. John was a terrific lawyer, and I never thought his murder was related to us in any way."

"We didn't either," Bennie shot back.

"But now you know, right?" Mary asked, pointedly.

"Because we're sure of it," Judy chimed in.

Anne nodded. "And we need your help."

"Well . . ." Jim and Sanjay exchanged glances, then Sanjay said, "Ladies, I'm not going to lie. You're springing this on us, and it sounds so out of left field. Some sounds like speculation, but some of it doesn't, I admit." Sanjay gestured to the corporate papers cluttering the black conference table. "But I don't know what you expect us to do. We would never go against the police."

Jim shook his head. "Right, we're not experts, they are. If they think this Shanahan guy killed John, we're inclined to go with their judgment. We don't know how we can help you."

Bennie leaned forward, urgently. "You don't have to do anything. You don't have to even believe us over the police. All you have to do is not fire us for a few days."

Mary added, "That's all we're asking. We need the time to investigate Machiavelli on our own. We need to use your case as a cover and we don't want Machiavelli to know we're onto him, in any way. We even took the step of offering to hire the plaintiffs in the reverse-discrimination suit, so he wouldn't think we suspected anything. The minute you fire us, or go looking for another lawyer, our cover is blown and we lose our basis for proceeding."

Anne said, urgently, "Sanjay, Jim, please give us three more days, that's all we ask. You have depositions coming up tomorrow and the day after, and I'm prepared to take them both. You won't have to cancel or postpone them. You haven't found a replacement counsel yet, have you?"

"No," Sanjay said, frowning.

"We were just discussing our next move when you came in." Jim's face fell. "We were crunching the numbers, too. We were probably going to have to abandon the litigation and withdraw our Complaint."

"So then you have nothing to lose," Mary blurted out. "Please, let us just go forward."

Anne nodded. "Guys, you won't be sorry. I've worked this case from day one, and we got through the time when you didn't see me as the one who could represent you. I am, and you know that now, and please let me finish what we started. I swear, in the end this will bring Machiavelli down *and* benefit London Technologies. We have the facts and the law on our side. This case is a sure winner. If we just keep the pressure on, he has to settle and he knows it."

Judy cleared her throat noisily, and Mary looked over, surprised to see tears glistening in her best friend's eyes, though Judy's attention was riveted on Sanjay and Jim. "I know that you're entrepreneurs, but I know that you're about more than money. You came up with a genuine innovation that opened your market up to newcomers, just like you. You saw that it was unjust and you put your company on the line, trusting in us, filing that lawsuit, and trying to break up a monopoly."

Sanjay listened, and so did Jim, and Mary could see that Judy was reaching them, with the power of her words and the authenticity of her emotions.

"So I guess I'm saying to you that this is not about law, but it's about justice." Judy's eyes brimmed with tears, but she held them back. "We all knew John, some of us better than others. We can't let Machiavelli get away with murdering him with impunity. We have a chance to do the right thing. You know how hard he fought for your company, how loyal he was to you. So please show the loyalty to him, even in death, that he did for you, in life." Judy swallowed hard. "I'm asking you, I'm *begging* you, to give us three more days. Will you do that, for us and for him?"

"Of course," Sanjay answered immediately, his eyes nearly wet. "Judy, when you put it that way. Mary, Bennie, Anne, we can do that, we have to, don't we?" Sanjay looked at Jim. "Right, we can't say no."

"We can't say no, not after that!" Jim burst into nervous laughter, wiping his eyes. "Hey, you guys don't pull any punches, do you?"

"Why start now?" Bennie laughed.

"Thank you so much!" Mary jumped out of her chair, unable to contain herself, and went around the table and gave them both very pregnant hugs. "We really appreciate it!"

"It's okay, it's all right." Sanjay let her go, with a sweet smile. "We have your back. We wish you luck."

"We sure do." Jim grinned. "Just be careful. Fighting crime doesn't go very well with being pregnant, does it?"

"So far, so good." Mary patted her belly, again instinctively, but the baby was still asleep. It struck her as unusual, but she didn't know if it was anything to be worried about. Probably not.

Meanwhile, Bennie was beaming, Anne was hugging Sanjay, Judy was hugging Jim, and Mary could feel the palpable warmth of the relationship returning, all of them newly bound by John's death and a common cause. Suddenly she caught sight of a young tall, redheaded man in jeans and a black T-shirt looking into the conference room, then continuing on his way down the hall.

"Who was that, Sanjay?" Mary asked, since something about him seemed familiar.

"That's our intern, Paul Patrioca. He does coding for us."

"I know that family!" Mary said, feeling a happy bolt of recognition. "The Patriocas live in my parish in South Philly. I went to high school at Maria Goretti with his sister. Paul's the baby of the family, there were seven of them. I knew him when he was little."

"You recognize him?"

"He hasn't changed that much. He's a Patrioca. They have that nose and bright red hair that sticks up. You don't see it that often." Mary thought back to Paul and his family, feeling her smile fade. "You know, come to think of it, that's funny."

"What is?"

"It's a funny coincidence that he works here." Mary started to wonder, putting it together.

"How so? He's new. Newish."

"When did he start? About six months ago? About the time that you filed the complaint against Home Hacks and EXMS?"

"Yes, exactly. How did you know?" Sanjay nodded, with a puzzled frown. "We hired him because we were getting too busy with the litigation, the meetings and all. We needed somebody to take up the slack."

"And he's in college? He goes to Drexel?" Mary looked down the empty hallway, but Paul had vanished. "Somebody go get him."

Bennie looked over. "DiNunzio, what's up?"

"The Patriocas live next door to the Machiavellis."

Chapter Thirty-Nine

Mary opened the door to the conference room, while Sanjay approached with Paul Patrioca. "Hi, I'm Mary DiNunzio," she said, shaking Paul's hand, when he crossed the threshold, looking plainly nervous. Up close, Paul had a long, narrow face, with prominent cheekbones and the hawk-like Patrioca nose, which he had grown into over the years. He came off as good-looking, but ill at ease, and his frame was thin and his arms geek-soft.

"Hey, hi." Paul scanned the room with his pale blue eyes, and Mary introduced Bennie, Anne, and Judy, sitting with Jim on the opposite side of the table.

"Paul, I know your family from way back. Your sister Teresa went to Goretti with me."

"Oh, okay."

"Why don't you sit down?" Mary rolled out a black ergonomic chair and gestured

Paul into it, while she sat down catty-corner to him.

"What's this about?"

"Oh, I just thought I'd call you in. You don't know us, but we're the lawyers for London Technologies in this antitrust lawsuit. We meet from time to time to discuss it, but when I saw you going by, I wanted to say hi."

"Oh, hi," Paul said slowly.

"I remember your family. The youngest of seven, aren't you?"

"Yes."

"You live next door to the Machiavelli family, don't you?"

Paul hesitated. "My parents do, I guess. I don't live there now. I live in West Philly. Powellton."

"Right, near the Drexel campus." Mary kept her gaze on him, in her best deposition mode, which is like being someone's best frenemy. "You probably know Nick Machiavelli, he's a lawyer in town."

"Um, yes, I guess I heard of him."

"But you knew them from the neighborhood, didn't you?"

"Yes, I mean, I knew of the family." Paul swallowed hard, his Adam's apple prominent in his long neck.

"But you've met Nick, haven't you? You

459

must have. His family lives next door to yours. He's about my age, he's your sister's age. He went to Newman when we went to Goretti."

"Oh yeah, I think I know him." Paul frowned, glancing again at Jim and Sanjay, and Mary could see that he was too young to be a good liar, which came with practice, or a law degree.

"You probably see Nick from time to time when he goes home. He visits his mother all the time. She still lives in the same house, just like my mother. So South Philly, right?"

"Yeah, I think she still does live there."

"And your mom, right? She still lives there, doesn't she?"

"Yes, my father passed eleven years ago."

"I know, I was at the wake. You don't remember, you were too little. But I went to pay my respects, for Teresa."

"Oh." Paul flushed under his freckled skin and Mary could see she had struck a chord, namely guilt, which always worked with her people.

"Nick goes home to visit his mother all the time. He brings all the neighborhood kids presents. He even gives out turkeys on Thanksgiving day, in the church parking lot."

"Oh, right."

Mary blinked, feeling for him. "You and your family probably got one of those turkeys, didn't they, Paul?"

"Yes." Paul swallowed hard, looking down at his fingernails, which were bitten off at the end of long, slim fingers.

"We did, too." Mary put her hand on his arm. "I know what it feels like to need a hand, from time to time. But it's not a crime to have less money than somebody else. Most people have been there, or they will be at sometime in their lives."

Paul nodded, downcast, but didn't raise his head.

"And it's not even a crime to have somebody put you through college. I would've taken that, too. I had student loans until about last week." Mary chuckled, patting his arm, though she didn't take her hand off. "And somebody who's really your friend, who *really* wants to help you, steps up and doesn't ask something in return. It's not a gift when somebody gives it expecting something in return." Mary paused to let the words sink in. "Is it?"

Paul shook his head.

"So." Mary moved her hand and let the moment pass. "Now's your chance to talk to us and come clean. I know you want to, because I know how you were raised. You

461

were raised just like Teresa and me. We all believe in the same things. Sometimes we lose our way, but we can forgive each other if we just come clean."

Paul sighed heavily, his skinny chest rising and falling in his T-shirt.

"All you have to do is answer my questions and tell the truth. Okay, Paul?"

"Okay," Paul mumbled, then after a moment, he raised his head, looking at Jim and Sanjay with glistening eyes, his young forehead wrinkling into agonized lines. "I'm really sorry. I really am. I had to do it. I didn't have a choice."

Sanjay didn't answer, glowering, but Jim nodded. "We understand. Let's straighten this out now. Let's clear the air."

"Okay." Paul nodded, jittery, then wiped his eyes, leaving pinkish streaks on his face.

Mary smiled at him in an encouraging way. "I know this is hard but we're going to get through this and we're gonna make it better. So let me just ask you, is Machiavelli putting you through Drexel?"

"Yes," Paul answered, with a deep sigh.

"How did that come about, did he approach you at some point and offer?"

"Yes, when I was a junior at Newman. My mom could barely afford the tuition in high school. I was on the assistance program. I didn't think I'd ever go to college. There was no way."

"I understand."

"And he didn't tell me I had to do anything for it, that was what was amazing. It was like Santa Claus." Paul flushed again. "But it was like a miracle. He said he would foot the bill, full ride. And he did. He does."

"How does he do that, physically?" Mary hadn't figured that out yet and was dying to know.

"Some company of his pays the tuition bill directly."

Mary could have guessed as much. "What's the name of the company?"

"Dilworth Corporation, LLC."

Mary made a mental note and she knew that Bennie, Judy, and Anne would never forget the name. In fact, if they could get on the phone to Lou now, they would have. "And Dilworth Corporation pays Drexel directly?"

"Yes."

"Have you ever done any favors for him before this one?"

"No," Paul answered, after a moment.

"But I'm guessing that one day, probably sometime in October or November, he came to you and asked for a favor, isn't that right?"

463

"He called me, yeah."

"And what did he say?"

"He said I know you do some computer stuff, can you go try to get an internship with this company, London Technologies? Say you'll work free." Paul glanced at Jim and Sanjay again, his lower lip puckering with regret. "I really am sorry guys, I mean it."

Sanjay didn't reply, and Jim merely nodded.

"Paul, what did Machiavelli ask you to do, specifically?"

"A couple things." Paul looked down.

"Which were?"

"Basically, let him know what's going on around here, about the lawsuit with Home Hacks and EXMS." Paul began picking his fingernails. "Like if the lawyers ever come in and meet, let him know. Try and hear something. Make copies of anything that the lawyers send and get it to him, like that . . ." Paul let his sentence trail off, and Mary waited for him to finish, knowing there was more.

Sanjay interjected sharply, "Paul, did you give him our code? For the software?"

"Yes," Paul admitted, hanging his head.

"Oh God." Sanjay grimaced. "That's it! Game over!"

Jim shook his head in disgust. "So they'll become us, once they drive us out of the market."

"Not so fast, gentlemen," Mary said, to them. She needed more information from Paul, so she resumed the questioning, in the same quiet tone. "So Paul, you gave him the code for the data integration software?"

"Yes."

"Do you remember when you did that?"

"The first week I worked here." Paul looked down, still picking his fingers.

"Did you give him anything else with respect to the software?"

"Bug fixes, patches, and code that I wrote for 2.1."

Sanjay shook his head, saying nothing. Jim rubbed his forehead.

Mary asked, "Other documents about the software or anything like that?"

"Emails, but we don't work that way."

"So most of the documents were on the lawsuit?"

"Yes."

"What were they, emails or letters, things like that, relating to the lawsuit?" Mary glanced at Anne, whose green eyes flashed with anger.

"Yes." Paul looked up, pained.

"How did you give him these documents?

You didn't email them, did you?"

"No, nothing by email. He didn't want anything traced."

"You didn't meet Machiavelli directly, did you?"

"No. He sent somebody to meet me, and I gave them to her."

"Who was she?"

"I don't know. She was short. Cute. Hot. I think she was, like, his assistant or something."

"Do you know her name?"

"No, we never even talked."

"But she met you in person?"

"Yes."

"How often did you meet her in the past six-month period?"

Paul paused, in thought. "Probably ten times."

"Where did you meet?"

"Always in the same place, Rittenhouse Square at lunchtime. On a bench. She would be eating her lunch, and I would sit down and put the documents inside a newspaper, then get up and go." Paul rolled his eyes. "It was like I was CIA or something, like a spy."

Mary thought it sounded exactly like Machiavelli's modus operandi. He probably had a network of these kids, doing his bidding in all sorts of enterprises, with him pulling the strings on an interconnected web of favors, like a second-rate Godfather. She felt appalled by the theft of business information, but she really wanted to focus on John's murder. "Did you ever go to Machiavelli's office and meet anybody else who worked for him?"

"No."

"Have you ever been to his office?"

"No."

"So the only contact you had lately with Machiavelli was when he made you this offer?"

"Yes."

"So the only other contact you ever had with Machiavelli is through this woman?"

"Yes."

Mary thought it over, because it wasn't helping on the murder case. "Did she ever come with anybody in his organization, whom you think he used for security?"

"No, she always came alone."

"How did you arrange the drop-offs?"

"She texted on a burner phone. It was never the same number."

"Okay, so, Paul." Mary leaned back, linking her fingers together. "I'm not well-versed in this area of the law, but I know enough to say that what you did is unlawful. It's industrial espionage and theft of trade secrets. You probably know that, too, don't you?"

"I *had* to do it," Paul said, stricken. "I owed him, and he said I owed him. He said I had to pay him back for the tuition he paid, plus interest. I don't have that kind of money, I don't have any money."

"You didn't sign a contract to that effect, did you?"

"No."

"Then he lied. If he offered you tuition money, he's legally considered a volunteer, and you owe him nothing. Did you keep any notes of what you told him?"

"No."

"So you're going to need a lawyer."

"Where am I gonna get a lawyer?" Paul practically wailed. "I don't have the money for that. Can you be my lawyer?"

"No, I can't be your lawyer and neither can any of us, because we represent London Technologies."

"Um, can I just ask you a question?" Paul asked, with a new fear in his eyes. "Are you going to tell my mother?"

Mary blinked, not completely surprised. Italian-American mothers and sons were connected not by an umbilical cord, but a bungee cord.

"Dude," Sanjay chuckled, dryly. "I think Mommy's going to find out. If we sue you or *prosecute* you."

"Oh no." Paul's lips parted, stricken. "She doesn't know anything about Machiavelli."

Mary didn't get it. "But she has to know that he pays your college tuition."

"No, she doesn't, she would kill me if she thought I took money from Machiavelli." Paul's words sped up as he got more upset, and Mary touched his hand, not wanting him to panic and shut up.

"But who does she think pays your college tuition? She had to see the checks, didn't she? Or some kind of receipt?"

"Yes, she saw a check once, but they say Dilworth, so I lied to her. I told her that Dilworth was an IT company in Center City, like, IT consultants? I told her I work for them part-time during school. I said they have a tuition payment program, and she believed it. She would never let me take the money if she knew it came from him."

"Why?"

"She hates his guts. My whole family does. All her friends hate him, too."

"They live right next door —"

"That's why. Machiavelli's mom still lives in their house and she didn't want to move, so Machiavelli wanted to make it bigger. He tried to buy my mom's house, but she said no."

Mary knew it rang true. Many wealthier South Philly residents, including the Philly Mob, would buy a few rowhouses, then knock out the interior walls to make one big house, though the façade remained unchanged. Partly it was to keep a low profile, but not even a mobster could convince his mother to move. Mary had tried to get her own parents to move to Center City or the suburbs, which they viewed as moving to Pluto.

"Her house is only worth about $75,000, and he offered her $200,000, then he raised it to half a million, then a *million dollars.* In *cash.*" Paul's eyes flared in giddy wonder. "But she still wouldn't take it. She won't move. My dad passed in that house, and she thinks his spirit lives there, like, his ghost. She's not going anywhere for *any* amount of money."

"Really." Mary could see that Sanjay's mouth had dropped open, but she was getting a hunch. "I'm going to bet that what Machiavelli did next was threaten her."

"Yes." Paul's expression darkened, his face falling. "She started getting phone calls from some guy, saying 'she better move if she knew what was good for her.' "

"Oh no." Mary shuddered. "So what happened?"

"My brother Joey moved back home in case anything happened, and, like, a week later when my mom was out, some guy came over the house, beat Joey up, and put him in the hospital."

"Ugh." Mary recoiled, but it could have been exactly what she was looking for. She felt her heart beat quicker. "Do you know who the guy was?"

"No, I wasn't there."

"Didn't you ever hear his name?"

"They called him Stretch. I don't know his real name or his last name."

"Why do they call him Stretch, is he tall?" Mary asked, though she should have known better than to make sense of South Philly nicknames.

"I don't know. I never saw the guy. I was young when it happened."

"Did your mom or Joey call the cops?"

"No, we don't snitch."

Mary let it go. "So then what happened?"

"After Joey got out of the hospital, he called Machiavelli at his office and told him that Stretch could beat him up every night, but it wouldn't make any difference, our mom would never sell. So he bought the houses on the other side of his mom's house. My mom's the only holdout on our side of the street, I think." Paul's forehead buckled. "I felt bad taking his money for tuition after what he did to Joey, but it was the only way I could go to college. I figured what my mom didn't know wouldn't hurt her."

"Do you think Joey would remember Stretch? Can we call him?"

"No, Joey's in Afghanistan. Third tour."

"What about your mom? Think she knows anything about Stretch, like his real name?"

"Don't know." Paul frowned, his eyebrows sloping unhappily down. "Are you really gonna tell her about me?"

"No, you are."

CHAPTER FORTY

Cullen Avenue, read the sign on the street where Machiavelli's mother and Paul's mother lived, but Mary didn't want to use the front entrance, to avoid being seen by Machiavelli's mother or Machiavelli, in case he happened to be visiting. She directed the cab to go around the block, since Paul's family had the corner property, with a side door on the cross street, Evergreen. Of course there were no evergreens in sight, only the typical block of redbrick rowhouses, gum-spattered sidewalks, and dirty gutters, though there was plenty of parking because there were fewer families, since Machiavelli's mother, Flavia, occupied the west side exclusively, except for the Patriocas.

Mary and Paul got out of the cab, beelined for the side door, and entered his house through the back, greeted by a noisy hubbub. Older women filled the kitchen, laughing, talking, and having a great time as they baked cookies, pasted magazine pictures on homemade greeting cards, gift-wrapped hand-knitted baby hats and receiving blankets, and packed paper plates, water bottles, and soda in brown-paper bags. The kitchen was warm with the aroma of fresh coffee and baking chocolate chips, and there were so many fluffy heads of gray hair that it looked like a stormfront had rolled in.

Paul moaned under his breath. "Oh Jeez, I forgot. She's got the Rosary Society today. Please don't make me tell her in front of everybody. It'll embarrass her."

"Paul!" "Paulie!" "Yo, Paul!" The older women came clucking toward Paul and Mary with open arms, a moving mass of bifocals, painted sweatshirts, and polyester pants, wearing slippers loose enough to accommodate bunions. "How you been, Paul? You got so tall!" "And who's that? Mary DiNunzio!" "Mare, you're havin' a baby?" "Look, Lil, she's havin' a baby!" "How's your parents, Mare?"

"Great, thanks!" Mary recognized her clients Margie Moran and Ann Butchart, accepting their fragrant hugs, which smelled of fading rosewater and hot glue gun. "Margie, good to see you! How's that new boiler working out? Ann, how's your shoulder? Better after the operation? Lorraine, is Brian doing okay at Pathway? It's one of the best schools around."

"He's so happy, thanks!" Lorraine chirped. Margie said she loved her water heater, and Ann's shoulder was on the mend, so Mary had completed her client relations for the day.

"Paul, you're home! How's school?" Paul's mother, Conchetta, hurried delightedly toward them, from the living room. She had the Patrioca nose, hooded blue eyes behind her pink acetate glasses, and a sweet, warm smile. Her orange-red hair looked freshly colored, set in spongy pink rollers, and her long, lined face revealed that she was probably in her seventies but she moved like a fifty-year-old in a white T-shirt, wide-leg jeans, and white Keds.

"Mom, you look nice." Paul gave her a hug. "What are you all up to?"

"Me and the girls are goin' over to Pennsylvania Hospital. We're bringin' the sick kids and the families some treats. You know, cheer 'em up!" Conchetta turned to Mary, engulfing her in a hug. "Hey, Mare! Long time, no see! Teresa will be sorry she missed you! She's on a business trip, big shot now."

"Hi, Conchetta!" Mary smiled, releasing her from the embrace. "Tell Teresa I said hi."

"Look at you!" Conchetta beamed, patting Mary's belly. "About seven months now, right? How you feelin', honey? You're carryin' high. It's a girl."

"You think?" Mary realized that she was with a bunch of mom experts, for a change. "But you know what, usually the baby kicks a lot, but for about a day and a half, no kicking. Is that weird? Or bad?"

"This is your first baby, isn't it?"

"Yes, why?"

"Because you worry too much. You can take your temperature every five minutes, Mare. I was that way with Teresa, she was my first, but by Johnnie, I knew better. And my fourth, you know Elizabeth, was like that too, slept all the time, she still does. She couldn't get out of bed in the morning, missed the bus all the time." Conchetta patted her arm. "You know what you gotta do? Eat. Did you eat."

"No, but I'm not hungry."

"Still, you gotta eat. Here, we made cookies. Sugar will perk the baby right up." Conchetta plucked some chocolate chips off a cooling rack, put them on a paper plate, and handed them to Mary, with one for Paul, too. "Mare, eat that cookie, and I'll get you a cuppa decaf. I'll make fresh."

"Good." Mary chowed down on the

cookie, which was soft, warm, and delicious. She tried not to worry about the baby. She'd been so preoccupied, she hadn't focused on her. Or him.

"It's fine, Mare, sometimes they sleep. Paulie was like that, too. He stayed still, *all the time.* I couldn't wake him up." Conchetta ruffled Paul's hair with a loving grin. "And now, he sits for hours at that computer and he's a big success!"

Paul forced a smile. "Ma, I came home because I was telling Mary about that guy named Stretch, who Machiavelli sent over? You remember that? He beat up Joey?"

"*Do I?* Ha! Those Machiavellis are a disgrace to the neighborhood! Rotten to the core!" Conchetta gestured in the direction of Flavia Machiavelli's house. "Who does she think she is, trying to take my home right out from under me? Our *family* home? Just because she has money, she thinks she can push me around? She picked the wrong family! Her and her crooked son! *Crooked!*"

"Right!" The other women started nodding in vigorous approval. "She's got *some* nerve! Sits in that place like it's a palace!" "How selfish can you be? Try to force everybody out on the *whole* block!" "She's greedy, just like her husband was! Just like her son is! All that money and it's never enough! And they call themselves *Christians*!"

Mary wanted to get to the point. "Conchetta, I need to know Stretch's real name. Do you know it?"

"Stretch? Yeah." Conchetta nodded, so did women behind her, adding to the chorus. "Stretch!" "I know Stretch!" "I heard a Stretch!" "My mother went to West Catholic with his mother! Now you're taking me back!"

"Okay, good," Mary said, hopeful. "So what's his real name? And his last name? I need to find him."

"Uh, um, I don't know." Conchetta shook her head, frowning. "I used to know, but I forget. They just called him Stretch."

The other women chimed in, "I forget his name!" "I never knew it in the first place!" "What's the difference?" "His last name had an L in it, that's all I can tell you!"

Mary hid her dismay. "Did it *start* with an L?"

"I don't know." Ann scratched her head. "I just know there's an L somewhere."

Mary felt stumped. "I really need to know his name. It's very important."

"Aha!" Conchetta eyed her, knowingly. "Is this about the murder I saw on the TV? You think Stretch had something to do with it? He's a thug, and I wouldn't put it past him."

Lorraine scowled. "I saw that on TV, too. Mare, Machiavelli was saying you and the other lady lawyers *killed* somebody, another lawyer! I said to myself, Mary should *sue* him! That's a terrible thing to say! We know it's not true!"

"Of course it's not true!" Ann waved her off. "I called your mother, Mare, and I told her we knew better! Between you and Machiavelli, we know who's the *good* one!"

Margie scowled. "I told my Chiara, 'that Machiavelli, he'll say or do anything to get himself in front of a camera! He's just jealous of Mary! Because everybody loves her!' "

"We love you, Mare!" they all chorused. "We love you, Mary!" "We know you're a good girl!"

"Thanks." Mary started to feel better, rethinking that saying, it was better to be loved than feared. She kinda preferred being loved and she was getting an idea for a way to find out Stretch's real name, especially since there were few alternatives. It would take too long for Lou to find out, and the police were preoccupied with Shanahan. She didn't know what other choice she had, and she wanted to take a flyer.

Mary turned to Conchetta. "Do you think Flavia would know who Stretch is? I'm going to ask her."

"She might." Conchetta nodded. "Stretch works for Nicky. Nicky's over all the time. What mother in South Philly *isn't* in her son's face?"

"Let's go ask Flavia!" Ann called out, then Margie and the others chimed in. "Let's go over!" "Let's give her a piece of our mind!" "Yeah, she's had it too good for too long!" "We got eleven minutes before the next batch comes out!" "The baked ziti's got another half hour." "Let's walk over, girls. We don't have to drive or nothing! Because none of us can!"

Paul grimaced, nervous. "Mom, no, don't go next door. You've never even been inside that house."

"It's okay, Paul." Mary realized he was worried about his secret coming to light. "I'll just ask about Stretch. You can deal with the rest another time." She turned to the other women. "But I'm not sure *everybody* needs to go —"

"We want to go!" they said. "We want to help you! We're goin'!" "We're backin' you and Conchetta!" "We're gonna stand up to the Queen, once and for all!"

"Damn right!" Conchetta started pulling

her spongy curlers out. "I never see *anybody* go in there! She's too good for everybody!"

Paul still looked nervous. "But Mom, Joey said stay away from her and Nick. You don't want to make her mad."

"I'm not afraid of her! Anyway what am I waiting for? Joey didn't want me to, but so what? I'm not getting any younger! I shoulda gone over there a long time ago! Mary needs the information. If Mary needs the information, we're going to get her the *information!*"

"Yes!" Ann cheered, and Margie and the others joined in, "Mary would do anything for us, and this is our chance to do something for her!" "Let's help Mary!" "Mary needs us!" "Let's go see that witch and find out what Mary wants to know!" "Yes, let's go!" "Here we go!" "Get your coat! It's chilly!"

They marched toward the front door, a senior-citizens mob on estrogen replacement, missing everything but the flaming torches and clubs. Mary didn't know whether to be delighted or horrified, but she realized how very strong these women were, each of them so quietly powerful in their own families, but too often marginalized outside of the house. They spent their time taking care of their grandchildren, their children, and their children's dogs, plus sick babies they didn't even know, but they wanted to take care of her, and in that moment, she felt grateful for them, walking examples of pure goodness in the world, in contrast to the Machiavellis.

"Let's go!" Mary charged ahead, taking Paul by the arm.

CHAPTER FORTY-ONE

Mary stood on the step with Paul and Conchetta, knocking on the black-lacquered door, which had a beautiful brass knocker. The façade of the house looked otherwise normal, of red brick, though it had been newly repointed and the front stoop was a fancy flagstone. The other women were trying to peek into the front windows, and Mary sensed that it wasn't solidarity that made them want to come, but nosiness.

The heavy door opened, and Flavia peeked out, blinking, her round brown eyes behind equally round bifocals and a bubble of gray pincurls, set with old-school bobby pins. Mary had remembered her bigger, but Flavia seemed to have shrunk, collapsed into herself. She couldn't have been five feet tall, with a short little nose, and her mouth was bow-shaped. She didn't seem scary or intimidating, and on the contrary, came off as timid as a baby snow owl in a white

Eagles Super Bowl shirt and sweatpants.

"Hello?" Flavia said, eyeing the crowd with alarm.

"Flavia, I don't know if you remember me. I was in the same grade as Nick and I think I met you once —"

"Mary DiNunzio." Flavia's eyes darted to Conchetta and Paul. "Conchetta? Paul?"

"Hello, Flavia," Conchetta shot back. "Surprised you even know who I am."

Mary interjected quickly, "Flavia, I was wondering if we could come in and speak with you."

Flavia looked uncertain, her gaze returning to the other women. "What about them?"

"What *about* us?" Lorraine called back. "What, you can't let us in? You don't have enough room for us? You got ten times more room than anybody else!"

Ann added, "Flavia, we won't stay long. We got cookies in the oven. And baked ziti but that takes longer."

Mary kicked herself for bringing them all. "If you wouldn't mind, Flavia. I would appreciate it if we could come in for a quick visit. There's something important I need to talk to you about."

"Uh, okay. Hold on a minute." Flavia slammed the door shut, and when she opened it again, she had taken out her bobby pins and fluffed up her pincurls. She opened the door wide and stepped aside, somewhat timidly. "Please, come in."

"Thank you." Mary entered the house, with the others filing in behind her, hushed by the awesome interior, which was like stepping into a cool, cavernous Tuscan villa. It was the size of four rowhouses, with the living area on the right and the dining room on the left, and the most remarkable feature was hand-painted Florentine murals that covered the walls on all sides, featuring tall green cypress trees, red-clay roofs, gold-stucco houses, and winding backstreets of cobblestone, like a Vegas version of the city.

Formal couches covered with gold velvet filled the living area, encircling a gold-painted coffee table and end tables, topped by ornate lamps with shades of golden silk and tall millefiori glass bases, obviously authentic, from Murano. Heavy brocade curtains with generous swags and deep maroon-and-gold tassels covered the windows, and the single sunbeam that slipped through fell on the lustrous mahogany dining table, which had carved chairs on either side. The house was decorated to perfection, but so devoid of clutter and other signs of domestic life that it seemed hollow, as if no one lived here at all.

"Holy *shit,*" Conchetta said under her breath.

"Your home is so lovely," Mary said quickly, and Ann, Margie, and the other women started walking around, oohing and aahing, looking at everything in amazement.

Conchetta cleared her throat. "Flavia, I just want to say that I've been angry at you all this time for what your Nicky did to my Joey."

Flavia blinked behind her glasses. "What did he do?"

"You know, about my house and about sending Stretch over to my house to beat my Joey up."

Flavia recoiled, aghast. "I don't understand," she said quietly. She clasped her hands together in front of her, as if she were holding her own hand.

"Don't act like you don't know," Conchetta shot back again, though her tone had softened. "You don't fool me."

"But I don't know. I didn't know. If you'll tell me —"

"You wanted to buy my house, and when I wouldn't sell it to you, you and your son sent Stretch over to beat Joey up."

"Your son Joey, the one in the Army?'

"Yes."

Flavia shuddered. "I didn't do that. I didn't know that Nicky did that —"

"Oh you're gonna tell me that he's such a good boy?" Conchetta's anger flared. "That he'd never do such at thing? That I'm crazy to think that?"

"No." Flavia shook her round gray head. "I know my Nicky is not a good boy."

"You do?" Conchetta asked, surprised.

"You *do*?" Mary repeated, equally surprised. "By the way, Flavia, what's Stretch's real name?"

"Sam Fortunato. Nicky calls him Stretch because he always stretches after he eats." Flavia scowled. "Him, I don't like. I tell Nicky all the time. That Stretch, he's no good. He's got a bad temper. I saw when he drove me once. He's got road rage. It scared me."

Sam Fortunato. Mary felt the name burn into her brain. Fortunato was probably the man Machiavelli had sent to kill John. She felt her pulse quicken. Now she had to decide what to do next.

Meanwhile, Flavia had resumed talking to Conchetta. "I wish Nicky were a good boy. I thought I raised him right. I tried to, after his father died. But he didn't turn out good. I pray every day that he changes his ways."

Paul took his mother's arm. "Mom, okay,

we're done, you said it, we should go now —"

"No, I'm staying." Conchetta pulled her arm back, her eyes remaining on Flavia. "Are you trying to tell me that you didn't know that Nicky did that?"

"I didn't know, my hand to God." Flavia raised her hand, swallowing hard. "I'm very sorry that happened. That's a terrible thing to do. And to a man in uniform, serving our country? I'm so ashamed."

Conchetta frowned. "And you believe me, just like that?"

"Of course. You have no reason to lie." Flavia tilted her head. "Now Nicky, he lies. He lies all the time. But I can tell when he lies. I know, I look right in his eyes, in his *soul.* And I'm gonna talk to him about Joey and see what he says. I'll know if he's lying."

Conchetta seemed nonplussed, disarmed by Flavia's response. "He said you wanted my house. He told me. He told Joey. Was that a lie or the truth?"

"A lie. I never wanted your house. I never wanted anybody's house but my own. What I wanted was *neighbors.*"

Listening, Mary felt her words ring true. Conchetta's frown turned sympathetic, as Flavia continued, her soft voice quavering.

"Nicky says he wants to treat me like gold, like a princess. But I don't want to be a princess. He wants things for me, but I don't want them." Flavia gestured aimlessly, a flailing of her short arms. "I don't need a house this big. I live alone. I only have Nicky, I don't have any other kids. I never use any of these rooms. I get nervous when there's too much room, like it's outer space. I like to be where it's cozy. I never leave the kitchen."

"Oh yeah?" Lorraine called, from behind them. "You stay in the kitchen? Then how do you explain *this*?"

Mary looked over to see Lorraine pointing at a wooden folding chair placed against the wall, next to a table tray that held several upside-down water glasses of various shapes and sizes.

Lorraine scowled, folding her arms. "You use the glasses and listen in to Conchetta's house through the wall, don't you, Flavia?"

"You *spy* on us?" Conchetta frowned, dumbfounded. "On my family?"

Paul recoiled. "You spy on my *mom*?"

Ann, Margie, and everyone else turned to Flavia, who flushed under her papery skin. "I'm sorry," she said quietly. "I'm not spying. I'm just . . . listening. I can't make out the words."

"But why do you *listen*?" Conchetta asked, but her tone wasn't accusatory, just bewildered.

"There's always something happening at your house, Conchetta." Flavia shrugged her little shoulders. "You have such a big family, so many kids. Their wives and husbands and babies, and the new puppy."

Paul flared his eyes. "You know about my cousin's *puppy*?"

Flavia looked up. "I didn't mean anything bad by it. I'm allergic to dogs, so I can't have one. I won't do it anymore."

Mary and Conchetta exchanged glances, and Mary wasn't sure what to say.

Conchetta pursed her lips, looking down at Flavia. "That's creepy, Flavia. Not gonna lie."

"I know. I'm sorry."

"Did you hear us today?"

"Yes." Flavia nodded, with a shaky smile. "You dropped the cookie sheet. Everybody laughed."

Conchetta chuckled. "Not *everybody*."

"I'm sorry that Nicky is so horrible to your family. I really am. I know nobody in the neighborhood likes him, and I think that's why they don't like me. But there's nothing I can do about it. It's too late. I can't spank him anymore. I can't punish him anymore. He's a grown man. All I can do is tell him I'm disappointed in him. That makes him feel bad. But it doesn't change him. I can only pray it's not too late to change him." Flavia gestured at the group of women, who had fallen abruptly silent. "I'm sorry if he did bad things to you, to any of you, or hurt your family. I see you in church, sitting together. I got Conchetta's flyer once in my door, by accident. You're the Rosary Society, right?"

They all nodded, and Conchetta answered, "We meet every week at my house. Today we're going over to the hospital. We're gonna leave in an hour."

"That's nice."

Conchetta paused. "You wanna come? We can always use an extra hand."

Flavia didn't say anything, but got misty behind her glasses.

Conchetta smiled. "Flavia, what do you say? Tick tock. The cookies are gonna burn."

"Okay." Flavia laughed, clapping her little hands together.

"Okay, ladies?" Conchetta turned around, facing the rest of the group. "You don't mind if Flavia comes with us, do you?"

"She can come." Ann smiled.

"Fine with me." Margie grinned, and everybody else chimed in, "No problem."

"She can come." "She can bring extra napkins." "Don't forget your sweater."

"Thank you." Flavia beamed. "Thank you all. I can even take us, if you want."

"You can *drive*?" Lorraine blurted out, delighted.

"No, I have a driver. Nicky makes me. He says it's safer. I have macular degeneration, I can't see so good."

"You have a *chauffeur*?" Paul's eyes widened. "In a *limo*?"

"No, in a normal car."

Conchetta looked at Flavia like she was crazy. "But there's fifteen of us. We don't fit in one car. We usually take the bus."

"He has a bus, too." Flavia smiled slyly. "They use it for bachelorette. There's booze in the back."

"Party!" Lorraine shouted, and the others joined in, laughing and cheering, "Let's do it!" "Woohoo!" "Let's go!" "We're ridin' in style!" "The Rosary Society is movin' on up!"

Mary couldn't join in their happiness, now that she had the name of the man who killed John. All she could think of was what she could do next to bring Machiavelli and Fortunato to justice. Suddenly she heard a text come in on her phone and she stepped away from the celebration. She slid her phone out of her purse, and the text was from Lou: **Here's the enlarged video but it's no better. Also tried but can't find more cameras. Shanahan still at large. No new news.**

Her heart sank, but she quickly ran the video. It was still dark and grainy, except that the image of the silhouette was bigger, but had no detail to help. She didn't know what Stretch looked like, but the shadow had no distinguishing facial features whatever. The height and weight, again, looked average. She watched with disappointment as the silhouette on the video pulled up the window, which she could see better since it was bigger, then left via the fire escape. She hit Stop and put her phone away, with a frustrated sigh.

Flavia caught her eye, puzzled. "Mare, is something the matter?"

"No." Mary forced a smile.

"What about with Stretch? What did he do something bad? I know he musta. If he did, I wanna know."

"Um, nothing," Mary answered, off-balance.

"Then why did you ask me his real name?"

"No reason. Just curious, because he beat up Joey."

"You're a bad liar. Nicky's a much better

liar than you. I answered your question, so you should answer mine." Flavia glanced at Conchetta and the others. "You girls mind if I talk to Mary, alone?"

Chapter Forty-Two

"So." Mary sat down at the glistening dining-room table. "You really want to know why I asked you Stretch's real name?"

"Yes." Flavia folded her hands in front of her. "Stretch works for Nicky. If Stretch did something wrong, Nicky should know about it and I wanna know about it."

Mary paused. "But what if Stretch did something wrong because Nicky told him to, like when Stretch beat up Joey?"

Flavia glowered. "Believe me, I'm gonna talk to Nicky about that."

"But do you still wanna know?"

"Yes." Flavia straightened in the chair, lifting her chin. "I wasn't born yesterday, Mary. I've been through a lot, more than you know. So tell me straight."

Mary decided to level with her. "I think that Stretch might've murdered John Foxman, a lawyer at my firm. And I think Nick might have told him to."

"Murdered?" Flavia gasped, her lined hand flying to her lips. "That can't be. Nicky wouldn't do that."

"I think he would. And I think he did."

"No, no, no." Flavia shook her head, jittery, placing both hands on her papery cheeks. "He's done a lot of things, but not that. A beating is one thing, but a murder, no. Not *that,* not *murder."*

"I know, it's awful. But I have good reason to think so and I'll tell you why, quickly. Nicky owns companies that make a lot of money, and to protect them, he filed the lawsuit against me and my partners —"

"The one he talked about on TV?" Flavia frowned deeply, trying to recover her composure. "I told him he shouldn't of said that about you on TV. I told him that wasn't nice. I knew it wasn't true. You could tell he was lying when he said it. He doesn't even believe that. I could tell."

Mary thought Flavia was right, but didn't say so, since the big picture was so much worse. "More importantly, I think Nick had Stretch kill John, to get rid of the lawsuit against his companies."

"I can't believe it." Flavia shook her curly little head.

"I can."

"Did you go to the police?"

"Yes, but they don't think Nicky is behind it. They think somebody else is."

"Thank you, sweet Jesus." Flavia looked heavenward, clasping her hands together in prayer.

"But I don't agree with them and neither do my partners."

"Why?" Flavia frowned.

"All of the facts point to Nick and Stretch."

"We'll see about that." Flavia leaned over, slipped an iPhone, from her pocket, and began to make a call.

"Wait, what are you doing?"

"I'm calling my Nicky."

"Wait, what?" Mary hadn't seen this coming. "You can't just call and ask him if he had somebody murdered."

"I know that. Shh, I don't want him to know you're here." Flavia set the phone down and put it on speaker, and when the call connected, the screen changed to read BABY BOY. "Honey, how you doing?"

"Good, Ma," Nick answered, his tone more affectionate than Mary had ever heard. "How's my Baby Girl?"

"I'm fine, honey. Can you come over?"

"Sure, I'm in the neighborhood. Be there in five minutes. You need anything?"

"No, just come home. And don't talk on

the phone when you drive."

"Okay, love you."

"Love you, too, honey." Flavia pressed the button to end the call, and Mary willed her heartbeat back to normal. She didn't know what was weirder, that Flavia was calling Nick to ask him about John's murder or that their nicknames for each other were Baby Girl and Baby Boy.

"Flavia, I don't know what's going on." Mary thought of her plan, going to hell now that their cover was about to be blown.

"What don't you understand? I'm going to ask my son if he had Stretch kill your friend."

"His name was John," Mary supplied, as if they were singing the birthday song and didn't know the name of the birthday boy. "Flavia, this is a murder case. You just can't ask somebody if they're responsible for murder."

"You can if you're his mother."

"But I didn't want him to know that I was onto him."

"So?" Flavia looked at Mary directly, from behind her round bifocals. "He's going to find that out sooner or later, if you're going to accuse him."

Mary had no immediate reply, since it was true. "But he's going to lie to you. He's not just going to admit it. He's going to say he had nothing to do with John's murder."

"I can tell when he lies," Flavia stated, as if it were a scientific fact.

"Flavia, with respect, no, you can't."

"Yes, I can.

"You're not a lie detector."

"I'm better than a lie detector. I read the newspaper. I know they're not reliable."

Mary thought she might have a point there too. "So you really think you can tell when he's lying?"

"I know I can. I know him better than anybody in the world. I carried him for nine months, just like you." Flavia gestured at Mary's belly. "You'll see, when you have that baby."

"What will I see? What do you mean?" Mary's hand went to her belly, but the baby still wasn't kicking, so the chocolate chip hadn't helped. She was going to call the doctor, after this debacle was over.

"Nobody knows a child better than its mother. Let me tell you something. You may not always get along with your child. You might fight with your child. You might not speak to your child for a year, maybe two. But a mother always knows her child."

Mary couldn't buy in. "But every day on the news, you see mothers saying what a good boy their son is, when he's a killer. Like Conchetta thought you were."

"But I didn't say that about Nicky, did I? *This* mother knows her son, the bad and the good." Flavia waved her off. "And those mothers on the news, the ones you were talking about? They're not lying to themselves. They're lying to the camera. They know the truth, inside. They know it in their heart. They can't bring themselves to say it out loud."

Mary blinked, thinking Flavia was either a genius or completely delusional.

"I *know* that boy. I raised him on my own. His father was never around. That's why he listens to me."

"But you said before that he doesn't listen to you."

"On the important things, he does. I'm the only one he listens to, and it doesn't get more important than this. Murder is a *mortal sin.*" Flavia leaned forward urgently, placing her wrinkled hand on the polished table. "I would never believe he could do that, or have Stretch do it, but I'm going to ask him, right to his face."

Mary didn't know if it was a good idea, but it was about to happen. "I guess it can't really do any harm. He's going to find out I suspect him sooner or later."

"Like I said." Flavia cocked her head. "Anyway, what is it with you and Nicky?"

"It's like he has it in for me. He's tried to do me in, so many times. It's like he's out to get me." Mary didn't add that Machiavelli had also tried to kiss her, in his office.

"It's on account of he's so confused, like his father." Flavia shook her head.

"What was his father like?" Mary had never met the man.

"Don't get me started. I shoulda left him so many times, but I kept the family together." Flavia rallied. "Nicky has a crush on you. He always has, from high school. He told me. He always liked you."

"He never told me." Mary wasn't completely surprised, given that kiss, but still.

"I think he's acting out to get your attention, for all these years. Like in the olden days, when the boys put the girl's pigtail in the inkwell. He told me you were out of his league."

Mary felt relieved to be considered too good for a murderer, but didn't say so.

"Now, he can't take it that you're having a baby, that you married Anthony. You said no to him, and he's used to getting what he wants." Flavia sighed. "I spoiled him, that much I did. He thinks he's entitled."

"Well, he's not."

"I know." Flavia's face fell into deeply sad lines. "It's gone too far."

"Yes, it has," Mary said, which was the understatement of the year, since they were talking about John's murder. "I'm not kidding around, Flavia. You and I, we're both adults. I'm telling you, right now, that I think Nick killed my friend John and I'm not going to let him get away with it. He's not *entitled* to commit murder. I want to put him away."

Flavia fell silent a moment, then looked at Mary evenly. "I agree with you. And if my Nicky committed murder, or had Stretch commit murder, I'll help you."

"You will?" Mary asked, astonished. It was the right thing to do, but she didn't know many mothers who would say as much, in her position.

"Yes, I will."

"But he's your only son."

"It's the right thing to do, and at the end of my life, I have to answer to my God." Flavia patted Mary's hand, and just then, the front door opened, letting a shaft of light into the large, dark room. Machiavelli appeared in the threshold, his mouth dropping open when he saw his mother sitting at the table with Mary.

"Hi, honey," Flavia called out, motioning him over. "Come sit with us."

"*Us?*" Machiavelli strode toward them, composing himself. His mouth reverted to its typical smirk, and he buttoned his suit-jacket as he swaggered over. "Hello, Mary, I didn't expect to see you here."

"I figured." Mary didn't know if she had the upper hand but it felt like it, from his reaction.

"Anyway it's a good thing you're here." Machiavelli reached the table. "I just got off the phone with the Pennsylvania Human Relations Commission. We're rejecting your settlement offer. My clients don't want to work for your firm."

"Oh that's too bad." Mary felt her theory confirmed, as if it needed it.

"So we'll see you in court." Machiavelli walked to his mother, put a hand on her shoulder, and kissed her lightly on the cheek. "Hi, Ma. You didn't tell me Mary was here."

"No, I wanted to surprise you." Flavia pointed to the chair catty-corner to her. "Sit down, please."

"Am I in trouble?" Machiavelli pulled out a chair, smirking.

CHAPTER FORTY-THREE

Mary sat directly across from Machiavelli, and Flavia linked her hands in front of her, dead calm. "Nicky, we have something very serious to talk about. I want you to tell me the truth, no matter what. And you know I can tell when you're lying."

"Okay." Machiavelli folded his arms, still smirking.

"And don't make that face. This is very serious."

"Okay." Machiavelli frowned, probably embarrassed. Mary would've been too, but it was too serious to make jokes.

"Mary says her friend John got murdered. Did you have anything to do with that?"

"No," Machiavelli answered flatly.

Flavia paused, her lips pursed. "Nicky, I want you to look me in the eye. I want you tell me the truth. Because you know I can tell when you're lying."

"I'm not lying." Machiavelli blinked, and

Mary couldn't tell if he was lying, but she knew he had to be.

Flavia leaned closer to him. "Do you swear to God?"

"Yes." Machiavelli kept a completely straight face. "I had nothing to do with John's murder."

"Did Stretch? Did you send Stretch to kill John?"

"No," Machiavelli answered, again flatly.

"Do you swear to me, Nicky? On my eyes?"

"Yes."

"Because if you're lying to me, you'll burn in hell. I will too. That's a mortal sin."

"Ma, I would never murder anybody."

"Stretch would."

"Maybe, but I didn't ask him to murder anybody. I didn't ask him to murder John." Machiavelli shot Mary a look. "Is *that* what this is about? You came here asking my mother this question? Making these accusations? It's *absurd.*"

"Is it?" Mary shot back. "You sent Stretch to Conchetta's because she wouldn't sell her house to you."

Flavia's hooded eyes stayed glued to her son. "Is that right, Nicky?"

Machiavelli frowned. "Okay, *that* I did, but I offered her a million bucks first. Why didn't they take it? It's not worth a tenth of that."

Flavia gasped. "Nicky, that's terrible! That's a terrible thing to do! I'm so ashamed of you. Joey is in the Army. He's serving our country."

"I wanted the house."

"But *I* didn't want the house." Flavia gestured at the big vast, cavernous room, as she had before. "I don't want any of this. I don't want you to *beat up* anybody for it. A man in uniform!"

"I wanted it for you."

"I told you, I don't want any of this, I don't need any of this."

"I let it go, Ma. They live there, don't they? It's all good." Machiavelli turned to Mary. "What's one have to do with the other, anyway? I had nothing to do with John's murder. You can't think I did."

"I sure can," Mary shot back, angering. "You might be able to convince your mother, but you can't convince me."

Machiavelli looked at her like she was crazy. "Why would I kill John?"

"You sent Stretch to do it."

"Why would I do *that*? It's still murder if I solicited it, and I never would. Murder?" Machiavelli's brown eyes flared. "Mary, I draw the line. I've done a lot of things, but murder, no. Never."

"Oh really?" Mary couldn't believe his nerve. It was time to bust him. "Let's go back a few days. You manufactured that reverse-discrimination lawsuit against us. Those three plaintiffs have worked for your businesses. You paid their college tuition and put them up to the Complaint against us."

Machiavelli's eyelids fluttered. "That's not true."

Flavia shook her head. "Nicky, you're lying. I can tell. You just lied to her. Did you do what she said or not?"

"Yes, he did," Mary interjected.

Flavia held up a hand to Mary. "I'm talking to my *son.*" She returned to Nicky, flushing behind her papery skin. "You said you would tell me the truth and you just lied. I can tell when you're lying and when you tell the truth. If you lie, Nicky, I swear, you will pay for the rest of your life —"

"Ma, don't get upset, your blood pressure." Machiavelli put his hand on hers, frowning with genuine concern.

"You want to give me a heart attack? Then keep lying. It'll be on you." Flavia went red in the face, the veins in her stringy neck bulging. She turned to Mary. "Ask him the question again."

Mary faced Machiavelli. "You manufactured the reverse-discrimination case against us, didn't you?"

"Yes."

"Those three plaintiffs worked for you in your businesses, isn't that right?"

"Yes," Machiavelli said, pursing his lips.

"You put them through college and then called in the favor."

"Law school. I put them through law school."

"I stand corrected. Otherwise, that's a yes?"

"Yes," Machiavelli answered, apparently unremorseful.

"You're vaguely aware there's a code of ethics for attorneys, aren't you? You can't manufacture litigation. It's abuse of process. You're not allowed to recruit plaintiffs, they're supposed to come to you."

"Oh really, Pollyanna?" Machiavelli rolled his eyes. "Tell that to the class-action bar."

Mary ignored it. "You filed a bogus lawsuit, completely fraudulent. You can get disbarred for that."

"Suspended, at most." Machiavelli shrugged.

"I would see to it that you got *disbarred,* if I didn't have bigger fish to fry. You did it because you wanted to neutralize John, because you thought he was the brains behind the antitrust litigation we brought on behalf of London Technologies against Home Hacks and EXMS, both of which you own, one way or another."

"Yes," Machiavelli admitted, his brows lifting in surprise. "How did you figure that out?"

"It doesn't matter." Mary inhaled deeply, feeling powerful and validated, for once in her life. "And you placed Paul Patrioca at London Technologies as a spy and made him steal their software code and documents relating to the antitrust litigation."

Machiavelli scowled. "How did you find *that* out?"

"Yes or no?"

"Yes."

"Home Hacks and EXMS are guilty of everything that London Technologies alleged, aren't they? They're gouging their customers to maintain monopoly power?"

"Yes." Machiavelli looked at her coldly. "You done yet?"

"No." Mary realized something. "I thought you sent those plaintiffs to us to set us up for litigation, but really you sent them to us as spies. When we didn't hire them, you improvised.

Machiavelli smirked. "You handed me an

ace and I know how to play it."

Mary saw Flavia, who looked appalled, but she didn't stop now. "You sent that female freelancer Amanda Sussman after us, didn't you?"

"Yes."

"And you even sent protesters to John's memorial service, didn't you?"

"Yes."

Listening, Flavia bowed her head, shaking it slowly back and forth, but she said nothing. Mary noticed Machiavelli glance at his mother, betraying just the slightest microexpression of regret.

Mary asked Machiavelli again, "You sent Stretch to kill John that night in his apartment, didn't you?"

"Asked and answered."

"Stretch walked in the front, wearing a suit, maybe even said he was from your office, to talk about the reverse-discrimination suit. He knew he would kill John in the end, so he didn't worry about a witness."

"No."

"And they went upstairs to John's apartment, where Stretch killed him with a lamp base and then left by the fire escape."

"No." Machiavelli shook his head. "I didn't do any of that. Neither did he."

"Where was Stretch the night of the murder?"

"With me."

"Where were you?"

"At the office. I was working. He stays until I go."

"Were you with anyone else beside him, who could prove it?"

"No."

"No security guards around?"

"Stretch is security. I was working late."

"Any cameras?"

Machiavelli rolled his eyes. "I don't surveil my own offices."

"Then you have no proof, and no alibi." Mary didn't believe a word Machiavelli said about his involvement in John's murder, no matter whether Flavia did or not.

"Mary, I don't know what to tell you." Machiavelli looked at her evenly, his brown eyes frank. "I didn't kill John Foxman. Neither did Stretch. I had nothing to do with it. I would never do that."

"I don't believe you."

Suddenly Flavia moaned, and Machiavelli leaned over, putting his hand on her arm.

"Ma, are you all right?"

"Flavia, are you okay?" Mary asked, worried. She didn't want to give Flavia a heart attack.

"I'm fine," Flavia answered, clearing her throat. "Nicky, I believe you didn't kill John. I believe Stretch didn't kill John. I don't think you could ever do a murder, but that *doesn't* excuse the other terrible things you did."

"I know, I'm sorry, Ma."

"No, that's not good enough. You have gone too far, for too long. I should have stepped in, years ago. Now, you have to make everything right." Flavia turned to Mary, her face drained. "Mary, what can he do to make this right? *Can* he make this right?"

Mary felt sick to her stomach. "John was killed, Flavia. How can you make murder right? Only by going to the police and confessing."

"He didn't do it."

"I didn't do it," Machiavelli repeated.

Flavia touched Mary's hand, squeezing it. "Mare, I know you're sad about your friend, you miss him and you want to see his killer go to jail. But can you put that aside, for just a minute?"

"No, I can't *put it aside,*" Mary answered, barely able to suppress her anger. She couldn't stand to see Machiavelli slip through her fingers. She hadn't come this far to come this far. "I don't believe him, and it's murder. You can't put murder *aside.*"

"Just for a minute." Flavia shook it off, jittery. "What about the cases you talked about? Did he commit crimes? Were they crimes?"

"No, they were civil wrongs."

"So he doesn't go to jail for them?"

"Not for them, no. But for murder, or conspiracy to murder, he sure does, and that's what I want." Mary's chest tightened. "That crime matters more than everything, Flavia. To me, and to everybody else. And it should to you, too."

"What if he takes away the lawsuit against you and your law firm?"

"He could do that. He *should* do that. You just heard him, he made the whole thing up!"

"He will do that." Flavia turned to Machiavelli. "Nicky, you'll do that, right?"

"Fine." Machiavelli folded his arms, with an unhappy frown.

Flavia returned her attention to Mary, her expression pleading. "What about what you said he stole? The computer? What if he gave it back?"

"He should give back the London Technologies software, plus the documents and any copies he made of those things."

Flavia nodded. "He'll do that too. Anything else? Wasn't there another case? The big one? I'm not a lawyer, but my husband was a lawyer and he settled cases when his clients did wrong. Can't Nicky settle that case?"

"Flavia, really?" Mary had an obligation to London Technologies to answer, but she felt as if she were bargaining over John's body. "Yes, he should negotiate a reasonable settlement with London Technologies because he just *admitted* that his companies did everything we alleged, and if he does that, we will end the litigation."

Flavia nodded again. "He'll settle then, too. How much do you want?"

"Flavia, are you brokering this deal now? I can't begin to answer that because I don't know. It would be up to my partners, Bennie and Anne."

Machiavelli grimaced. "Ma, no, wait, there's *millions* at stake —"

"So what?" Flavia whipped her head around to her son. "Nicky, you have enough money. You have *plenty* of money, more than you can spend in twenty lifetimes! How much do you need? What's the matter with you? I raised you better than that! Stop it, stop it right now!"

"But Ma —"

"Don't you *dare*! Don't you dare say anything except, 'I'll do it.' "

Machiavelli sighed theatrically. "Okay, whatever, I'll do it."

Flavia raised an arthritic index finger. "And you'll pay what they want."

"I'll *negotiate. She said negotiate.*"

Mary leaned forward, looking Machiavelli directly in the eye. "Hold on, let's be clear. You're not agreeing to this because your mother is making you. You're agreeing to this because I *got* you. You're not doing me a favor, I'm doing *you* one. Me and my partners found out what you were doing, and we can prove everything we say in court. We could have you disbarred after what we found out about the antidiscrimination lawsuit. And we would win *London Technologies,* especially with Paul Patrioca's testimony. So you're not giving me anything that I didn't *earn.* You're giving it to me because in the end, I'll get it anyway, and *then some.* And that's the power of the *law.*"

"Whatever." Machiavelli shrugged, but Mary knew it bothered him.

"And finally, your alleged ancestor, the real Niccolò Machiavelli, said it's better to be feared than loved. But let me tell you something. It *isn't.* Your mother is isolated in this neighborhood because everybody is afraid of you." Mary pointed at Flavia, whose face fell. "She lives her days alone in this big house, listening to the Patriocas through a *wall.* She doesn't have any friends because of you. She doesn't even have any neighbors because of you. Neither do you, but maybe you don't notice it or don't care. But with her, you care. I *know* you care."

Machiavelli blinked, his expression darkening just the slightest, and Mary got the impression that he was listening.

"Today, all that changed for her. She's joining the Rosary Society. They're going to give her another chance, and you know why? Because love is better than fear." Mary felt her heart lift, unaccountably. "This whole neighborhood is full of love, everywhere. And love is what gives you a second chance. They're willing to give her a second chance, and she's going to take it. If you ask me, you should too. This neighborhood, these people, even me, all of us will forgive you, but you have to change. You just have to *change.*"

"Right!" Flavia chimed in, frowning at her son. "Nicky, everything Mary said is true, and this thing you have with her has to stop, here and now. You have to get over her. You lost your chance. She married Anthony.

She's having a baby. You don't get everything you want. Only babies do. *Capisce?*"

"Yes." Machiavelli nodded, avoiding Mary's eye.

"Now, Nicky, say you're sorry to her."

"I'm sorry, Mary."

Mary felt her chest tighten, reaching her limit. "I'm not accepting your apology. You can't say you're sorry for murder."

"Mary, give it up!" Machiavelli threw up his manicured hands. "I didn't kill him, and you can't prove I did. You have no evidence."

"I have a video!" Mary blurted out, raising her voice. She hoped she could parlay it into something more. Maybe she could trick him into confessing. "It shows Stretch leaving the apartment by the fire escape. Or *you*!"

"It *can't*! I wasn't there and neither was he! Where's the video? At the office? I want to see it!"

"No, right here!" Mary got her phone, scrolled to the text, and set it on the table, playing the video. She knew it wouldn't deliver, and the very thought made her want to throw up. Machiavelli leaned over to get close to the phone, and Flavia adjusted her glasses. They all watched the video in silence until the end, when the shadowy silhouette climbed out of the window and vanished.

"Ha!" Machiavelli laughed, cruelly. "Mary, that doesn't show anything. That could be anybody. It could even be a woman. You can't tell *anything* from that."

"Mary, he's right." Flavia eased back into her chair, troubled. "I don't understand. Is this why you think it's Stretch? It's just a shadow. You can't see a face."

"Flavia, it's Stretch, I know it is, I just can't prove it. I know they did it, and you're in denial because it's Nicky." Mary began to feel nauseated, but she didn't know if it was physical, emotional or both. She put her hand on her belly, but the baby wasn't moving.

"Let me see that again." Machiavelli picked up Mary's phone, watching the video closer. "There's *nothing* here. It really could be anybody."

"No, it's Stretch." Mary wiped her brow, newly damp.

"Wait. Look, Mary." Machiavelli pointed excitedly, freezing the video, enlarging it even further, and showing her the screen. "See that bump, on the killer's left wrist? Maybe it's a woman, wearing bracelets, with, like a pendant or a charm. It could be a woman in pants."

"Don't be ridiculous." Mary tried to focus on the video, and since it was enlarged, she saw what Machiavelli meant. There was a small bump on the shadow's left wrist, visible only when the killer opened the window and his sleeve rode up.

"Or it could be a man with a big watch, who wears it loose. A man's watch, but oversized —"

"Like Nicky's." Flavia pulled up her son's sleeve to reveal a clunky stainless-steel watch. "I gave him this watch, but lots of men have them. The murderer could be a man with a big watch like Nicky's."

"My Panerai?" Nicky said, with a note of pride. "I love this watch. It's a real diver's watch, designed for the Italian Navy. I don't wear it loose, but maybe the killer did. He could've been wearing another type of big watch."

"You did it, not Stretch! It was *you!"* Suddenly Mary felt terrible. She didn't know what was wrong with her, then she felt a rush of warmth in her underwear.

"Mary?" Flavia squeezed her arm. "You're so pale. What's the matter?"

"Um, I think I need to go to the doctor." Mary rose, nervous.

"Nicky, get her to your car!"

CHAPTER FORTY-FOUR

"Is the baby okay?" Mary asked, her heart in her throat. She lay on the examining table in the examining room, holding her breath while Dr. Foster read a long continuous paper graph inching out of a fetal monitor machine, which sat next to the examining table on a rolling cart. A plastic fetal heart rate monitor and a contraction sensor had been taped to Mary's belly, as soon as she had gotten to the office.

"The baby is fine." Dr. Foster smiled, looking up from the tape. Her heavy black glasses slipped down her nose, and her pearl earrings matched her long, white coat. "The heartbeat is normal and steady."

"Thank God!" Mary felt tears come to her eyes, but held them back.

"You had a scare, but it's over now." Dr. Foster came to Mary's side, letting the monitor tape drop.

"But the baby hasn't been kicking for,

like, a day and a half."

"I know, you told me, and that can be worrisome. It doesn't always mean something."

"But the spotting? This is the second time."

"Again, I'm not overly worried, but I think it's time for you to go on restricted activity, for two weeks. Stay home, off your feet for a week. Then check back with me."

"You think?" Mary couldn't process it fast enough.

"Yes, I know your job is important to you. But I play it safe, always do. You told me how active your day was yesterday and today. I'm hearing that you're very busy." Dr. Foster frowned. "I even saw you on TV the other day, in the middle of a mob scene. It was all I could do not to text you."

"What you saw was a protest after a memorial service. A friend of mine was murdered. It's just been such a busy time, and everything is so important."

"My condolences." Dr. Foster nodded gravely. "And believe me, I understand that you have a lot of things to juggle, all important. Welcome to motherhood."

Mary managed to smile, wiping her eyes.

"But that doesn't change my orders. Please stay home for two full weeks. Then call me and come back in. We'll see where we stand." Dr. Foster smiled in a professional way. "You're going to be here for a few hours. I want a full reading, so we have a complete picture. So rest now, and we'll keep monitoring the baby. After you leave today, go directly home to bed. I'll have the receptionist tell your friend that you'll be awhile longer."

"My friend?" Mary hadn't called Judy or Anthony in Boston, because she didn't want to alarm them until she knew what was going on.

"Your colleague. The guy in the waiting room."

"He's here?" Mary hadn't thought that Machiavelli would wait. He'd dropped her off at the doctor's office, parking his big Mercedes-Benz illegally. They hadn't spoken on the way here, since she'd been disgusted to be in such close quarters with him. "He's not my friend. In fact, he's my enemy."

"Really?" Dr. Foster gave her a final pat on the arm. "He's pretty worried about you, for an enemy. He's already asked the receptionist about you twice. With enemies like that, who needs friends?"

Mary managed a smile, because she couldn't say, *oh yes, he's a prince of a murderer.* "Dr. Foster, would you do me a favor? Could your receptionist tell him to leave? I can get a cab home."

"Are you sure?" Dr. Foster checked her watch. "It's the end of the day, rush hour. You might not get a cab so easily."

"I'll be fine. He's the last person I want to see right now." Mary hadn't had a choice on the way here, but she sure as hell had a choice on the way home.

"Okay, I'll tell her." Dr. Foster nodded. "I'm going to leave you for a while. I'll come back later to check on you."

"Thank you so much."

"Be back in a bit." Dr. Foster left the examining room, and Mary took a deep breath, exhaling slowly. She rested her head back on the crinkly paper, keeping an eye on the spiky graph as the tape kept ticking out of the monitor. The razor-thin black line remained basically flat until it peaked like a tiny mountain range, and she saw that it came at regular intervals, a sight that eased her to her marrow. She sent up a prayer of thanks, that the baby was still okay.

Mary's attention stayed glued to the graph paper, and suddenly she felt drained and exhausted. She had been so active lately, too active, even if she hadn't been pregnant, and she felt it catch up with her, as she lay there. She looked away from the monitor, so she wouldn't obsess, and scanned the mint-green walls, the pretty floral watercolors, and the inspirational poster. I SET MY WORRIES ASIDE AND LET MY BODY DO ITS JOB.

Mary thought back to the first time she had seen that poster, on her last visit. It had made her worry about *her* job, and everything that went with it. But that was before John had been murdered and everything else happened. She had tried so hard since then to catch Machiavelli. She had come so close to getting him, even today, with Flavia. She had come *so close.*

A wave of frustration washed over her, and she closed her eyes. A tear slipped out, she could feel its wetness on her cheek. She didn't try to wipe it away. Instead, she let herself go. Her arms fell back, her chest rose heavenward, and she felt everything she was feeling. She tried to set her worries aside, like the poster said, but it wasn't so easy to set that burden down. She sensed that was part of being a mother, too.

Another tear rolled down her cheek, but she had to surrender. It was so hard to stop now, but she needed to rest, even she had to admit it. Her body was trying to tell her something, so was her baby. And now, her doctor.

Mary couldn't deny it anymore. It was common sense. She had to go home, go to bed, and slow down.

The very next thought that popped into her head was that she could work from home, then she stopped herself before she went mentally further, checking her thoughts the way the monitor checked her baby's heartbeat. She couldn't work from home, or she didn't want to. She didn't have the energy. She was out of gas. She didn't even have the strength right now to call anybody and fill them in on what had happened at Machiavelli's.

Mary had to face the fact that she certainly couldn't catch Machiavelli from home. Maybe that was why he had stayed in the waiting room. He probably wanted to relish his victory or throw it in her face. Or maybe he was still nursing his crush, regardless of the promise he had made his mother. She had to believe that he would adhere to what he'd said about the lawsuits, and Bennie and the others would accept that as a consolation prize. But they all wanted John's killer brought to justice and would settle for nothing less.

Mary resolved to hand that baton off to them. Bennie, Judy, Anne, and Lou were more than capable of functioning without her, and Mary had come to a fork in the road, one she had been avoiding thinking about. It was time to let them go too, and all of the things that came with them, things she loved so much, things that were a part of her work life and her personal life, which had been knitted together like the yarn of a favorite sweater. Or that beautiful baby blanket that Judy had weaved for her, on her loom.

Mary kept her eyes closed and let her thoughts run free, and so many memories bubbled to the surface of her consciousness, the endless containers of take-out lo mein during trial prep, the silly notes passed during client meetings, and the wacky adventures they had gone on together, over the years. She remembered the clients that had been so much a part of her, her old friend Simon Pensiera, whose little girl Rachel had ultimately pulled through, and adorable Patrick, a dyslexic boy who had touched her heart so much that she wanted to adopt him, and even the time that Pigeon Tony had been accused of murdering his lifelong rival, from back in the days of Fascist Italy.

Mary opened her eyes, and her wet gaze returned to the graph paper of her baby's heartbeat, and she realized what she had been doing wrong. She had been focusing so much on what she had to leave behind that all she thought was how much she was losing. Her only consolation to date had been the pregnancy, which was nauseating, literally.

She looked at that heartbeat and realized that she wasn't on her own anymore. There really was another human being living inside her, and their hearts were beating together, inseparable now and probably forever, if her mother was an example, or even Machiavelli's mother, or Conchetta, or Marshall, or any of the vast tribe of mothers she knew in her life.

Mary felt a rush of gratitude that the baby was okay, because in the car on the way here with Machiavelli, she had entertained so many darker possibilities. She had taken for granted the baby's life within her, and she could never do that again.

Her hand went to her belly, this time not trying to test if anything was wrong, but cradling the baby. She found herself wondering if it was really a boy or girl, since all of the poll results were different, and either way, what it would look like, if it would have thick hair like Anthony, or be nearsighted like her, or be short like her parents, or bedazzled like El Virus. Her heart filled at the thought of how happy everybody would be when the baby finally came, especially her and Anthony.

And when she focused on that little child, curled up within her, it was easy to set her other worries aside, to fight the impulse to call Bennie and others, check her phone, read her email, or do anything else in the world. Somehow along the way, Mary had forgotten that the most important thing to her was family.

And now she had a family of her own.

This was where her family started, right here, right now.

With a mother, and a child.

CHAPTER FORTY-FIVE

Mary got home exhausted and let herself into the house, which was quiet, still, and darkening as twilight fell, though she didn't bother to turn on a light. She felt like she needed to sleep for about three days and she was going straight to bed. She'd called Judy and Bennie from the cab, filling them in on everything that had happened, and they'd felt just like she did, torn. It was maddening that they couldn't prove Machiavelli's involvement in John's murder, but they were amazed to hear that she'd been able to get Machiavelli to withdraw the reverse-discrimination Complaint and settle *London Technologies.*

She dropped her purse on the floor and walked over the mail scattered on the floor of the entrance hall, which had been delivered through the slot in the front door. She didn't care about the bills or anything else. She was leaving everything behind, but in a good way, especially since she had handed off the baton to Judy and Bennie. They had probably already sprung into action, calling Machiavelli, drafting the withdrawal papers for the reverse-discrimination Complaint, and starting negotiations on *London Technologies.*

Mary climbed the stairs wearily, holding on to the railing. The only sounds were her padded footfalls on the carpeted stair and the creak of the wood beneath, since it was an old house. She tried not to think about the fact that she hadn't been able to prove that Machiavelli was behind John's murder. She told herself that he would be brought to justice, especially with the others on the case, or that sooner or later, the police would realize that Shanahan was a false lead. She reminded herself that not everything could be accomplished as fast as she wanted. She soothed herself by saying that she had made incredible progress in a very short time.

She reached the second floor, but she had a bitter taste in her mouth, no matter what she told herself. The truth was that she had tried so hard to make it happen, and she had come so close, but she had failed. John had been brutally murdered, and she hadn't been able to do anything about it. She thought of William at the duck pond, and how anguished he had been. She thought of the Hodges at the memorial luncheon, and how forlorn they had been. And in the end, she thought of John, who came through so beautifully for her when they had worked together. He had never left her side, not for a minute. And though Judy had told Sanjay and Jim they should be loyal to John in death, in the end, Mary had been unable to show him the loyalty he had shown her.

She felt tears well in her eyes, not happy tears but miserable tears, and by the time she got to her bedroom, all she could do was crawl into bed in her clothes, curl herself around her baby, and cry them both to sleep.

She didn't wake up until after seven o'clock, when her phone pinged with an excitable text from Judy: **WE HAVE AH-HHMMMAAAAAZING NEWS!!! WE'RE COMING OVER TO CELE-BRATE!!! SEE YOU IN 15 WITH PIZ-ZZZAAAAAAA!!!**

Mary texted back, **Great, what happened? Let yourself in. I'm upstairs.**

OK, YOU'LL SEEEEEEEE!! XOX-OXXOOXOXXOXOXO

CHAPTER FORTY-SIX

Mary sat up happily against her headboard, since her bedroom had been invaded by complete chaos, bearing carbohydrates. Bennie, Judy, Anne, Lou, and Roger had stacked pizza boxes on her dresser, with several bottles of champagne, soda, water, paper plates and napkins. The aroma of hot pizza and cold champagne filled the air, an unexpectedly fragrant combination. Corks had been popped, gooey pizza had been distributed on sagging plates, and everybody stood grinning in a circle around Mary's bed, refusing to tell her the good news until everything was ready.

"So what happened?" Mary asked, delighted. "Tell me!"

Bennie raised a plastic glass of champagne. "DiNunzio, we toast to you, even though you can't drink the good stuff."

"To Mary!" Judy beamed, holding up her paper cup.

"To Mary *and* her baby!" Anne held up her cup, grinning ear to ear.

"Yes, to Mary and her baby!" Lou and Roger joined in, standing together, raising cups of champagne.

"To me, the baby, and Anthony!" Mary raised her bottle of water, hoping that the good news had to do with John's murder. "Now tell me what happened!"

Bennie sipped her champagne, then took a deep breath. "We have reached a settlement with the other side in *London Technologies,* and it's a whopper."

Mary masked her disappointment with a smile. "That's great news! What did you settle for? And how did it come about?"

Bennie practically wriggled with delight, warming to the story. "Well, after we got the call from you, Anne and I called Marcus Benedict. You know, from Barrett & Tottenham."

"Yes, I met him when I defended Alex Chen's deposition."

"Oh, right." Bennie nodded, still buoyant. "It took the whole night to hash it out, but we reached an agreement in principle. We can't say they were difficult negotiations, as we'd like to take the credit. We know you get the credit, behind the scenes."

Anne interjected, "Yes, we know that,

Mary, and if you ask me, I thought Benedict was *relieved* to talk settlement. He knew it was a loser and we're both guessing that was Machiavelli who told him that they could settle."

Mary agreed completely. "It must have been, that's why he did what he did. He didn't want to pay to settle, but he also knew he'd lose."

Bennie nodded. "Right, that's true. We know that he had marching orders from Machiavelli to settle, thanks to you."

"Thanks to Flavia." Mary forced a smile. "I didn't want to bargain with him. I wanted to put him behind bars, for John."

"Understood, and I agree, we all do." Bennie's smile evaporated, and so did everybody else's. Judy's face fell, which was so heartbreaking that Mary was sorry she'd said anything, ruining the happy moment.

"Sorry, honey," Mary said, trying to recover, and Judy set her plate on the night table and sank onto Mary's bed, her shoulders slumping.

"It's okay, I felt strange too. It's hard to celebrate. It's hard to be happy about anything, now." Judy swallowed hard. "William is still at the hotel with the Hodges, so sad and disoriented. I don't think he should go back to Glenn Meade until Shanahan is found, just to be on the safe side, but it's so sad to see him."

"I bet. The poor guy."

Judy took a deep breath. "But we're allowed to be happy about the settlement. I know how much John cared about the case and he would've been thrilled that all of his hard work paid off, so I think we should enjoy this for him. If we don't, the terrorists really will have won."

"You're absolutely right," Mary said, meaning it. She was so proud of her best friend, for showing such bravery and heart in the worst possible circumstances.

Bennie rallied, straightening. "Yes, I think John would've been astounded with the settlement, which is, are you ready — $11 million!"

"Wow, that's incredible!" Mary perked up, and so did everybody else, their grins returning.

"It's amazing!" Bennie beamed, proudly. "And we'd only just started discovery. It's a terrific result. We couldn't be happier. Sanjay and Jim are over the moon. Benedict agreed that Home Hacks and EXMS would return the software they stole, including all copies, and agree not to use it. Sanjay and Jim will agree not to sue them over it, but we're fine with that. We're totally vindi-cated."

"I'm so happy!" Anne practically jumped up and down, her gold bangles jingling. "We have to go back to work and draft the settlement agreements tonight, if it takes all night. We want the agreements signed and executed, so Machiavelli can't pull a fast one."

Lou winked. "That's the move. I *still* don't trust him."

"Me neither," Judy said, flatly, then brightened. "And we have more good news, Mary, which is why Roger's here. Roger, do you want to tell her?"

"What is it, Roger?" Mary asked, turning to him with a smile, since she liked him better than she used to. In fact, she liked him well enough not to feel embarrassed that he was in her bedroom, which luckily, she'd had a chance to straighten up before they'd arrived, picking up the dirty clothes over-flowing the hamper, decorating the door-knobs, and making an attractive tent on the handlebars of her stationary bike.

Roger stood taller, smiling in his stiffly formal way as he held his champagne cup. "Thanks to your handiwork, the reverse-discrimination suit against you, Bennie, Judy, and the firm has been dropped."

"That's wonderful!" Mary felt her heart lift, even though she had assumed it was coming.

"In addition, Machiavelli has agreed to issue a press release that there was 'absolutely no merit to the discrimination allegations' " — Roger made air quotes — "and that his filing of the Complaint with the Human Relations Commission was 'a passionate advocate's overzealous reaction to the plaintiffs' failure to be hired.' So he managed to absolve you of any wrongdoing — and promote himself at the same time."

"That's great!" Mary said, surprised. "I didn't even think to ask him for that. You never see anything like that in a settlement. It does absolve us and it undoes his smear campaign."

Bennie nodded. "It sure does, and I'm delighted."

"Me too," Judy chimed in, beaming.

Mary turned to Roger, marveling. "How did you get Machiavelli to agree to that?"

"I threatened to get him disbarred."

Mary burst into startled laughter. "That's exactly what I would've done! I threatened him with that, too."

"That doesn't surprise me, Mary." Roger shrugged happily. "When we were together at the interview today, you said you learned

537

something from me. Maybe I learned something from you, too."

"Aw." Mary felt a rush of happiness, bubbling out of nowhere. "You know, I have to tell you, when I went down to South Philly and saw my former clients, they all knew about it and what Machiavelli had said about us. They all had something to say about it. Some of them even called my mother."

Roger's smile broadened. "Is that a South Philly thing?"

"No, it's a Mary DiNunzio thing," Judy interjected, and they laughed, including Mary.

"Anyway, I didn't realize how important my reputation was to me, truly. And it wasn't just about my client base or whether they're going to keep giving me business. It was just about what people think of me, in the world." Mary heard herself talking, realizing that she hadn't acknowledged how much Machiavelli's smears had gotten under her skin. "And now I'm going to have this baby and I don't want him, or her, to hear bad things about me. I don't want her tainted with any of that. So thank you, Roger, for restoring our reputation."

"You're welcome." Roger bowed mock-comically.

Bennie smiled. "I feel the same way, even though I don't have a child. We're *known* in this city. Our names stand for something. Integrity. Hard work. Quality. Justice."

"Don't forget attitude," Lou added, chuckling.

Judy grinned. "You mean swagger."

Roger smiled slyly. "However, do you know what the Sage has to say about reputation?"

Judy looked over. "No, what?"

Bennie snorted. "Who cares?"

Everybody laughed, and Mary was inclined to agree, but didn't say so because Roger looked like he was warming up to tell them, whether they wanted to know or not.

"Lao-Tzu said, 'Reputation should be neither sought nor avoided.' "

Bennie looked at Roger like he was crazy. "Oh please, enough with the Sage. What does he know?"

"He's a sage," Roger answered, good-naturedly. "That means he knows *everything.*"

Everybody burst into new laughter, and Lou threw a napkin at Roger. Mary felt happier than she had in a long time, surrounded by people she would miss, but without the panicky feeling she'd had before. She knew she wasn't going to lose them and that the baby was just the next chapter in their lives together. She felt an ease inch over her and she sank back in the pillows.

Judy caught her eye. "You tired, honey?"

"Just a little."

"I bet. Okay, we're out of here." Judy rose, businesslike. "Bennie and Anne are going back to the office to draft the settlement papers. Lou is going back to John's to keep looking for cameras, God bless him. Roger and I are going to clean up this mess because we're sharing a cab home, since he lives near the hotel."

Mary waved them off. "No, you and Roger go, too. I can do it later, don't worry about it."

Judy shot her a look. "Don't even start with me. We're not leaving you with this mess."

Roger looked around. "We need a trash-bag. Do you have some, Mary?"

"Roger, please, you don't have to clean —"

Judy interrupted, turning to Roger. "Trashbags are in the kitchen island, top drawer on the left."

"Be right back." Roger left the bedroom, then Bennie and Anne headed for the door, too.

Mary smiled. "Thanks for the pizza, guys."

"Thank *you*, DiNunzio. Bye now."

"Bye, Mary." Anne left with Bennie, and Lou started picking up paper plates from the dresser, but almost dropped them.

"Lou, let me do that." Judy crossed to him, taking the plates. "You go."

"Okay, you convinced me." Lou went to the bed and gave Mary a warm hug. "By the way, did you see the video I texted you? It wasn't much help, eh?"

"It was, a little. I didn't notice anything, but Machiavelli did. Look." Mary realized she had forgotten to tell the others about it on the conference call, but she could do that tomorrow. She scrolled to the text and played the video, freezing it at the window. "See the outline on the left wrist, with the bump?"

"Yes." Lou nodded. "Hmmm."

Judy came over to see. "I do, too. What do you think that is?"

"Machiavelli tried to tell me it's a woman's bracelet with a pendant or a man's oversized watch, worn loose. He was even wearing one, but still denied it was him."

Judy snorted. "He says it's a *woman*? Gimme a break."

Lou frowned, puzzled. "Why would he even point out that he had a watch on like that? Is this a game? Cat and mouse?" He straightened with a grunt. "I'll check it out later. Bye now." He left the bedroom, and Mary set the phone down beside her, turning to Judy.

"Judy, really, please go. I can clean up later."

"No, you should take it easy. I want to save the crusts for the dog."

"You're going to take garbage to a hotel?"

"When you're a mother, you'll understand," Judy said, and they both laughed. "And you do have to start taking it easy. Bed rest means bed rest."

"Not literally."

"Yes, *literally.*" Judy smiled, stacking the plates. "So how are you going to do this? You have to stay home for two weeks."

"I know."

"Will you be okay?"

"Yes." Mary rubbed her tummy, with a contented sigh. "I feel better about it now. I think I was being negative about the pregnancy. Anthony said so and he was right."

"It happens." Judy set the stacked plates on the dresser.

"Maybe it's good that it takes nine months, so you can get used to the idea."

"Right. I'm so glad you're okay, and the baby is too." Judy puckered her lower lip. "But I'm going to miss you."

"I'll miss you too." Mary felt a pang.

"But I'll bring dinner over and hang with you guys."

"I know you will."

"You won't be able to get rid of me." Judy gathered the crumpled napkins.

"I won't try."

"It's not the end of anything."

Mary felt touched. "No, it's just the beginning of something else."

"Aww, that's deep."

"It kind of is." Mary heard Roger coming upstairs, and in the next moment he entered the bedroom with two trashbags.

"I got one for recycling, too," he said, breaking the mood.

Chapter Forty-Seven

Mary listened to Judy and Roger laughing and talking downstairs as they took out the trash, finishing up their cleanup. A text alert pinged on her phone, and she glanced over on the bed to see that it was Anthony. She picked up the phone and read his text: **Research went well. Will call later. Love you**. She texted back, **Great! I had a big day too. Love you too.** She set the phone down, then leaned back in the pillows against the headboard, resting her hand on her belly, and in the next moment, she felt the baby kick.

"Ah!" Mary yelped, thrilled. She kept her hand on the same spot, trying to figure out if the baby had kicked her with his heel or its toe, but she couldn't tell. Relief washed over her like a warm wave. It made her so happy to feel the baby move again, and she wondered if the pizza had done the trick. She made a mental note to eat more pizza, purely for medicinal purposes.

Mary heard Judy and Roger coming up-stairs to say good-bye. "Guys, I felt the baby move!"

"Yay!" Judy cheered, entering the room with Roger. "Were you worried?"

"I was trying not to, but I was." Mary looked up at Judy, who looked down with sympathy, her expression soft in the warm light from the lamp.

"Aw, let me feel." Judy put her hand on Mary's belly, and Mary moved her hand over to the spot.

"Wait for the magical pizza trick." Mary felt the baby move again. "Ha! Did you feel it?"

"Yes!" Judy burst into laughter, turning to Roger. "Feel this! It's the coolest!"

"That's intrusive." Roger recoiled, amused. "I would never do that."

"I'm fine with it, by now." Mary smiled. "Roger, have you ever felt a baby move before?"

"No, unfortunately, I'm not a father."

"Go ahead then, I don't mind. Here's the spot." Mary took his hand and placed it on her belly. He leaned over, and his jacket sleeve edged up his forearm, revealing a chunky bracelet of wooden beads, with a large silver medallion hanging down.

"I don't feel anything." Roger smiled, cocking his head. Judy was standing behind Roger's shoulder, beaming.

"Just wait." Mary looked at his bracelet again and did a mental double-take. She flashed on the enlarged video, with the bump on the left wrist. The outline of Roger's bracelet was the same, with the medallion hanging down. It could have been *his* bracelet on the video.

"I still don't feel anything." Roger kept his palm against her belly.

"You will." Mary's thoughts raced, but she had to stay calm. If she was right, then *Roger* had killed John. But she couldn't let him know she suspected him. And she couldn't let Judy take a cab with him.

Roger smiled. "It's amazing to think that there's new life, inside you."

"Damn, I think the baby fell sleep." Mary forced a regretful smile. "Roger, if you don't mind, you should probably go, but I'd love for Judy to stay awhile. We can catch up —"

"Of course." Roger withdrew his hand from Mary's belly. "You must be exhausted."

"Mare, the baby can't be asleep, it was awake just a second ago." Judy stepped closer, and her gaze fell on the bracelet. Her eyes widened in shock, and she glanced at

Mary, frozen.

"Judy?" Roger straightened, frowning. "Is something the matter?"

"Uh, no." Judy faced him, stricken. Her fair skin flushed. Tears filled her eyes. "I, um, just noticed your . . . wrist mala."

Mary slid her hand to her phone to call 911. Judy was blowing their cover, too emotional to keep it together. She had lost the man she loved and was looking into the face of his killer.

"Judy?" Roger frowned. "What's upsetting you?"

Judy tried to speak, but her hand flew to her trembling lips. She burst into tears. "Roger?" she blurted out, horrified. "Did *you* kill John?"

CHAPTER FORTY-EIGHT

"What?" Roger recoiled, appalled. "Why would you ask me that? What a question!"

"Roger . . . I can't believe . . . you would!" Judy sobbed, her hand to her mouth, trying not to break down completely. "I admired you . . . you're so cool . . . and smart . . . why did you . . . why *would* you?"

Meanwhile, Roger was so focused on Judy that Mary could sneak her phone onto her lap and touch the screen to wake it up.

"I didn't, of course I didn't!" Roger stepped toward Judy, as she kept edging away. "Why would you say such a thing?"

Mary swiped her phone, and it asked for a passcode.

"Your wrist mala . . . we saw it . . . on the new . . . video."

"There's a *video*?" Roger asked, his tone changing so dramatically that it was as if his voice emanated from another man.

Judy nodded, her hand over her mouth.

Her agonized eyes shifted to Mary, and Roger whirled around just in time to catch Mary keying in her passcode. Her mouth went dry.

"Give me that phone!" Roger flew at Mary, grabbing the phone from her hand.

Mary scrambled away from him, her heart beating hard. Her hand flew protectively to her belly. She tried to think of what to do. There was nothing she could use for a weapon. If she screamed, help would come sooner or later, but he'd have time to kill one of them. She had to reason with him, stall him until she thought of something better

"Mary, were you calling the police? On *me*?" Roger stood over the bed, breathing hard. The look in his eyes was pure outrage. "What a terrible mistake! How could you make such a terrible mistake?"

"Roger, you scared me, that's all." Mary struggled to stay in control. "But I won't call again. I won't tell anybody. You probably didn't mean to kill him."

"*Of course* I didn't!" Roger shouted back, losing control. "I *didn't* mean to! It's not like I *planned* it! But I just got so *sick* of it, all of a sudden! All of you lawyers, you think you're so damn *smart*! But you make mistake after mistake! I get *so sick* of cleaning up after your mistakes! I've had a career of it, a *lifetime* of it! Can you imagine what it's like to be a *legal malpractice* lawyer? The clients are the *worst*! They're *all lawyers*!"

"I can imagine," Mary said, calmly. She held her hand out, keeping him back. He looked down at Mary as if he weren't really seeing her, his fury driving him. Judy sobbed against the dresser, watching them in horror.

"*That's* why I didn't want to take your case!" Roger shouted down at Mary, prone on the far side of the bed. "I *knew* you wouldn't listen! And John wouldn't listen, either! He was going to ruin everything! I only went there that night to tell him not to quit, to come back to your firm! But no, he wouldn't listen!"

"I did listen to you, Roger." Mary was trying to placate him. Her heart was beating out of her chest. He had to be deciding what to do with her and Judy. He couldn't kill them both at once. He needed an exit strategy. Mary was trying to give him one. "Roger, I listened to you, and that's why we stayed the course on our case."

"You didn't *want* to listen to me! You fought me every step of the way!"

"But I came around, in the end," Mary said quickly. "You showed me the way. You

550

changed my mind. Remember, what I said to you before the interview with Vanessa? I told you, 'I learned from the master,' and I did. You. And Judy listened to you too. We listen to you. We admire you."

"I *know* what I'm doing! Lawyers come to me because I know what I'm doing! If they knew what *they* were doing, they wouldn't be getting sued for malpractice, now would they?" Roger laughed, without mirth. "You would think that would be a wake-up call, wouldn't you? You would think that would cause a lawyer to question his judgment, wouldn't you? You would think that would *make a lawyer learn to take direction* from somebody who knows better, wouldn't you? Lawyers hire me when they're in trouble, but they don't listen to *a word* I say!"

"You're absolutely right, they should listen to you —"

"If John quit the firm, we would've lost that case! The press *never* would've let it go! It was damning! And I never lose! So I tried to get him to come back! He wouldn't listen!"

"I totally understand, Roger." Mary saw the fury burning in Roger's eyes, out of control. Her plan wasn't working. He was getting more worked up, not less. He had killed John in a murderous rage like this.

Fear bolted through her body. She fought the panic tightening her chest.

"I *told* him he was making a mistake!" Roger started breathing harder, shaking his head. "I said, 'just *listen* to me,' but he wouldn't change his mind! He told me to get out! He tried to throw me out! *Me!* He thought he *knew,* but he didn't! He was just a *kid*! And he wasn't *half* as smart as he thought! As *you* all thought —"

"Stop talking about him!" Judy shouted suddenly, sobbing, and in the next moment she was flying across the room at Roger.

Chapter Forty-Nine

Mary screamed, terrified, as Judy raced toward Roger in blind hatred.

Roger backhanded Judy, connecting with her cheek, then pivoted and punched her hard in the forehead.

"Judy!" Mary screamed, watching in horror as Judy staggered backwards from the impact, then fell against the dresser, banging her head. Judy collapsed to the floor, unconscious.

Roger whirled around, coming after Mary. She scrambled to the other side of the bed, ran out the door, and reached the hallway. Her mouth had gone bone-dry. Adrenaline coursed throughout her body. She had to get help.

Roger overtook her in the hallway, pulling her back by the hair. She cried out in pain. Her hair felt like it was coming out at the root. She tried to free herself, hitting Roger's arms. Her breath went ragged with fear and exertion. She heard panting and realized it was her. Roger was going to kill her and the baby. He'd lost control.

"Help!" Mary screamed, but Roger clamped a hand over her mouth to silence her. Tears of fright came to her eyes. Her heart hammered like a piston. She bit down hard, grinding the flesh of his palm between her front teeth. She tasted metallic in her mouth. She had drawn blood.

"Bitch!" Roger sprang away, startled and in pain.

Mary raced forward toward the stairway, praying she wouldn't fall. She had to live. She had to survive for the baby. She grabbed the banister just as Roger caught her, yanking hard on her shoulder and her silk T-shirt, trying to pull her back into the bedroom.

Mary held on to the banister for dear life. Her shirt collar pulled tight against her throat, cutting off her air. She writhed this way and that, trying to get him off, but she couldn't. Roger grabbed her shoulders again and tried to pull her back. She clung to the banister with both hands, squeezing the wood as hard as she could. Her fingers kept slipping. Her arms ached. Her shoulders felt like they were being pulled out of their sockets. She looked wildly around for something to use as a weapon.

She spotted a framed photo of her and Anthony hanging on the wall, to the left. She let go of the banister and lunged for the picture, tearing it off the wall. Roger grabbed her and tried to get her in his arms, but she whirled around and whacked him in the face with the photo.

The glass on the picture shattered against his cheeks and eyes. Roger cried out, his hands flying up. The picture fell to the floor. Shards of glass were embedded in his cheeks and forehead. He brushed them away, making bloody cuts as Mary raced back to the stairs.

She reached the top and raced down the staircase, half-stumbling, trying not to lose her balance. She prayed she didn't fall. Nothing could happen to the baby. She had to get out of the house. She had to save them both. And Judy.

Roger ran down the steps after her, right behind her. Suddenly he kicked her in the back of the head.

Mary's skull exploded. She cried out in agony. She saw stars, stunned. She reeled and slipped on the step, losing her balance. Her arms flailed, but she caught the banister, hanging on tight. She forced herself to stay conscious. She had to keep her wits about her. It was do or die.

Roger clambered downstairs and squatted next to her, grabbing her arms and trying to pry them off the railing. He pulled one arm off and tried to shove her down the stairs. She grappled with him, not letting go, wrenching him back and forth.

His leather shoe slipped on the stair and his leg came out from under him. She saw him pitch forward, then whipped him downward with one hand, holding on to the railing with the other. The sudden motion knocked him off-balance and he started to fall, but held tight to Mary. She didn't have the strength to keep her grip on the railing. He took her down with him.

Roger rolled ahead of her down the stairs, unable to hold on to Mary. She managed to slide down on her back, protecting her belly. She landed on top of him, then scrambled over him and darted to the front door.

"Help!" she screamed, praying her neighbors heard. She reached the door and grabbed the knob, twisting it open.

Roger grabbed her ankle from behind, dragging her backwards. Fear electrified every fiber of Mary's being. She couldn't fall facedown on the baby.

Mary grabbed the small console table to break her fall, dragging it back with her.

The lamp, the mail, and the key basket scattered everywhere. The door swung partway open.

"Help!" she screamed in desperation. She was almost safe. Somebody had to have heard her. She prayed they would come before it was too late. The table legs skidded on the hardwood, and Mary held on to the table, riding it backwards.

She tried to climb over it to the door, but her belly was in the way. Roger clambered to his feet, grabbing her from behind by the shoulders. She screamed, ramming her elbow back into his chest, again and again. She couldn't get him off of her. Terror and effort exhausted her. Sweat slaked her face and neck. She felt weaker and weaker.

Roger put his hands around her throat, choking her from behind. She tried to scream but no words came out. She gasped for oxygen. She heard herself gagging.

"Mary!" Judy screamed, and Mary looked up to see her best friend racing down the stairwell, holding her phone.

"Roger, no! Stop!" Judy shrieked in terror. Mary couldn't keep her eyes open. She was losing consciousness. Judy had probably called 911 but they wouldn't get here in time for her, or the baby.

Suddenly the front door opened and

standing in the threshold was Nick Machiavelli, holding a Pyrex dish with a tinfoil cover. His dark eyes widened in shock. He dropped the dish, slipped a hand inside his jacket, and pulled out a gun.

"Hands up or I shoot!" he shouted, aiming the gun at Roger.

"Don't!" Roger raised his hands, releasing Mary just as Judy reached the bottom of the stairs.

"Mary, are you okay?" Judy shouted, frantic, and Mary nodded, coughing as she tried to get her breath. Her knees buckled, and she sank into the arms of her best friend. Judy hugged her and eased them both onto the floor, where they clung to each other as Mary's coughs subsided.

"Roger, hit the floor! Don't move!" Machiavelli advanced on Roger, pushing him backwards into the living room. Roger got down on his knees, then lay facedown on the rug. Sirens blared nearby.

"I called 911, that must be them." Judy hugged Mary, whose breath started to return to normal. Her throat hurt, her head was killing her. She held her belly, thanking God she felt the baby moving. The sirens sounded closer, and she hoped they had an ambulance. Judy had a cut on her face, and her right cheek had begun to swell, her eye gradually closing. They should get checked out at a hospital.

"How are *you*?" Mary asked, hoarsely. "You had a concussion."

"I'm fine. We made it, girl." Judy hugged her tighter.

"Yes, we did." Mary felt a rush of gratitude that they had survived, as well as sympathy for Judy. "I'm sorry about John."

"Thanks. But we'll put Roger away. That helps."

Machiavelli glanced over, holding the gun on Roger. "So ladies, lemme guess, Roger's the bad guy?"

"Yes," Mary answered.

"*Told* you it wasn't me." Machiavelli snorted.

"Sorry, and thanks." Mary managed a smile. "Meanwhile, since when do you have a gun?"

"Don't worry, I got a carry permit, Pollyanna."

"You were almost right about the video."

"*Almost?*" Machiavelli lifted an eyebrow. The sirens sounded less than a block away. "Lucky I came by when I did. My mother was worried about you. She made you spinach lasagna. Now it probably broke in a million pieces, and she loved that dish. She wanted it back."

"Uh-oh. Who's going to tell her?"

"Baby Boy, of course," Machiavelli answered, with a sly smile.

Chapter Fifty

The next few hours were a blur of activity, starting with the previously unlikely trio of Mary, Judy, and Machiavelli standing together as a cadre of police officers swarmed Roger. They hoisted him to his feet and handcuffed him, still bleeding from his facial cuts, then hauled him out of the house into a waiting police cruiser. He didn't look back, but it was a moment that Mary and Judy would never forget. Seeing him get his comeuppance gave them both comfort, though Mary noticed that he'd left bloodstains on her living room carpet. She made a mental note to deduct it from the legal fees they'd never pay him. And to remember that at least once in her life, she had been totally badass.

Then she and Judy were whisked into ambulances, taken to the hospital, and wheeled into the emergency department. Judy was sent for testing, which came out fine, and Mary was examined, put on a fetal monitor, and cried tears of joy when she was told that the baby was fine. Detectives Krakoff and Marks appeared, and Mary and Judy gave them preliminary statements, enabling them to charge Roger with John's murder, attempted murder, and other offenses. Mary's home was officially a crime scene, so she was secretly happy she had cleaned up.

Bennie, Anne, and Lou arrived, and Mary and Judy had filled them in as much as they could before they got sent out to the waiting room, since they weren't immediate family. Her parents came, horrified and distraught, and she and Judy had to comfort them, get them some water, and make sure they were okay, a turnabout of the typical hospital visit. The Hodges and William were happily teary to learn that John's murderer was in custody, and they thanked Mary and Judy. The Tonys and El Virus arrived but they had to stay in the waiting room, too. Mary had no problem with her mother-in-law's being outside, though she missed The Tonys. She heard that the Rosary Society showed up, and Tony-From-Down-The-Block had his eye on Conchetta Patrioca so love was in the air.

Except that Anthony wasn't here yet. She

hadn't had her phone, so she hadn't been able to call him herself and let him know what was going on. The cops had taken Judy's phone for evidence, so Machiavelli had stepped up to call him, which must have blown his mind, not only hearing that his wife was almost killed but being told by her former enemy. Anthony hadn't been able to get a flight from Boston until early the next morning, but sent his love.

Mary and Judy were admitted to the hospital overnight for observation, and, after some doing, they even got the same room, for the best/worst slumber party ever. Mary called Anthony using the landline in the room, but wasn't able to reach him. Her parents insisted on staying the night since he wasn't there, and they'd conked out in chairs. Judy had fallen asleep after the Hodges and William left, leaving Mary not completely surprised to learn that her best friend snored. Still it was one of the loveliest sounds Mary had ever heard, and she thanked God that Judy was alive.

Mary couldn't sleep and lay in bed, her eyes open, her thoughts racing, and her palms resting on her belly. She couldn't help but replay the events of the night, even as horrific as they were, but it helped her to process them, now that she and Judy were safe. She could feel the baby moving through the cottony blanket, and every kick made her feel better.

The room was dark and quiet, and the only light came from the sharp greens and blues of the monitors keeping track of her vital signs, since she'd been given IV fluids and had a plastic clip on her index finger. Moonlight streamed in through the window next to her bed, bathing the room in a soft glow, and instinctively she turned her head to look outside, toward the sky.

The night was darkly black, the stars ghosted by the haze over the city, but the moon hung low in the sky, a mottled whitish-gray as perfectly round as a child's marble. Mary had always liked the moon, and Judy had told her that it had a female energy. But Mary didn't know if she was allowed to think that anymore, or if it violated gender discrimination laws.

"Babe?" somebody whispered, and Mary startled, turning from the window to see Anthony walking toward the bed, hardly visible except for his smile.

"What are you doing here?" Mary asked softly, marveling. She raised her arms, and Anthony came to her, scooping her up and holding her close. She burrowed into his chest, even though the zipper of his windbreaker rubbed against her cheek, and she breathed in the familiar smells of hard soap, faded aftershave, and oddly enough, pencil lead. Anthony was the only person she knew who still used pencils, which left a sooty bump on his index finger, and inexplicably, their scent.

"I couldn't get a flight until morning, so I rented a car and drove. I would've called you but my phone died." Anthony released her, sitting on the edge of the bed, holding her hand and looking into her eyes. Mary could see his agonized expression in the moonlight, which touched her.

"Aw, you didn't have to do that."

"What happened, honey? It sounds like a nightmare."

"It was, but it's over now."

"You could've been killed."

"But I wasn't, and the baby is fine."

"Thank God. I want to hear everything, but not now, you have to rest." Anthony's eyes glistened. "I'm so sorry I wasn't there, babe."

"But you were, honey." Mary heard herself say, her heart speaking for her. "You were —"

"No, I wasn't."

"Yes, you were, you're always there for me, and I have so much to tell you. I've done so much thinking, but there's one thing I know and it's that you have always been there for me. All the time." Mary tried to explain. "Whether it's by my side, or waiting for me at home, or sleeping beside me. You've been there for me all along, and everything you said that night, about the baby, and about how I felt about the pregnancy, it was true." She felt tears come to her eyes. "But that's changing, it already has, I feel it. I'm so happy that we're having this baby, and so grateful that I'm going to be home with her, or him, at least in the beginning. After that, we can sort out anything we need to sort out —"

"— I know, and we don't have to worry about it now —"

"— and we'll figure this out, even though I know it won't be easy —"

"— we'll do it with our families, and they'll help —"

"— no, *we're* the family." Mary heard the truth of it, just as she said it aloud. "*This* is the family, the three of us. This is where it starts. We're the center. If we just start here, and remember that, then everything else will fall into place, whether it's work, my parents, your mother, The Tonys, the Rosary Society —"

"The what?" Anthony smiled, puzzled.

"Never mind, whatever it is, anything that's not the three of us will find its own orbit."

"Its *orbit*?"

"I can't explain it, I just know I'm right. The moon told me."

"Then I agree with you and the moon, sweetheart," Anthony told her.

And he rewarded her with a long, loving kiss.

EPILOGUE

It was a beautiful Sunday afternoon in May, and Mary stood at the kitchen sink in her parents' house, washing the dishes after dinner. Anthony, her father, and The Tonys had gone into the living room to watch the Phillies game, leaving Mary and her mother in the kitchen to clean up and do other things that you needed ovaries to perform. Anthony had tried to help, but her mother had shooed him away, to preserve decades of DiNunzio tradition. Meanwhile, Mary could barely reach the sink over her belly, since she had passed her due date four days ago and was mentally counting down to delivery, every second of every day.

"Here, Ma." Mary handed the wet plate to her mother, who dried it with a faded dish towel.

"Grazie." Her mother smiled sweetly, wiping the plate until it was drier than it had been out of the factory.

"You know, we can let it dry on the rack."

"*Si, Maria,*" her mother said, again sweetly, and Mary knew that even though she had said yes, what she really meant was no.

"And I wish you would let me get you a dishwasher."

"*Si, Maria.*"

"Or a garbage disposal."

"*Si, Maria.*"

"And an air conditioner, it could go right in the window. It would work better than a fan."

"*Si, Maria.*"

"You know we're not Amish, right?"

Her mother laughed, if only to humor Mary, who'd made the joke about a thousand times before. She didn't really mind washing the dishes, but she wanted to make her mother's life easier. Right now, it felt perfect, with a soft breeze coming through the kitchen window, the smell of tomato and basil scenting the air, the background music of baseball play-by-play, and she and her mother standing side by side the way they always had, having some quiet time together. Mary would've said it was Zen, but Roger had given that a bad name.

Mary picked up the next plate and washed it with a sponge, trying not to think about Roger. She had been relieved that he had pled guilty to murder and two counts of attempted murder, and though he hadn't been sentenced yet, she hoped he would get at least twenty years. Judy was beginning to emerge from the grief that had enveloped her after John's death and she had become William's guardian, which had helped them both. Machiavelli's settlement had more than compensated London Technologies and refilled the coffers at Rosato & DiNunzio. Shanahan had been fired from Glenn Meade, after he'd returned from a week-long bender. And Bennie had already talked to Mary about when she'd be coming back after maternity leave, and it looked as if they'd have to hire a new associate. Whether it would be a boy or girl, nobody knew.

"I think is a boy, Maria," her mother said, out of nowhere, with a smile.

"You think?" Mary asked, smiling at the irony, then suddenly she felt as if she had to go to the bathroom, urgently. In the next moment, a gush of warm water started to run down the inside of her legs. She looked down, almost dropping the plate. "Ma, I think my water just broke! Is that what happened? My water broke?"

"Maria, si!" Her mother's hooded eyes flew open behind her bifocals, and family chaos erupted.

Anthony, her father, and The Tonys swarmed into the kitchen, leaving Mary without any shred of gynecological dignity, and she tried not to panic, though this wasn't the way their delivery was supposed to happen. Their car was parked a block away, her go-bag was at her house, and she and Anthony had hoped it would be only the two of them who went to the hospital, but instead, it was the two of them plus her parents and The Tonys, who had parked in front of the house.

Anthony, Mary, and her parents piled into their ancient Bonneville convertible and raced to Pennsylvania Hospital. Mary called Dr. Foster and Judy, while Anthony navigated the massive car through the warren of South Philly streets like a captain steering a cruise ship through the Thousand Islands. The Tonys followed in Anthony's Prius, and Mary hoped they and the car arrived in one piece.

They reached the hospital entrance and left the Bonneville with her parents while Anthony commandeered a wheelchair and rolled Mary onto the Labor & Delivery floor, where they were given a room, the baby was monitored, and Mary's contractions eventually began. They were deceptively easy until they became agonizing and unbearable, and Anthony and a saintly nurse held Mary's hand while she did her breathing exercises, which didn't help at all. Neither did ice chips, focusing on a single spot, walking up and down the hallway, or squatting like a yogi, and as soon as Dr. Foster said it was okay, Mary asked for every drug legally available.

And a mere twenty-five hours of back labor later, Mary and Anthony were delivered a beautiful baby boy. They put him in Mary's arms, and she looked down at him, her eyes brimming. She'd never seen anything so adorable, this tiny pink baby with wet, dark hair, his eyes looking up at her, unfocused and pure.

"He's beautiful." Anthony looked down at the baby, teary and tired.

"I love you both," Mary whispered, feeling every word was instantly true.

"I love you both, too." Anthony kissed her on the cheek.

It wasn't long before Mary was moved to another room and it was filled to bursting with visitors. Judy and William, Bennie, Anne, Lou, Mary's parents, El Virus, The Tonys, and even the lucky lady from the Rosary Society who had been dating Tony-From-Down-The-Block. Flowers, balloons, and pastries covered every surface, and

Mary did the best she could to make sure everybody got to see the baby, but didn't give him every communicable disease known to man.

William grinned from ear-to-ear. "I *told* you it was a boy!"

"You were right!" Mary laughed, her heart full and light, both at once, which seemed happily paradoxical.

Judy laughed, too. "So what are you going to name him?"

"YEAH, MARE. WHAT'S HIS NAME?"

"Maria, che?" her mother asked, and everyone waited to hear.

Mary looked at Anthony, and he looked back at her, since they'd already decided the baby's name. "We're naming him Anthony, after his father," she answered, with a smile.

"It's a Tony!" The Tonys cheered, and everyone else joined in.

ACKNOWLEDGMENTS

Here's where I get to say thank you, and my first thanks go to you, my reader. You have supported me in so many ways, for so many years now. I never take you or your loyalty for granted, and I never will. A writer is nothing without a reader, and I'm grateful to each and every one of you.

And now, thanks to the experts I consulted in my research for this book, who are named below. I owe them a huge debt of thanks, and of course, if there are any mistakes in the novel, it's on me, not them.

Thank you so much to Detective Thomas Gaul of the Homicide Division of the Philadelphia Police Department, my homegirl Kathleen Tana, Esq., and Jerry Hoffman, Esq., my mentor as a lawyer. Thanks to Linda Redding of Cerebral Palsy Association of Chester County, and to Drs. Nora Demchur and Annelise Wilhite. And thanks to my dear friend Nicholas Casenta, Esq.,

Chief Deputy District Attorney of the Chester County District Attorney's Office.

Special thanks also to Margie Moran and Ann Butchart.

Thank you to my goddess editor, Jennifer Enderlin, who is also the publisher of St. Martin's Press, yet she still finds the time to improve my manuscripts. And big love and thanks to everyone at St. Martin's Press and Macmillan, starting with the terrific John Sargent and Sally Richardson, plus Don Weisberg, Steve Cohen, Jeff Dodes, Lisa Senz, Brian Heller, Jeff Capshew, Brant Janeway, John Karle, Erica Martirano, Jordan Hanley, Tom Thompson, Erik Platt, Anne Marie Tallberg, Tracey Guest, Rachel Diebel, and all the wonderful sales reps. Big thanks to Rob Grom, for outstanding cover design. Also hugs and kisses to Mary Beth Roche, Laura Wilson, Samantha Edelson, and the great people in audiobooks. I love and appreciate all of you!

Thanks and love to my terrific agent, Robert Gottlieb of Trident Media Group, for his unflagging dedication and enormous expertise, and thanks to Nicole Robson and Trident's digital media team.

Many thanks and much love to the amazing Laura Leonard. She's invaluable in every way, every day. Thanks, too, to Nan

Daley for all of her research assistance and everything else, and thanks to her and Katie Rinda for "running the ranch," so that I can be free to write.

Finally, thank you to my amazing daughter (and even co-author) Francesca, for all of her support, laughter, and love.

How lucky am I?

Very.

ABOUT THE AUTHOR

Lisa Scottoline is a *New York Times* best-selling and Edgar Award-winning author of thirty novels. She has 30 million copies of her books in print in the U.S., she has been published in thirty-five countries and her thrillers have been optioned for television and film. Lisa writes a weekly column with her daughter, Francesca Serritella, for *The Philadelphia Inquirer.* Those stories have been adapted into a series of bestselling memoirs. Lisa lives on a Pennsylvania farm with an array of pets.

The employees of Thorndike Press hope you have enjoyed this Large Print book. All our Thorndike, Wheeler, and Kennebec Large Print titles are designed for easy reading, and all our books are made to last. Other Thorndike Press Large Print books are available at your library, through selected bookstores, or directly from us.

For information about titles, please call:
(800) 223-1244

or visit our website at:
gale.com/thorndike

To share your comments, please write:
Publisher
Thorndike Press
10 Water St., Suite 310
Waterville, ME 04901